THE ARES TRIALS

THE COMPLETE COLLECTION

ELIZA RAINE

ROSE WILSON

Editors: Christopher Mitchell

For all those who feel they don't belong.
Your tribe is out there.

THE WARRIOR GOD

1

BELLA

"Bella, please, put me down."

I barely heard the words over the blood pounding in my ears. But I knew the voice.

"Bella, I'd really, really appreciate it if you could just let go of my neck."

The red mist was making my vision cloudy, obscuring the man in front of me, who was pinned to the wall by my hand across his throat.

But I knew his voice.

"Bella, please." The voice was scratchy and choked but...

"Joshua!" I cried, dropping my rigid arm immediately, the fury raging through my body dissipating as guilt swamped me. "Shit, shit, shit, I did it again, didn't I?"

Joshua slid down the magnolia-painted wall opposite me, clutching at his throat, his eyes red.

"Yeah. Yeah, you did."

"Why? Why am I like this?" I couldn't keep the bitterness from my voice as I crouched down to him, pulling him to his feet.

"That's what therapy is going to help you with, Bella," he said, blinking slowly and twisting his neck as we walked back toward his desk, and the long couch I always sat on.

"But I've been seeing you for months, and I'm no better." Anger started to rekindle in my gut, the frustration of not being able to control myself a delicious fuel for my rage. Nothing set off the rage like frustration.

"Anger management therapy is a long process. You're doing great," Joshua said, and sat down in his chair.

I slumped down on the patient couch and cocked my head at him. My skin was still fizzing from the adrenaline that always accompanied me getting mad.

"How many times will you let me attack you before you quit on me?" I whispered. I didn't actually want to know the answer. He was the only man who had ever tried to help me, and I couldn't face watching him suffer at my own hands over and over again.

"I'm tougher than I look, Bella. I'm not going anywhere."

He smiled at me, most of the strain on his face now gone, and I so badly wanted to believe him.

I knew it was wrong to have a crush on your shrink. But, in my defense, he was freaking hot. Dark hair flopped over his forehead and curled around his ears, and his hazel eyes were permanently calm and soothing, a balm to my own constant million-miles-an-hour energy. And he looked tough enough to me. My eyes flicked over his body.

Broad shoulders.

Rounded biceps.

Big red mark on his neck... I'd done that. I'd *just* done that. Guilt made me feel sick, twisting my stomach in knots. Joshua was the only person who had ever truly tried to help me.

But when the red mist descended, I was no longer Bella; mostly decent, if a little hyper, human being. I was a freaking maniac. And strong to boot. It was as though my anger made me physically more powerful, and dangerous. Rational thought abandoned me, my normal senses overtaken completely.

And the worst part was, I desired it. When I was younger, I hadn't tried to fight it. The feeling of strength and control was like a drug, and I allowed the craving for confrontation to run wild. I reveled in every fight I won, no matter if the person I kicked the shit out of deserved it or not. Every time someone underestimated me, at five foot two with my pixie-face and blonde hair, I took pleasure in smashing their preconceptions to bits. And it wasn't just their preconceptions I smashed. I smashed *everything*.

When I got too old for the cops to keep letting me out, I got more careful. But I didn't stop.

When I was busted for fighting in the underground gambling rings, they gave me a six-month sentence. When I fought with every cellmate I had, I was put in solitary confinement.

And then I got sad. Like really, really sad. Being completely alone sucked. But in the absence of anyone to pick a fight with, I could think clearly for the first time in my life. I realized I needed to control my anger, and I needed to vent it on the right people. The people who deserved their asses booted into next week.

"Tell me more about your foster parents," Joshua said.

"But what if it triggers me again?"

"We need to work through your problems. I accept the risk that comes with that," he replied, gently.

I shook my head.

"No. No, I don't think we should carry on. I've already hurt you once today."

"You're not a bad person, Bella. The anger in you is chemical, it's not part of your soul. Remember that."

I said nothing. Because he was wrong. My issue wasn't a chemical imbalance. It was more than that, I was sure. I'd known something was wrong with me my whole life.

Joshua sighed. "Will you join us for the group session today?"

I nodded. I hated group therapy. Everyone there pissed me off. But Joshua insisted it was good for me, and I felt bad about what I'd done to his neck.

"Sure," I said.

"Good. Are you sure you don't want to carry on now?"

"I'm sure," I told him. Like hell did I want to keep talking about being abandoned by my asshole parents, and then being passed between money-grabbing, child-hating families for the next ten years. "I'll go for a quick run round the block, burn off some energy 'til group starts."

"Good idea," he smiled. "See you in twenty minutes."

∽

"You're a decent human, you're a decent human," I chanted to myself as I jogged down Fleet Street, avoiding tourists and biting back impatient comments. God, but those morons moved slowly.

Maybe I should relocate. London was filled to the

brim with angry energy. It couldn't be helping me calm down.

But I couldn't leave London. Not because I had family there or anything. Hell, I didn't even have any friends, let alone family. No, the reason I couldn't leave London was the theaters.

Since I'd moved to England from New Jersey ten years ago, I'd saved every spare bit of cash I could scrabble together from the menial, shitty jobs I could never hold on to and my bouts in the underground fights, to spend on the theater. I didn't have the patience for books, and I could barely sit still through an entire movie, but there was something completely mesmerizing about the theater to me. I attributed every moral fiber in my being to what I had learned through plays and musicals. Empathy seemed to pour into me from nowhere when I watched the fictional stories play out so vividly before me, the actors giving it everything they had and every second sucking me in further.

No, I couldn't leave London. Although since losing my last shitty job I couldn't actually afford the theater any more. But at least I'd learned a valuable lesson; I did not have the right temperament to be a bartender in a city. Drunken assholes were a big fucking trigger for my temper. I sucked in air as I jogged faster.

I'd find another job. Soon. I had to, or me and my stick-up-her-ass cat would end up hungry and homeless.

"You're a decent human," I repeated through clenched teeth, flipping my middle finger at a cyclist who was swerving around me on the wrong side of the road and swallowing back the desire to yell something obscene at him.

. . .

When I got back to Joshua's building I headed straight for the washroom and changed my t-shirt. I let my hair out of its knot on top of my head and tried to make it look somewhat attractive, then gave up, glaring at my reflection instead.

Why the hell would a man who I regularly attacked and knew how much of a freak I was, be attracted to me?

I blew out a sigh. At least he *knew* I was a freak. Unlike all the other poor bastards I'd dated. The first they'd known of it was when something innocuous triggered the mist and I went freaking crazy on their ass. Me and dating did not go well together.

But Joshua... There was something in his eyes when he looked at me, I was sure of it. Something deeper than just professional patience. He cared about me.

"Yeah, keep telling yourself that, freakface," I muttered at my reflection. But that was fear talking. Fear manifesting as shit-talking and aggression. He had taught me that, in our sessions.

I was scared he would turn me down, and then I wouldn't be able to face him again. I would lose him, and his help.

But I couldn't stop imagining how much better my life would be if he *did* like me. Imagining having someone to share each day, and night, with. Imagining him kissing me...

I stood straighter as I made my decision. I was going to tell him how I felt.

If he wasn't interested then he wouldn't be a dick about it, that wasn't his way. I would just go home with a red face, eat my bodyweight in ice cream and then spend a few hours with my punch-bag. Maybe avoid him for a week.

But if he said yes... Those soft eyes, that gentle voice, those expressive hands.

The best-case scenario outweighed the worst-case. I was going to do it.

I was early, so there was nobody else around as I pushed the double doors to the lecture room open. My heart hammered in my chest as I stepped into the room. I was really going to do it. I was going to tell him how I felt. Maybe not that I was in love with him, I didn't want to scare the shit out of him. But definitely that I was into him.

Joshua was a part-time university psychology lecturer, part-time anger management shrink. The university let him use his office for one-on-one sessions, and one of their larger lecture rooms for group. I'd never made it to university. Surprise, surprise.

Sadly, Joshua's building wasn't one of the many beautiful old university structures that dotted London and looked like something out of a fairytale. It was a concrete monstrosity built in the seventies, and the lecture room looked like any other boring office, just a bit bigger, with lots of cheap plastic chairs.

I stumbled as I reached the ring of seats set out for us crazies in the middle of the room.

Someone was lying on the floor, in the center of the circle of chairs.

Joshua.

"Joshua?" I ran forward, dropping to my knees beside him, about to turn him onto his back when I froze. *Blood.* There was blood, pooling beneath him. I watched in dazed slow-motion as the surreal-looking red liquid spread, approaching my knees. Logic seeped through my shock. If the blood was spreading now... this must have just happened.

I leaped to my feet, my fists raised, my muscles swelling as instinct took over.

"Where are you?" I roared at the unknown threat. "Show yourself!"

The air in front of me shimmered, and then there was a blinding white flash. My hands moved to cover my eyes instinctively, and I could feel the anger building inside me.

I was ready to fight.

I dropped my arms and blinked rapidly, clearing my eyes.

And gaped.

A man was standing on the other side of Joshua. And he looked like no man I'd ever seen.

He was seven feet tall at least, and was wearing gleaming golden armor like a freaking Roman soldier. His face was covered by a massive shining helmet with a red plume, and his arms and legs were made of muscle, thick ropes of it wrapping around his limbs like Arnold fucking Schwarzenegger.

He reached out with his sandaled foot and poked at Joshua.

"What the fuck are you doing?" I yelled, darting toward him. "Why have you done this?"

The eyes in the helmet snapped to mine.

"You are more interested in challenging me than saving him? That confirms it. You are the right one," the man said, his voice deep and abrupt. His words took me aback, and I realized he was right. I needed to help Joshua.

I shoved my hand in my jeans back pocket, pulling out my cellphone and fumbling to unlock it.

"Stay right there! I don't know why you've done this, but I'm calling the police!"

The man ignored me, flipping Joshua over with his foot, and there was an awful squelching noise. Blood soaked the front of his shirt, and his eyes were glassy and staring. I froze, senses swimming.

"Is he dead?" Please, please, please don't let him be dead, I prayed, the backs of my eyes burning.

"Yes. He is dead."

I felt a wave of dizziness wash over me, my stomach flipping.

"No, no, he can't be." I dropped to my knees again, feeling for a pulse in his neck.

There was nothing.

"His human body is dead. The police will think you did this," said the man simply.

"What?"

"You are here, alone with the body. And human police are fools."

"*Human* police? Who the hell are you?"

I stared up at the armored giant, my head swirling, red seeping into my vision. This couldn't be happening.

"I am Ares, God of War."

"Ares? The fucking Greek god?"

"Yes. Stop saying fuck. It is unladylike."

"Unladylike?" I realized I was yelling as I got unsteadily to my feet. "Why did you kill him?"

"Stupid girl. I did not kill him. And only his human body is dead. His soul has been stolen, taken to Olympus."

I felt myself sway slightly, then a surge of adrenaline shot through my veins, steadying me.

"You need to start talking sense, right now," I hissed.

The huge man glared at me a few seconds, then sighed.

"I am Ares, the God of War. And you are Enyo, Goddess of War. I did not kill him, but I am here to kill you."

2

BELLA

A normal person, on being told that an armored giant was there to kill them, would run a freaking mile, as fast as possible.

But true to form, my instincts kept me slap-bang where I was, fists raised, red mist taking over.

"Just try it, armor-boy," I snarled. All sensible thoughts, the ones about Joshua and the police and how the hell this guy had appeared out of nowhere, or what he'd just said about me being a damned *goddess*, were relegated to the back of my mind, to make space for the swell of anger and violence that was spreading through me.

He may be bigger than me, but I was stronger than I looked. *A lot stronger.* And I didn't always fight fair.

Slowly, he drew a gleaming sword from a sheath at his side. It was almost as long as I was, and my aggression wavered just a tiny bit. I'd never fought anyone with a sword before.

First time for everything.

I dropped my stance, bending my knees, ready.

"Are you not going to run away?" he asked me, his voice still calm.

"No, I'm not, you fucking maniac. I'm going to keep you here until the police arrive."

"At which point I would vanish, and you would be arrested," he said.

"We'll see about that," I spat, though part of me knew he was right. But that part of me had no control whatsoever over the rest of my body.

My legs were almost vibrating with pent-up energy, my vision now completely red.

The giant lifted his sword.

A flash of green light filled the room, and I saw a new figure directly in front of me, small and... furry. Shock rocked through me as I blinked, and the giant gave a bark of anger.

"Zeeva?" I stammered.

My cat was sitting between me and the giant.

My short-haired, uptight, tuna-eating Siamese cat. Just sitting there, like it was totally normal.

"What in the name of sweet fuck is going on?" I breathed, blinking hard.

The man I was secretly in love with being murdered by an armored giant was something my violence-addled brain could react to. But my fucking cat appearing out of thin air at the scene of the crime?

Nope. Too much.

My fists dropped to my sides in bewilderment as Zeeva turned to me, her amber eyes as disdainful and aloof as they always were.

"Bella, you are a fool," a cool woman's voice sounded in my head. *"Next time you are faced with fighting a god, run."*

I opened my mouth to speak but nothing came out.

I'd lost it. I'd actually lost it. Maybe none of this was happening, and Joshua was fine. Maybe he'd visit me in the lunatic asylum.

Maybe not.

Zeeva began glowing turquoise, and my jaw hung even lower as she began to grow, not stopping until she was the size of a freaking lion. But her head was still that of a Siamese cat, her pointed ears and almond shaped eyes just larger.

"Ares, you may not just take her power from her by killing her. You must earn it."

The woman's voice issued from the cat loudly, and I felt my knees wobble.

"You do not understand the seriousness of the situation!" barked Ares.

"I understand perfectly. Hera has informed me. Zeus attacked you and you lost your power. But you may not take Enyo's without first earning it."

I felt my mouth opening and closing like a freaking goldfish as I stared between them.

The giant glared at my huge cat, fury in his eyes, then slammed his sword back into its sheath.

"Fine. We go to Olympus then," he snapped, and the world flashed white around me.

When the light cleared from my eyes for the second time in five minutes, I was absolutely positive I had gone mad.

I was standing on a white marble floor, and instead of

walls either side of me, there were giant flames. And they weren't orange, like normal fire, they were multi-colored – purple and green and red, dancing together mesmerizingly. A cough drew my attention, and my dumbstruck gaze shifted to what was in front of me.

Thrones. Two thrones, with people sitting on them. Well, one person. A beautiful young woman with white hair, a green dress, and a crown made of roses with gold thorns. The other throne, the one apparently made out of freaking skulls, was occupied by a figure made completely of smoke.

"Ares, what have you done now?" a hissing male voice asked, coming from the smoke person.

"How did you flash without your power?" added the woman, then gave me a small smile as she ran her eyes over me. "Don't panic, it's all real, and you'll get used to it," she said quickly to me.

I opened my mouth wider to answer, but nothing but a small squeak came out. I closed it again. The red mist had abandoned me for the first time in my life and my brain had just frozen, along with my body. Whatever was happening simply couldn't be happening.

"This is Enyo," the armored giant grunted, pointing at me. "The power of war was split between us, and then she was... lost to the mortal world." I blinked at him. "When I am with her, I can access that power, as it is the same as mine." He ground the words out like they were being forced from his lips.

What the hell was going on?

"The power was split between you?" asked the woman, and Ares nodded.

"Yes, Queen Persephone." Persephone? Did that make the smoke guy on the skull throne Hades?

This was fucking crazy. I mean, I love a bit of Greek mythology as much as the next girl, but this couldn't be real.

"Why was the power split? Are you two related?"

A weird spluttering sound bubbled from my mouth as I looked in horror between them, the absurdity of the idea jolting my reactions back to life. I had no family.

"For the love of sweet fuck, do not tell me that we are related," I breathed. He glared at me through the eye slits in his helmet, and I noticed the color of his eyes without meaning to. They were the hue of chocolate, rich and dark and... lost.

"We are not related. We could not be further from each other in lineage. I am descended from..." he paused and took a deep breath. "I am descended from Zeus. She is descended from an unknown Titan."

"I'm what now?" I asked, my eyebrows so high they were making my face hurt. Confusion was making my head swim, and the shot of adrenaline that usually came with my anger and made me rock-steady before a fight just wasn't coming.

Just treat it as a play, I told myself. *They're actors. Don't freak out.* "You're talking about Zeus and Titans. And my cat can speak." I put my hands on my hips, and closed my eyes as I sucked in air, dizziness pricking dangerously at me. "My only friend just got killed, and I'm fairly sure armor-boy did it. Someone, please tell me what the hell is going on."

When I opened my eyes Persephone was glaring at Ares, a faint green glow around her.

"Did you kill a mortal?" She asked him, her voice laced with steel.

"No! He was already dead. And besides, he wasn't

mortal. There was guardian magic around him. Only his human body was destroyed."

The word 'destroyed' used to describe Joshua made me feel sick, but I clung to his words, trying to make sense of them.

"If he's not dead, where is he? What the fuck is going on?" I said, louder this time. Frustration was whipping through me like a storm, battering at my disbelief.

"Sorry, Enyo," Persephone said, with a small nod.

"Bella," I snapped, correcting her automatically, then regretting interrupting her. "My name is Bella," I mumbled.

"OK. Bella. Here's the short version. I, like you, once lived in the mortal world without knowing about Olympus. This is a world run by gods, filled with immortals and magic and creatures we knew as myth and legend. Zeus, the King of the Gods, recently made a very big mistake, and now my husband, Hades, rules in his place, in turn with Poseidon."

I stared at her until she carried on.

"Zeus is missing now, but before he left he fought with Ares, and took his power away. Zeus is extremely strong, and something like that can't be reversed."

"Yes, it can. If I kill her I can take her power," interrupted Ares. I threw him my best 'shut the hell up' look and turned back to Persephone.

"What happened to Joshua?" I had a hundred other questions, but that one was the most important.

Persephone frowned, and looked at the smoky form next to her. When he spoke again, the hissing sound was gone from his voice.

"This is not the first report I've heard of guardians being taken from the mortal realm," he said.

"Guardians?"

"There are many of them, all making sure that people like you - with power that does not belong in the mortal realm - don't cause, or attract, any trouble."

Indignation spiked in me, but faded fast. I both caused and attracted trouble all the time. There was little point in denying that.

"So Joshua knew about all this?" I waved my hands around the room, and the flames either side of me leaped and danced in response.

"Yes. He will have known you had power and would have been trying to help you manage it. I doubt he knew who you truly were. Just that you were of Olympus."

Disappointment speared my gut. Along with a dull sense of betrayal.

"And my cat?"

"I don't know," answered Persephone, looking curiously at Zeeva. I looked down at her too, normal-sized now and sitting a foot away from me. As usual, she didn't deign to look back at me.

"I was assigned to watch over Enyo a long time ago," the woman's voice from earlier said.

"By who?" asked Persephone, before I could ask the same thing.

"Hera," she answered, and Persephone smiled.

"Hera is a kind goddess and a fair ruler," she said to Zeeva, and the traitorous freaking cat actually nodded her head at the Queen.

"So..." I rubbed my hands across my face. "Just to confirm, you're saying me and my cat have magic powers and are from a secret Greek mythology world?"

"You have the power of war. It is mostly anger, strength and violent tendencies," said Ares gruffly.

Well, I mean, that would explain a lot. Like, a hell of a lot. Maybe this wasn't so cream-cracker crazy after all.

"And Joshua and other... *Guardians* have gone missing?"

"We do not have time for this!" Ares snapped, stamping his foot on the marble. I didn't flinch, straightening my own spine instead as a response. Other people's rage triggered my own, and I clung to the solidifying feeling, the sharpening of my focus. "I need my power back, before my realm discovers what has happened and rebels against me!" Ares shouted.

"We need to find Joshua!" I protested, looking at him. "Fuck your stupid powers; a man has been kidnapped!" A vision of Joshua's lifeless face flashed through my mind, and I clamped my jaw shut, trying to hold on to my fragile focus.

I needed to concentrate on one thing at a time, and that had to be finding Joshua. He may have lied to me about who or what he really was, and who or what I was for that matter, but he *had* been helping me. And now I was the only person that knew what had happened to him. I was all he had.

Understanding all this other madness would have to wait; I needed to make sure he was safe first.

"My powers are significantly more important than the disappearance of some minor guardian," said Ares. My fists clenched, but Hades spoke, and we both turned to him.

"Ares, you may not kill Enyo for her power. I forbid it."

The god of war snarled, and I failed to stop myself giving him a sarcastic smile and a middle finger flip. He bared his teeth at me.

"There is another way you can gain your power back,

as we have already discussed. Oceanus is the only being stronger than Zeus. Ask him for help."

"Hades, I am not a puppet and I will not ask a Titan for help!" Ares said loudly. His enormous body was practically bulging out of his armor as his muscles tensed. I recognized the signs of trying to contain a fierce temper.

"Then you are destined to be powerless forever," shrugged the smoke figure. "Unless she agrees to share her power with you voluntarily."

"Why would I help him?" I exclaimed. "He's an asshole! For all I know, he kidnapped Joshua himself!"

"He is not guilty of that crime," said Hades.

"Being an asshole, or kidnapping my friend?" I snapped back.

"The kidnapping," Hades said after a pause, in which I was sure I heard a chuckle. "A number of demons escaped the Underworld in the chaos of Zeus' fleeing. I have reason to believe that one of these demons is responsible, and I have heard they are seeking refuge in Ares' realm."

"That is not my problem," barked Ares.

"As ruler of Olympus, I am making it your problem. I want you to find this escaped demon and the stolen Guardians. I have no authority in your lawless land. It must be you."

"If I return to my realm, I will be overthrown without my power!"

"Then you and Bella must work together."

"No. I want no part of this," said Ares.

"It is my command as your King, Ares," said Hades, and the slither was back in his voice. An icy fear began to creep over me, and an impulse to hide clawed up my throat. The feeling was alien to me, and panic started to grip my chest, my breath coming fast.

"She's still human, my love," said Persephone gently, and the fear lessened quickly. She turned back to us and spoke clearly. "Ares, you must do as your king commands. Bella, if you want to find your friend, the assistance of Ares, one of the twelve rulers of Olympus, will be invaluable. You would be foolish to turn down help such as that."

The finality, and sense, of her words were impossible to ignore, despite every part of me railing against the idea of working with this giant idiot. He was as likely to kill me as help me.

But I had no choice.

"I have to find Joshua," I said. "I'm the only person in his life who knows he's gone missing. I'm all he has."

Persephone's eyes softened, and she laid her hand on the arm of the smoky form beside her. Their love was almost tangible, it rolled from them like physical power. I felt a little bolt of jealousy, and turned it fast into resolve. If I found Joshua and kicked the ass out of whoever had taken him, maybe I could have some of that for myself.

"Then it is settled. There will be a small ceremony to see you both on your quest," said Hades, then there was a bright flash and he disappeared.

"Ceremony? What? We have to find Joshua! We don't know why he was taken, we have to find him now, before he's..." I trailed off, not wanting to finish the sentence. I couldn't bring myself to say 'dead', not after seeing his body on the floor in a pool of blood.

The weirdness of the whole situation rocked through me again, making me shiver, and I forced it down. *Focus on one thing at a time, Bella. Laser-focus.*

"All in good time, Bella. We must wait for Hades. In

the meantime, I think you need a bit of background on your new surroundings," said Persephone.

"What I need is a fucking big drink," I answered hotly, then instantly felt guilty. She was trying to help me. To my surprise, she grinned at me.

"When I first got here, a big drink was just what I needed too."

3

BELLA

Persephone flashed us to a huge room with enormous arched windows all along one side revealing a green forest beyond. I hadn't expect Ares to accompany us and I glared at him.

"Why are you here?" I asked, as Persephone made her way to a long counter. The center of the room was dominated by a long, grand dining table.

"I can't use my power without you," he answered, sounding like he'd rather be anywhere in the world than by my side.

"Well I need some time alone. To find out what the hell is going on, and to organize myself," I said firmly. It was true. But mostly I just wanted him gone.

"You swear too much," he said, after a pause. I heard Persephone laugh as I felt myself scowl.

"I'll swear as much as I fucking like," I snapped.

"You called me an asshole. That is rude."

"You were planning to kill me! I'd say that's more rude than calling someone who is clearly an asshole an asshole!" Anger was pumping through me and his eyes narrowed.

"Stop calling me an asshole," he snarled.

"Alright. How's fuckwit?" A favorite insult in London. "Or maybe shitface?"

He took a step toward me and I raised my fists, but Persephone's level voice cut across us.

"Here's that drink you wanted, Bella." I turned to her, reluctant to take my eyes from the armored giant. "Ares, we need some girl-time," she said, and flicked her hand. I heard Ares shout as light flashed, then he was gone.

I let out a sigh of relief.

"Thank god for that. He's freaking crazy."

"He's not the worst of them," she smiled at me.

"Really?" I took the drink she offered me, and she held up her own in her other hand.

"Really. I know how you're feeling. But trust me when I tell you, accepting it quickly is easier than pretending none of it is true."

I gulped down half of my drink, and a pleasant warmth flooded from my throat down my chest.

"Actually, I've always known something was wrong with my life. To be honest, this sort of makes sense." Persephone chuckled, and sipped from her own glass.

"I wish I'd found it that easy."

The truth was, it felt more right than it should have. Perhaps the need to find Joshua wasn't the only thing keeping a total meltdown at bay. I actually felt like I'd been waiting for someone to come and drop a shitstorm like this on my head all my life. Admittedly, 'Bella, you've got magic war power' was not the form I had expected the shitstorm to take, but it made sense right down to my core. The more I thought about me being from somewhere that wasn't the shitty world I lived in, where I simply didn't belong, the more something pleasant and right tingled through my body. It was the same part of me that fueled my anger and strength. The part of me I'd spent my life trying and failing to understand and control.

It was almost a relief.

Plus, it might explain why my parents abandoned me.

"Erm, thank you, and Hades, for not letting Ares kill me," I said to Persephone.

"You're welcome. Bella, you should talk to your cat. Hera wouldn't have assigned someone to watch over you personally unless you were important."

"Ares said I was the Goddess of War. Is that important?"

"I don't know. There *isn't* a Goddess of War," she said slowly. "I can't tell you anything about your past, but I can tell you a little about Olympus. All of the Olympian gods here rule their own realms. There were twelve, until Hades created a new one, and gave it to Oceanus, who is a Titan. That's a big deal because the Olympians and the Titans fought a war a long time ago, and they still don't really get on. Zeus hates Titans."

"Didn't Ares say I'm descended from a Titan?" I felt guilty for drinking and asking questions about myself whilst Joshua was out there somewhere, but I couldn't see what else I could do. I may as well use the time to learn something useful.

"Yes. Many citizens of Olympus are. But it's only recently that they began being accepted in society."

"Great. I'm a freak here too," I muttered, and drained the rest of my glass. Persephone laughed.

"You won't be saying that when you see some of the creatures who live here. You'd have to be pretty special to stand out in Olympus. We're currently in Hades' realm, the Underworld, also known as Virgo. The realms are all star signs in the mortal world. Ares' realm is, unsurprisingly, Aries."

"Who owns Taurus?" I asked, before I could stop myself. That was my star sign.

"Dionysus, god of wine. And it's an awesome place. Unlike Ares' realm, which is home to the most violent tribes in Olympus. Everyone there is ruthless, well-trained and power hungry. It's dangerous enough that it's rarely visited by anyone."

"Right," I said, ripples of trepidation making their way through my body. Was it wrong that Aries sounded a little bit cool to me? "And that's where I'm from?"

"I don't know. Talk to Zeeva. She can probably help you more than I can. I'm only just learning a lot of this now. I've still not visited all of the other forbidden realms myself."

"There are forbidden realms?"

"Yes. Aphrodite, Artemis, Hephaestus, and Hades all have an 'invite-only' policy on their worlds."

"Have you been to Aries?" I asked.

"Yes. I've visited the Queen of the Amazons, in the south," Persephone nodded.

"Queen of the Amazons?"

"Yes. The queen is Ares' daughter."

"Huh. He doesn't look the dad type," I said slowly.

"Parentage is a bit weird with gods. My mother is a god, but I've never met her. They kind of drop kids and bolt."

"Doesn't sound that weird," I muttered, aware of my bitter tone. Persephone gave me an understanding smile.

"There's no familial attachment here. Gods are

immortal, and love and family are nothing like what we grew up with."

"You and Hades seem pretty tight," I said.

"We are bonded," she beamed, and I squashed down another stab of jealousy. "Hera, goddess of marriage, linked us with magic. It is as unbreakable as immortality itself."

"Sounds like a big commitment," I said, and set my glass down on the long table. Persephone picked it up, and carried it back to the counter.

"The biggest," she replied, as she filled it back up with amber liquid. "Speaking of Hera, I will leave you and Zeeva to talk until Hades returns."

"But what about Joshua? The longer we don't know where he is, the more chance there is that something awful will happen to him."

"Bella, if whoever has taken him wanted to kill him, they would have done so when they killed his human body. Hades says that Guardians have strong magic, I'm sure your friend is fine."

I scowled at her, but said nothing, sipping at my drink instead. If her precious Hades had been kidnapped, I bet she wouldn't be so damned calm. But she was being kind to me, and I had no way of achieving anything without the help of these people.

I had a lot of questions that needed answers, that was for sure, but the priority was saving Joshua. I was the only person who knew he was in trouble. Only after he was safe, would I be able to work out what all this meant for me.

Persephone left me with my topped-up glass of whatever-it-was, and I fell into one of the many chairs. A small flash of teal light shone from somewhere on the floor and I frowned.

"Hello, Enyo," said a woman's voice in my head, and I jumped in surprise so hard that liquid sloshed from my glass.

"Get the fuck out of my head!"

"Do not swear at me. I have watched you for longer than you can possibly imagine, and I know your bluff means nothing." Zeeva jumped up onto the table in front of me and sat slowly. Gracefully. I narrowed my eyes at her.

"Why have you never spoken to me before? And how are you talking in my head? And why are you even here?"

"I had no reason to speak to you before now. I am a creature of magic with the capacity for mental communication, it is common in Olympus. Why I'm here is not your business."

"Not my business? Are you joking? Of course it's my business!"

The cat let out a long mental sigh and flicked her tail. My head swam. Zeeva was definitely the part of this my brain was struggling the most with. I mean, she was hardly an affectionate house pet, but that had been part of why I liked her. She had as much of an attitude problem as I did. If I'd known she was a freaking... Wait, what *was* she?

"What kind of 'creature of magic' are you?" I asked her.

"I am a sphinx hybrid," she answered, after a pause.

"Sphinx? Don't they ask riddles?"

"Yes. If I were to ask you a riddle that you couldn't answer, I would then have to kill you, so please don't ask for one," she said dryly. My mouth fell open.

"You could kill me?"

"*Of course.*"

"Why are you here? I don't understand." I scrubbed my hands across my face for what felt like the twentieth time.

"*Drink more nectar. It will help you think more clearly,*" she instructed. I looked down at my glass. I was drinking nectar?

"Please tell me why you are here. Or at least that you can help me save Joshua," I asked, changing my tone to pleading as I picked up the glass. Aggression wasn't going to work with her, clearly.

"*I was assigned to watch you by Hera. She has a special interest in you. The power of war was split between you and Ares, as he said. Yours has been suppressed by such a long period in the mortal realm, but it will awaken the longer you are here. And Ares will be able to access it.*"

"Two questions," I said, holding up my hand to stop her. "One, how long have I been in the mortal realm? I'm twenty-nine and I don't remember being a baby, so I'm guessing it was around then?"

Zeeva blinked at me. "*What is question two?*" she asked.

"How does this power-sharing thing work? If Ares is using my power, can I use it at the same time? Or is it like a take-it-in-turns scenario? Because Ares doesn't strike me as the type of guy to share his toys."

"*I have no idea. I didn't believe he would ever come for you, or that you would return to Olympus.*"

"Right. Great." That's helpful. *Not.* "So... Question one? How long have I been away?"

"*That is inconsequential.*"

Anger spiked in my veins. "If you won't answer my questions and you don't know how any of this works, what exactly can you help me with?" I asked her sharply.

"I am not here to help you. I am here to report back to my Queen on your activities."

"You're a spy?"

A gleam of something dangerous flashed across her amber eyes. *"Call me whatever you wish, Enyo, I will be keeping my eye you until this is resolved."*

"My name's Bella, not Enyo," I snapped, swigging angrily at my nectar.

"Which is short for Bellona, the Roman name for the goddess of war, which is derived from the word 'bellum', the Latin word for warfare."

I gaped at the cat. "How can you possibly know what my name is short for? I never even met the people who named me."

"I have been with you for a long time."

"No, I bought you eight years ago. You couldn't possibly have known my parents. Could you?" I couldn't keep the hope from my voice, and I could swear the look in the cat's eyes softened.

"There is too much for your mostly mortal brain to process right now. When you have proven to me that you can handle it, I will tell you more," Zeeva said eventually. I scowled, opening my mouth to protest, but the dangerous gleam flickered back instantly, and her body glowed teal. *"Do not push me, Enyo, or I will tell you nothing."*

I clamped my mouth shut, clinging to the resolve I had earlier. I couldn't do anything in Olympus without help. If the cat knew things I wanted to know, I couldn't force her to tell me. I'd have to win her trust.

"Fine. But can you please call me Bella?" I said.

"Very well."

"What's your real name?" I asked her.

"Zeeva."

"But... that's what I named you. You must have had a name before that."

"I did. Zeeva."

"Wait, did you get inside my head and choose your own name?" I asked, gaping.

"That's enough conversation for one day," she said, and jumped down off the table. *"Hades is back."*

"Wait! That's not fair!"

There was a little flash of teal light, and my traitorous magic cat was gone.

4

BELLA

I didn't know how she knew, but Zeeva was right about Hades. Before I'd even finished the rest of my nectar, Hades, Ares, and Persephone appeared at the other end of the room.

Ares' presence instantly set my nerves on edge, my anger responding to his instinctively. I stood up.

"The Olympians and a few guests are on their way. You will be leaving within a few hours," Hades said, his smoke figure turning to face me.

"They love a bit of drama here, Bella. You'll get used to it," Persephone added.

And she wasn't kidding.

After a few minutes of nervous waiting, no less than thirty people appeared out of nowhere, and boy did they test my not-freaking-out abilities. A long dais lined with thrones had appeared with them at the end of the room, and eight of the grand seats were occupied. I ran my eyes fast along the row of what I was sure were the other Olympians, my suspicions confirmed when everyone else in the room bowed low to them. I quickly did the same, desperate to take in everything around me and not knowing where to start.

Start with the gods, I decided, as I straightened. They emanated power, and my knowledge of Greek mythology was decent enough to give a pretty good guess at who they all were. Poseidon was in the middle, and the most obvious. He was wearing a toga the color of the ocean, had black hair streaked with grey, and was holding a trident. The hot-older-guy look was seriously working for him. Next to him was a severe but beautiful-looking woman with blonde hair wrapped around her head like a crown and a white toga. The owl on her shoulder gave her away as Athena. On Poseidon's other side was the most stunning woman I'd ever seen. Her skin was the color of mocha and her hair was candy pink, rolling over her shoulders and sheer blue dress in waves. She had to be Aphrodite. I was squarely into guys, but just looking at her made my insides feel weird. Next to her was a hunchback guy with a leather apron on, who must have been her husband Hephaestus. On his right was a young girl with an enormous bow and tube of arrows and gleaming armor, and next to her a ridiculously pretty guy in matching armor. He was wearing a beaming smile. The twins, Artemis and Apollo. Back at the other end of the row was a guy in tight leather trousers and an open denim shirt, with long wavy black hair and a lazy grin. Next to him was a man with a red beard and scruffy red hair, wearing a plain black toga that only made the fluttering silver wings on his sandals stand out more. Dionysus and Hermes.

I had already been told that Zeus was missing, but I

was disappointed not to see Hera. I wanted to know why she'd sent a miserable freaking cat to keep an eye on me for years.

"So. You're the reason Ares has been so secretive," said a voice behind me, and I spun around.

A woman with boobs so big they barely fit in the corseted red dress she was wearing was giving me a narrow-eyed look, a half-smile on her handsome face. "Interesting."

"Who are you?" I asked. I didn't have the patience or inclination to be polite to her if that's how she was going to start a conversation. A more genuine smile tipped her lips up, and she brushed a strand of black hair out of her face.

"I'm his sister, Eris. Who are you?"

"Bella."

"Bella," she repeated, and a sudden urge to do something completely outrageous, like take all my clothes off, gripped me. Eris gave a tinkling laugh. "Oh, you're a susceptible one," she grinned, her eyes sparkling with either mischief or malice, I couldn't tell. "I like you."

"Erm," I said, concentrating hard on stopping my hands from undoing the snap on my jeans. "Are you doing this?"

"Doing what?" she purred innocently, then a cackling laugh bubbled from her lips. "Sorry, it's too easy, I'll stop," she said, and the feeling vanished. I scowled at her.

"Don't fucking do that again."

"But I'm the Goddess of Chaos and Discord, I can't help myself," she pouted. "What are you a goddess of? I hope it's something fun. I can tell you have power, and you don't come across very innocent."

"Erm, war, apparently," I said, my eyes widening as I

saw *something* walk behind her. "What in the name of sweet fuck is that?" I breathed. Eris ignored the question, her eyes lighting up.

"War? You're the goddess of war?"

"So I'm told. Seriously, what *is* that?" I pointed at the creature who had now stopped loping across the room and was talking to a woman with a lopsided face and leathery wings. Eris turned and waved her hand dismissively.

"That's a griffin talking to a harpy. Who told you that you were the Goddess of War?"

"Ares did. What the hell is a griffin?" I'd heard of a harpy, but not a griffin. He had a beak for a nose, huge torn wings, and legs like the back legs of a lion.

"Lion-eagle cross. Let me get this right. Ares told you that you were the Goddess of War? This is too good."

She was beaming as I dragged my attention from the griffin back to her face.

"Why?"

"Oh, I'm sure you'll find out soon enough. Come, let me show you some more beasties of Olympus. That over there is a minotaur, he's Hades' captain of the guard in fact, and that is a centaur. They're reclusive creatures, never leave that stuck-up bore Artemis' realm if they can help it."

My mouth fell open as I stared at the centaur. She was freaking magnificent. The bottom half of her body was that of a white mare, and rising from the horse's chest was the torso of a warrior woman. Gleaming silver armor and a belt hung with axes and war hammers wrapped around her body, and white hair the color of the horse's coat was pushed back from her stern face with a silver band.

Strength and fearlessness and battle-bravery stirred inside me as I stared at her.

"She's ready for war," I breathed, without even realizing I was speaking aloud.

"Well, you would know," said Eris. "Being Goddess of War, and all that." She said the words with barely-contained delight, and suspicion roused me from my fascination with the centaur.

"Why are you so excited about this?"

"Because my brother can be a complete fucking asshole, and you might just provide me with some entertainment."

"Well, we agree on that at least. Your brother is an asshole. He wanted to kill me."

"Wanted? I would amend that to *'wants'*, sweetie. Present tense. I highly doubt he's stopped wanting to kill you; Ares wants to kill most things."

"Great. Any tips on *not* being killed by him?"

"Nope. But I look forward to seeing if you survive."

"Thanks," I said, loading my voice with sarcasm.

"You're welcome," she smiled, and an urge to run over and slap the serious centaur on the ass gripped me so hard my feet started to move.

"Stop it!"

"Eris, whatever you're doing, stop," I heard Persephone's voice say, and mercifully my feet stilled. The grin on Eris' face vanished.

"Of course, oh Queen of dull," Eris said with an over the top bow. For a moment I thought her huge boobs would spill out of her top, but she straightened in time. "Good luck surviving my idiot brother, sweetie," she said to me, then turned and strode away.

"Thanks. You keep rescuing me," I said, turning gratefully to Persephone.

"Not for much longer. You're needed," she said.

She walked me the length of the room to stand in front of the dais with the thrones, Hades now occupying one. Ares glared at me as I approached, and as before, his anger seemed to steel me rather than intimidate me. I could take his bullshit. I gave him a potent 'fuck-off' look as I came to a stop beside him.

The other gods' eyes bore into me too, and I avoided looking at any of them directly. I wasn't one to shy away from threats, but damn - they were intimidating. Energy thrummed from them, swirling through the air like heat over tarmac. It was weird. And I didn't like it.

The smell of the ocean washed over me suddenly, so strong I froze, then a cool breeze seemed to cut through the uncomfortable power-heat. I felt myself relax instantly, and a man shimmered into being just in front of the dais.

He looked like a completely normal man in his sixties, with a weather-beaten face, fierce blue eyes, and a pale green toga. Persephone and Ares bowed on either side of me, so I did the same.

"Oceanus," ground out Ares as he straightened, and I felt my eyebrow quirk. This was the most powerful being in Olympus? But he didn't exude power like the gods behind him. All he exuded, in fact, was a cheerful calm.

"Ares," Oceanus said pleasantly. "I am pleased to hear that you may have an opportunity to prove yourself a true ruler." Every muscle in the God of War's body tensed, and I wished I could see under his helmet. I was pretty sure his face would be as red as a tomato. He clearly didn't like Oceanus much.

"I have agreed to help Hades with his escaped demon," he said eventually, voice hoarse.

"And in doing so, you will also be helping this young lady whose power you covet. How selfless." Oceanus' eyes twinkled as he looked at me, and I instantly trusted him. Which was very unlike me. I folded my arms, suspicious.

Oceanus smiled. "I have a desire to prove myself an ally to the Olympians," he said loudly, and turned in a full circle, looking at all the gods on their thrones in turn. "So I have a gift for you. It is in everyone's interest to get Ares back to ruling his... unique realm. But I am bound by my own rules, and those do not allow me to just hand out power of that magnitude. Power must be earned. It is the most dangerous thing in the world."

Silence met his words. Ares shifted, his armor clinking.

"If you return to Hades with both the escaped demon and the missing Guardians, then I will forge you a Trident of power."

No silence this time. Loud gasps rang through the room, and all of the gods behind him moved in their seats.

"I..." Ares began, then faltered. "A true Trident of power?"

"Yes. You will be restored to full strength."

"I accept," said Ares, bowing his head. I looked between the two men, blinking.

"Then you must be on your way."

Before I could think another thing, light flashed around me.

∿

"Where the fuck are we now? And what is a Trident of power?" I said, anger getting the better of me as I blinked into bright sunlight and turned to Ares' hulking form. We were standing on sand, and all I could see behind him and around us was more sand. Piles of rocks and hardy plants that clearly refused to die in the desert heat dotted the landscape.

"We are in my realm. A Trident of power is extremely rare and grants its wielder power equal to that of an Olympian." Ares answered stiffly. The bright light was reflecting off his armor, making it hard to look at him, and for the first time I got an idea of what he might look like if he had his power and was truly godly. Except that he didn't have his power and he wasn't godly. He was an asshole.

"What do we do now?"

"We find the demon."

"Just like that? But we don't even have any supplies!"

"We don't need supplies, foolish mortal."

I scowled at him. "I don't give a flying fuck if you don't eat, but I sure do."

He let out a long, agitated breath. "Of course I eat. But I can use your power to flash us to food at any point," he growled. I paused, dropping my hands from my hips.

"Oh. Good. Because you don't want to see me hangry."

"What is hangry?"

I rolled my eyes. "Pray you don't find out," I muttered. He stared at me a moment through his stupid shiny helmet's eye slits.

"You are an idiot, and will likely get us killed," he said eventually.

"I'm not an idiot," I replied. Which was partially true. I

couldn't argue the bit about getting us killed though. "And anyway, I thought you wanted me dead?"

"That depends," he said, turning and looking out over the nothingness.

"On what?"

"How irritating you are, and if you are at risk of killing me along with you."

Well, I was dead then. If I irritated him even half as much as he annoyed me, we were fucked.

There was a slightly pink shimmer in the air between us, and Ares froze, hand on his sword.

"I need to attend to some business before we embark upon this quest. I shall return shortly," he said, then vanished in a flash of pink.

5

ARES

"Who the hell does that washed up old has-been think he is!" I raged, stamping my foot against the marble of Aphrodite's throne room floor as I paced. The pink shimmer was her calling card, and I had been relieved to see it. I had expected her to want to see me before I left on my quest. I had *wanted* her to want to see me.

"Come now, Oceanus is hardly a has-been. And I think he's quite attractive," purred Aphrodite from her throne.

"Don't test me," I growled, turning to her. She gave me a sultry smile and all my damned resolve seeped from me as her beauty took over my senses. "Aphrodite, stop using your power on me," I demanded. "I can't withstand it with none of my own." Her smile vanished.

"I know, and I'm becoming bored. You're like a wolf with no fangs."

Anger, not with her but with myself, leaped through me, but none of my godly power accompanied it. It was just plain, useless fury.

How could I have been so fucking careless? How had I let Zeus take my power?

"I have a way to get my strength back now," I told her, my voice harsh.

"Yes. A Trident of power. How exciting." She didn't sound excited. She sounded completely uninterested. "You know, you could just kill the girl."

"I would love to kill the girl. She is infuriating. But I would still have to carry out Hades' bidding and find this damned demon. Why anger the new Lord of the Gods if I would have to perform the same task regardless?"

Aphrodite sighed, and lifted a peach from the bowl of fruit that was always next to her throne.

"I suppose," she said. "But you never used to care about angering Lords. In fact, you quite enjoyed it."

"Petty little Lords in my own realm, yes. Not Hades."

Her smile slid back into place. It was breathtaking. *She* was breathtaking.

"Well, now those Lords will get a chance to get even with you," she said. Trepidation rippled through me, and I cursed my loss of power for the millionth time. Trepidation was not something I was familiar, or comfortable with.

But the Goddess of Love was right. When the Lords of War caught up with me, they would likely be stronger than I was. Unless the girl came into her power fast and I could use it all, as I hoped.

My eyes raked over my lover's smile.

"You take pleasure in my plight?" I snarled at her.

"Yes, Ares, I do. It's your own stupidity that got you here."

Her words struck me like a dagger. They were true. But to know she enjoyed my pain...

"Then I will leave you," I said stiffly.

"No. You will do as you came here to do. You will take pleasure in my body, and I yours, before you set off on this boring quest."

She still wanted me. The knowledge buoyed me, and I slowly pulled my helmet off. I saw the gleam in her eyes, before she flicked her hand.

"On second thoughts, I'm tired. I'll see you when you return from Aries. If you return."

I felt my face burn, and rammed my helmet back onto my head. I could not even flash myself out of her blasted fucking throne room. I had no power.

With another flick of her hand I was back in my desert, dismissed.

6

BELLA

"You left me alone in a fucking desert less than five minutes into this damned quest!" I yelled, when Ares appeared out of nowhere on the sand beside me just ten minutes after he had left.

The giant god looked at me long enough for me to register the fury in his dark eyes, then roared, drawing his sword from its sheath.

I ducked into a low crouch, balling my fists, the red mist descending fast.

But Ares turned, and I rose slowly as he started smashing his sword into a large cluster of boulders as though they had just announced themselves his mortal enemy. He bellowed with rage as he landed his weapon again and again on the rocks, and they cracked and crumbled under his wrath.

"Your business went well then?" I muttered, the red mist leaking away. I cocked my head as I watched him hacking the shit out of the rocks, his sound of his armor moving and the steel clash of his sword ringing though the air.

Whilst it was quite amusing to see his fury with the inanimate objects, I was also reluctantly impressed. Power or no power, the man could wield a sword. I mean, a pile of rocks wasn't the ideal target but... I'd destroyed enough plasterboard walls that didn't really deserve it in my time to withhold judgment.

I wondered absently what had made him so mad as I flopped back down on my ass with a sigh. If we really did share the same temper, then it didn't matter what had set him off, as long as I let him take it all out on the rocks. Especially since I was unarmed. Which was the first of a number of things I had decided needed resolving fast.

He'd only been gone for ten minutes, but that was long enough to be completely alone in a strange place, and for the panic I'd so far kept subdued to make some headway.

I had been abducted by the God of War and taken to a world that by all rights shouldn't exist. It probably said a lot about me that until I was alone and unarmed, a secret little part of me had actually been excited by that. Something in my life finally felt right, even if it was kind of impossible, and my friend's life was in danger.

As long as the adrenaline was burning through me I could eliminate anything that made me weak, any self-doubt or emotion that wasn't helpful. But standing in a damned desert with nothing at all did the opposite of that. Worry had begun crashing through me unchecked, a whirlwind of doubt and the undeniable truth that I was in way, way over my head smashing into me like a wrecking ball. The reality of my whole life changing in one day, being wanted dead by a violent god and now being expected to chase down a demon escaped from the

Underworld finally hit me. And in a world where everyone was armed with dirty great swords or freaking magic, I was woefully under-equipped.

At that point in my runaway-train of panicked thoughts I had managed to latch onto something and steady myself. Weapons. I needed a weapon. With something nice and violent to focus on, I'd sat down on the hot sand, taken a deep breath, and forced myself to concentrate.

Joshua had once told me that list-making was a good way to feel in charge of a situation that otherwise felt out of my control. At the time this had seemed like good advice for when I lost yet another job, or my fuckwit landlord put my rent up for no good reason. But now that I knew Joshua was some sort of magic person from another damned world, I had to wonder under what circumstances he had really intended his advice to be used. It probably wasn't sat in a desert somewhere in Olympus trying to keep a panic attack at bay. None-the-less, I had made myself a list entitled 'things I need to survive in the realm of war'.

As Ares yelled again, his huge sword running out of rocks to smash, another stab of betrayal bit at me. Joshua had known I was different the whole time. He had known I really didn't belong, and that it wasn't a damned chemical imbalance. He had tried to help me believe that I was normal, instead of just telling me why I'd always felt so out of place, so trapped. So wrong for the world I was in.

I squashed the feeling with a snort, and went through my list again in my head. There was no point getting myself worked up about Joshua until I had at least saved his life. I could yell at him for lying to me after that.

. . .

When Ares finally stomped back to me, his shoulders were heaving and his sword hung limply from his right arm.

"Better?" I asked him.

"No. Let's go."

"Woahhhh there," I said, springing to my feet. "You got to take care of some business, so I think it's only fair that I do too."

"Your business is inconsequential," he said. I bit down on my tongue, hard. I would not swear at him. I needed his co-operation.

"It would make life a lot easier for both of us if I had a change of clothes and some of my stuff," I said calmly.

"Why do you need more clothes?" he scowled.

"Because I like to change my fucking underwear every now and then!" So much for not swearing.

"Use magic," he shrugged.

"I don't know how to."

"Then I shall do it."

"Not a chance in sweet freaking hell are you going anywhere near my underwear!"

"As if I-" he started angrily, but I held up my hands and spoke over him as loudly as I could.

"Just take me to my apartment so I can throw some stuff in a backpack, or I'll give you endless shit until you do. It's that simple, armor-boy."

I knew I would win eventually, and I was right. But I wasn't prepared for the feeling I got when Ares finally flashed us back to my apartment and I stared around at the dimly-lit space. A pang of something strong gripped me, and it wasn't sadness or fondness for my home. It was a gut-wrenching delight at the thought that I might never have to see the place again.

It may have been a little premature, but I was quite sure that whatever the hell was happening to me was the start of something that did *not* end with me returning to this dump.

"You live here?" Ares' tone held a note of disbelief, and something else I couldn't identify. Probably general assholery, I decided as I made my way quickly through my tiny kitchen, into my tinier bedroom. I was lucky to have a separate bedroom at all, living this close to the city center, but that didn't mean I liked the place. The neighbors were awful, always yelling at each other, fighting and throwing stuff that banged off the walls and set my temper humming. And everything was damp. The shitty landlord never fixed anything he was asked to, and no matter how much mold-removing product I covered the minuscule shower-room in, dark slimy mildew always crept back over the walls and ceiling in a matter of hours.

"Where do you sit, or eat?" Ares called as I pulled up the thin single mattress on my bed to get to the storage space beneath it.

I ignored him, finding an old khaki-colored backpack and yanking it out. The answer was that I ate sitting on the bed, the bare walls closing in around me as I tried to watch Netflix or read on my phone. I was an outdoors kind of girl, and ADHD levels of hyperactivity meant I was ill-suited to a space this cramped. But I couldn't afford more. Hell, right now I couldn't even afford this. The only saving grace of the entire building was the basement. It had been slowly filled over the years with tired but functional second-hand gym gear, including a punch-bag. I couldn't pay for real gym membership, so even though it had no ventilation and got hotter than the freaking sun down there under the four-story concrete building, I never uttered a bad word about it. I *needed* it.

I started to throw t-shirts, two pairs of jeans, and a whole pile of socks and underwear into the bag, barely paying attention to what I was selecting. Other than my Guns N' Roses t-shirt. I made sure I had that. I slipped off my sneakers and shoved them into the bag, pulling my only decent-quality shoes on in their place. They were whacking great big walking boots, with hidden steel-caps, that did some serious damage to whatever they connected with.

Then I pulled open the drawer in the little unit by my bed and wrapped my hand around the thing I had really come for. My flick-blade. It may not be as big as Ares' sword, but the little knife and I had history, and it had never let me down. No way was I facing Underworld demons without it. Or hulking armored giants with no sense of humor.

"I am glad you came back here."

I jumped so hard in surprise that the blade slipped from my fingers and landed on the threadbare carpet.

"Zeeva!" The bastard cat appeared on my bed, her tail swishing.

"You are aware you are unlikely to see this place again?"

"Yes, and good riddance," I said, picking up my knife, pulse slowing.

"I mean London, not this awful apartment," she said, her mental voice laden with distaste.

I faltered. I wouldn't miss this shithole, but London? The city was special.

"Does Olympus have musicals?" I asked hopefully.

"Olympus has plays beyond your wildest dreams, but I doubt you shall ever see them," she answered.

"Why not?"

"Primarily because I would be surprised if you survive Ares and his realm," she said bluntly. I scowled at her. *"But even if you do, you can't stay in Olympus."*

A sick feeling churned through my stomach. The only reason I wasn't completely freaking out was that Olympus felt so right, even though I'd barely spent an hour there.

"Why can't I stay?"

"You are of the mortal world now. You need power to live in Olympus if you are not raised there."

"I have power! That's why Ares wants me!"

"But you can't use it yourself." Her tone was that of every teacher I had ever known when I failed to do what I had been asked, and at that moment I realized what she was doing. She was goading me.

"You want me to learn to use my power?" I asked. Her amber eyes flicked to the door, where Ares stood beyond.

"He will not teach you. You may only rely on yourself."

"Can you teach me?" She bared her needle-like teeth.

"Your power could not be more different than mine. I can teach you nothing."

I didn't think that was true, given that I knew fuck all. When you were starting from zero, anything at all was more than nothing.

"Well, as it happens, 'learn magic war power' was next on my list, right after 'arm myself'," I said haughtily. Her eyes moved to my knife, safely folded shut as I pushed it into my jeans pocket.

When she said nothing else, I grabbed my deodorant and a few other bits from the hanging shelves in my washroom, then zipped up my bag, mentally crossing the items off the packing list I'd made in the desert.

"You know, I might not *want* to stay in Olympus," I lied, as I slung one strap of the backpack over my shoulder and looked at the cat. She blinked slowly.

"You want to stay," she said. *"As a true goddess, you could explore a world that is truly limitless. Realms that float in the sky, reside in volcanoes, are submerged in golden domes in the ocean. Ships that soar through the sky. Magic that can provide endless experiences, tastes, feelings, desires. People, gods and creatures that will obliterate the boundaries of your imagination. Stories that will leave you desperate for more. And adventures that will never end if you do not want them to."*

The bag slipped off my shoulder as my muscles went slack. Zeeva was describing my greatest dream. A world where I could not get bored. Where my boundless energy and vivid imagination could be constantly absorbed. My eyes were glazing over as I imagined it, my drab, moldy, tiny apartment vanishing behind a vision of freedom and life.

"And I can only stay if I have magic?" I breathed.

"Yes." The vision cleared abruptly, my mushroom-colored walls slamming back down around me.

The idea of actually having or using magic was something my brain had so far refused to dwell on. The fact that I had heard my own apparent War power referenced countless times in the last crazy few hours didn't make it feel any more real or true.

I mean, it wasn't like I didn't believe it. Why the hell would Ares have shown up in my life otherwise?

But I didn't feel like I had any magic power. And as arrogant as it might have been, I had enough confidence in my ability as a scrappy but pretty accomplished fighter to not *have* to process the idea. I could survive without magic, I was sure, so I was focusing on Joshua, and arming myself. Things I knew about, could work with and control.

But if I ultimately needed the magic to stay in Olympus... That changed things. That was a motivation I could use, that I could force my brain to accept. I'd show that stuck-up cat I could learn magic.

If Ares could use it, then so could I.

I just had to find a way of getting him to tell me where to start.

7

BELLA

When I stepped back into my kitchen, which somewhat impossibly looked even smaller with the enormous god squished into it, Ares grunted and locked his eyes on mine. The red plume of his helmet was flattened against the grubby ceiling, and I failed to suppress a smirk. He looked ridiculous.

"Why do you live here?"

"It's all I could afford that came with a free punch-bag."

"Afford? You pay money to reside in this... box?"

"Jeez, you're clueless. Yes, armor-boy, I pay money to live here. Is Olympus rent-free?" The last question came out more hopefully than sarcastic.

Ares shifted his weight, looking disdainfully at my splintered gray cupboards. "In my realm you live under the rules of your Lord or King."

"And how do your Lords and Kings become Lords and Kings?"

Ares shrugged and the metal of his helmet scraped the ceiling at the same time his shoulder plates clanged against the kitchen unit. "The Lords are deities; they are born that way. They delegate power to the Kings."

"You got any Queens?" I asked. He nodded.

"Many. Hippolyta of the Amazons is my favorite." His eyes lit up as he spoke her name, and I remembered Persephone saying that that she was his daughter. The thought made me uncomfortable, so although this was the most amicable and useful conversation we'd had so far, I changed the subject.

"You ready to go? I need to find my friend." Ares' eyes darkened.

"Always you talk about your friend," he grumbled.

"Yes. That's generally what friends do. They give a shit. Do you have tequila in Olympus?" I asked, spying the bottle of booze on the counter behind him, next to the broken kettle.

"What is tequila?"

"My version of nectar of the gods," I muttered, swiping the bottle and tipping my bag forward to open it. When the tequila was safely stowed inside, I put my hands on my hips, and cast my eyes around the little apartment one last time. There was nothing at all that I would miss here. Which in itself was sad. But it only served to strengthen my resolve. I couldn't be more ready to move on, even if it was to something mostly unbelievable and very likely lethal. "Let's go."

"So... Why are we starting here, in the empty desert?" I asked when the light from the flash cleared from my eyes and I clocked my sandy surroundings again.

"Stop talking," Ares grunted.

"Hey, if I'm going to do this with you then you have to tell me what's going on," I said, as he began to stomp through the sand. "I'm not going to just follow you about like a damned puppy."

"If you want to survive, and find your godsforsaken friend, then you will do exactly that." He paused and turned to look at me, something malicious gleaming in his eyes. "You will behave like my pet."

Anger, hot and real, flushed through me. "Your pet?" I echoed, my voice low.

"Correct." He nodded, his stupid helmet plume bouncing.

"I am nobody's fucking pet," I growled. The red mist slammed down, energy soaring through my veins, filling my muscles.

"You will start by swearing less," he said.

"I will start by ripping your freaking head off, you overgrown jerk!"

I leaped at him before I could stop myself, and cried out as I hit an invisible wall, bouncing back and landing hard on my ass. Dusty sand flew up around me as I scrabbled to my feet. *Never stay down longer than you need to.* Ares folded his arms, self-satisfied.

But before I could try flinging myself at him again, I realized something. It wasn't just my shoulder and hip that had physically felt that wall of power. Something in my gut had too.

With a roar, I launched myself at him again, but dropped low at the last minute, aiming to swipe out his legs. I hit the invisible barrier again, as I expected, but this time I was concentrating. There it was! A flare of something, like a sharp yank on a cord deep in my belly. Was that him accessing my power?

I yelped as I was suddenly lifted off my ass, my distraction by the alien feeling giving Ares the upper-hand. Literally. He had my shirt in his fist like he'd scruffed a dog, and was picking me up off the ground. I struggled and thrashed, half-expecting my shirt to tear, but he set me back down surprisingly gently. I turned to glare up at him, and he glared back. He was at least two feet taller than me.

"Stop wasting time," he said.

"Stop being a prick," I replied. Sparks flew in his dark eyes, and I was close enough to see that they looked like burning embers. They were... much more interesting to look at than they should be. I snapped my eyes away.

"Why are you making this so difficult?"

"Oh, I don't know, probably because you introduced yourself with your intention to kill me? Or maybe because you don't give a flying fuck about saving Joshua and are only doing this to save your own ass? Or perhaps it's just because you're a humorless oaf."

"The fastest way to save your friend is to stop angering me," he said, and there was a new, very real strain in his voice.

"Tell me how to use my power," I said, finding his eyes again.

"No," he answered flatly, and turned around, resuming his stride.

"Then I'll keep being a pain in the ass," I said, almost jogging to catch up with him.

"You will do that regardless," he spat. I couldn't really argue with that, so I reluctantly fell in beside him. The adrenaline from my brief and unsuccessful bout with him was still churning through me, firing me up, but the red mist had melted away. The fastest way to help Joshua was to keep moving, not uselessly attack Ares.

"At least tell me where we're going," I said.

"We are going to one of Aries' busiest cities, to find out who knows anything of this accursed demon," he sighed, after a long pause.

"Oh." I said. That seemed like a good idea, but I wasn't going to tell him that. "Why aren't we flashing there?"

"Because the King of Erimos does not allow flashing into his city. Only out."

I moved my curiosity about Erimos and its king to a new list called 'things to ask about later'. "But if you're the god of this realm, can't you just break the rules?"

Ares took a long breath, then let it out slowly. I got the distinct impression he felt like he was talking to a child.

"Your power is a shadow of what mine was. It will strengthen the longer you are here, but right now, the most impressive thing that you can do is flash." I opened my mouth indignantly to defend my newly discovered magic, but Ares continued before I could speak. "Many in the cities of my realm would choose to take advantage of me, should they discover my lack of strength. To topple the God of War would be a legendary feat. So we shall not be revealing my identity to anyone."

A little ripple of excitement took me, and I really wasn't sure why. "You're going to move through your own realm in disguise?"

"I can see no other way." He did not sound happy about it at all, but for some reason, I was thrilled with the idea. It was like being in a spy movie or something. Maybe it was my love of theater, and the opportunity I was about to be given to be a real actress that was so exciting. Or maybe I was just more messed up than I realized I was.

"Won't they recognize you? You're pretty, erm... distinctive." I eyed his hulking frame as I asked the question. Ares said nothing, just stamped across the barren desert, his armor clinking. "Are you going to use magic to change what you look like?" I tried again.

"Your power is not strong enough for me to use it for a prolonged period like that. It would drain you and render you unconscious." I didn't like the lilt of happiness in his voice at the mention of me being unconscious.

"Then how are you going to disguise yourself? Surely everyone knows what you look like?"

Ares slowed to a stop, putting his huge fists on his hips.

"You have no idea how little I want to do this," he said quietly. "With you of all people."

"Do what?" A combination of apprehension and excitement skittered over my skin in the warm desert heat. What was he about to do?

"There are only three beings who have ever seen my face." I barely heard the words from behind his helmet, he spoke so low.

"Why?"

"The helmet of war is part of me. You would not understand." My mind jumped to my knife, and how wrong I felt when I didn't have it, but I dismissed the thought, concentrating on Ares.

"So, you never take it off?"

"Not in front of people, no."

"Are you really ugly?" I couldn't help the question, and his head snapped to me, embers in his furious eyes again.

"You mock me?" I swore I could hear the actual ring of steel in his words, and there was a tiny tug in my tummy. *I was making him mad enough to use my magic again.*

"It's just a helmet," I shrugged.

"You are an ignorant, selfish, weak child," he growled, the embers growing and coloring his eyes a dancing amber. I took a breath, the sight utterly mesmerizing. The longer I looked at the fire burning in his eyes, the more I was sure I could hear the ringing of swords and distant drums, the more the sensation of being flooded with adrenaline and the unbeatable feeling of victory tingled through me. He must have mistaken my awe for fear though, because his shoulders squared and he took a step back, giving a small, satisfied nod and breaking the spell.

Deciding that it was probably safer to let him think that I was scared of him than let him know he had the most beautiful eyes I'd ever seen, I kept my mouth shut, but residual tingling still pulsed across my skin. This was not what I needed. At all. But already I wanted to see the fire in his eyes again.

He just called you a weak child! Not cool! Get it together, Bella, I chided myself mentally.

"If I'm ignorant, then that's your fault. You won't tell me anything." I folded my arms across my chest, the tingling finally ebbing away.

Ares shifted his weight from one foot to the other, armor jangling. "I will tell you what you need to know about Erimos on the way," he offered eventually.

"I'm not interested in Erimos," I said, although I totally was. "I want to know why you're so attached to this helmet. Do you sleep with it?"

Ares gave a bark of annoyance, this time stamping his foot on the ground. "You are everything I hate about humans!"

"I'm going to take that as a compliment, on behalf of all humans," I said. Truth was, I didn't think I represented humans well at all, they mostly seemed to hate me. But he didn't need to know that.

"The helmet was a gift from my father," he snapped.

"Zeus? The same Zeus who stole your power?"

"Yes."

"Don't you hate him now?"

"No. He is mighty and strong and our true leader."

"Then... Why'd he take your power?" I felt the tug in my tummy before I saw Ares begin to grow, his armor shining and growing with him. My eyes went straight to his, with a spark of hope. *I wanted to see the fire.*

"My father will have had his reasons. And I will have an eternity to work them out. In the meantime, we will find this blasted demon, get your accursed friend, and deliver them to Hades!"

"And show the whole of your realm your real face," I added, with a small shrug.

A blast of power erupted from the god, and before I could blink, I was tumbling backwards. Heat and the sound of drums engulfed me as I lost my footing, but then my butt bounced off something soft, righting me on my feet again. I had my arms flung out, trying to regain sturdy footing as I looked up at Ares. Embers burned in his chocolate eyes and the stupid tingles started up again instantly. I could still hear the drums.

"You are impossible," he snarled. "Are you trying to force me to lose my temper?"

"No," I lied. *A little.* Though I knew how stupid that was. He probably would kill me.

I turned my head to see what had broken my fall, but there was nothing there. Had I somehow used my magic? Or had Ares stopped me falling on my ass again? I couldn't imagine he cared much about my ass though.

"Removing my helmet will be the hardest thing I have done in centuries. If you can't respect that, keep your mouth closed," he said quietly.

To my utter astonishment, his words actually made me feel guilty. If this really was such a big deal for him, maybe I should back off a little. *But he was going to kill you!* My indignant inner voice was right, but I couldn't bring myself to goad him again. Centuries was a long time. Plus, there was a curious part of me that wanted to see what he looked like under the armor.

In a flash, my sex-starved brain served me an image of him, under the metal. And I mean under *all* of the metal. Huge, hulking, and *naked*. I couldn't stop the heat spreading across my cheeks and blinked the image away quickly. Weirdly, naked Ares in my head still had the helmet on. It seemed it was easier for my imagination to conjure up a naked body than to invent the god's face. Bet a shrink would have fun with that one.

When I did indeed keep my mouth shut, Ares huffed an angry breath, and turned his back to me, taking a few long strides and putting a decent distance between us. I almost made a quip about him being a drama queen and clamped my jaw shut tightly to stop the words escaping.

But geez, the man was over-dramatic. What was he hiding under there? An image of Shrek popped into my head and I bit back a snort of laughter slightly too late. Ares tossed me an angry glare over his shoulder, then gripped the bottom of his helmet.

Anticipation skittered through me, unbidden. Why did I care what he looked like? He lifted his hands, pulling the helmet clear from his head. A mass of warm brown, slightly wavy hair fell down his back, and my eyebrows shot up in surprise. It was streaked through with white and reached well past his massive shoulders. I watched wide-eyed as he dropped the helmet onto the sand and began to tie it back into a tail with a leather strap. I really would not have guessed him as a long-hair-kinda-guy. In fact, I would have staked money on him being an angry-buzz-cut-kinda-guy.

When he finally turned to me, it took every ounce of willpower I possessed to keep my jaw from dropping.

Fuck me sideways, Ares was hot. Hot enough that this was the most evidence I had had so far that he wasn't actually human. No human looked like that.

Those chocolate brown eyes that stormed with fire were set in a face that could not have blended stern and sexy any better. His hard, angular cheekbones and jawline were offset by full soft lips, and his short, dark beard somehow made his wavy hair look intensely more masculine. He was perfect. Simply perfect.

"Well, I guess you won't need a paper bag," I breathed.

He frowned, dark eyebrows drawing together. "Why would anyone need a bag made of paper?"

Seeing his mouth move as he spoke for the first time gave me an inexorable desire to feel his soft lips, and I screwed my face up. *He was a god. Of course he would be hot. That didn't mean he wasn't still an asshole! Focus!*

"It's just an expression from my world," I said, shaking my head. "What are you going to do with that?" I asked, pointing to his helmet in the sand.

"I will hide it, along with this." He banged a fist on his massive chest-plate, and my cheeks burned as though someone was holding a flame to them. Great. The hottest asshole I'd ever met was about to undress.

. . .

I tried to distract myself by sitting and doodling in the sand, whilst Ares clanged about, removing his armor. *Joshua.* This was about saving Joshua, I told myself repeatedly, drawing a large spiral with my finger. I needed to stop delaying Ares and get a move on. As soon as he was ready to go, I'd start behaving myself; rein in the attitude, and focus.

"Let's go," Ares grunted, snapping me out of my self-scolding. I leaped to my feet, pulling my bag with me, then stumbled as I turned to the god. He was wearing simple black linen pants, and no freaking shirt.

"Why aren't you wearing a shirt?" I fixed my gaze on his face, his outrageously sculpted pecs burning into my lower peripheral vision.

"People in Erimos do not wear shirts," he answered simply.

"The women better wear damned shirts," I said, alarmed. I wasn't walking into an alien city with my boobs out. Not a chance.

Ares gave me a look as though I was ten years old. "It is clear you are a tourist. You may stay dressed as you are." Across his forehead was a gold band, the same material as his shining helmet. I pointed to it.

"Is that your armor? In disguise?" He nodded. "Neat trick," I said, impressed. "But you do look a little... regal."

He rolled his eyes and turned his back to me, striding through the sand. It was entirely impossible not to look at his massive shoulders, the way his toned muscles moved as he walked, the dimples in the small of his back. The low waistline of his pants... I gave myself a hard mental slap. *No more ogling, Bella. It's time to find Joshua.*

8

BELLA

We'd only spent about a minute walking, in complete and awkward silence, when a teal shimmer caught my attention, and I slowed to a stop. Zeeva appeared on the sand before me, gave a languid cat stretch, then sat neatly, tail wrapped around herself.

"Why is your cat here?" growled Ares, stopping and turning to glare at us both.

"Beats me," I shrugged, refusing to look at his bare chest. His muscular, tanned, hulking bare chest. "What's up, Zeeva?"

"I assume you are headed for Erimos?" she asked in my head. I nodded. She yawned.

"Unfortunately, my tether to you will not work once you are in the city. I must stay with you now."

"Oh." I didn't really know if I wanted her with me or not. She hadn't exactly been friendly or helpful so far. But she did know more than me, and I supposed her presence couldn't hurt. I looked up at Ares. "She's coming with us to Erimos," I told him.

Ares snarled. "You are not welcome, spy," he hissed at Zeeva. I didn't hear her reply to him, but he looked pissed as he stamped a leather boot, then turned and resumed his march, his delicious back somehow radiating anger.

"Well, you managed to piss him off again," I said to the cat. She didn't bother to answer me, just sauntered after him.

∼

"So, you were going to tell me about Erimos," I prompted when I caught up with them. I was getting hot, but I hadn't brought any water, only tequila, which on reflection wasn't very helpful in a desert.

"It is run by a particularly brutal king. There are fighting pits all over my realm, and he has the largest, and the most, gambling establishments. Erimos has money. Many come here to enjoy drink and women." Ares barked the words, a hum of anger still rolling from him.

"Lovely," I said. "What's a fighting pit?"

"A gladiator ring, in your world," Zeeva's voice sounded in my head, at the same time Ares shook his head.

"You are clueless," he muttered.

"You don't think that's where Joshua has been taken, do you?" All misplaced sexual thoughts about Ares vanished as images of Joshua chained up and forced to fight gladiators filled my mind.

Ares just shrugged. "If a demon has been spotted in my realm, someone in Erimos will know about it," he said. "That is why we are going there."

Anxiety pulsed through me, the reality check sharpening my focus.

"Your friend is a Guardian, not a fighter. It is unlikely he

would have been taken to the pits," Zeeva said a long few moments later. I looked at her gratefully, but she didn't turn to me.

"How do I talk back to you in my head?" I asked her.

"Just concentrate on projecting the words to me alone. But I'd really rather you didn't. You're annoying enough already."

"Charming," I muttered. Even in Olympus, nobody fucking liked me, not even my own damned cat.

I could kind of see their point though, I thought glumly as we walked across the sand, the vista around us still void of anything except the odd scrubby bush or pile of rocks. I just wasn't good at staying still, or relaxing. I put people on edge, irritated them. And that was the best-case scenario. I'd lost many friends just through the kind of trouble I seemed to attract. Or more honestly, I lost them when they saw my *reaction* to the kind of trouble I attracted. I couldn't walk away from a fight. I couldn't back down when challenged. I couldn't just work out what was best for me and make a smart decision. I ran on pure impulse and energy. And it scared people. Hell, some-times it scared me.

"We are here. I know it will be hard but try to keep your mouth closed and let me speak," Ares said abruptly, turning away.

I frowned around us at the endless sand. "Erm, is the city invisible?"

Ares looked at me like I was mental. "Invisible? And you have the nerve to call me an oaf." He shook his head yet again, then frightened the living shit out of me by bellowing so loudly I thought he'd been stabbed or something.

"What in the name of-" I started, but my shout was drowned out instantly by the sound of roaring wind, and my hair whipped up into my face as the sand around us began to spin into peaked tornadoes. Within seconds I could see nothing but the beige of the sand whirling around us, and even though there seemed to be a pocket of clear air surrounding the three of us, panic surged through me, instinct taking over. But as fast as the sandstorm had started, it stopped. The sand didn't fall back to earth like it should though, spinning off into the sky and disappearing into clouds instead. I looked back down to see that the sand had left a massive sunken clearing in its place, filled with the most magnificent walled city I could have possibly imagined.

My immediate impression was that it looked like Agrabah from the Disney movie Aladdin. But as I looked closer at the jewel encrusted walls that surrounded the shining metropolis before us, I began to notice the darker details. Skulls were set between the pale stone and the jewels, and the bulbous spires on the buildings that peaked high above the walls were decorated with swirling carvings of weapons. Swords and flails and axes and hammers were all intricately entwined in huge patterns across the impressive architecture.

From our elevated position I could see that the grand spired towers were mostly in the middle of the square city, and the further toward the walls I looked, the smaller the buildings became. But they were all made of the same stone, and they all glittered in the sun, as though wealth was built into the structures themselves. Broad courtyards filled with fabric marquees occupied the spaces between the buildings, and I could just make out figures bustling around. Surrounding the city, beyond the walls, were six or seven sunken pits lined with rows of stepped benches, with circular stages in the center. *The fighting pits,* I realized with a pang of morbid curiosity. Between the pits were hundreds of brightly colored tents in clusters and I frowned at them.

"Why are they outside the city?" I asked, pointing at the tents.

"You must pay to enter Erimos. The people who live in those tents can't afford to go inside the walls." Ares stamped down the sandy dune, and I followed him.

"I'm guessing you have money?" I asked, suddenly aware of how penniless I was. Ares just grunted.

"They use drachma here." I looked down at Zeeva, the cat seeming to almost float across the sand, effortlessly graceful.

"Right. Good to know," I said, even though it meant nothing to me at all. But I would take any and all of the information offered to me. Eventually some of it would surely be useful.

When we got to the bottom of the dune, the gates of Erimos loomed large and imposing in front of us. Up close I could make out lots of bones embedded in the stone walls, not just the skulls visible from further away. Diamonds glittered amongst femurs, sapphires glinted against ribs, and amethysts shone around collarbones. It was creepy as hell, but I burned to explore a city such as this. It called to me.

But when he reached the intricate iron gates and the two armor-clad guards collecting coins from the trickle of folk moving through them, Ares turned left sharply, walking instead along the outside of the wall.

"Why aren't we going in?" I asked, walking fast to keep pace with him. The sounds of people calling out, selling wares and greeting each other died out as we moved further along the wall.

"We may be able to get the information we need without entering the city."

"But I want to enter the city!"

"I don't care what you want."

"Clearly," I snapped.

"He is avoiding the King of Erimos," offered Zeeva.

"Why?"

"Ask him."

"Why are you avoiding the King?" I asked Ares, and he turned sharply, snarling at the cat.

"Meddling beast," he hissed at her. She flicked her tail. "He is not just a King. And it will be best if he does not know I am here."

"But you're in disguise."

"I will not take unnecessary risks!" he shouted, drawing to a stop and rounding on me. "This is my realm, my world, my rules, and you will stop challenging me!"

I glowered back at him, but stayed silent, remembering my resolve to behave. To an extent, he was right. At least about it being his world. He definitely knew best here, and the fastest way to get to Joshua was to let Ares do what he needed to do.

But there was no way I was playing by his rules.

It took another five minutes to reach one of the clusters of tents. I couldn't see the sunken fighting pit that I knew was just beyond the campsite because we were on level ground now, but my body hummed with curiosity.

"The people who live here are pit fighters. Many are

owned by slavers who stay in the city," said Ares quietly as we got close.

"Why don't they run away?"

"Most are bound and cannot. But not all of them. Some fight for glory," he answered. "They are a hard people. Keep your mouth closed and let me talk."

The tents were all of the colors of a circus, bright reds, blues, purples and yellows, and their inhabitants looked just as colorful. I made a sincere effort to keep my interest from showing on my face as Ares slowed down and we walked casually into the camp. Directly ahead of us was a large fire, an iron pot swinging over it, and about six people were seated around it on wooden stools. As far as I could tell, they were all dressed similarly, shirtless with baggy hareem pants in purple or red. But that was where the similarities ended.

Two of them, I was pretty sure, were minotaurs. They were as tall as Ares, covered in dark fur, had hoofed feet and snouted faces, and most impressive of all had giant horns curling up out of their foreheads. They were freaking awesome. As the group began to notice our approach, a creature with loads of spikes sticking out of his bald head turned to us, and I saw that he only had one amber eye in the middle of his deformed face. He stood up, and I realized with a jolt that *he* was a *she*. A badly torn rag was tied around her chest, and she fixed her single eye on Ares.

"State your business," she said as the whole group stared at us. The other three men looked human. I plastered a friendly smile on my face, whilst adrenaline streamed through my system.

"My... friend is missing. I am seeking information," said Ares. The cyclops nodded, and he continued. "Have you heard anything about an Underworld demon moving through Erimos?"

The cyclops' face was an unmoving mask, and one of the minotaurs kicked at the iron pot, making it swing. A waft of something meaty-smelling washed over us.

"We have heard nothing of the sort."

"No new demons on the fighting circuit?"

"We can't help you." Her voice was hard, and Ares tensed. I felt a pull in my gut as anger rolled from him.

He was a god. He couldn't be used to people refusing him. I couldn't help wondering if anyone less powerful than him had ever refused him before.

"That smells good," I said, before he could lose his shit and give us away. "What is it?"

One of the human men gave me a pointed look up and down, then answered.

"Alexsis lost her leg in the pits last week. She died this morning."

"Oh. Sorry to hear that," I said, confused. Why was he telling me about his friend dying? The man shrugged.

"She was our cook. This is all we have left now that she's gone."

"Shit," I said sympathetically.

"Can you cook?" asked the minotaur closest to me. His voice was like a rake on gravel.

I barked out a laugh. "No. Unless you count grilled cheese." I felt another wave of power roll off Ares, and guessed it was now aimed at me. Time to shut my mouth. "Well, thanks for your help and good luck learning to cook," I said cheerily, starting to turn around.

All of five of them stood up in unison. I paused in my turn, and my muscles clenched as my instincts kicked in, strength surging through my body.

"We need a cook," growled the minotaur. "And that will feed us for a week." He pointed at Ares' headband.

"I told you that you looked too regal!" I hissed at him. He looked at me, furious, and my words died on my lips. Embers burned across his irises. As if in direct response, the mist dropped over my own eyes. My vision sharpened even as it turned red, and the familiar feeling of being too large for my own body swamped me. My skin hummed with barely contained energy as I tore my eyes from Ares and turned back to the group.

"I'm not your fucking cook."

"We'll see about that, little lady," said one of the humans, then shimmered and morphed before my eyes into something... insane. It had the body of a panther, dark and sleek and powerful looking, and the glowing red tail of a scorpion was raised high over its back. Before my brain even had time to process that curveball, the thing snarled and launched itself at us.

As fast as lightning, Ares was between me and the thing, swinging his massive arm out as he side-stepped and dropped to his knees. His forearm slammed into the creature as it charged past him to get to me, and I felt a wrenching in my gut. The creature flew through the air like a freaking Frisbee. I watched open-mouthed as it crashed down into a tent thirty feet away, and shouts went up from inside.

"What the-" started the cyclops woman, but Ares cut her off with a roar as he charged towards the campfire. All sensible thought about escaping or not causing a scene abandoned me, and with a battle cry to match his, I threw myself in after him.

9

BELLA

I'd be lying if I said a part of me didn't enjoy the red mist. The thing about being a five-foot-two blonde with a big mouth is that people constantly underestimate you. And there are few things as satisfying as seeing their faces when they realize their mistake.

I went for the closest target to me, the minotaur who had suggested I'd be his cook. I slid my flick-knife from my pocket as I charged, my narrowing focus taking in his broadening stance and his snarling snout as I approached. I registered his shoulder moving as he drew back his arm and I turned up my speed, strength flooding my legs as I powered toward him. I managed to get under his elbow before he even realized how close I was, whipping out my hand and slashing at his rib cage. He let out a snorting bellow as my knife made contact and I pivoted on the balls of my feet, jabbing the blade back into anything I could reach. I got him square in the small of his back, and I forced as much of my anger-fueled strength into the jab as I could. It was enough to topple him, a cry of pain escaping his snout. But my elation was short lived. A wrenching in my stomach cut through my concentration completely, and I whirled to see the God of War picking up the cyclops by the neck, practically glowing with power. My peripheral vision clouded on one side and it was enough of a warning for me to just avoid the punch thrown at me by the other minotaur.

"What the hell did you do to him?" it said in a vaguely female voice. Prickles of guilt edged my anger, trying to derail my focus, but they couldn't get through. The focus was too strong.

"The same as I'm about to do to you," I hissed, drawing my knife back. But I didn't get a chance to do another thing because the cyclops came hurtling through the air, then smashed into the minotaur, both of them yelling as they crumpled to the sand. Ares had thrown the creature clear across the campfire clearing, into *my* minotaur.

"If I were you, I would leave now, before Ares gives you both away," said Zeeva's calm voice in my head.

"No way! We're just getting started," I answered her, throwing a glare at Ares, then looking around for the other two human men. They were nowhere to be seen. But movement registered on my right, and I saw the panther with the scorpion tail stalking through the tents toward us. I heard Ares snarl, and felt another pull in my gut, and my focus slipped again with the alien feeling. "Stop doing that!" I shouted, turning to the god. His eyes were dancing with red, gleaming with power.

"I have missed this," he breathed. Was he getting high off my war power?

"Well, you're putting me off!"

"I do not need your help."

A surge of anger bolstered me, an idea striking.

"Yes, you do. You're weak without me."

Exactly as I'd expected, I felt the tug in my tummy that accompanied Ares' anger at my words, but this time I turned my focus inward, and I tugged back.

He let out a shocked breath, then I felt a burst of *something* shoot through my hands, into my flick-blade. The weapon seared hot under my fingers, and the sound of war drums banged loud in my ears. Everything slowed around me, and it was like my normal fighting focus had been multiplied by a million. I could see what was happening around me in slow-motion. It was incredible. *I was invincible.*

Or at least, I would have been if I had eyes in the back of my head.

Pain lanced through my left shoulder blade, and the magical moment severed abruptly. I couldn't help the scream that tore from my lips as white-hot agony burned all the way down my spine, and my legs buckled. Sand flew up around me as I crashed to the ground, and my vision swam like I was underwater as I struggled to hold onto what was happening. I heard the drums redouble, a roar from Ares, the snarl of a cat, then my head hit the sand.

10

ARES

"I told you she would get us killed!" The girl was a dead-weight over my shoulder as I stamped through the entrance gates to Erimos. Nobody cast us a second glance. As long as you'd paid entry to the city you could be carrying five dead bodies on your back and no-one would care.

"If you hadn't accessed her power so much, she wouldn't have been tempted to try to use it herself," Hera's accursed cat answered me. *"You were foolish to fight those men. You should have walked away."*

"The God of War does not walk away from a fight," I spat.

"And now the God of War can't access any power because his only source has been poisoned by a manticore," she sang back at me. I screwed my face up, a sick feeling churning through my gut. Gods, I wished I had my helmet on. It felt so completely wrong to have my face exposed like this. But other than a few appreciative looks from the local whores, I was largely being ignored.

I knew where the sole apothecary was in Erimos and

turned left into the busiest of the many bazaars in the city. Hawkers shouting and the smell of spices consumed me as I strode through the square, Bella's cheek bouncing softly against the skin of my back as I walked. Something uneasy flashed through me again as I recalled her face changing from awe to shocked pain as the manticore stinger had sunk into her back. I'd barely had enough time to access her power and deal with the vile thing before she'd fallen unconscious. And as such, cutting off my access to her power.

That was where the uneasy feeling was coming from, I was sure. I was utterly powerless whilst she was like this. It was nothing to do with the fact that actual flames had burned in her eyes when she had looked at me in the camp, her muscles tense, her weapon ready.

She was rude, impulsive, unladylike, and embodied everything I disliked in a woman. She was the opposite of Aphrodite. So it did not matter that I had heard the drums of war when I looked into her eyes. What mattered was keeping her alive long enough to use her power to hunt down the escaped demon and getting my *own* blessed power back.

"She's blue," said the owner of the apothecary, when I slid the girl from over my shoulder onto the stone table in front of him. His store was lined with bottles of hundreds of colors. Some were so bright they made my eyes squint. Bowls of powders and ooze were interspersed with the bottles, and the whole place smelled like iron.

"I'm sure you've seen worse," I said.

"Hmmm," he responded, dipping his head to look at her face. He was a small human man, with thinning hair and spectacles. "Manticore sting?" He asked, looking at the blackening wound in her back.

"Yes."

He tutted. "And what is she?"

I paused, trying to work out the best way to respond. "Demigod," I answered eventually. The skinny man looked up at me over the rim of his glasses, disdainfully.

"I can see that, she'd already be dead otherwise. How strong? Will she be able to handle Ambrosia?"

"I, erm..." Anger rippled through me as I struggled to answer his question. Look at me! One of the twelve most revered beings in the damned world and a tiny human was looking at me like I was an idiot.

"She is powerful," I said eventually. But I had no idea if she could withstand Ambrosia. It sent those without enough power completely mad, and was highly addictive to those on the cusp. But it healed mortal wounds so it was a risk worth taking if required.

"Fine. I'll try something else first, but if it does not work, it will have to be Ambrosia. You can pay, I assume?" His eyes flicked to my headband as he spoke.

"Of course I can," I snapped. "Get on with it." He gave me a sarcastic bow.

"Voithos!" he barked, and a sprite appeared from a minuscule doorway in the back of the room. She was only two feet tall, and moved as fast as a cat.

"Yes, Giatros," she squeaked.

"Get me some epikóllisi, and hurry up."

"Of course," she said, and scampered off to the shelves. I watched absently as sheer wings popped out of her back, and she hovered up the shelves, scanning for whatever she'd been asked to find. Giatros had fetched a large stone bowl and was pounding an orange flower in it.

If the girl died now, could I find the demon without her power? The days after Zeus had left, when I'd had nothing, were some of the darkest of my extremely long life. What was the God of War without strength? My father had stolen the core of me, my essence, the thing that made me who I was. The thing that made the world both fear and love me. That made my subjects respect me, drove them to achieve great things.

If it hadn't been for that voice reminding me that my power existed in another form, in another world... I looked down at Bella, as Giatros smeared an orange paste onto her wound. The stuff made her skin look even more blue. The manticore toxins were spreading through her fast.

If she did survive, would she discover how she ended up in the mortal world to begin with? Did that damned cat know?

I looked around for Hera's spy, spotting her on the floor near to the stone table. Her gaze was fixed on the winged sprite as she flitted about the room, gathering bottles.

"Do you intend to pounce?" I asked her coldly.

She turned slowly to me, blinking. *"I have a vested interest in this girl's life. If she dies today, Hera will know that you are to blame."*

"Me? She got herself stung!"

"Because you goaded and distracted her."

"Why do you or your master care?"

"You know why, warrior god. And you had better pray that if she lives, she does not find out."

11

BELLA

Bright light penetrated my closed eyelids, and my first thought was that something furry had died in my mouth. Shit. I must have drunk too much tequila. I blinked, finding it hard to open my eyes, and a slight man with thick glasses hazily came into focus.

"What the..." Before I finished my croaky sentence, a rush of memories crashed through my brain. Joshua, dead on the ground. Ares, God of War, telling me I was a goddess. Hades, Persephone, Olympus... Escaped demons, huge cats with scorpion tails... "What happened?" I tried to sit up but my head swam and the dizziness stilled me.

"Drink this," the guy with glasses said, putting one hand behind my back and helping me to sit up. I did as I was told, recognizing the taste of nectar from when Persephone had given me some. Warmth and strength flowed through me as I sipped, and I concentrated on my surroundings. I was in a room lined with shelves on every wall, and it looked like a drugstore from a fantasy film. Glass bottles and stone bowls filled with crazy colored liquids and powders were everywhere. I jumped in surprise as a tiny woman with sheer pink wings appeared in front of my face, hovering excitedly.

"Erm..." I said.

"You got yourself stung by the manticore." My eyes snapped to Ares, standing a few feet from me, huge arms folded across his bare chest.

"What the fuck is a manticore?" The winged girl flinched at my cussing and I gave her an apologetic look. She gave me a hesitant smile and fluttered away.

"The cat with the scorpion tail," he said. I took another long sip as I tried to recall what had happened. We had been at the campsite with the fighters, and they had wanted me to be their cook. I replayed the scene in my head, until I reached the part where I'd tried to pull back on that tug in my stomach. Something had happened. I had felt something move through me, flow into my knife. But then... Pain. I guessed that was when the scorpion tail got me. Squashing the excitement that I may have actually used a little bit of magic, I looked at the thin man.

"Where are we?"

"My apothecary. I was able to heal you with epikóllisi paste, rather than using Ambrosia."

"What's Ambrosia?" The man's eyebrows shot up, and Ares coughed and moved toward me.

"Now that the poison is dealt with, we should get going," he said quickly. It appeared I'd put my foot in it again.

"Thank you for healing me," I said to the man. He shrugged.

"I do as I'm paid," he answered, but his eyes were warm and I didn't believe his indifference.

"Perhaps we should buy a few more things, while we're here," I said, turning back to Ares. "More of this paste seems like a good idea. I mean, we've only just started and I got hurt."

"You didn't just get hurt. You almost died," said Zeeva in my head. I gripped the edge of the stone table I was sitting on and peered down. Zeeva blinked back up at me, tail swishing.

"Was it that bad?" I asked her.

"You were blue, Bella. It was that bad."

"Then we should definitely buy more of that paste," I said, setting down my empty glass and pushing myself off the table. I felt surprisingly well for someone who had apparently nearly died. "Why don't I feel worse if I was so badly injured?"

"Your body expelled the poison very quickly, and the actual wound wasn't very deep."

"Oh. Good." I gave my body a mental high five for looking after me, then panic gripped me when I realized my knife was no longer in my pocket. As soon as I started frantically patting down my jeans though, Ares held out his open hand. My closed little knife looked tiny in his huge palm, and I snatched at it gratefully. "Thanks," I said, for some reason unable to meet his eyes now that he'd done something I was genuinely grateful for. His heavy shoulders lifted in a shrug, and I realized that avoiding his eyes meant I was staring straight at his nipples. Heat flushed through my cheeks.

"I know how it feels to lose a weapon," he mumbled.

"Right," I said awkwardly, and spun to the store-keeper. "So how about some more stuff that'll save my ass again if I need it?"

. . .

We left ten minutes later, Ares grumbling about puny mortals and lighter drachma pouches, and my rucksack heavy with tubs of paste and bottles of nectar.

"Look, we don't know how close to one of these apothecary places we'll be if we run into trouble again," I said, then froze in my tracks as I stepped into the bright light and the sounds and smells of Erimos hit me.

We were in a bazaar, fabric-covered stalls surrounding us, and each filled with more delights than I could ever want. Food, weapons and clothes were on display everywhere I looked and my stomach growled as the smell of cooking meat washed over us. "Can we get something to eat?"

"Fine," he muttered, and stamped toward the nearest vendor. A large barbecue was set up across the front of her stall, and a joint of meat was spinning slowly on an iron pole over the smoldering coals. As Ares asked the woman behind it for two portions, I ambled over to the next stall. It was selling armor, but nothing like Ares' gleaming, clanky gold stuff. This was all soft, supple leather, and it looked badass. I wondered as I stroked my fingers down a leather corset top if the manticore stinger would have had more trouble penetrating my skin if I'd been wearing something like this. The t-shirt I had been wearing was torn and bloodstained, and I'd had to change it in the tiny washroom in the apothecary.

"No," said Ares from behind me. I spun, and he held out a piece of meat on a small wooden skewer. I took it from him and clamped my mouth around it immediately. I was freaking ravenous.

"No, what?" I asked him, once I'd swallowed a few mouthfuls.

"No clothes shopping."

"But if I had armor I might not have been hurt," I protested.

"I am not wearing armor," he said, gesturing to his ridiculously perfect chest. "And I was not hurt."

"No, but you seem to be happy using my magic power as a shield whenever you damned feel like it," I snapped back. He glared at me for a few seconds, then tossed his empty hand in the air in annoyance.

"Fine. Buy yourself some armor. You'll still end up dead in a damned day."

"Ooh, first time I've heard you use a naughty word," I said, grinning and holding out my hand. He shoved the rest of his meat, minus the skewer, into his mouth, then pulled the drachma pouch from his pocket and dropped it moodily into my hand.

"Damned doesn't count as a swear word," he muttered as I pulled the corset from where it was hanging.

"It does where I come from."

"You're a long way from home, Enyo."

"My name is Bella," I corrected him. And as I stared past him at the thriving, angry city, I couldn't help the feeling that the rest of his statement was wrong too.

After the stallholder enthusiastically demonstrated the magically reinforced quality of the leather armor by stabbing it repeatedly with a sharp knife, and allayed my concerns about the corset's lack of upper coverage by producing wide shoulder straps that laced into the bodice, I was sold. It was awesome. I wanted to put it straight on, but Ares grumbled something about finding a caravanserai for accommodation and gossip, and stamped off before I had time to unlace it.

"I think we should talk about what happened," I said as I skipped along beside him, trying to keep up as I rammed my new leather-wear into my bag. It was too big, and I eventually gave up, draping it over my arm instead as we weaved through the crowd.

"You are angry with me that you were injured? It was your own fault."

"Why would I be mad with you that I was injured? I was the one careless enough to get stabbed," I said. "I'm mad with you because whenever you use my power it throws off my focus. And that's what makes me good. My focus. I need it. I can't have you messing it up every two minutes."

Ares let out a long sigh. "It is called war-sight. Not focus."

"What?"

"Everything slowing down and you being able to anticipate other's moves and block out distractions. It is called war-sight."

I frowned up at him. I'd relied on those abilities to keep me alive countless times over the years, and it was weird as hell hearing someone else describe them. "So, it's part of the war magic?"

"Yes."

"And I've been using it in the normal world all these years?"

"A small part of it, yes."

"When I got that burst of tingly energy, was that me using a large part of it?"

"Yes."

"Why did it go into my flick-knife?"

Ares slowed, finally turning to look at me. "We will not discuss this here," he said. "There is a child stealing from you."

"What!" I whirled, tearing my rucksack away from a skinny, shirtless kid who yelped in surprise. "Fuck off and steal someone else's shit!" He looked down at the bit of fabric in his hand that he'd managed to pull from the bag at the same time I did. My panties. He was clutching a pair of my damned panties. "Give those back!" But he was off, racing through the crowd like a whippet. Before I could tear off after him, Ares gripped my shoulder.

"We do not have time for this."

"He stole my godamned underwear!" I spun to Ares, outraged, and for a moment I swear I saw the corner of his mouth quirk up. But his words carried no hint of humor at all.

"Then I regret not informing you of his presence sooner."

"You knew he was trying to rob me and you said nothing?"

"You were being annoying."

"I was asking questions I need answers to!"

"You were being annoying," he repeated.

I bared my teeth at him. "You know, I'd almost forgotten that you were a giant asshole." Dark embers danced through his eyes, and I realized that insulting him when he didn't have his helmet and armor on was quite different than before. I could see the muscles twitch in his jaw, the skin across his forehead and eyes tighten, his hair move against his shoulders as he swelled and tensed. His anger resonated in me, the excitement and challenge of it intoxicating.

"Do not call me an asshole," he ground out.

"Or what?"

"Or-" he started, but I never found out what my alternative was. At that exact moment, the two us were lifted clean off our feet.

12

BELLA

"That's them," barked a voice, as I kicked and flailed my feet as I spun in the air. The minotaur from the fighters' camp came into view as I twirled uselessly, an armored guard next to him holding a tall staff that glowed.

"Put me down right now!" roared Ares.

"You're coming with me," the guard answered from under a purple fabric helmet. He turned and began to march through the courtyard, people moving out of his way with sideways glances, and I began to bob through the air behind him. The minotaur gave me a vicious smile as we passed her.

"How are we floating?" I ground out, as I bounced against Ares' enormous arm. A spark of electricity zipped between us and he scowled as his hair fell over his shoulder.

"The staff. All the guards have them. They encase people."

"Right. How do we get out of being encased?"

"We don't. They're designed to restrain people in a

world inhabited by the strongest and most violent fighters in existence."

I gritted my teeth, panic beginning to coil in my stomach. I didn't do well with being trapped. Not since my stint in prison. "I assume they can't hold gods?" I asked, angrily.

"Of course not. But you do not have the power of a full god, and therefore neither do I."

I balled my fists as I drifted too far from Ares to hear him, and a small creature that I guessed was a satyr walked underneath me. He was a little two-legged goat, his bearded face the only human-looking thing about him. Nobody seemed surprised or concerned to see us floating through the bazaar after the guard. It must be a common occurrence in Erimos. When I drifted close to Ares again, I spoke. "Where is he taking us?"

"Hopefully not to the King," he muttered. My arm bumped against his again, and more sparks fired. "Is that the staff's magic?"

Ares just grunted. I glanced down at the ground, wondering where Zeeva was, but I couldn't spot her. I wasn't sure if that was good or bad.

Energy was coursing through me with nowhere to go, and I knew I needed to calm it, to slow my panic. I took a long breath, flexed my fingers, and patted the pocket with my knife in it. Enjoy the scenery, I told myself. Learn about where you are. When you're in a situation you can't control, make a list.

After ten minutes of being bounced through the air of Erimos, my 'things that will help me survive in the city' list didn't have much on it. There seemed to be an endless array of creatures living in Erimos. Beautiful women were everywhere, some with skin that looked like water, others with skin that looked like tree-bark. Muscular human men mingled with creatures that appeared to be made up of the most bizarre animal combinations imaginable. Many had wings and tails, and all looked like they could take a punch or two.

The guard marched on without pause, so I was only afforded fleeting glimpses. We were heading toward the center of the city and the buildings around us were becoming more opulent as we went. There were no more noisy bazaars, but the shady doorways we passed were definitely selling trade. Several appeared to be drinking establishments, men and women stumbling in and out, clutching goblets. More were brothels, I was guessing from the number of scantily clad bodies leaning against the jewel-encrusted building-fronts. And they were certainly not all women. This place looked to be a pervert's dream, I thought as I stared wide-eyed at a four foot tall creature with six arms, and six breasts. She gave me a little finger wave as I passed, and I mutely returned the gesture.

The next part of the city we passed through felt different again. The buildings were taller, and a number of them reminded me of churches or temples, bulbous spires over grand arched doorways inviting folk in. It was clear the guard wasn't heading for any of these though. The enormous central tower that dominated the view above us was clearly our final destination.

Eventually we slowed, and as I turned gently in the air, I tipped my head back and gazed upward. The tower was massive. It glittered and gleamed with colored gems in the bright light, and the curved main body of the structure was adorned all over with intricate carvings of weapons. Small arched windows were cut out of the stone in a curving spiral and I couldn't help my burning curiosity about what was inside.

We floated over a shining blue walkway, which morphed into grand steps leading up to an even grander doorway. Columns that mimicked the shape of the tower lined our path, and as we entered the magnificent building, my breath caught.

We had floated into an oasis. In the middle of the huge round room was a pool, the most luscious and inviting turquoise color. Around it were daybeds draped in soft white fabric, and vividly green palm trees offering their inhabitants privacy. I could hear birds calling as we carried on down the blue walkway toward the pool, and the jewel-encrusted walls were giving off light high above us, dappled and soft. Three or four naked women were in the water that I could see, and waif-like girls scuttled between the daybeds carrying trays of drink and small bowls.

The guard stopped abruptly, dropping to one knee, and Ares and I bumped against each other again as our invisible tether to the staff went slack.

"I have the man you asked for, my Lord."

I felt Ares stiffen before we drifted apart again.

"Are we about to meet the King?" I hissed.

"You are indeed," boomed a voice, and the palm trees fluttered as a figure stood up from the largest daybed. I felt my mouth open in surprise when instead of walking around the pool to us, he stepped onto the surface of the water, barely leaving a ripple where his feet met the liquid.

He was tall, slender and gorgeous. If Aladdin aged as

well as George Clooney, this man would be the result. His black hair was thick and full, and he was wearing long purple robes, tied loosely at the waist and exposing most of his chest. Row upon row of gold bands hung around his neck, and there were too many pendants for me to make out what they all were. As he reached our side of the pool I could see his face properly, and my heart began to hammer in my chest the second our eyes made contact.

Something about this man was wrong. I knew it as surely as I knew my own name; I could see it in his dark eyes as though it were tattooed on his forehead.

The man flicked his hand, and whatever was holding us in the air vanished. I failed to get both feet steady under me as we dropped to the floor, and my pride burned as I stumbled onto my knees. After so long off the ground, both my feet were tingling and numb. I leaped back up, hoping my cheeks weren't giving away my anger that I had fallen, but the man's gaze was fixed on Ares.

"Well, well, well," he said, a cruel smile crossing his handsome face. "I never thought I'd see the day."

"Hello. I'm Bella," I said, loudly. His eyes flicked to mine. My heart pounded in my chest, my pulse racing. I would not look weak in front of this man. I would go on the offensive early. Establish myself as strong.

"I know who you are."

"I doubt that," I answered. "But I have no fucking clue who you are. Help a girl out?"

His eyes narrowed and he cocked his head at me.

"He is the King of Erimos," said Ares. His voice was loaded with pent-up anger, and my own energy responded instantly, fizzing through me.

"Now, now," the King said smoothly. "I'm a little bit more than that. As you well know," he smiled at Ares. "I am one of the three Lords of War," he said, looking back to me. "Appointed by the great god, Ares." My heart skipped a beat. "Pain, Panic and Terror. Together we walk in the mighty god's wake, basking in his deadly power." He spread his hands as he spoke, then looked slowly back to Ares. "That is to say, when he *had* power."

Shit.

My stomach dropped as I looked at Ares. It seemed that taking his helmet off hadn't made him as invisible as he'd hoped it would.

13

BELLA

"**A**s your ruler, you must bow to me," snarled Ares. The King stared back into Ares' furious face.

"Make me," he hissed. I felt the tug in my stomach at the same time the King cried out, doubling over into a painful looking bow.

"Do not play games with me, Pain," Ares said.

Pain? My head whirred as I tried to piece information together. The King had said there were three Lords of War; Pain, Panic and Terror. And Ares had just called him Pain? But he was so beautiful...

"So the rumors are not entirely true," the King croaked as he straightened. "You have some power remaining."

"Has an Underworld demon passed through Erimos in recent weeks?" barked Ares, ignoring the statement.

"Yes," Pain answered.

"Really?" I couldn't help my excited response, and the King looked at me. His gaze bore into mine, and I instantly regretted showing my enthusiasm.

"Why do you seek this demon? Are you are here on Hades' bidding?"

"Why we are here is none of your business. Tell me where the demon went," Ares said.

"Was he alone?" I added quickly.

"You assume this demon is a *he*?" Pain smiled at me, and an uneasy feeling rippled down my spine. That smile held a malice that I didn't possess. I was filled with anger and energy and a desire to physically feel the world around me, but I did not yearn for pain, nor to inflict it. This man however... It oozed from him.

"Answer the damned question!" shouted Ares, and Pain whirled to him.

"You are in my domain now, holy one, and your little show of power only served to confirm that you are indeed weak," he hissed, the tower darkening around us. "My brothers will be here momentarily, and we shall decide together what to do with our once mighty leader. Until then I suggest you take a seat." I felt movement behind me and glanced back to see two large wooden chairs appearing out of nowhere. I had my knife in my hand, though I had no recollection of taking it from my pocket, and my racing pulse was causing blood to pound in my ears.

"Bella, listen to me." Zeeva's voice in my head almost startled me into dropping my weapon. *"This is Ares' fight. It is Ares' realm, his subjects, and his pride you face. If you want to find your friend, you must let him lead this."*

Every instinct in my body ached to throw myself at creepy, hot Aladdin. But her words rang so clear in my head they drowned out my other thoughts.

This was Ares' fight.

I looked at the two men, Ares refusing to sit down and

an epic stare-off in progress. She was right. I would be pissed if someone stole an important fight from me.

I slowly put my knife back in my pocket. I wanted to ask Zeeva where she was, but I couldn't mind-speak like she could. I remembered her saying that I had to project my thoughts to her and folded my arms across my chest. With a pointed sigh, I sat down hard on the seat behind me. Both men broke eye-contact with each other to flick glances at me. I gave them a sarcastic smile.

"Don't mind me," I said. "Please, continue eye-fucking one another." Ares bared his teeth, but they went back to staring at each other.

"Where are you?" I thought the question as hard as I could whilst holding an image of my stuck-up cat in my head.

"By the closest palm," came a reply a moment later. Giving myself a mental high-five for managing to make contact, I scanned the pool fast, and saw a tiny flicker of a tail behind the nearest tropical tree.

"How'd you get in here?"

"I followed you. People do not notice small cats here. Listen to me. The Lords of War are powerful, each able to inflict the power they embody with so much as a look or a word. Do not goad Ares whilst in the presence of the Lords. It is extremely important that they do not realize his volatility. Do you understand me?"

"Gods, you sound like my old teachers," I answered, rolling my eyes.

"Bella, do you understand me?" she repeated, her mental voice hard.

"Yes!"

"Good."

· · ·

The air before me began to shimmer, interrupting us, and with a flash of red two more men appeared. Two men who could not have looked more different from one another.

One was a similar stature to Pain, tall and slender, but instead of being dressed like an Arabian sultan, this guy was dressed like Robin Hood. He was wearing leafy green breeches, had a white linen shirt on that was also open to his navel, and tall leather boots. Sandy colored hair curled over his ears, and when he looked at me his green eyes shone with something just as dark and unsettling as I saw in Pain's eyes. The third man... The third man was so striking that once I started looking at him, I couldn't stop. He had no features at all. He was a humanoid mass of something solid; smooth and hard and mesmerizing. Whatever he was made of was covered in a marbling effect, black and white swirling and moving and blending over what I guessed was his skin. His blank face fixed first on me, then on Ares.

"My Lord," a hissing voice issued from him, like nails dragged down a blackboard. It made my skin crawl.

"Terror," responded Ares stiffly, before turning to the Robin Hood guy. "Panic," he acknowledged just as curtly.

So, these were Ares' three Lords of War. I resisted the urge to stand up and introduce myself. I was going to do exactly what Zeeva had told me to do. For once in my life, I was going to behave myself. Avoid trouble. Not be a dick.

"Now you are a delectable little surprise," said Panic, turning to me. "Where have you been hiding?" I bit down on my lip to stop myself responding.

"Aw, she's shy," hissed Terror. "Maybe we can find a way to liven her up." Fear shot through me, his innocuous words laced with a threat I never, ever wanted to see fulfilled.

"Maybe you can find a way to back the fuck up," I said, leaping to my feet and whipping out my knife. The two men with faces smiled.

"I see she is perfectly susceptible to our power," Terror said. I clung to the words as my heart hammered. He was called Terror. He embodied fear. I wasn't really scared of him, he was just using magic. I repeated the sentence in my head, drawing on it to calm the fear.

"I'm sure you're perfectly susceptible to my foot up your ass," I said, parroting him.

"Bella!" Zeeva's voice hissed through my head. Shit, I was supposed to be keeping my mouth shut. This was Ares' show. I sat back down as Terror cocked his head at me. The black and white swirled and swished across him, like black oil over a marble statue.

"Delectable was a good choice of word, brother," he said quietly. Another stab of fear gripped me, and I bit down too hard on my lip this time, tasting blood. Pain let out a long, satisfied breath, his eyes widening as they focused on my mouth.

For the first time in my life, I did not want to be at the heart of the action. I very badly wanted to be anywhere but where I was. I wasn't used to feeling afraid, or out of my depth, or weak. But power oozed from these three men, and it was dark and foreboding and just plain fucked up.

"You are here to tell me about the Underworld demon who is hiding in my realm," said Ares loudly, and all three Lords looked at him.

"I must say, you're rather dashing under all that armor," Panic said to him. "Who'd have thought the God of War would be so pretty?"

Ares was hot as hell, but not pretty. The word had

been used to rile him. But I felt no tell-tale pull in my gut, the indication that Ares was getting mad and using my power.

"Tell me about the demon," he demanded.

"The trouble is, we don't take orders from anyone weaker than we are. Nobody in this realm does," Terror said slowly. "That's the way you designed it. He who is strongest, rules. And by all accounts, you are no longer the strongest."

Ares stepped forward, but not rashly or angrily. Deliberately. I felt my pulse quicken. "I am the son of Zeus, God of War, one of the twelve Olympians and most revered beings in existence," he said, and thrills shuddered through me at the tone of his voice. When he wasn't stamping around like an overgrown toddler, he was freaking *fierce*. "Make your decision carefully, my Lords. For I am eternal, and you only exist within my realm and my power."

I could see the doubt cross the faces of Pain and Panic, fleeting but real.

"There is nothing in this realm that cannot be won in a fair fight," said Terror eventually. He was clearly the ringleader of this little trio. "We know of the demon you seek. We know of their plan, and who they are working for."

I opened my mouth, but Zeeva hissed loudly inside my skull and I closed it again.

"Prove that you are still our true leader. Pass a trial that each of us set for you, and demonstrate your dominion over Pain, Panic and Terror."

"You will regret this," the God of War growled.

"We are only living by the standard you have set," said Pain, bowing low. Oceanus's words came back to me, about Ares earning his power back by being a true ruler within his own realm.

"If you can pass the tests, then we will hand over your demon. All wrapped up with a bow," grinned Panic.

Ares stared at him, then pointed at me. "The girl doesn't leave my side." Terror's statuesque form turned to me, and I gave him the finger.

"Fine," Terror said.

"Excellent!" exclaimed Panic, clapping his hands together. "As we're already here in Erimos, would you like to start us off with your trial first, Pain?"

"It would be my pleasure," the Lord grinned. "I've got just the thing.

"I believe something so heroic should not go unwatched," said Terror, moving his hand to his feature-less face thoughtfully. "We shall host a feast tonight, in honor of these..." He paused. "Ares Trials. Yes, I like that. Then you may embark upon Pain's test tomorrow."

"There will be no feast," growled Ares.

"Oh, but there will, mighty one," Terror said. His voice was harsh and sing-song at the same time, and I hated it. "Or we won't allow you to take the girl with you. And we both know that would be a serious blow to your chances."

Did Terror know who I was? And that Ares only had power around me? Or did he just think I was important to Ares somehow?

Either way, we didn't have time to screw around at feasts. "What about the demon and the people he's kidnapped? We don't have time for feasts," I said, standing up. Not one of the four men looked at me. I heard Zeeva sigh in my head. "Can you at least give us some proof that you do really know where the demon is?" I tried. The thought of being this close to finding out if Joshua was OK and being forced to wait uselessly was more than I could handle.

"Are you questioning our integrity?" asked Pain, looking at me.

"Well, based on what I have learned so far, yeah. You all seem like a bunch of twisted jerks," I said. "I get bad vibes from the lot of you."

Pains lips curved up into a smile. "Few insult the Lords of War so freely, and without repercussion," he said. A stabbing pain started in the bottom of my skull, and although I stopped myself making a sound, I couldn't help the flinch of my face. Slowly the pain moved down my neck, my muscles tensing and warping as my nerves reacted.

"Stop. Her request is fair. You are all dishonest." Ares voice was loud and hard, and mercifully, the pain stopped. I took a deep breath and straightened my body, sweat beading on my forehead and chest. Fury was simmering inside me, my instinctive reaction to pain. The desire to destroy things burned through my blood, and my gaze fixed on Pain as red shrouded my vision. Hot older Aladdin or not, this guy was going to get a kick in the balls the first opportunity I got.

"Fine. Once you are satisfied, I shall summon the guests and we shall see you back here in two hours." Terror waved his hand, and a huge iron dish on a stand appeared before him. Gently flickering orange flames danced in the center, and they suddenly flared white and bright.

An image materialized over the dish, amongst the white flames. A hooded creature was reaching out, touching the face of a woman laid out on a dark stone slab. She didn't look dead, her skin was a healthy color and her mouth moved as she breathed. But she didn't react when a blackened claw raked over her cheek, leaving the faintest red mark. My stomach twisted into knots as I stared.

There were rows and rows of slabs surrounding her, all with bodies stretched out on them. And directly to her left, looking for all the world like he was in a restful sleep, was Joshua.

14

BELLA

"Joshua! Take us there, now!"

"Calm down, little girl. All in good time." Fury stormed inside me, fear for Joshua, outrage that this had happened to him, guilt that I had spent a single moment since getting here not thinking about him, was all building into an uncontainable rage within me.

"He doesn't have time! Look at him!"

"I don't know who 'he' is," said Terror, waving his hand and the image in the flame dish vanishing, "but I can assure you that the demon's plans are not immediate."

"What is it? And who is it working for?" Ares barked the questions as fury and fear pounded through me. Normally I would have hurled myself at someone by now, but these three... Their power was enough that my instincts were frozen. I knew that they would tear me apart before I moved a foot.

But that didn't stop me wanting to.

I would find a way to make them pay. Once I'd rescued Joshua, I would find a way.

"You have not earned those answers yet, mighty one. We have made a deal. Complete the Ares Trials, and we will hand the demon over. See you in two hours."

We were escorted roughly from the tower, and I barely saw the people or stone around me for the red haze. "Don't fucking touch me!" I bellowed at a guard as he tugged at my elbow once we were out of the grand doorway. He jumped backward, then scowled and strode away.

"We need to-" began Ares, but now that I was no longer in the presence of the Lords, the need to hit something was too great to restrain. With a roar, I smashed my fist into the nearest wall, the bite of pain as my knuckle split on the sharp gems only spurring me on. Before I could land another punch, there was a bright flash, and I froze, heart crashing against my ribs as I looked about. We were back at what was left of Ares' pile of rocks. Where we had started.

"Go ahead," he said, and sat back on his heels, just as I had done when he had gone apeshit with his sword. I blinked at him, then with a roar, booted the pile of rocks as hard as I could with my steel-capped boots. Over and over I kicked at the boulders, unbridled rage brimming up and flowing out of me as the rocks flew and smashed beneath my feet.

Eventually, exhausted, I fell back on my ass, rubbing my hands across my face hard enough to hurt.

"They know where he is, and they won't tell us," I said hoarsely. I felt utterly powerless. Frustration was the worst feeling in the world. "They could end this right now, but I can't do a thing."

"Nothing comes for free in Olympus."

"All those people though!" I turned on the ground, looking at Ares. "They're just letting all those people be held captive, so that they can play games with you?" Ares said nothing. "That's fucked up! Do you understand how fucked up that is?"

"When the great gods were allocated power, many shared the parts of it they didn't want with others," said Ares quietly. "Some power is too great and complex to be wielded by one. For example, Athena has the power of war strategy, a refined version of what I..." He paused, then corrected himself. "We have. Which is the rawest form of the power of War. Anger, glory, valiance, courage, strength." I stared at him, trying to work out what he was telling me. "But War is about much more than valor. War involves Pain, and Panic, and Terror. War involves Death and Violence and Discord."

"So, those powers all live in different beings?"

"Yes. My sister is the Goddess of Chaos and Discord. Keres demons, who reside in the Underworld, are the spirits of violent death. They swarm over battlefields, feasting on the souls of those most brutally killed." A shudder rippled through me. "And the Lords of War... They are directly of my creation. They are of my power."

I shook my head. "No. No, you don't feel like them. I don't feel like them, and you said we share the same power."

"You do not understand," Ares said, and pushed himself to his feet.

"No, you're right. I don't." I stood too. "Explain it to me."

He let out a long sigh. "All you must know is that your friend is in no imminent danger, and that the Lords cannot be blamed for their behavior. They exist purely to behave as they do. And they are necessary."

"It's necessary for your world to have twisted assholes in charge?"

Ares raised one eyebrow in an uncharacteristic quirk. "Olympus would not be Olympus without twisted assholes in charge," he muttered.

I could feel my anger dissipating fast, hard resolve replacing it. If those pricks were telling the truth about the demon, then Ares was right, and Joshua wasn't in any immediate danger. And at least I now knew he was still alive. Nobody in the image over the dish looked like they were in pain, messed up as all the stone beds were.

And now we had some sort of plan. If we completed these Ares Trials, we would get him back, and capture the demon. As fucked up as it was to play with people like this, I needed to accept that we were in a better position than we had been before we entered Erimos.

"You just swore," I said to Ares.

"Hmmm."

"Do we have to walk back to the city now?"

"Yes."

"Will you tell me how to use my power on the way?"

"No."

As we began trudging back to Erimos, I thought about what Ares had said. He said the Lords of War were 'directly of his creation'. Did that mean he had literally created them? Or fathered them perhaps? Or just that his godliness came with a side of Pain, Panic and Terror?

I considered asking him, but I had too many other things to straighten out in my head first, and this was probably the only stretch of silence I would have for a while. I had to adjust my game-plan. I was no longer on a demon hunt with the God of War. I was now partaking in three Trials designed to defeat him. Maybe kill him. Could he even die?

I had a lot to add to my 'questions to ask later' list, I realized. Like why was my useless cat so keen that I didn't land Ares in trouble when the Lords showed up? In fact, why was she with us at all? I still had no idea. A bolt of worry for her moved through my chest, and I hoped she had made it out of Pain's tower safely. The fact that she had been my only pet, and company, in London was impossible to shift, despite her disinclination to tell me anything helpful. Although my many evenings spent stroking her did seem pretty weird now.

I looked up at Ares' muscular back, his shoulders flexing as his arms swung, his tied ponytail moving against tanned skin. Why am I attracted to a miserable, humorless brute? I should add that to the list of questions.

If I was being honest though, I was lacking evidence that he actually was a brute. My initial impression of him, dressed in armor and wielding a sword over the bleeding body of my only friend, may not have been entirely representative. So far, even when I'd deliberately annoyed him to the point of lashing out, he hadn't hurt me at all. And as far as I was aware, he'd given up on his notion of wanting to kill me for my power pretty quickly.

He *was* miserable and humorless though. And he was using my power and not telling me how to. Which meant he was definitely still an asshole. Just not quite as asshole as these new assholes.

I let out a sigh, and he turned his head to me as he walked.

"You are tired already?"

"Fuck no," I retorted. "I was just lamenting there being so many assholes in the world."

"Why do you swear so much? I dislike it."

"I swear so much for exactly that reason. People like you, who think they can dominate me, dislike it. Plus, there are many situations in life where only a creative swearword will do."

"Like what?"

"Well, there was an old homeless man in London I once heard call someone a wankwaffle for throwing a sandwich at him. I thought that was an excellent use of creative swearing."

"Wankwaffle?" The word sounded so ridiculous coming out of Ares' mouth that within seconds my small chuckle had turned into full on laughter.

"Say that again," I gasped, through cackles, and to my sheer delight, he did. Hysterics took me completely, tears streaming from my eyes as my brain replayed the mountain of seriousness before me saying the word *wankwaffle*, over and over.

"You are very strange," Ares said eventually, when I'd recovered myself enough to resume walking beside him.

"I needed that," I breathed, my cheeks aching slightly.

"You needed to hear me saying wankwaffle?"

A snort of fresh laughter escaped me, and I reached out and punched him in the arm. "Stop saying it! You'll set me off laughing again!"

"I do not understand how you can be furious and fearful for your friend one moment, and laughing hysterically another," he said, shaking his head.

"I think it has to do with being so overwhelmed that

it's either laugh or drink all the tequila and cry," I
told him.

"Tequila makes you cry?"

"Sometimes," I admitted. Though I had never shed a
tear in front of another person. Not since my first foster
family. I mean, tears of laughter or pain notwithstanding.
I'd been in many fights that had caused my eyes to water.
But never tears of sadness.

"Then why do you drink it?" I looked up at the huge
god, the bewilderment on his stunning face obvious.

"To escape."

"Escape what?"

"Boredom, mostly."

The confusion cleared from his expression as he
glanced down at me. "Your mortal world is extremely
boring," he said with a nod.

"Yeah," I said. And now I had a chance to live where I
truly belonged, and never be bored again. I just had to
work out how to use magic.

15

ARES

I usually enjoyed feasts in my own realm, thrown in my honor. Especially when the other Olympians attended, and they could see the deference my subjects gave me first-hand. But this was not one of those feasts. Aphrodite attending was the only upside I could see to the entire circus.

She looked even more stunning than usual, if such a thing was possible. Today her skin was dark and rich, and her hair a pale blue, in masses of curls that framed her soft face. I longed to run my hand down her cheek, to run my fingers down her throat, to feel her stomach tense beneath my touch as I moved lower. But she had been seated at the other end of the long table in Pain's dining hall when we had eaten, and since the gathering had been moved to the opulent oasis, she had not yet approached me. My pride still stung from her dismissal of me the last time I had seen her. I would not look weak by going to her first, like a keen puppy.

So, I stood still by a large palm tree, with my arms folded across my armored chest, and glared at everyone who walked near me. It felt good to have my helmet back on. Really good.

"Brother."

I barely moved my head an inch, to see my sister, Eris, sauntering toward me. "Must you wear such revealing clothing?" I asked her.

"Yes. It upsets, delights and confuses people in equal measure. Besides, they're naked." She gestured at four mer-women, swimming seductively in some sort of dance in the clear water of the pool. Many guests were watching them appreciatively, including Pain.

"I see you haven't killed the girl yet." Eris said.

"Of course I haven't," I grunted.

"And is that because Hades forbade it, or because she's so pretty?" She smiled at me and took a long sip of her drink.

"Keep your mouth shut, sister."

"Not one of my strengths," she said, mock apologetically. "And if I did, I wouldn't be able to tell you what I came over here to tell you."

I let out a long breath. "Fine. What did you come to tell me?"

"I know what Zeus is doing with your stolen power," she whispered, her eyes shining.

Every muscle in my body froze, her words spinning through my head. Zeus was using my power?

"What?"

"Did you think he just stole it just for fun?"

"He stole it to stop me defeating him," I growled. Eris pouted and tilted her head to one side.

"Oh, little brother, you can't defeat daddy, even with

your power. He's far, far more powerful than all of us. Silly boy."

Anger rumbled through my gut, and I only just stopped myself reaching for Bella's power. There was no point alerting her to this conversation. I looked automatically across the pool, to where she was having an animated conversation with the same severe white centaur who had been at Hades' ceremony. Well, Bella was having an animated conversation. The centaur was barely moving as the girl threw her hands around as she talked excitedly.

"What is Zeus using my power for?" I ground out instead, looking back at Eris. There was a very good chance she was lying. My sister was not known for her honesty.

"Come now, I'm not going to just tell you! Where's the fun in that?"

"This is not a game!"

"Actually, thanks to your lovely Lords of War, that's exactly what it is now. You know, I was going to put my drachma on her dying in the second Trial, but now I'm not so sure. There's something about her..."

Curiosity flashed in her eyes, under the casual tone. She was desperate to know more about Bella.

"She is human. She will likely die in the first Trial," I snapped.

"She may be mostly human now, but I'm not stupid, or weak, Ares." Eris' tone had changed, no longer playful. "There's power under the mortal layers. And if she sheds those and reaches it, she could be strong." I said nothing, and she continued to stare at me. "She told me, Ares," she said eventually. "She told me that she is the Goddess of War. That's what you're using her for, isn't it?" Still, I said nothing, staring out over the pool. "But there is no Goddess of War. There never has been. So, I'm left wondering, however did you find her?"

"Leave me be, Eris," I said, unfolding my arms and looking at her. "I have business to attend to." Before she could respond, I strode away from her, looking like I knew exactly where I was going. The truth was though, I just needed to be away from her. My sister was one of the most shrewd and dangerous women in Olympus. And I knew what she would say next. She would offer me more information about Zeus and my power, in return for information about Bella. Information that was too valuable for me to give up, even if the thought of someone else using *my* power burned a hole in my insides. It wasn't like me accessing Bella's power, because that was the same magic. It was a part of both of us. But using a god's power that had not been properly allocated to you?

It was a gross violation of everything deities held close. And Zeus, whilst wrong in his most recent actions, was our immortal leader. There was no way he would stoop so low. She was lying.

"I told you that your Lords might have some revenge planned," cooed a voice. I felt my pulse leap as I whirled around.

"Aphrodite," I said, giving her a curt nod, that belied my racing heart.

"Are you worried about the Trials?" My eyes were drawn to her full lips as she spoke, and desire washed through me. She lifted a long-stemmed glass to her mouth, the movement slow and impossibly sexy.

"Stop it," I said. She rolled her eyes at me, but the fierce need to touch her lessened. "Of course I am not worried about the Trials. I created the Lords. Anything they design will be to my strengths."

"Has it occurred to you that that means they know your weaknesses too?" She raised one perfect eyebrow as she looked at me and I faltered before answering her.

"No. They are driven by valor as much as anyone else in my realm. Their tests will show off their power."

"And your first one is Pain? That should be fun to watch." Her beautiful eyes sparkled.

"Would my pain arouse you?" I asked her quietly.

"Not explicitly, no. But I long to see the beast in you again. And maybe a dose of pain will bring it out."

I clenched my teeth. I longed to feel the beast in me again. But there was nothing there but hollow rage. "I will have my power back soon."

"And you expect me to wait for you?"

"I expect nothing from you." That was a lie. As long as I could remember, I had expected things from the woman who dominated my thoughts day and night. And she had never, ever fulfilled any of them outside of lust.

"Good." Her usually warm voice was clipped and cold, her soft beauty hardening before me. The Goddess of Love was not all sugar-sweet whispers and sensuous caresses. Love was one of the most cruel things in the world, and Aphrodite embodied it all. But the side of her that was attracted to a man like me was rarely on display in public, and true-to-form, a beaming smile replaced her hard look as Pain approached us.

"Lord Pain," she said, as he reached her. He took her hand and bowed low as he kissed it.

"Oh, divine goddess, you are a vision," he said smoothly. She gave him an appreciative nod.

"Your brothers are here tonight?"

"Indeed." He turned and pointed to where Terror was sitting in a large chair, a tree-dryad girl on his lap and an Erimosian girl dancing before him.

"Tell me, what is it that he is made of?" Aphrodite asked curiously.

"Marble." Her eyes darkened, and jealousy fired through me instantly. I knew that look well.

"So hard to touch... I wonder..." she whispered, and Pain's smile spread slowly wider.

"An audience with the goddess of love would be an honor for the Lords of War," he said. "All three of us would be at your disposal, day or night."

"Now, there's an idea," she said, voice like sweet honey.

The need to lash out gripped me, almost intolerable, and as Pain's eyes flicked to mine, malice dancing in them, I turned away. For the second time that evening, I strode across the tiled floor with faked purpose, needing to be anywhere else.

The goddess toyed with me as though I were a plaything. An image of her laying naked on her bed, the three Lords around her, aroused and hungry, filled my head and a hissing snarl escaped my mouth. I changed direction, heading for the large doors of the tower. I did not care if Pain had the satisfaction of causing me to leave my own feast. I was done for the night.

16

BELLA

"Oh dear. The goddess of love has upset my brother. Again." Eris gulped down more of her drink as I watched Ares storm out of the tower doors.

"Are they friends?" I asked, as casually as I could.

"Why? You interested?"

I gave a slightly too loud snort. "Hell no. I mean, he's hot. Like really hot. But so is everyone here." Too much delicious fizzy wine had followed too much delicious rich food, and I was feeling dangerously talkative.

Joshua. Lords of War. Manipulative goddesses with massive boobs. Remember what's at stake. Keep it together, Bella.

"Well that's true. Folk are either gorgeous or half wild-animal in Olympus. Although I suppose some men are a bit of both." She waggled her eyebrows at me and I laughed.

I knew I shouldn't, but a large part of me couldn't help liking the Goddess of Chaos. I mean, I wouldn't tell her my secrets, but I'd sure as hell party with her.

"Do you have a partner?" I asked her.

"Many."

"Oh."

"One of the perks of being immortal."

"I'd have thought that would make it harder to find love," I said.

"Love? Gods, I thought you were less naive than that, sweetie," she exclaimed. "Love is a concept best left to those less... volatile. And anyway, it's dull."

"How can you find anything in a world like this dull?" I asked her. She gave me a long look.

"Sweetie, I thrive on discord. Shit going wrong. Look around you. With Hades and Poseidon in charge and 'Oceanus the long-lost Titan' playing nice, there's not a lot for me to do. Zeus fucking things up for a while was excellent, but now he's gone. You, and these new Ares Trials are the most exciting thing to have happened around here in a while."

"Well, I can't wait to see the rest of Olympus," I said, draining what was left in my glass. When I looked back at Eris, she had a strange, almost pitying look on her face.

"I'm starting to hope you get the chance," she said eventually. "Tell me about your world, where you grew up."

"Sorry, I'd better follow armor-boy," I said. "He may be a giant asshole, but we're kinda bound to each other until this is over."

"He'll just be sulking in his room; stay and have another drink."

I eyed her, her smile too wide, her eyes too narrow. I wasn't drunk enough or stupid enough to trust her, no matter how much I liked her company. "Thanks, but no. See you later."

Before we had left for the feast, my bag and new leather armor had been left in a plush room in a small but grand tower I was informed was called a caravanserai. Basically a Erimosian hotel. As I stepped out of the tower to make my way back there, I saw that the bright sunlight had disappeared completely, and although I could see no actual moon above me, a cold blue light that could easily be assumed as moonlight glinted off the embedded gems in the buildings around me. The streets were busier now than they had been earlier, many more young men and women leaning against walls of buildings, offering 'exotic delights' or 'magnificent returns' or 'wild rides'. The buildings I had assumed to be drinking establishments earlier had humans and creatures alike streaming in and out of them, some looking elated, more looking desperate. I channeled my best 'back the fuck up, I'm a badass even though I'm not dressed like one' energy. Everyone I was passing was armed, and all either wore clothing appropriate for a desert, or barely anything at all.

"Well if you don't have it by this time tomorrow, we'll have to find another way for you to pay," snarled a voice from the darkness between two buildings on my right. There was a loud slapping sound, and a gurgled shout. I forced myself to carry on. I wasn't there to meddle in other's business.

But the knowledge of an impending fight called to me, and my feet slowed of their own accord. Someone screamed, shrill and loud, and a man's laugh accompanied it.

I stopped walking.

"This is no business of yours, little girl," rumbled a

voice far too close to me, and I leaped to the side, away from it. Something stepped out from the shadows at the end of the alleyway.

"How did I not see you there?" I breathed, staring. It was only a little taller than me, but had massive leathery wings that were torn and covered in spikes. Its body was leathery too, with a small piece of fabric hanging from a belt to cover its genitals, and it had legs that looked more like a bird's than a human's. But my eyes were drawn back to its mostly human face. It was as though half of it had been melted, all the features on the right-hand side a good inch lower than those on the left. Tufts of thin hair stuck out over its skull and I couldn't have told you the thing's gender if my life had depended on it.

"It's my job to blend in." I felt my eyebrows rise. How could a creature like this blend in to anything? I heard a thump from behind him in the alley and another scream, this one muffled.

"What's going on back there?" I asked. Energy was swirling through my middle, building fast.

"None of your fucking business."

True. But not good enough.

"So, do you just guard alleys while someone else does the beating?"

"The boss only hits on folk who don't pay," the thing grunted. So, this thing was a mob-heavy. This really wasn't any of my business. Maybe I should just walk on.

"You can go and screw yourself, you fucking bully! I'd rather you killed me than took everything away from her," I heard a voice in the alleyway cry.

They were giving themselves up to defend someone else. A lover, a wife, a child? Either way, my interest was piqued. From those words I knew that this person had courage and honor. Another thumping sound echoed from the alley, along with another cry.

Red slowly descended over my vision. I cocked my head at the thing in front of me. "Move."

The thing just snorted, its lopsided mouth quirking into a smile. I shrugged, then darted forward, dropping into a crouch and hitting out hard with my fist. I caught it exactly where I wanted to, right in the muscle in the side of its thigh, and it gave a small shout as its leg crumpled beneath it. Before its knees had hit the ground I was back up, kicking out hard and catching it under the jaw, which was now waist-height. There was a sickening crunch, then the thing's eyes rolled back into its head and it tipped slowly backward, unconscious.

I turned and strode into the alley. As I got further into the gloom I could see a large man, shirtless and tanned, dark hair slicked back from his hard face, pinning a boy against the rough wall.

"Hi," I said, and the older guy's head snapped to me.

"Grothia?" he called loudly.

"If that's wing-thing back there, they're gonna need some medical attention," I said. The boy's eyes widened as the guy's narrowed.

"This is none of your business. Leave."

"I can't," I said, with another shrug. "You're right, this has nothing to do with me, but I can't help feeling that your punishment of this young man exceeds his crimes."

"You think you're some sort of vigilante?" he said, a cruel smile spreading across his face. "It's been some time since we've had one of those in Erimos."

"Put him down," I said. I was painfully aware that not twenty-four hours ago I had been holding Joshua against a wall in the same position. My guilt morphed into anger, more strength pulsing through me.

Slowly, the guy slid the kid down the wall, and the boy's own hands went to his throat as soon as he let go. One side of his face had a long red line running down it, and I immediately looked for the blade that must have caused it. Sure enough, the glint of metal shone in the guy's left hand as he turned fully to me.

"You don't look like you're from around here, little girl," he said. "So I'm going to give you a chance to turn around, and walk away."

I squinted past him, to see if the kid could escape down the other end of the alleyway while I distracted the jerk, but it was too dark for me to see. The boy stayed where he was, hand on his throat. Oh well. I'd have to knock the goon out then, same as I had with wing-thing. "No, thank you," I said, and slid my flick-blade from my pocket.

"That's a little knife," he said, holding his own up and twirling it, showing off its size. It was curved, like a scimitar.

"Little knife for a little girl," I answered, and threw it at him.

He didn't move fast enough, and it sank into the top of his shoulder as he yelled. The kid sprang to his feet, but before I could feel any sort of relief for his escape, he launched himself at the mob-boss.

"Wait!" I started, then froze as I realized what he was doing. He yanked my knife from where it was deep in the guy's flesh, avoiding the wild stabbings from the scimitar in the wailing man's other hand. The kid moved fast, and my stomach lurched as he threw me a backwards glance, then ran.

"Shit!" I raced after him, ducking under the useless swipe from the bleeding mob-boss, and powering after the kid. There was no fucking way I was losing that knife. "Come back, you ungrateful little thief!" I bellowed, as he flew out of the other end of the alley, which I could now regretfully see was not a dead-end after all.

He banked sharply to the left, and I pivoted on the balls of my booted feet, chasing after him. There were more people on the streets here, colored lanterns casting soft light over the glittering walls, and the smells of meat wafting through the air. We were moving toward the bazaars.

I followed the kid through more twisting, turning streets, until we burst into one of the wide courtyards filled with fabric-covered stalls. Panic rushed through me as I took in the sheer number of people and places to hide. If I didn't catch up to him soon, I would lose him - and my knife - for good.

"I saved your damned life, you shit!" I hollered, forcing more energy into my legs, turning up my speed. How was he so damned quick? Not many people could outrun me. The idea of losing my weapon, the only thing I'd managed to hold onto my whole life, the thing that had saved me countless times, was making anger build inside me, and my vision darker.

My eyes locked on the kid as he slowed down, reaching a three-way crossways between stalls. I watched as his body began to shift, his weight moving from one side to the other, and made a desperate guess at which way he was about to turn. I banked fast to my right, praying he was going to do the same. I could cut him off.

With a surge of speed I flew around the stall, and just as I'd hoped, he barreled straight into me, his head turned to search for me behind him. I swiped at his neck as he stumbled backwards, and he cried out as I gripped him. That familiar bolt of guilt ripped through me as I noticed the already red marks from the mob-boss' fingers around his throat, but the red mist blocked it out.

"Give me my fucking knife back, now!" I roared, as I lifted him up. He was taller than me, but my grip was iron, and his feet scrabbled on the ground as he beat at my hand with his. "I can keep this up all night, kid. Give me back my property." When purple began to tinge his face, he finally reached into his hareem pants pocket, and pulled out my flick-blade. I held out my other hand and he dropped it into my palm. I let go instantly. "I was trying to help you, and you stole from me. What gives?"

"I don't need your help," he croaked, backing away from me. eyes red.

"It kinda looked like you did, kid."

"He was right. You're not from round here," he spat, then turned and raced away, into the crowd. I cocked my head after him. This place really was full of tough people.

No vigilantes required.

And still no friends for me.

"I'm pleased you recovered your knife without killing anyone." Zeeva's voice sounded in my head and I scanned the ground for her, spotting her prowling from behind a stall selling meat skewers.

"Why would I kill someone?" I answered her, shoving the flick-blade possessively into my pocket. "And why was he such a shit?"

"Even those with good in their hearts are different in the realm of war."

"Huh. Well, I'm glad you're here. I have no idea where I am."

17

BELLA

All the way back to the caravanserai I asked Zeeva questions, and all her answers were vague and unhelpful.

"As I told you, the longer you are in Olympus, the more of your power will be accessible to you. I am guessing being in this violent place may speed things up." I could hear the distaste in her voice, and wondered briefly what Hera's realm was like compared to this one. But I dismissed the question in favor of more useful ones.

"If I get more power will I still be human?"

"Right now you would be termed a weak demigod. Mostly human, with some divine power. The stronger you get, the higher class demigod you will become. I do not know if it is possible for you to lose enough of your humanity to become a full goddess."

"But if I started out as the Goddess of War, with the same power as one of the twelve Olympians, how the hell did I become human?"

Zeeva didn't answer me for a long time, silently stalking through the busy streets. *"The story of your origin is not mine to tell. And I could not tell it fully, even if I wanted to.*"

"The story of my origin?" I repeated, glaring down at her. "You make me sound like a fucking super-hero." Despite being accused of being a vigilante once already that day, I couldn't see myself wearing a cape and fighting crime.

Perhaps super-villain would be more fun.

"*You are no hero, Bella. But you could be something. Something more than you could ever have been in the mortal world.*"

"I know," I said quietly. And I did know. I knew it to my core. I was meant to be here. I belonged in a world where even the good guys were dicks.

When I finally reached the place I was staying I was still buzzing with energy. A woman with tree-bark skin was standing in a grand hall hung with luxurious burgundy and gold fabrics and an enormous staircase stretching up the center of it. The woman smiled when I told her who I was, and gave me a small orb that shone ruby red. I followed her up the impressive staircase and was sure that we must be at the top by the time she stopped and pointed to a door. A small round hole in the center of it glowed red, and I looked at the orb in my hand, then at the tree-woman. She nodded at me, leaf green hair falling over her shoulders. Hesitantly, I pushed the orb into the hole and there was a little click, and the stone door swung open. The red orb popped suddenly back into my hand.

"Huh," I said. "Thanks. Do you know which room my friend is in?"

She nodded mutely at the door next to mine, then turned and made her way back down the stairs.

I knew Ares wouldn't want to see me. But I had questions for him, both about my power, and about whatever it was we would be doing the next day. So instead of entering my room, I strode to his door, and knocked loudly.

"No!" came the immediate shout.

"I need to talk to you," I said through the door. There was silence, followed by a thud, and then the door opened abruptly.

"The terms will be set out by Pain tomorrow. There is nothing I can tell you now."

"Erm, I was kidding when I said about you sleeping in the helmet," I frowned, staring up at his gleaming gold-covered head. I squashed an urge to reach up and flick the red plume.

"I just put it back on to talk to you," he grunted defensively.

"Why? I spent all day with you without it."

He glared at me through his eye slits, peering closely. "You have too much energy. Why?"

"How do you know how much energy I have?"

"You are swaying and bouncing and flushed."

"Oh. I tried to save a kid from getting beaten up by a mob-boss and a really ugly thing with wings, and he stole my knife."

"Who stole your knife?"

"The kid."

He shrugged after a short pause. "You were careless to let it get stolen."

"He stole it from where it was embedded in the mob-boss' shoulder!" I protested. Ares let out a long sigh, then stepped to the side, holding the door open.

I gave him an over-the-top grin and stepped into his room. It was one hell of a room. I'd never been to Morocco, but I'd drooled over plenty of five star hotels on the internet, and this was exactly what I had seen pictured. Soft, dim light came from painted glass set in the stone walls, which were draped with deep, rich yellow and red fabrics. A dresser, large closet and enormous bed were all made from wood so dark it was almost black, and the cushions on the mattress shone like they were made from real gold.

"Nice room," I whistled. There was a clanking noise behind me, and I turned to see Ares lifting his helmet from his head. All the pent-up energy in the world couldn't stop my body from momentarily freezing, as my pulse rocketed.

There was something so sexy about his face being revealed, something so beautiful about his hair falling over the metal chestplate of his armor. Something so strong and fierce and just freaking hot about all of him.

"What is a mob-boss?" he said, snapping me out of it.

"Erm, a gangster."

"What?"

"You know, lends people money, knowing they can't afford to pay it back. Then blackmails them and beats them up."

"A gambling hall owner?"

"That would fit, yeah."

"There are many in Erimos. Which one did you kill?"

"Woah now, armor-boy. I didn't kill anyone."

He almost looked disappointed as he frowned at me. "Then why are you here?"

"Because I have questions for you. I want to be able to use my power."

"No. Leave."

"You can't just march about using my power and not letting me have any of it!" I threw my ass down on the bed, to make a point that I wasn't going anywhere. Ares pinched the bridge of his nose, and I took the opportunity to examine his lips. They were freaking excellent lips.

"I should not have let you in here. I thought you needed my help with the guards because you had killed someone."

"I don't kill people. To be honest, I'm not thrilled that it sounds like you do."

"I am over three thousand years old, and the God of War. How is it you thought I would not be responsible for some death during my life?" There was a grit to his voice that was obviously meant to intimidate me, but, as seemed to be the case with his anger, it just fired me up more.

"I guess when you put it like that, it's not really your fault," I shrugged.

"You belittle my achievements? Say they are not really my fault?" He stared at me, muscles twitching under his gold armor.

"Look, I get that you have to do a certain amount of nasty stuff, it's your job. But I wouldn't call killing people an achievement."

"What if the person I am killing is a tyrant? A murderer? A threat?"

We were back to that vigilante idea again, I thought, pondering his words. Did anyone ever deserve to be killed? "We all deserve a second chance," I said eventually.

"You are mistaken," he snorted. "Many here deserve nothing but death."

"Here in Olympus, or here in your realm?"

"Both. Leave me now."

"But you need to tell me how to use my power before tomorrow. If you distract me again like you did today at the camp we could fail Pain's Trial."

"All you need to do is stay out of the way, and I will win."

"Look, armor-boy," I said, standing up. "Do I strike you as the type of girl to 'stay out of the way'?" Ares said nothing, just glared at me. Gods help me, he was even hotter when he was angry. I shoved down the desire to see the fire in his eyes again. "I'm going to take your silence as a no. Pain is going to put us through something unpleasant at best, lethal at worst, and asking me to do nothing is unfair and quite frankly, not going to happen."

"Why are you making this so difficult?" Ares barked.

"Difficult? You are asking me to go against every instinct in my damned body!" I could swear when I said the word body his eyes flicked down my advancing torso. I jabbed my fist into his breastplate when I reached him. "You need me, and I need you. So, we work together or we both fail."

"No." He glared down at me. "I will repeat myself as long as I have to, irritating little human. I am over three thousand years old. I *created* Pain, Panic and Terror. With access to my power, their tests will be no match for me at all. If you want your friend back, do as you are told." He hissed the words, and I could see the burning orange starting deep in his eyes. A distant drum beat found my ears.

"Access to *your* power?" I repeated. "You mean *my* power!"

"Our power."

"My power! It's my damned power!" I shouted the words, the drums beating louder, and fire exploded in Ares' eyes. For a second the world around me vanished, the ring of steel sounding loud, a rush of adrenaline flooding through me as a blissful need for glory took me. Ares gripped my shoulders with both hands, pulling me into him, and heat ripped through my core as something fiery and fierce and untamable burned in his expression.

But with as much force as he'd pulled me to him, he pushed me away, taking a huge breath.

"You will leave now."

"Not until you tell me how to use my power." I half choked the words, drums and steel and heat and fire clouding my mind. And a rare throbbing between my legs that radiated through the rest of my body, fueling the powerful energy and throwing me completely.

He moved to the door, swinging it open hard and avoiding looking into my eyes. Was he feeling this too? "Get out."

I did as he said, not because he had told me to but because I didn't trust myself with him a moment more. When he'd pulled me to him... I'd wanted him to kiss me. What the fuck was I doing wanting him to kiss me?

"This isn't over." I managed to fling the words over my shoulder as I stormed out, hoping to hell he thought I was talking about the argument about my power and not the fact that I apparently had the hots for a three thousand year old giant asshole warrior god.

18

BELLA

I hadn't realized how tired I was until I threw myself down on my own equally plush bed. My eyelids drooped as I stared at the cloth-covered ceiling above me, my churning brain and fired up body slowing down fast.

I'd never had a problem falling asleep. Except when I was in solitary confinement. But that wasn't emotional, that was physical. I had so little to do, so little to vent on, so few ways to expend energy in that fucking awful place that I didn't need to sleep.

Today, I needed to sleep. Perhaps it was my war magic at play all this time, making sure my body got what it needed to be a good fighter. I thought about the laser focus that I now knew was actually called 'war-sight', and yawned. I forced myself to sit up and pulled my shirt off over my head, then reached down to untie my boots. Sleeping in boots was not cool.

A flash of curiosity whipped through me about what Ares wore to bed, and I rolled my eyes.

Joshua. Think about Joshua. You're going to save him from

whatever the fuck that rotten-handed demon was, kick his ass for lying to you, then see if he wants to be your boyfriend, I told myself firmly.

My jeans soon followed my boots onto the floor and I tipped backwards again, letting out a sigh as I hit the mattress. Where had all this sexy stuff in my head come from? I rarely thought about sex at all, writing it off as something I could only do with guys who meant nothing because they all bolted when they found out what I was really like.

That's not to say I didn't enjoy it. But I'd never understood why people went so nuts for it. My admittedly fairly limited experiences had left me pent-up and hyper, craving something I couldn't get. I had to assume that I either wasn't doing it right, or I hadn't found the right person. Someone caring and patient like Joshua might be the exact sort of lover I needed to get me to wherever it was I couldn't reach.

Someone hot and fierce and untamable could get you there a hell of a lot quicker, my confrontational inner voice quipped. I shoved it down. Maybe I was hormonal. Maybe it was avoidance. I probably shouldn't underestimate the psychological impact of being told you're a goddess and being kidnapped to a fantasy world.

Yes, that was probably it. Ares had turned my world upside down and awakened a possibility that I didn't have to live the life I hated anymore. And my overwhelmed brain was confusing my excitement about everything I had yet to discover about magic and Olympus with him. Joshua would call it 'projecting' in our sessions. I was projecting my burning desire for a new life in a world where I belonged onto Ares, in a different form of burning desire.

I pulled the thin silk sheet over myself as I nodded. That was definitely it. And now I knew that, I could ignore it completely, and concentrate on getting through the Trials and saving Joshua.

But it wasn't Joshua's eyes that burned with promise in my mind as I drifted off to sleep.

Waking up in the softly lit Moroccan-looking room took me so much by surprise the next day that I was sitting bolt-upright, searching for my knife before I had even blinked the sleep from my eyes. The events of the last - I didn't even know how many hours - tumbled through my head as I stared around at the beautiful room.

I was once the Goddess of War. I was meant to be like this. I finally had a reason for all the fuck-upery in my life. And there was power inside me that could make me even better.

Guilt doused out the excitement rippling through me as the awful image of that blackened hand on the girl's face came to me, Joshua laid on the stone table beyond. This wasn't about me. Once Ares had his own stupid power back I would be free to learn how to use mine, and then I could get excited. But first, I had to save my friend.

Guilt-driven determination settled over me as I swung my legs out of bed. If Ares was going to refuse to let me use my own power, I would have to find a way of working with him that wouldn't get me killed, like it almost had at the fighters' camp. I pulled on my jeans and unzipped my bag, looking for a t-shirt.

"It would be a shame not to wear that leather armor you were so excited about," said a lazy female voice. This time I

didn't jump in surprise. I was starting to get used to Zeeva showing up in my head uninvited. Plus, she was right about the armor. I'd clean forgotten.

"Morning, Zeeva."

"It's in the closet over here." I looked around for her, finding her sitting in front of one of two large dark-wood closets.

"Thanks," I said. "Am I supposed to wear something underneath it?"

"That's up to you."

I thought about it as I opened the closet wide. There were dresses in there. Lots of very pretty, brightly colored flowing dresses, covered in sparkling jewels. I paused, cocking my head at them. I literally couldn't remember the last time I had worn a dress. With a small shake of my head, I pushed them along the rail until I came to the brown leather corset.

It took me a full ten minutes to work out how the many metal catches and thick leather cords could be adjusted, but eventually I had the thing on. I stood in front of the mirror that lined the inside of the closet door and moved experimentally, watching as a massive grin overtook my face.

I looked like I felt, for the first time in my life.

My black skintight jeans were more like leggings anyway and moved with me, but my top half... The wide straps that had been added to the corset made it feel secure as well as protecting my shoulders along with my ribs and other important organs. I had chosen to wear nothing underneath the armor because the body of it came high enough that I wasn't at Eris levels of cleavage, but it still made me feel... well, sexy as fuck. The material lining the inside was intensely soft, not rubbing or moving at all as I bent over and stretched, testing it.

"I look badass, right?" I asked Zeeva.

The cat flicked her tail. *"Yes,"* she said. My eyebrows shot up. I had expected her to mock me.

"Really? You really think so?"

"Yes. You are beginning to look as you are supposed to look."

"I knew it!"

What would Ares think of it? The question was in my head before I could help it, and I replaced it quickly with, what would Joshua think of it? Probably that it would encourage my violent psyche, I thought with a frown. I gave a small shrug and closed the closet. My violent psyche might just be what saved his life, if I could survive Ares' Trials.

A loud bang on my door told me that I was about to find out what Ares thought, whether I wanted to or not.

"We must leave," his gruff voice hummed through the heavy wooden door. I grabbed my knife off the night-stand, pushing it into my pocket, and opened the door. The God of War stood huge and hulking before me, armor and helmet in place.

"Good morning to you too," I told him, turning back into the room. He stayed put just outside the door as I grabbed my boots, pulling them on. "Do we leave all our stuff here?" I asked him. He nodded, his red plume bouncing. "I see you're talkative as ever today," I muttered, as I tied my laces.

"You are hoping for an apology?" he said.

"No. But if you've changed your mind about not letting me use my own power being dangerous then-"

He cut me off. "Hurry up, or we will be late."

"Late for what?"

"The Trial announcement."

Panic fired through me, not at the imminent news of our fate, but at something much more alarming. "I haven't eaten yet!"

Ares let out a long breath. We'd been together five minutes, and the sighing had already begun.

"We will get something on the way."

He got me more of the tasty meat skewers from a stall as we made our way through the stone streets toward Pain's tower, and I tore into one as soon as he passed them to me. Now that he was in full armor, gleaming and gold, many people in the streets were staring at him. The hawker hadn't even charged him for the food.

"I have a question," I said, around a mouthful of delicious greasy meat. He didn't say anything, so I carried on. "Is the reason I can always sleep and eat, no matter how upset or in danger I am, part of my power?"

"Yes," he grunted. "You need to be battle-ready, always."

"I thought so! It makes so much sense now. I just thought I was a bit heartless."

"You were likely that too, until you became human." I looked sideways at him.

"And how did I become human?" I asked the question as casually as I possibly could, but his eyes darted to mine and there was nothing at all casual about them.

"I don't know." I scowled, and shoved more meat in my mouth.

"What is this?" I held up my last skewer.

"I don't know."

"You know nothing, Jon Snow," I quoted, shaking my head and eating more.

"My name is not Jon Snow. You are irritating and confusing," Ares said tightly.

I sighed. "At least I have a sense of humor, armor-boy."

"I have plenty of humor."

"Really? Tell me a joke."

"I do not know any jokes."

"You shock me," I replied sarcastically. "What do you find funny then?"

"Many things."

"Like what?"

"People falling over." I looked up at him, licking my fingers.

"I should judge you for that, but to be honest there are whole TV shows of people falling over to laugh at where I'm from."

"TV shows?"

"Yeah. Plays shown on screens you can watch from anywhere."

"You mean a flame dish?"

"What?"

"A flame dish. Like the one the Lords used to show us the demon."

So those flame dishes were the Olympian equivalent of a TV? I thought about that a moment, throwing a glare at a scruffy kid whose eyes lingered on me too long. There was no way I was getting robbed again. The streets of Erimos had already cost me a pair of panties and almost my knife.

"Can you see anything you like in these dishes?" I asked Ares.

"Gods can use them to broadcast images, and they can be used to communicate with one another. But they are rare, only the wealthy and powerful have them."

"Huh. What do you think Pain's Trial is going to be?"

"Gods, do you ever stop asking questions?" he groaned.

"In my defense, I have been here one day. There is a lot to learn."

"Find someone else to ask. Like that insolent cat." Zeeva, as usual, was nowhere to be seen.

"But how would she know what your Lord of War would be thinking? Do you think whatever it is will be painful?"

"Given that he embodies pain, yes," he answered, slowly, as though I was stupid.

It was a fairly stupid question, I supposed. Of course it would be painful. I mean, I wasn't scared of pain, but I certainly didn't crave it, or get off on it. In fact, I would go pretty far to avoid it. Anticipatory nerves tingled through me and I changed the subject. "Do you like your sister?"

Ares gave a loud bark of annoyance, throwing his hands in the air. "Be quiet! I am trying to mentally prepare myself for battle and you will not shut your mouth!"

"I talk when I'm nervous," I said.

"You are the most irritating being I have ever met! I should have just killed you in that damned human building, before that cursed cat showed up!"

The memory that accompanied his words, of the shock of finding Joshua and then seeing him towering over the body, sent me instantly from nervous-energy-mode to pissed-off-mode. I felt the skin on my face tighten, and my hands ball into fists.

"You couldn't kill me if you wanted to," I snarled. Ares

said nothing, but his pace increased. My much shorter legs couldn't keep up with him without skipping, and he knew it. More anger fizzled through me. "Without my power, you're just a big muscular brute, and nothing more. I bet I'm faster than you."

"Pray that you never find out which of us is the better fighter," he hissed, whirling on me suddenly. I squared my shoulders, glaring up at him, but his eyes flashed inside his helmet, and he spun back, marching off down the street again. I gave him as vicious a finger flip as I could manage, and then stormed after him.

19

BELLA

Pain's tower looked just as it had the last time we had entered it, he and his creepy brothers standing in front of the oasis, a huge flame dish between them. Servants lined the entrance, all shapes and sizes, and all dressed in purple robes.

Ares didn't pause as he strode toward the Lords. I was annoyed that I was trailing slightly behind him, so I put on my best 'couldn't-give-a-flying-fuck' face and slowed down instead, so that I didn't look like I was chasing after him. I glanced about myself like I owned the place and tried to ignore the unpleasant feeling tingling through me. I knew that if I looked over, Terror's featureless face would be trained on me. I could feel it.

"Let's get on with this outrage," snapped Ares, and I was forced to look at him and the Lords.

Pain wore a smile from ear to ear, and Panic winked at me. My lip curled up, and something dark flashed through his eyes.

"Good day to you, mighty Ares," said Pain, giving him

a slow bow. "Are you ready to face the worst of your realm?"

"Get on with it!"

"As you wish."

There was a blinding white flash, and we were no longer in the tower. I could hear sound before I could see anything, the brightness from the flash replaced with harsh sunlight. As the world came back into focus around me, my jaw hung open.

The sound was hundreds of people cheering and shouting, from row upon row of stone seats, ringing a massive sandy stage.

We were at the top of a gladiator pit.

"You intend to make me fight in the pits?" snorted Ares. "You set me no challenge at all." He sounded cocky and sure of himself, as I continued to blink around. We were in a high box, lined with soft fabric and comfortable looking chairs, that overlooked the whole pit. The crowd were mostly human, but there were plenty of creatures I could make out in the crowd who had wings, or fur, or animal limbs. I swear I could see one person with her hair on fire.

"This is a particularly special fight," Pain smiled. "Hence the excellent spectator turn-out." He gestured to our right, and I turned to see another well-furnished box, occupied by a figure made of smoke, and a beautiful white-haired woman. Hades and Persephone. She gave me an encouraging smile and a finger wave. I dumbly held up my hand in response, but my fingers didn't move.

I'd fought in rings back home most of my life. I fought for money, for glory, to tame an un-scratchable itch. But this...

This was no dark and dingy basement with shitty boxing ropes marking the boundaries. This was no stinking, cheaply-made aluminum cage, surrounded by bellowing drunks that made a grab for my sweaty ass every time I left a fight victorious.

This was the real fucking deal.

I gaped down at the sandy stage in the middle of the ring. Though far away, I could see dark smears that were surely blood. Iron bars blocked five or six gates surrounding the stage, and I wondered what they kept behind them, below the stepped rows of benches. Animals? Warriors? Monsters?

"Good day, Olympus!" called Pain, and his voice was somehow amplified, filling the huge space. Everyone in the crowd fell instantly silent. "Welcome to a rare spectacle indeed. Your warrior God, Ares, is here today to prove his strength to us all." He paused to throw a smile at Ares. "And he will be fighting with a human companion!" Mutters rumbled through the assembled folk. I shifted my weight, a hand going instinctively to my knife for comfort. "There will be three rounds, two today, and a finale tomorrow, provided they live that long."

Ares gave a small hiss as laughter and louder chatter rippled through the fighting pit.

"As a divine God of your stature, we need to put you at a disadvantage of some sort," said Pain, and Ares stiffened. Was Pain not going to acknowledge the fact that a god with no magic powers was already at a freaking disadvantage? Did the crowd know Ares had no power? "You may either wear your armor into the ring, or take your sword."

"I will not fight without either," growled Ares. I felt a small tug in my gut, and even though his size didn't change, he seemed to loom larger in the box. Terror's stone face turned my way, and my skin crawled instantly.

He knew. I was sure he knew that Ares was using my power. Instead of asking about fucking flame dishes, or arguing about using my power, I should have been asking more about the Lords, more about what the rest of Olympus knew about Ares' loss of power. Frustration filled me as I realized how woefully under-informed I was.

"Then you forfeit," said Pain with a shrug, snapping my attention off Terror.

"Never."

"Then choose. Armor or Sword."

I knew which he would choose, even before Ares yanked his sword from its sheath. I couldn't see his eyes, but I could feel the fury rolling from him.

"You will regret this," he said through clenched teeth, before crouching and laying his weapon on the carpeted floor. I saw that same flicker of doubt that I had seen the day before cross Pain's face, but Terror spoke.

"So you keep telling us," he said lazily. "We are acting exactly as you have trained us to act, mighty one."

Ares straightened, and I felt a sudden jerk in my stomach. A tiny crack appeared down the side of Terror's face, and he took a step backwards, a sharp intake of breath escaping his stone exterior.

"I want to begin now," said Ares, and with a sideways glance at Terror, Pain clapped his hands and we flashed again.

～

"What the fuck did you do that for?" I hissed, as soon as the second flash cleared and I saw that we were now standing in the middle of the sandy ring. I walked slowly in a small circle, looking up at the now roaring crowd surrounding us.

"He needed to be reminded of his place," said Ares, his voice still loaded with fury.

"Save it for the Trial!" I pointed at the crowd. "Do they all know that Zeus stole your power?"

"No. Absolutely not. Hades and Poseidon have forbidden all knowledge of Zeus' actions to be public."

"Well, your Lords worked it out pretty quickly. I reckon your rumor mill is pretty busy," I muttered. "What are you going to do without a sword?"

"The same as you," he grunted.

"I have a knife," I said, pulling it from my pocket and flicking it open.

"I have these," Ares said, and smashed his fists together, making the armor over his forearms ring loudly.

My instinct to compare him to the Incredible Hulk died on my lips, as his eyes sparked. He *was* pretty impressive, if I was being honest.

And his strength and anger was doing something to me. My usual adrenaline hit before a fight felt like it had been multiplied by ten, delicious energy coursing through my body, making it hard to stand still. My eyes were flicking between each of the barred gates around us, and slowly everything before me became tinged with red. I was ready.

A booming rumble began, and the sand-covered stone beneath my feet began to move. Large jagged bits of rock began jutting up from the ground and I looked fast between them, noticing metal shining in all of them.

"Are they... swords? Like actual swords in stones?" I called over the noise.

Ares moved toward the closest one as the rumbling stopped. "Yes."

"Mighty Ares! This will be your only chance to procure yourself a weapon! If you cannot remove the weapon from the stone, you shall continue the competition unarmed!"

"What about me?" I protested, and Ares flashed me a look.

"I thought you had a weapon," he said snarkily, then pulled himself up the nearest rock. It was about five feet high and uneven, but he made short work of getting to the shining sword hilt buried in the top. A deep scraping sound made my head snap to the left, and I saw one of the iron gates barring the doors into the ring start to lift.

"Ares, something is coming," I called, as another scrape followed it, and a second gate lifted.

One by one they all started to rise, and I looked back to the warrior God as he closed his hand around the hilt of the sword and screamed.

I could actually see the electricity around him, it was so intense. Purple and yellow sparks of power leaped and danced across his metal armor, and he tipped his head back as he wrenched his hand from the weapon.

"Careful now!" sang Pain's voice across the pit. The crowd roared with laughter.

.   .   .

It's a test of pain, I reminded myself, as Ares stared down with burning eyes at the sword. And this god would back down from nothing, of that I was sure.

I couldn't help flinching as he moved again, closing his fist for the second time around the sword hilt. This time his scream was more of a groan, but just as much sparking electricity bounced over his body.

The sword moved though. Only an inch before Ares let go again, chest heaving, but it did move.

I looked warily back at the open gates. If Ares didn't get the sword out before whatever it was we were supposed to fight came out, then I might just have to show him how much he had underestimated me.

20

BELLA

As Ares pulled on the sword for the third time, a figure stepped out of the gate on my left. Heart pounding in my chest, I turned to face it. Taller than Ares by a few feet, the thing had one gleaming blue eye in the center of a flat face, shrouded in a deep hood. The cape dropped all the way down its body but was open enough for me to see that it was wearing a small white wraparound garment held over its thighs by a leather belt. In one hand was clutched a tall staff, sparking with the same energy that was tearing through Ares from the sword.

In time with a yell from the God of War, the staff stopped glowing. I looked between the two fast. The staff had stopped glowing when Ares had let go of the sword.

They were connected. The staff was the source of the electricity, I was sure.

"We need to destroy his staff, then you can get the sword!" I shouted.

"I will get the sword myself," Ares barked, and lunged for the hilt again. I screwed my face up as two more cyclopes stepped out of two more gates, each with glowing staffs. Shit.

"You're an idiot! Let's deal with these guys first, then getting the sword will be easy!"

Ares let go of the sword with a snarl, his chest heaving even harder than before. "I will get the sword, pain or none!" he roared.

"Pig-headed fucking moron," I snapped, not quite loud enough for him to hear, and turned back to the nearest enemy. I would bet all the drachma in the world that I could disable all these one-eyed bastards before he could get that stupid sword out of the rock.

Challenge set for myself, I ran at the first cyclops.

It was like hitting a brick fucking wall. I smashed my fist into its chest as I launched myself at him, but instead of him reacting, or my fist sinking into flesh, I bounced backward five feet. The damned thing didn't even look at me. I staggered backward, stumbling as I tried to stop myself falling, and my bruised pride caused more anger and strength to surge through me.

"You're getting it this time, asswipe," I hissed through clenched teeth. Taking a bigger run up, I tried again, but instead of going for the cyclops, I made a grab for the staff as I reached him.

This time he did react. Fast. His single blue eye locked on me, and he moved, swinging the staff out of my reach and bringing it swiping toward my legs. But my focus, or war-sight, had kicked in, and I saw his muscles move, his body shift, the momentum of his actions, all before the actual event. I knew exactly what was coming. I jumped early, clearing the staff and coming back down just in time to land on the metal, bringing the thing crashing to the ground. The cyclops let out a hiss as instead of letting go of the staff, his body followed. He tumbled onto the sand, and I moved fast. With as much strength as I could muster, I brought my boot down on the glowing end of the staff.

I heard the scream rip from my mouth, but it didn't sound like me. Agony was tearing through my body, every nerve ending on fire, every sense totally overloaded, as electricity coursed through me. With a mammoth effort, I threw myself back, breaking the contact, and the pain abated instantly. Sweat rolled down my back and my forehead, as I panted for breath. The cyclops was struggling back to its feet, lifting the staff high, as Ares shouted again. I looked dizzily at him as he gripped the sword up on the rock. Now that I knew how fucking awful the shocks were, I couldn't believe that he was still up there. The sword had only moved another inch or so.

I looked back at the cyclops, trying to think of another way to rid him of his staff, and paused. He was staring in dismay at the end of his staff, which was no longer glowing. It was no longer doing anything at all.

I'd broken it. My big fucking boots had broken it! Giving myself a mental high-five and the cyclops a sarcastic grin, I raced towards the next one. He didn't follow me, just dropped the useless staff to the sandy floor and folded his arms. Weird. But definitely not a bad thing.

To my relief it looked like only three of the creatures had come out of the six gates. I wasn't sure I couldn't handle another one of those shocks, let alone six of the fuckers.

"Why aren't you guys fighting us?" I asked the second cyclops loudly, as I neared him. His eye stayed trained on

Ares, on top of the rock, just like the last one had. "I mean, you're helping me out with this whole statue thing you've got going on, but I'm a little suspicious," I said. The cyclops didn't react. "OK," I shrugged. "Your job is to guard the electricity staff thingy and nothing else. Fair enough."

With a lurch, I darted under the arm that was holding the staff, kicking out at the bottom of the long pole. He moved it out of my way in time, but in doing so leveled it out, so that it was parallel to the ground. After a split-second of apprehension about how much it was going to hurt, I grabbed at the glowing end, and yanked it with all my strength to the ground, forcing it hard onto the sand-covered stone. I faintly heard a smashing sound as pain engulfed me, then it was drowned out by the sound of my own blood pounding in my ears. I was on fire. I couldn't breathe. With a scream, I wrenched my arm away, moving my legs too, instinctively carrying myself farther from the vile staff. Thankfully the cyclops did exactly as the first had, dropping the other end of the now broken staff with a scowl and folding his muscled arms in front of him.

I swiped at the fresh wave of sweat rolling down the back of my neck, my ears ringing. The only positive I could draw as I stumbled toward the last cyclops was that at least the shocks left no residual pain. They left me dazed and sweating and breathless, but once I broke contact, the agony stopped immediately.

"Are you ready to get your shitty staff smashed too?" I panted as I reached the third creature. I glanced back at Ares, as the cyclops ignored me. The sword was half way out now, and I was sure there was much less electricity sparking over him. Certainly he had stopped yelling. He must have been taking the shock powered by all three staffs, until I started destroying them.

I had just felt the shock from one each time, and that was bad enough. All three in one hit? I couldn't help the teensy bit of admiration that welled inside me. *He's an idiot for not just helping you,* I told myself. If he had, I wouldn't be about to get another one of these hurt-like-hell shocks.

But he hadn't helped me, so I was.

Dredging up more energy, I leaped high, kicking at the cyclops' hand that was holding the staff. He turned, moving it out of the way, but I saw the adjustment coming, and twisted in the air. A small shock gripped me as I made contact, and the cyclops actually made a grunting noise as the staff slid from his grip. I landed awkwardly, but rolled to the staff before the cyclops could scoop it up again, bringing the back of my heel slamming down on the glowing end.

Instead of the final shock I was expecting, I heard a roar of triumph from Ares, and no pain wracked my body at all.

"I told you I would get the sword!" the warrior God bellowed from behind me. But I didn't look at him. My gaze was fixed on the cyclops, just as his huge eye was on me. He was only a couple of feet away from where I was sitting on the ground, the smashed staff beneath my boot. He hadn't straightened and folded his arms like the others.

"Well done, little girl," the creature said, baring sharp teeth as he grinned at me. "Now those staffs are out of the way, we can play."

.   .   .

I barely rolled out of the way fast enough, his own massive boots crashing down where I had been sitting. I scrambled to my feet whilst still moving, seeing the other two creatures charging towards me on both sides. I darted for two lumps of rock, and heard a loud thud behind me. Pulling my knife from my pocket and flicking it open, I whirled.

Ares, gleaming and gold and magnificent, was wielding a fine silver sword and landing blow upon blow on the three cyclopes surrounding him. Indignation that the idiot man only had the damned sword because of me, but was now getting all the glory, swamped me, and I cried out as I charged into the melee.

But before I even got close, I felt a huge wrench in my stomach, and Ares glowed gold, his movements speeding up so much I could barely see him. Fatigue and dizziness washed over me and I staggered, my charge broken like I'd hit a wall.

The golden blur in front of me wobbled, my eyelids suddenly heavy, and it took everything I had not to fall to my knees.

"Fucking... asshole..." I tried to say, but the words came out as a whisper.

I felt as though I'd been hit by a truck, and to my dismay, I couldn't stop my knees from buckling. The blur of gold that was Ares faded from my vision as the red mist leaked away, everything replaced by a pale haze.

He was draining me. I didn't know how I knew that, but I was sure it was happening, because the only solid thing my fast receding senses could still feel was the fierce pull in the pit of my stomach.

He was using all of my power. Everything I had. To

defeat the enemies I had disarmed, with the weapon I had enabled him to get.

A tinge of red crept back into the edges of my vision, the white haze clearing ever so slightly.

A gong sounded, so loud I half-lifted my hands to my ears, but found they were too heavy to get that far, so I let them fall again, my whole torso swaying. The roar of a crowd penetrated my ears, and the pull in my stomach lessened so abruptly that I lost my balance somehow, pitching forward onto my elbows.

I took a shuddering breath, trying to see clearly, but everything was too blurry, and my eyelids simply wouldn't do what I needed them to do. A shadow moved over me, and my instincts kicked in. Blind and half immobile or not, today was not the day a one-eyed fuckwit killed me. I dropped onto my side, my limbs feeling like they weighed a ton as I dragged them into myself, and kicked up pathetically at the figure looming over me. My steel toe caps rang against metal, and I heard Ares.

"Stand up."

I tried to roll again, but I simply didn't have the strength. That kick had finished me. Frustration and anger hit me so hard that the back of my useless eyes burned hot with tears. I was fucking laid on the ground in front of the world I wanted to belong to, weak as a damned kitten.

"I hate you," I whispered. "You fucking did this to me." Then for the second time in two days, I passed out.

21

BELLA

"**Y**ou really are a fucking moron, Ares. Learn to control yourself." The voice was vaguely familiar as it pushed its way through my consciousness.

"That's rich coming from you! I didn't know she was still so weak," I heard Ares snap back.

"I'm not weak," I said, but it came out a thick mumble. I pushed myself up onto my elbows and looked around. I was lying on another damned stone table, but this time the room was gloomy and bare, the surrounding walls all the same color as the stone the gladiator pit was made from.

Eris stepped into my line of vision, holding out a simple stone cup.

"My brother is a fool," Eris muttered.

"Why are you helping me?" I croaked, gulping at the liquid. It was nectar, and knowing how much better it would make my exhausted body feel, I glugged it greedily. I felt like death warmed up, every muscle aching like hell.

"As much as I like to watch him flail around like a child, I don't actually want to see him killed. And without you, he has fuck all."

"You know he's using my power then?" I glanced sideways at Ares. Fierce fury leapt inside me but my exhausted body couldn't fight and rage like it usually did, and a wave of pain beat through my head as I gripped the stone cup hard enough to make my fingers ache.

I looked away from him, back to Eris.

"Yes," she said. "Everyone out there does now, too. It was pretty obvious when you went down like a sack of shit."

I heard a hiss from the God of War, and forced myself to drink more nectar instead of looking at him. Zeeva jumped up beside me as I swallowed the smooth liquid. It wasn't working yet.

"Why are you here? You always show up too damn late," I said to the cat.

"I have changed my position on helping you." I paused, raising my eyebrows at Zeeva. Even that small movement made my head hurt more. *"Do not respond out loud. We will talk more later."*

I did as she said, finishing what was left in the cup and feeling a tiny surge in strength. Enough for my simmering rage to take hold.

"So just to recap, Ares drained all of my energy and power to defeat three cyclopes that I had already disarmed alone," I said loudly.

"Yes. And now neither of you will have any power at all in the next fight," said Eris, in a patronizing tone I knew was meant for her brother.

"I-" started Ares, but trailed off.

"How long until the next fight?" I asked.

"Half an hour."

"I want a moment alone with Ares."

The words surprised me even as I said them. I didn't even want to lay eyes on him, never mind be alone with him. But the fury whirling through me needed an outlet before my head exploded, and if I couldn't physically expend it, I would have to do something else.

"I'll bet you do," Eris said, then wheeled away from me and strode through a rough stone doorway. I watched her curvy leather-clad ass swing out of the room and took a deep breath, trying to channel some of her sass through my fatigued system. Zeeva jumped down off the stone table, gave me a lingering look, then sauntered off after Eris.

"If you are expecting an apology-" began Ares, but as my eyes snapped to his, he stopped speaking. He wasn't wearing his helmet so his reaction on seeing my face was clear.

"You are surprised by how angry I am?" I hissed. "You, who shares my power, who knows what it is like to fight and win, to revel in strength and victory, are surprised to see me so angry when you drained me of all my strength and let me crumple helpless to the ground in front of the fucking world?"

More blood pounded in my head, the rage making it throb harder. Ares' mouth set in a hard line, and he dropped his gaze from mine.

"I have not been able to use my power in a fight for some time," he said quietly, still not meeting my eyes.

"You're a fucking god, not a child! How can you have so little control of yourself? And at someone else's expense?" I spat. I mean, I'd lost control before, of course I had, but I hadn't hurt someone who didn't deserve it since I was a teenager.

I saw anger in Ares' eyes as they flicked to mine, but it died out fast as I glared at him. "What is done is done. We must now work out how to survive," he said flatly.

"Fuck you, Ares. I can't fight with you. I can't work with you. If you had helped me smash the staffs in the first place you'd have got the sword faster, and we both could have taken out the cyclopes, but you insisted on acting like an arrogant asshole."

"We have to work together," he ground out.

"Why? I'm no damned use to you like this!" I yelled, gesturing at my aching body, anger reaching fever pitch. Feeling so useless was burning a hole in my gut, in my *soul*. I always had my fighting spirit, my speed and strength. Not having it was unbearable. "You've taken everything out of me, right before a fight! Do you know how that feels?"

"Yes!" He shouted back at me so loudly that my churning fury was momentarily halted. "I know exactly how that feels," he roared. "I have been living with it for months! Zeus stole my power and to taste it again from you is-" He stamped his foot, snapping his mouth closed as if he'd said too much. He rubbed a hand across his face, his long hair falling over his shoulder, and an unexpected stab of empathy jolted through me.

He'd gotten carried away in the fight. He got a taste of the thing he missed most in the world, and he got carried away. I could understand that, on some level.

But not at another's expense.

"I won't fight with you. I won't help you. I can't. You were right before. We'll get each other killed."

Joshua's face filled my mind as I spoke, pouring guilt over my boiling anger, but I knew my words were true. We *would* get each other killed if we carried on like this, and then I'd be unable to help anyone. Ares was rash and selfish and impossible. I would just have to rely on his huge ego to be justified and pray he could defeat the Lord's tests without power. There was no doubt he was a good fighter and could withstand pain, magic or none.

I felt sick as I thought about watching him from the sidelines, Joshua's life at stake and me doing nothing, but I couldn't see another way if he was going to treat me like this.

"I do not believe I can win this fight without your help," Ares said after a long pause, almost too quietly for me to hear.

"I have no power left for you to use! And that's *your* damned fault!"

"That is why I need you. With no power, I need your help. To fight whatever we are to face next."

I blinked at him. Had I heard that right? He was looking down at his feet, his huge arms folded across his chest.

"You need my help to fight? Not to just use me as a fucking battery whenever you feel like it, but to actually fight?"

He looked up at me, and the look in his eyes made my eyebrows rise even higher. He looked... normal. Like a normal guy, asking for something he hoped he would get.

"I do not know what a battery is," he said.

The simplicity of his statement took me by surprise. "A battery is a power source in my world," I said quietly.

"Oh. Then yes. I would like you to help me fight whatever Pain is going to put in the pit with me next, not as a battery."

I stared at him. I wasn't getting an apology, that much was clear. But I reckoned this was as good as the same thing from a god. He was asking, politely, for my help and he wouldn't do that unless he wanted me to get killed, or actually thought I could fight.

I narrowed my eyes at him. "Are you trying to get me killed so that you get my power that way?"

He pulled an affronted face. "If I was going to kill you, I would do it with honor."

"Like over the dead body of my friend?"

"That is not how I had planned to kill you," he answered gruffly. I held my hand up, signaling him to stop.

"Look, if you actually want my help, telling me how you had planned to kill me is a bad idea."

"Agreed."

"Would you look at that. We actually agree on something," I muttered. The sincere look in his eyes, the absence of angry defensiveness, along with my intense desire to *not* walk away from all of this had mounted up, and somehow my anger was melting away. It was almost as though him turning his anger off had also turned off mine.

Truth of the matter was, I wanted to fight. I had a point to prove to that crowd now. If Ares really was willing to work with me, instead of getting us both killed, we could likely give them a show to remember.

"After this test, we need to talk properly about my power. And you are never, ever to drain me like that again."

I saw him bristle at being spoken to so authoritatively, the muscles in his jaw working. "It was an accident," he said eventually.

"Is that you swearing not to do it again? 'Cos it didn't sound like it."

His eyes locked on mine and a new intensity burned in his irises. I couldn't tell if it was anger or regret or something else completely, but whatever it was he was feeling it hard. I resisted the urge to look away.

"I swear," he said, through gritted teeth.

"Fine. I... I'm very tired," I said, tearing my eyes from his uncomfortable gaze and swinging my legs awkwardly over the table. I tested my weight on them. My thighs felt like I had run three marathons and my feet throbbed, but I could stand. "I don't actually know how much help I can be."

"Have more nectar. It should take effect before the next fight, though it will probably not have time to restore your magic." He moved toward me, leaning close to pick up my empty stone cup. It was impossible not to notice that he smelled of fresh sweat and sand and metal. I closed my eyes a second, getting a grip on myself, then pivoted to watch him move to another table in the long room, where a jug stood.

He poured me a drink and passed it over, and I drank, relieved to have something to concentrate on. My stomach was tying itself in knots. Residual adrenaline, anticipation for the next fight and lingering shame at my public display of weakness all crowded for space in my head. But the thing that was taking up the most space in my fuzzy brain, the thing stamping around and sending my rational thoughts scattering?

Bone-deep confusion over the mountain of muscle kicking at the sand before me.

What he had just done was selfish, dangerous, and made me so angry that I thought I was going to explode. But I was connected to him somehow, in a way that made everything else lose its sense.

22

ARES

"What is this place?" Bella asked me, as she sipped more nectar.

"It is where the fighters used to eat when they lived under the pits," I told her. The remnants of her power were still coursing through me, and just keeping my voice level wasn't easy. To feel the blissful elation of speed and strength and movement when I'd been fighting the cyclopes and drawing on her magic... I had told her the truth. I had never meant to drain her of all her power and energy.

But now I was worried that my lack of power was doing something else to me. This girl meant nothing to me, yet an alien feeling was gripping my entire chest every time I looked at her now.

Guilt.

I felt guilty about what I had done to her.

Before Zeus stole my power, I would not have given a second thought to it. I didn't kill her, I just left her weak, so that I may demonstrate my power. Bask in glory. That was what I did best. So why did I feel like I had done something wrong?

Because I knew the shame she would have felt, collapsing weak to the ground. I knew the thrill of the fight that I had denied her. I understood it in a way that only she and I could.

I shook off the thought, disliking what it might mean. My lack of power must have been affecting my head, as well as my body. It was making me weak everywhere. I could not afford to worry about others, when I had such a difficult goal to achieve.

But that was exactly why I did have to worry about her. As much as I hated it, I couldn't do this alone.

I just wished it wasn't her. I wished that the fire in her eyes didn't linger there in my memories for hours after each fight I had with her. I wished that I didn't hear the drums of war every time she lost her temper. I wished that her fierce tenacity didn't spark respect inside me.

No, my feelings were wrong. So wrong. She was a human. An annoying, tiny human. I compared her to Aphrodite in my mind, picturing the two side-by-side. The Goddess of Love and most beautiful woman in the world was not even comparable to Bella. Clearly what I was feeling was a product of my situation. When I had my power back, my mind would strengthen again, and Aphrodite would love me again.

"Why don't the fighters live under here anymore?"

"They chose to live in their own camps." For once, I was grateful for her questions distracting me.

"Huh. I can understand that," Bella nodded. "If I was a slave, I wouldn't want to live under rock. You'd feel more trapped wouldn't you?"

"I don't know," I answered.

"What do you mean you don't know? Think about it, if

you were told you had no freedom at all, and you had to do everything someone else told you to, including fight for your life, you'd already be pretty miserable, right?"

"I- I don't know. I have never considered it." She gaped at me.

"Your realm allows slavery and you've 'never considered it'?"

"Well... No."

"Then consider it right now! Consider a life where you are somebody's damned toy! How can you never have put yourself in their shoes?"

"I don't need to. I'm a God."

"You're a ruler. These people are your responsibility."

"That is not how my world works. I let every King or Queen rule as they wish. It is not easy to earn a kingdom and it is even harder to hold on to one. They deserve to rule as they like." I folded my arms, satisfied with my answer.

"Survival of the fittest," she said thoughtfully. "I think it's wrong."

Anger surged through me. "You have been here two days! How can you possibly think you know more than me about my own world?"

"I don't, but it appears you're incapable of empathy. So you're not fit to rule."

Red tinged my vision. "You dare to tell me I am unfit to rule?"

"Until you consider what it is like to live the life your subjects do, yes. If you can imagine what they go through every day and still decide to rule that way, then that's different. I mean, you'd be an asshole, but a better ruler."

"Stop calling me that." Every time she used that word a frisson of energy moved all the way down my spine. I thought it was anger, but somehow the fact that she felt strongly enough about me to use such a word was oddly satisfying.

I didn't like it at all.

She shrugged and finished her drink. "I'm just saying, in a world like this you wouldn't have a problem filling the fighting pits with people who actually wanted to be there. Slavery is not necessary. You'd see that if you could understand what it would be like to be someone's slave."

Her words buzzed loudly in my mind. Sometimes, on my dark days, I did feel like someone else owned me. And I hated it. I instantly dismissed the thought though. Aphrodite loved me, she did not treat me as a slave. I made her happy when we made love. That was not the relationship of slave and master. I shook my head.

"You are infuriating," I said.

"I'm feeling better," she answered.

"Knock knock," called my sister's voice from the open doorway, before she strode in. "Not interrupting, are we?"

"How do you make your hair stay up on top of your head like that?" asked Bella, cocking her head at Eris' mountain of curls.

"How is that important?" I asked her incredulously. The girl was insane. "Will you ever stop asking questions?"

Eris laughed. "I'll show you one day. If you survive this." I heard the undercurrent of nerves in her voice. And she was right to have them. Bella didn't seem to be aware of how unlikely it was that we could defeat a magical creature without any power at all. More guilt and shame trickled through me. It was my fault. Getting so caught up in that blissful feeling of her magic might cost us our lives.

And now I had asked her to join me in a fight I wasn't sure we could win. If she died, it would be my fault completely.

But I'd seen her fight and the truth was, I had a better chance of winning with her than without her.

When I'd had my power I would not have mourned the loss of one human in a bid to strengthen myself. I had to be strong, like I used to be. I had to win back Aphrodite's respect.

And besides, if Bella found out how she became human, I would have to kill her anyway, before she killed me.

23

BELLA

The doubt in Eris' eyes was seriously unsettling.

"Surely we can defeat whatever Pain throws at us?" I said, my usual bluster and confidence returning now that I'd finished my second cup of nectar. Thank god.

"It will be a creature or being with power, designed to face a god. Fighting with no power at all will be... difficult," said Ares. To hear doubt in his voice was far, far more worrying.

"Then we'll have to be smart as well as tough," I said. "If you'd listened to me last time-"

He cut me off. "Then I would have got the sword easier, I know!"

"Christ on a cracker, calm down armor-boy," I said, giving him a look.

"I must say, it's more fun to see you get pissed with your helmet off," said Eris with a smile. "Your jaw does this excellent twitching thing."

"You've seen my face many times before," he grunted.

"Yeah, but not with someone else around who riles

you as much as she does. It's fun." She grinned and hopped up onto the stone table swinging her legs. Her enormous boobs were squished into a leather wrap-around thing that she must have been sewn into, it was so tight.

"Look, my point is that I don't think Pain's tests will just be about brute strength. He embodies pain, they will be endurance tests, that will hurt. In the last test, it was about taking the pain of smashing the staffs to get ahead. We can handle that without magic, right?"

"I can handle any pain," said Ares, standing straighter.

"You're about to find out what it feels like to be human, little brother," drawled Eris.

～

By the time I was following Ares through a maze of rock tunnels, heading for the sandy stage and whatever foe awaited us, I was feeling much better. I didn't know if I would get any of my usual focus, or accelerated speed or strength, but the sheer volume of adrenaline buzzing through me would hopefully make up for that.

Knowing that Eris and Ares, ancient all-powerful deities, were worried about our ability to win this fight was only spurring me on. I had a point to prove to both the crowd and the godly siblings.

The thing about years of fighting people much, much bigger than myself was that I'd had to develop a confidence in the skills I had that they didn't. If it weren't for my inexorable need for confrontation, I would never have stepped into the ring with most of my opponents. On paper, I should have lost every single fight. And that's why people came to see me. It took four or five fights in every shady shithouse I found to compete in before the bookies realized what they had on their hands.

I'd smash my first opponent to bits and they would think it was a fluke, a lucky break. They'd pitch me against somebody harder, and when I made short work of them, the odds against me would decrease just a little, but I would still be far from the favorite to win. After seeing me knock out another three guys twice my size, pumped up to the eyeballs on steroids, the odds would finally tip, and I would become the favorite. At which point I always left, to find a new challenge, a new group of lowlifes and adrenaline junkies to shock and delight.

The reason I always won wasn't because I was stronger or faster, although I often was. It was because I had learned what made me different. I didn't start out winning. I had my ass handed to me plenty of times at the beginning. But slowly I realized that fighting wasn't just about having big muscles. Pain wasn't just about taking blows.

Strength of mind was what had always given me the edge; unbending confidence, and an ability to see from another's point of view. And that would be what gave me the edge in this fight too. I had to be the reason Ares won this.

I had to be. Because if I could make him see how good I was, he would have to help me with my power. He would have to concede that I was more useful with it than without it.

I repeated that in my head as I walked, trying to make it louder than the traitorous part of me that wanted him to see how good I was simply because I was desperate to impress him.

. . .

The roar of the crowd as we stepped out of one of the gates onto the sandy stage was deafening. They were cheering for Ares of course, the golden blur who had devastated the three cyclops half an hour earlier.

I stood straighter as he waved the sword he had won at the crowd. The red plume on his helmet fluttered as he moved, and I couldn't help rolling my eyes. I was developing an unnatural resentment of his helmet, and I had no idea why.

It's because it covers his beautiful face, the sex-starved part of my brain piped up. I ground my teeth together. Maybe the extraordinarily high levels of excitement and adrenaline I had experienced since coming to Olympus had done something to my sex drive.

Or maybe I had just met the first man in the world who could handle me.

"Are you ready, mighty God of War?" boomed Pain's voice, and I pulled my knife from my pocket, focusing. It was time to prove to everyone what I was made of.

"Hephaestus has provided me with a monster fit for a God for your second round!" Pain's voice was filled with glee.

"Hephaestus makes creatures from metal," Ares said to me, moving so that his back was to mine.

"More electricity then?" I asked.

"I doubt he would use the same trick twice," he growled back. The ground rumbled for the second time, but when I looked to the gates, they remained closed. "Move!" barked Ares, and I realized with a jolt that the center of the pit was dropping. We both moved fast, reaching the edge of the ring where the ground was stable and turning back. The middle section of the pit had dropped too far to be able to see what was down there, and I began to step cautiously toward the edge, to peer down. Ares' arm shot out across my front, stopping me.

"But-" I started and he shook his head, plume bouncing.

"It will rise again in a moment. Carrying our foe."

"Oh." This must be common in the pits then. "Should we spread out?"

"No. If it is entering the pit this way, then it is too large for the gates. We should stay where we can communicate."

My surprise at his willingness to work together was only dampened slightly by my alarm that we would be fighting something too big to fit through the gates. They were eight feet tall at least. What the fuck was coming?

I didn't have to wait long to find out. I saw its head first, rising from the hole in the middle of the pit. Made from shining metal, the back of its serpentine head was ringed with vicious-looking horns, and black oily liquid dripped from silver fangs. Adding to its snakelike appearance, the head was attached to a long neck, and I held my breath to see if it would be followed by a body with limbs, or if it actually was a snake.

It wasn't a snake. It was much, much worse than a snake.

The neck *was* attached to a body. A huge hulking body with four legs ending in lethally clawed feet. But that wasn't what was causing my pulse to rocket and my heart to pound in my chest. There were two other heads attached to the body. Three long necks wound around each other as the heads snapped and snarled at us and very real fear trickled down my spine, my breath quickening.

"Say hello to my new Hydra!" sang Pain.

"Don't cut off any heads!" Ares said urgently. I gaped at him.

"What the fuck do you think I'll be cutting them off with?" I held up my tiny flick-blade as the Hydra made an awful screeching sound. Ares' eyes darted to the little weapon, then back to me.

"For every one head removed, two grow back," he said.

"You're the one with the sword," I snapped. "How the hell are we going to kill it?"

"I've only seen one before, and it was disabled by someone pulling out the power source in its head."

The pit floor was almost level again, and I didn't think we'd have long once it was flat before the Hydra charged. "How do we get up to its head?" I was estimating its height at about twelve feet easily. My usual red mist, and calm focus wasn't coming. My breath was short, and my hyped up heart-rate was making my limbs shake.

I dragged at the blind confidence I had felt just moments ago, trying to fill myself with it. I had to prove myself. *I had to prove myself.*

"I don't know. And we have to work out which head."

"Shit."

"Are you ready?" Ares asked, dropping his stance and leveling his sword at the Hydra.

Nope, but I sure as fuck wasn't going to admit that to him. "Course," I said, mimicking him, trying not to think about how under-armed I was. I loved my knife, I really did, but it had never, ever felt so inadequate. I was up against a twelve foot tall monster made of metal. It would *so* not be my first choice of weapon.

The thought actually hardened my resolve though, as the Hydra screeched again, and the pit of the floor finally clicked into place. Shoving my knife back into my pocket, I flexed my hands into fists, and the creature stamped and shuffled on the sand. This would have to be about speed and agility.

Your body is a weapon, your body is a weapon, I chanted. It was what I had told myself in prison, the only time I had been separated from my blade.

All three Hydra heads stopped squirming and locked on us. My skin tingled and my limbs shook with adrenaline, blood crashing in my ears. Before it could charge us though, Ares bellowed a roar, and launched himself forward. Abandoning all doubt to the dust, I screamed and followed him.

I saw instantly what he planned to do. As the metal beast powered forward to meet us, Ares dropped, skidding across the sand and raising his sword high above him in a point. He was going for the underbelly. Seizing the opportunity he was giving me by distracting it, I veered to the right. If I could get behind it, I would have a shot at climbing up its back. That had to be the easiest way of getting to one of the heads.

But I underestimated the creature. The head closest to me darted out as I reached it, and I heard Ares' sword make contact with the metal. A shriek accompanied the shredding sound, but I couldn't see if the cry had come from Ares or the Hydra because a freaking horned snake head twice the size of my own was snapping at me, metal fangs as long as my forearms glistening with black ooze. I tried to turn on a burst of speed but none came, and the thing caught the back of my ribs as I raced on. The impact was enough that I went flying forward, mercifully out of the thing's reach, but painfully hard enough to totally screw up my landing. Pain lanced up through my ankle as I stumbled and fell, twisting it. I felt my face screw up as I rolled, turning so that I could see if the Hydra was still after me.

It wasn't. All three heads were now trying to get under its own body as Ares crouched beneath it, slashing and stabbing with his sword.

"Get on its back!" he hollered.

I threw a glare at him as I scrabbled to my feet. Thank fuck for the toughened leather armor. If it was a fang that had caught my back, it would have gone straight through flesh. I tested my weight on my ankle, and though darts of pain sprang up my shin, it wasn't debilitating. I first jogged, then ran toward the Hydra, taking care to stay behind it, out of reach of its long necks. But as I got close it began to stamp its feet hard, and a wave of heat washed over me.

I kept running as one head shot up high, reaching over the creature's back and locking eyes on me. It opened its jaws wide, and an unearthly glow shone from deep in its throat. Uneasiness gripped me, and I tore my eyes from the head to its tail. I needed to climb up its tail to its back, and I could worry about why its mouth was glowing later.

I was only a few feet away. Spikes jutted up along the Hydra's whole spine, and the metal it was made of what looked to be millions of tiny interlocking scales. I threw myself at its haunches as I reached it and cried out at the fierce heat of the material under my touch. But I held on, jamming my fingertips into the tiny gaps between the scales, and kicking with my feet to try to push myself higher.

I could hear Ares yelling but I couldn't make out the words over the shrill screeching noise the Hydra was making. With an effort, I managed to pull myself up onto the thing's back, just in time to see all three heads twist over to look at me. The wailing noise wasn't coming from any of them, I realized. It was coming from three small glowing metal stumps at the creature's shoulders. I watched with horror as the metal scales duplicated themselves out of nowhere, the stumps rapidly turning into necks.

I had about thirty seconds until heads formed on the end of them, I realized. And then there would be six freaking sets of fangs to deal with. I lurched forward, trying to reach for the central neck whilst staying low enough to avoid the snapping jaws, but the heads on the left and right had different ideas. They swooped in on either side of me, and I conceded with a second to spare that I couldn't avoid them. I gritted my teeth and threw myself off the Hydra's back, hearing a satisfying crunching sound as the left and right head smashed into each other, before my shoulder smacked into the ground, swiftly followed by the rest of me.

"Where did the new heads come from?" I heard Ares yell, then felt a tug on my arm that stopped me rolling through the dust. Within seconds he had yanked me to my feet, and we were running to the edge of the pit.

"I don't know," I panted, looking at him. Dark oily stuff covered his gleaming armor. "But I can't get to one head while the others aren't distracted. They're too quick."

"We'll have to try something else." We both looked at the Hydra. If it wasn't trying to kill me, I'd have thought the last metal fangs clicking into place as the new heads finished building themselves was cool as hell. As it *was* trying to kill me, I was stuck somewhere between crazy impressed and freaking terrified.

"How the hell are we going to get past six heads?" I breathed. As if hearing me, the creature pawed at the ground, its claws scraping on the stone, then took a slow step toward us. All six fanged jaws snapped in unison, then opened wide. They were glowing again. The sound around us changed, and I realized it was because the steady roar of cheers and whoops from the crowd had hushed.

The Hydra was getting ready for the kill.

24

ARES

The feeling burning through my body as I watched the Hydra heads rear back up before us was not fear. I knew that for certain. But it was nothing I had ever experienced before.

It was connected to fear, perhaps. A kind of fear-fueled excitement? It made my heart hammer against my ribcage, my stomach clench in anticipation, my breathing quicken. I could feel sweat on the back of my neck, cool on my skin. I could hear blood rushing in my ears.

Eris' words rang through my head. "You are about to find out what it feels like to be human." Was that was this was? This visceral, physical reaction to the threat before us? It was... intense. Never, ever before had I not known I could beat my opponent. Never before had I been so out of control of my own fate. And contrary to everything I thought I would feel, *it was delicious.*

I could die. Actually die. The towering creature before me could end my life if I wasn't smart enough, strong enough, fast enough. The thought set my heart racing even harder, as though it were trying to remind me that keeping it beating was my challenge.

I felt a twisted grin take my face, resolution coursing through my body, hardening my muscles. This was a real fight. A real, true, life-or-death fight. Could there be anything more thrilling than overcoming death itself? How had I never known this desire for glory, this need to believe in my own ability? If I could beat the Hydra, the six-headed, twelve-foot-tall monster that by all rights should crush me to dust, I would be an actual hero. A deserved hero.

Fiery excitement caused a noise to bubble from my lips, and Bella snapped her head to look at me. Was she feeling this too? Did she feel this every time she fought?

The idea was intoxicating.

A wave of heat rippled through the pit, grounding me ever so slightly. Something was about to happen. In a sudden blur of movement all six heads shot forward, black liquid firing from the lethal jaws. The oily substance coated the ground, not quite reaching us but spreading fast.

"I'm gonna guess that we don't want to touch that stuff," said Bella. I glanced at the exposed parts of her arms, then down at my own solid armor. Even without my magic, my armor would withstand more than her human-made boots and leather. If the liquid was acid or lava, she was in trouble.

"Climb onto my shoulders. From up there you may be able to reach the heads, and you will not make contact with the liquid.

She stared at me. "Climb on your shoulders? Seriously?"

"Yes. Do it now."

"But-" she started, then yelled and looked down, leaping sideways. The liquid had reached her boot, and as I had feared, instantly began burning through the material, acrid smoke sizzling from her shoe. I looked down at my own divinely created boots, relieved to see they were not reacting to the acid. "Get it off me!" Bella kicked and shook her leg, bending to untie the shoe fast, until a shriek from the Hydra made us both look up. It was charging.

With a fierce curse, Bella gave me a glare, then reached for my shoulder. I bent as she lifted the boot that wasn't covered in the black liquid, cupped one hand beneath it and lifted. I heard her intake of breath as she clambered across my shoulders, then felt my own breath constrict as her thighs moved around my neck. But I had no time to deal with the new increase in pulse rate her thighs were causing. The Hydra had reached us.

I slashed with my sword, no longer caring if I severed a neck, as I raced to my left. Bella shouted, one of her hands gripping my helmet as I ran. The black acid splashed up around me as my gold boots pounded the earth, the Hydra stamping and shrieking behind me.

"We need to get under it!" shouted Bella. Her voice sounded strained.

"We need to go for the heads!" I roared back. I saw one of her boots, only half of it remaining and smoking, fly to the ground in my peripheral vision.

"No, this is a test of pain, and the burning acid is on the ground. We have to endure the acid to win, the answer is low, not high!"

I processed her words as I darted out of the way of a

snapping jaw, trying to ignore the feel of her legs squeezing around my neck. She was right before, about the staffs, though I wouldn't admit it. It made sense, I decided. I would do as she bid me.

"You can't touch the ground, you'll burn. Let me slide under, and you can stand on my armor."

"You're sure you can take the acid?" She gripped my helmet harder as I pivoted one-eighty and held my sword high. I felt her move on my shoulders, her feet coming up to where her thighs were.

"My armor is divine. It can withstand anything!" I roared, and ran full-pelt at the creature.

Excitement set my insides alight as the myriad horned snake heads snapped down toward us and I dropped, putting my trust in Bella to both stay off the acid and avoid the fangs. She jumped as I slid from my rear-end to my back, flying under the belly of the beast as scaled necks collided with each other, acid splashing up in waves either side of me.

Bella gave a true battle cry, raising her arms above her and grabbing onto the scaled underbelly of the creature. I jammed my sword into the ground to stop my movement, trying to maneuver myself underneath her as she hung from her fingertips, keeping her legs bent and feet from touching the acid below. Finding one of the gashes I had made earlier with my sword, she pushed one arm deep into the creature, holding on with a strength I hadn't thought her small frame capable of.

Her body convulsed suddenly, in time with a shriek from the Hydra, and the four clawed feet around me began to stamp and jump in earnest. A scream, high and long ripped through my skull, and when I realized it was coming from her I shouted her name before I could stop myself.

"Bella!" She didn't respond, her body convulsing again, but her arm moving further into the mechanical creature, then wrenching back hard. She dropped, slamming into my armored chest in an awkward crouch, and the brief glimpse I got of her agonized face, tears streaming down her cheeks, set a boiling swell of rage through me, before she began to slide on the gleaming metal.

I dropped the sword, flinging both arms out to stop her falling, pulling her body flat to mine. "Hold on to me!" She cried out in pain, and for a moment I thought she had touched the acid. Then she pulled her left arm free of my vice-like grip, the one that had been inside the Hydra. The skin was searing red and blistered, but clutched in her fist was a pulsing purple orb.

"It's dead," she gasped, and with a flash of light the metal beast above us vanished, a gong sounding loud in my ears.

25

BELLA

Ares sat up, gripping me around the waist with one arm and gently moving my legs with his other so that he could scoop them up, clear of the black acid. Tears of pain still leaked from my eyes, but I didn't care. The agony of my burned arm was blocking out everything other than the fact that I'd killed the Hydra.

"How did you do it?" Ares asked me quietly as he stood, still cradling me.

I screwed my face up against the fierce burning, and concentrated on answering him. "Followed the heat. Put my arm in, went to where it was hottest." A wave of nausea took me and I clamped my mouth shut. Agony or none, I didn't want to throw up on the God of War's fancy armor.

"Pain! We have defeated your test!" Ares bellowed. The crowd erupted in response to his words. "That is enough for today."

"Indeed. Good show," came Pain's magnified voice, then everything flashed white.

We were in the caravanserai, in my room, and Ares set me down on the bed quickly. More nausea crawled up my throat.

"I feel sick," I croaked, and he dropped to his knees beside the bed, before popping back up with my rucksack clutched in his huge fist. He rummaged through it fast, his armor clanking, then pulled a tub of the paste that we had got at the apothecary out of it.

"This may hurt," he said, putting the tub next to me on the bed, then pulling his helmet off. The pain was so all-consuming that I couldn't even focus on his face. I felt like my arm-bones themselves were burning, my entire forearm and hand a mass of fire and agony. I was getting flashes of brief and blessed numbness, but I knew on some level that that was not good. "Are you ready?" Ares asked me. I nodded.

He was right. It did hurt. In fact, it hurt more than anything else I'd ever experienced in my life. More than when I'd broken my ribs, my collarbone, my ankle. I was sick. I cried. I screamed. I was a damned mess.

But Ares sat beside me patiently, applying more thick paste to my raw and scalded skin, and saying nothing but the words, "You can sleep soon."

After what felt like an eternity my arm was completely covered in the stuff, and thank all the gods, I stopped feeling like I was being flayed alive and started to feel the cooling effect of the paste. Within a minute of the pain lessening, I was unconscious, the sleep Ares had been promising taking me completely.

. . .

When I woke, the first thing I registered was pain. But it wasn't agonizing, just dull and uncomfortable. With an instinctive delicacy, I lifted my arm clear of my body, and sat up slowly. Although very similar, this room was not my own. The closet and washroom door were the wrong way around. I looked around slowly, stopping as my gaze fell on Ares. He was sitting in a large and extravagantly uphol-stered chair, wearing an open linen shirt and leaning one elbow on the armrest. He looked... disheveled.

"How is your arm?" he asked me. I blinked at him, then looked to my raised limb. The paste had hardened, forming some sort of cast. I was grateful for that. I didn't want to see the state of my skin underneath.

"It hurts," I said. "But not as bad as before."

I felt a tiny tug in my gut and I snapped my eyes to him. "What are you doing?"

"Helping you," he said gruffly. "Zeeva said I had to let you sleep for your power to restore properly." Anger started to bubble inside me.

"You've just been helping me so that you can get to my magic?"

He gave a hiss of annoyance and stood up, coming to the bed. *His* bed, I realized with a start. If we weren't in my room, we must be in his. "No. You needed your power back for me to do this." He leaned over me and took my other hand. My body reacted to his touch immediately, my pulse quickening of its own volition. I felt a stronger pull in my stomach, but before I could open my mouth to protest or question him, delicious soothing pulses washed through my arm. A tingle that wasn't tickly or exciting, but completely relaxing, moved all the way from my spine and down my arm, and every muscle in my body went slack as I melted into the mattress.

For the first time since we had entered the gladiator pit, nothing in my body hurt.

"Gods have healing powers," Ares said quietly, then let go of my hand. He didn't move away though, his hair falling forward as he leaned over me.

"Even Gods of War?" I whispered, the soothing warmth fading, but no pain returning.

"Especially Gods of War. I had to wait until you regained your magic to use it though."

"Why didn't you do that with the manticore sting?"

"You were unconscious. I can't use your power whilst you're unconscious. And besides, healing a burn is not the same as healing poison. You're still not that strong."

I tried to get indignant about being told I wasn't strong, but failed. He wasn't insulting me. He was stating fact.

He had helped me. Nursed me. Why? For my power, obviously. But who'd have thought he would be so gentle? I looked into his eyes, wondering how anyone could look so sad and fierce at the same time. But then, I had been both sad and fierce most of my life. "Thank you," I said.

He straightened, moving away from me a little. "You were injured with honor. You killed the Hydra."

"You're damn right I did," I grinned at him. "Who needs magic, eh?"

"We do, to heal you," he said, and my elation drooped a little. "You need to wash off the paste, it is no longer necessary."

I frowned at my arm. "Shouldn't I leave it there to protect the skin a bit longer?"

"Your skin is healed."

"What?"

"The healing doesn't just take away the pain, it heals your wounds. Your arm is fine now."

I stared at Ares, the impact of his words crashing into me. "You can instantly heal wounds here?"

"Not everyone can. My sister can't, for example. Her power is too destructive."

"But... What's the point in fighting if you can just heal?"

Ares faltered, his gaze dropping from mine. When his eyes found mine again, embers were dancing in his irises, but I felt no anger from him. "I am immortal. Today was the first time in millennia that I fought with the real risk of not just injury, but death." The excitement in his low voice was infectious, and I felt my stomach tense as I recalled the rush of adrenaline that accompanied the build up to a challenge. "It was glorious."

"So for thousands of years you've never been at risk of losing?" He licked his lips as he shook his head, and heat flashed in my core. "No wonder you're so fucking miserable," I said on a long breath. "It's one of the best feelings in the world. The knowledge that if you best your opponent, you've earned it. The challenge laid out before you, the odds stacked against you." All my muscles were tensing now, my pain gone completely, and my energy returned in force.

My chance to bask in the glory of my victory over the Hydra had been stolen by my injury, and now the elation was flooding me in a blissful tidal wave.

"I felt truly alive today," Ares said. "And watching you fight with such courage despite having no power at all..." He stared into my eyes and the beat of a drum banged in the depths of my mind.

I had done it. I had won the God of War's respect.

Only it wasn't his respect I wanted now. The energy pouring through my body was all going to one damned place, and I couldn't stop my eyes moving from his, down to his mouth, then further down, tracing the lines of his abs, the V of the muscles cording his stomach and hips, the low band of his pants.

The drums got louder, and when Ares took a ragged breath I knew for certain that he could hear them too. Before I could stop myself, I wrapped my good hand around the back of his head and pulled him to me, closing my lips over his. His hands came to my face immediately, his fingers pushing into my hair as his tongue found mine and pleasure exploded in my center, so fiercely I ached. My skin sprang to life with a sensitivity I'd never felt, every caress of his fingers on my neck and jaw sending shivers of pleasure through me.

He kissed me with the ferocity of a man starved, as though he had never tasted anything like me before, and I knew that because it was exactly how I felt. Never, *ever* had a kiss been so consuming, so full of promise, so damned *right*.

26

BELLA

I pulled him closer to me, his soft lips moving harder against mine, and he half-fell to the bed. His hand moved to my ribs as he rolled, the movement breaking the kiss, and fevered panic gripped me at the void he left. But his strong arms dragged me back to him, one hand now up my back, the other in my hair, pulling my head gently back so he could trail kisses down my throat.

I couldn't even comprehend how much I wanted him, shivers like electricity shooting from wherever his lips landed to all the places my body was screaming to be touched. As my nipples hardened I became vaguely aware that I was still wearing the supple corset. We were on our sides, my good arm now beneath him, and my left useless in its paste cast. I needed to feel his hard chest, his muscular back, his tanned skin. I longed to touch him, to feel all of him. The drums beat louder as my breath caught, his kisses reaching the bottom of my throat and moving toward my breasts. His hair brushed my skin tantalizingly as he moved.

He reached the top of the corset and stopped, looking up at my face, breathing as hard as I was. Flames, huge and fierce and hot and beautiful, were dancing in his eyes, and the sight was so fucking perfect that every single thing in my life that wasn't him faded into nothingness. Every thought, every doubt, every fact, even the freaking mattress beneath me ceased to exist - there was just him and me, our bodies belonging together, the need between my legs now painful in its intensity.

A deep moan left his lips, and he moved to kiss me, even hungrier than before.

"Ares? Persephone has come to heal Bella."

Eris' voice through the door startled us both, and Ares shot backwards so fast that he fell clean off the side of the huge bed. I scrabbled up to a sitting position, heat and arousal making my thoughts too slow to do anything useful. Ares got to his feet fast, and his eyes met mine. Though they were still filled with longing, the fire in his irises was dying out.

"We... We should not have done that."

The drums stopped.

I stared up at him, his words snapping my attention from the screaming need in my core.

"Why not?" I was breathing hard.

"Many reasons. We should not have done that." His words felt like a slap to the face. Did he need to say this whilst my lips were still swollen from kissing him?

My feelings must have shown on my face, because his wild expression softened a second, before a hammering began on the door.

"Ares? Let us in," Eris called from the other side.

I pushed myself up from the mattress fast, feeling my cheeks beginning to burn. There was no way I wanted

Eris or Persephone seeing me like this. And if this idiotic lump of muscle that called himself a man wanted to make me feel unwanted, he had succeeded.

"I'm showering," I mumbled, jumping off the bed and moving awkwardly fast to the washroom door. I slammed it shut behind me, hearing no protestation from Ares, then slumped against it, taking deep breaths and begging my body to settle down. After a moment's pause, I heard him speak.

"I used her own power to heal her, but thank you for coming, Queen Persephone."

I only just caught the Queen's response, something along the lines of being glad I was better and looking forward to seeing us at the ball in a few hours.

A ball? Fuck that. There was no way I was going to a damned party. I stamped across the beautiful bathroom to where an enormous sunken bath was set into the floor. I barely noticed the intricate orange and teal tiles lining the little pool as I yanked the faucets on.

How the fuck could I have been so stupid as to kiss him? More worryingly, how the fuck had it been so unbelievably good? If just a kiss was that sensational then what the hell would my body do if he got my clothes off?

He doesn't want to take my clothes off, I remembered, the thought like a bucket of ice-cold water on my arousal. He just got carried away, again.

The man had no self-control at all. First he drained my power because it felt so good to have it again. Then he let the thrill of winning a fight he might actually have lost get the better of him. And me.

I kicked angrily at the water in the fast-filling pool, and snarled as my jeans got splashed. Tugging the tight denim off with one hand was hard enough, but getting the corset off was a freaking nightmare. By the time I was naked, I was ten times angrier than I had been before I started.

I sank into the pool, and my frustrations were momentarily halted when my arm met the water. The solid paste fizzed on my skin, and I flinched, expecting pain. But none came, and slowly the cast melted away. I gazed in wonder at my forearm, wiggling my fingers and lifting it from the bath.

It was perfect. As though I'd never hurt myself. An unstoppable excitement surged through me as I considered what being able to heal wounds like that would mean. Desire to get to my power swelled inside me, fighting for room with my anger.

In an effort to calm down, I tried to work out how I would feel if every fight I fought carried no risk at all. There was an array of powder blue and pink soaps on the side of the bath, and as I used them to wash the rest of the paste off my arm and then the sand and sweat from my body and my short blonde hair, I concentrated on what it would be like to be a goddess. Like really, properly thought about it, for the first time since this rollercoaster of chaos started.

Sure, being immortal would have its benefits. And being able to flash myself anywhere in the world would be cool as hell. So would the wealth and power that came with the position. Who didn't want to live in luxury?

But Ares had all of those things, and he was miserable. I didn't know exactly what it was that made him so humorless, but I knew it ran deeper than the loss of his power. His demeanor wasn't new, it was clearly deep set. He had no empathy at all. When we'd talked about the slaves earlier, he had obviously never even considered a life different than his own. Was that what power that mighty did to a person? Were all of the gods so deluded and out of touch?

And the kick he got from fighting the Hydra... He said he had not felt that feeling for millennia. Did I really want to give that up?

I let out a long sigh as I rinsed the suds from my hair. Ares was an ass. He had the body of a man, and the temperament of a teenager. Before I could think too long on just how manly his body was, I dragged my resolve firmly into place. If he thought us hooking up was a mistake, then so did I. Even if it *was* the hottest kiss known to man.

I was not interested in a guy who told a woman who was literally panting for him that he regretted kissing her.

No. Ares was a douche-bag. I would work with him to finish the Trials and save Joshua, but no more ogling, drooling or fantasizing over him.

As far as my magic went... If I needed it to stay in Olympus, then so be it. But I was sure as hell not going to let it turn me into someone as messed up as him.

I pushed the washroom door open firmly, wearing my best 'fuck-off-I-don't-care-what-you-think' face. To my surprise, Ares was nowhere to be seen, but Eris was sitting on his bed instead.

"Thank the gods, I thought you were never going to leave that room," she drawled, standing up.

"Erm, why are you here?"

"Your hoity-toity cat asked me to help you get ready,"

she beamed. "I'm not usually up for helping people, but you fascinate me."

"Zeeva? Where is she?"

"Busy, apparently. Probably talking to someone else like they're complete shit, I suspect. Now, I've moved the clothes in your closet to this room."

"Wait, why?"

"Ares offered to swap rooms. Yours needed cleaning up after..." She trailed off, and I got an unpleasant flashback of heaving all over the floor as Ares treated my ruined flesh. A stab of something that wasn't anger for him knifed through my chest, and I screwed my face up.

"I don't need help getting ready. Where's my bag?"

"Sweetie, you definitely need help getting ready. Have you ever been to a ball in Olympus?"

"You know I haven't," I answered, my eyes flicking down to her ridiculous cleavage. She gave me a silky smile.

"I'm not going to put you in anything like this, I swear," she said. "You couldn't pull this look off anyway." I frowned and looked down at my boobs, wrapped in a large blue towel. They weren't as big as hers, granted, but they were OK. "No, I think we'll go for something feminine, yet badass," she mused.

Against all instructions from my brain, my mouth opened. "Like what?"

"There's plenty to choose from," she said, sauntering over to the closet and opening it. "Pick a color and I'll make it work." I cocked my head at her suspiciously.

"You're the Goddess of Discord and Chaos. I'm not sure I should be wearing anything you give me. It'll probably disintegrate half away through the evening and I'll be standing there naked."

"Now there's a thought!" Eris clapped her hands together. I rolled my eyes.

"Besides, I'm not going to any damned ball. I'm tired. And your brother is an asshole."

"You have to go, you're one of the guests of honor. And the aforementioned asshole is the other. So suck it up, and pick a color."

I was about to argue with her, but I already knew there was no point. Plus I wasn't really tired at all, and a part of me really wanted to find out what I might look like 'feminine, yet badass'. Ignoring the fact that it was the same part of me that wanted Ares to see me looking good, I stepped toward the closet.

"This one?" I pointed at a pale blue garment that had too many bits of fabric for me to work out what it was.

"Yes, that should work with your hair color," Eris mused, reaching out and picking up a lock of my wet hair. "But shoulder-length isn't right for you, sweetie."

"I'm not going any shorter," I said, stepping out of her reach, the hair slapping onto my cheek. It had taken me years to get it to grow this long, after I'd had to cut it super-short in prison. Long hair was too easy for others to use against you in a fight.

"No, no. Not shorter. Longer."

I felt a tingle across my scalp, then movement down my shoulders and back. I spun with a yelp, gripping my towel with one hand to stop it falling, and reaching around the back of my head with my other.

"What are you doing?" Eris grabbed my shoulder with one hand, stopping me turning in panicked circles and moved me in front of the long mirror that hung inside the open closet door.

I froze. My hair was long. Like waist-length long. And

no longer one yellowish blob of color, but weaved with platinum and ash streaks, highlighted by the gentle waves it fell in. "Holy shit."

"Yeah. It's definitely an improvement. And I promise it won't all fall out."

"It's like supermodel hair," I breathed, too scared to touch it. "How did you do that?"

"Sweetie, I'm fucking ancient. There's not a lot I can't do."

"Ares said you can't heal," I said, remembering his words. A darkness crossed her face briefly.

"It's true my powers are mostly on the more destructive side." Her voice was slightly too hard as she spoke.

"Then how can you make beautiful hair? That's not destructive at all."

"Bella, making you look hot as hell will wreak plenty of havoc, trust me," she said, her sassy tone returning.

"What do you mean?" She stared at me, eyes full of mischief. I couldn't work out if it was a cruel or playful delight she was experiencing.

"I assume you are not aware that Ares has been engaged in a centuries long affair with Aphrodite?"

I swallowed hard, a distinctly unpleasant feeling crawling over me, then settling in my stomach like a rock. "Aphrodite? The Goddess of Love?"

"That's the one, yes."

Well, fuck. Fuck, fuck, fuck. I'd seen her twice now, and she was beyond beautiful. Painfully stunning. No wonder Ares didn't want me.

"She's married to Hephaestus, so it's not like they're an actual item or anything, but everyone knows they're at it," Eris continued, pulling the blue thing from the closet and holding it up.

"At it," I repeated dumbly. "So, the Goddess of Love isn't faithful to her husband?"

Eris paused her examination of the garment and looked at me, eyebrows high. "Sweetie, nobody in Olympus is faithful to their spouses. Except Hades. That delicious specimen of a man is fucking exceptional."

"Right." If the folk around here weren't bothered about being faithful, then hopefully that meant Aphrodite wouldn't smite me into oblivion for kissing her boyfriend. For some reason, I found the idea of upsetting the Goddess of Love a lot more frightening than upsetting the God of War. Go figure.

"Aphrodite has been toying with my little brother for as long as I can remember, and I've never, ever seen him even a little bit interested in anyone else." Another sucker-punch to the gut. Why the hell did I care? *It was just a damned kiss!* "Until you."

My eyes snapped to hers. "Me? What do you mean?"

She gave a tinkling laugh. "Sweetie, if his awkwardness around you wasn't enough, or the way he fought alongside you in the ring, then the man sitting and tended your fucking wounds should be a bit of a clue. Ares does not play well with others, and he is certainly not the nurturing type."

I swallowed down the wave of hope and elation that accompanied her words. Ares had turned me down. He was with Aphrodite. And Eris was *not* to be trusted. No matter how much I couldn't help liking her.

"So you're trying to make me look good to cause friction between Aphrodite and your brother?"

Eris shrugged. "I don't like her, but she creates more disruption than most of the other Olympians put together. She's incredibly fickle, easily bored, dismissive of the rules and more manipulative than I am. Angering Aphrodite is positively a sport for me. The fallout is always worth the effort."

I pursed my lips as I looked at her. "Remind me not to get on the wrong side of you," I said. She grinned at me.

"When Aphrodite realizes you've got the attention of her pet warrior, you'll be begging me to be your best friend."

27

BELLA

"You know, for a woman who hasn't worn a dress in twenty years, you look damn good in one," Eris said, as we both stared at my reflection.

I didn't reply. I couldn't. I was too busy trying to work out how I felt about both what I was looking at, and what I had learned about Ares and Aphrodite.

Eris had made a whole load of alterations to the dress, and she had totally nailed her earlier goal of 'feminine, yet badass'. It was in the Erimosian style, a floaty silk skirt falling almost to the floor, but the band around the waist and hem were decorated with a gold pattern of intertwining swords, rather than the flowers it had before. The top half of the dress had been changed from blue to gold, and was wrapped tightly around my torso like mummy bandages, the gauzy fabric layered up expertly. Little capped sleeves covered my shoulders, in a shape that looked almost like armor. My newly long, wavy hair was pulled back from my face with a blue headband that matched the skirt, with hundreds of tiny gold beads hanging from it.

"Have you deliberately made me look like I'm wearing gold armor?" I asked her. *Armor like Ares,* I left unsaid.

"I've made you look like the Goddess of War," she said. "Do you like it?"

"Yes."

I loved it. There was no point pretending I didn't. I'd spent my whole life trying to understand how my violent, confrontational urges and fierce temper could exist within a person who loved the theater, who loved Disney. And here she was, staring back at me from the mirror. The two halves of me that had never worked together properly, finally, melded. A freaking warrior princess.

I turned to Eris. "Thank you."

"You're welcome," she said with a smile. "Now, I must go and get ready myself. Ares will collect you shortly."

"Wait-" I started, but she gave me a finger wave, and vanished with a flash.

I closed my eyes and took a deep breath. For someone who didn't scare easily, I'd take a freaking acid-breathing Hydra over going to this ball any day of the week.

The knock on my door a half hour later made my heart leap in my chest, and I forced down my trepidation as I stood up. *It was just Ares.* I'd spent the last two days with him. There was nothing to freak out about.

Fire, drums, heat, passion. The flashback to our kiss tore through my mind, and I bared my teeth. *Get a grip, Bella!* I forced myself to picture Aphrodite's beautiful face instead, as I reached the door and pulled it open.

Ares was in full armor and helmet, exactly as I had expected him to be. But I was clearly not dressed as he had expected. A slightly odd noise came from under his helmet, and I saw his eyes widen.

"Just flash us to the party," I snapped, surprising myself with how angry I sounded.

"Your hair..."

"Is longer, yes. Ten fucking points for observation. Get on with it." I could feel my face heating just being in his presence, and I was suddenly desperate not to be alone with him.

"Bella, I-"

"I said let's go, armor-boy!" I cut him off loudly. His eyes hardened, and he straightened.

"Fine." There was a familiar pull in my stomach, a flash, and we were back in the fighting pit.

I blinked around myself, registering the changes from when I'd last been there. The sky above us was no longer bright and clear as it had been during the day. An inky blanket of navy was lit by swirls of glittering clouds corkscrewing over my head, pastel pinks and oranges sparkling in the gloom. The sandy stage had changed too, now dotted with tall marble columns, each with orange flames flickering on top which cast a soft, animated glow over the other folk milling around. Short satyrs and slight young women moved between the guests carrying trays of drinks, and I could hear a harp playing, though could see no musicians. It was beautiful, and unexpectedly calm.

"Bella! I'm so glad you're OK." I turned at Persephone's voice, the Queen hurrying toward me in an exquisite leaf green dress that had a high choker neckline, and black vines embroidered across the edges.

"Oh, yeah, thanks. I heard you came to help."

"Queen Persephone," grunted Ares, then strode away, his armor clanging.

"He's as cheerful as ever then," Persephone said with a smile. "You look amazing! I got a bit of a makeover when I got here as well."

"Thanks, you look awesome too. How do I get one of those drinks?"

Persephone flagged down a satyr and I gulped down most of the drink he handed me in one go. Persephone raised her eyebrows at me. "One of those days, huh?"

"Definitely one of those days."

I chatted to Persephone a while, but I struggled to keep my attention from wandering. Now that my strength was restored, my awareness of the things around me was in full-force, perhaps even more so than usual, and everything was setting me on edge. I didn't know if it was my constant low-level shame and anger about the kiss and resulting rejection, or my trepidation about Aphrodite. Eris had done a good job in setting me up to worry about seeing the Goddess of Love, that was for sure.

"So, the man the demon took, are you two together?" Persephone's words slammed into me, drawing my attention fully back to her. Guilt swamped me.

"No, no, he was my, erm, anger management shrink."

"So no romantic feelings at all? It's just you seemed very upset when you first got here." Her voice was gentle, and not probing. Unlike Eris, who I believed was always trying to get to some information she could use, I got the feeling Persephone actually cared.

"He was the only person who didn't get freaked out by my strength or my temper," I said quietly. "But I guess if he knew what I really was, then that makes sense now. I thought he was my friend."

"Just because he knew you were from Olympus doesn't mean he wasn't your friend."

"His job was to keep an eye on me. He spent eight months trying to convince me that my issues were chemical." I could hear the hurt in my voice as I said the words aloud. "All that time he knew that my temper was part of my soul, my strength part of what made me who I was. Why did he lie? Why not just tell me?"

"I'm sorry," Persephone said softly. "That must be hard."

I shook my head, embarrassed. "No, I'm sorry. I guess I've been avoiding thinking about it much." A little too much, I thought, that damned kiss firing in my memory again. "I have to find him, I'm the only one who knows he was taken. I can worry about our relationship once he's safe."

"Good plan. Things have a way of changing here. Oh, here comes trouble." I glanced to where she was looking over my shoulder, and my heart skipped a beat. The woman walking toward us had raven black hair, alabaster skin and scarlet red lips to match her lace sheath dress. Even though she looked completely different than the last time I'd seen her, I knew at once she was Aphrodite.

"Queen Persephone," she said as she reached us, and her voice was like a caress. She turned to me. "Bella, is it?"

I bowed my head as I answered her. "Yes, that's right."

"You were impressive today."

"Oh," I said. I hadn't expected her to compliment me. "Thanks."

"Have you seen Ares? I need to speak with him."

"No, he went off as soon as we arrived." Relief that she

wasn't going to use her divine power to punish me for kissing her lover was washing through me, along with a tiny, unjustifiable glimmer of satisfaction that he hadn't gone straight to her when we got here.

"No matter. I'm sure he'll come to me soon enough," she said. Her eyes moved slowly up and down my dress, and I suddenly felt an overwhelming desire to impress her. I needed her to like me, to love me even. I wanted to be like her, have eyes as deep and mesmerizing, have lips as full and soft, skin as smooth and touchable-

"My, my, you are still mostly human," she said with a small smirk. The feeling broke, and fresh embarrassment pricked at me as I realized she'd been using her power on me.

I had wanted to worship her. Hell, I had wanted to *be* her. The thought of her invading my mind like that, making me want to change who I was, made the nervousness Eris had instilled in me tip dangerously toward anger. I didn't take well to being played with.

"Yes, I am still mostly human," I answered stiffly.

"You really should learn to use the mediocre power you have to guard yourself, little girl," she said quietly.

"Little girl?" I repeated. My hearing had narrowed to just us, and my vision was tightening, red tingeing the edges.

"Yes. You are little, Bella. Do not forget how little you are. I am one of the twelve most powerful beings in the world, and you are tiny. Tiny in size, power and influence. Tiny in the mind of the God of War."

"You're pissed because you know he likes me," I snarled, the red mist descending, and the knowledge that goading a goddess was a seriously bad idea abandoning me completely.

Aphrodite laughed. "Likes you? He worked well with you today because he has no choice. He needs his power back. And I'm the reason he wants it back so badly. I won't fuck him until he's strong again." She whispered the last words as she leaned close to me, a cruel smile distorting her beautiful face.

Every instinct in me wanted to punch her, but my arms seemed to be glued to my sides. Before I could say another word she spoke again. "Whatever it is you think you have with him, forget it. Little Bella in her ugly little war dress will never be able to compete with the Goddess of Love. This is one fight you will lose."

"He's not a fucking prize," I snapped, and her smile widened.

"Oh, but he is. And a fine one at that."

"If you're not going to let me hit you, fuck off," I hissed. Aphrodite chuckled.

"I can see why you might think you two have something in common," she said, straightening and moving back. "You are as impulsive and idiotic as he is."

"I'd rather be impulsive and idiotic than cruel."

"Bella, dear, Ares is all three. You are out of your depth."

Without another word she turned on her heel, striding away across the sand, beaming at everyone she passed. I felt my arms loosen by my side and they sprang up automatically, fists balled. My heart was hammering, fury rolling through my body.

"Woah there," said Persephone, and her voice startled me. Her presence had faded to nothing when Aphrodite had been taunting me.

"How can she talk about him like that? She doesn't fucking love him, she's playing with him!"

Persephone touched my arm, glancing around us as she spoke in a hushed voice. "Bella, the gods can mask conversations from others. Only you two know what you just said to each other, and it sounds like it should probably stay that way."

"Everyone should know how nasty she is!"

"Bella, please, listen to me. Making a scene is not going to end well, I promise you. She's not a goddess you want to go up against."

The anger had eased enough with Aphrodite's departure for me to know Persephone was right, but frustration replaced the fury fast. If Ares and Aphrodite were together, fine. But for her to talk about him like he was just some toy, some shiny trophy? Telling him she would only sleep with him when he had his power back was the same as saying she didn't want him for what he really was, only for his strength. It was cruel. If a man told me he wouldn't sleep with me unless I had bigger boobs or longer hair or a bigger bank balance, I'd tell him to go fuck himself. Why was Ares letting her treat him this way?

I bit down on the inside of my cheek, hard.

Why did I care?

Whatever it was between me and Ares that made the drums bang and the fire dance was physical. Nothing deeper than that. I had no right at all to get involved. He was a grown-ass man, he didn't need his freaking honor or heart defended by me. And if Aphrodite was jealous of us spending time together, or whatever it was that had made her go all mighty-goddess-bitch on me, there was nothing I could do about that.

The knowledge that she could call me names and belittle me, and I couldn't do a thing about that either, bothered me though. Of course it did. She had basically just challenged me to a fight I couldn't win. That was like offering freaking drugs to an addict. But it wasn't a real fight. When you won a fight you earned money, respect, a title. You didn't win a fucking man. That wasn't how it worked.

I glared into the crowd where she had disappeared, trying to let my anger go. I needed to help Ares win the Trials, catch the escaped demon, and save Joshua. Aphrodite's love-life and bad fucking attitude was not my problem.

28

ARES

I could feel Bella's anger as she stared after Aphrodite. Unease was gripping my muscles in a vice-like hold as I watched the Goddess sashay through the crowd.

She knew. I knew that she would sense something if she spoke to me, which was why I had done my best to melt into the shadows since arriving.

But somehow she knew before she even saw my face.

"It's not like you to play so well with others."

The voice belonged to my sister, and my stomach sank. "Eris, not now."

"You know, that lover of yours is going to make Bella's life a misery if you fight so well with her tomorrow."

"I have to work with her," I grunted.

"Not necessarily."

"You're suggesting I work against her now?" I turned to Eris, scowling. "Earlier today you yelled at me for draining her power."

"That's because you had another fight to complete straight away," she shrugged, her burgundy gown rippling as her shoulders moved. "Tomorrow is the last one. Drain her all you like."

"It's only the last one until the next Lord's Trial," I snapped.

"I'm sure she'll have time to recover before then."

I narrowed my eyes at her, and she sipped from her glass. "I thought you liked Bella," I said. "Why are you telling me to do this? She'll hate me."

"Ares, I don't like anyone, you know that. And what's your problem? You've already done it once. Do you like her?"

Eris' eyes sparkled as she looked into mine.

"I just want my power back."

"You *do* like her," Eris breathed, delight on her face.

"Don't be stupid." My eyes flicked to Aphrodite instinctively, and Eris caught the look and snorted.

"Sweetie, last I checked, you two were not exclusive. You know she's with someone different every night, right? She's the Goddess of Love, for fuck's sake."

Heat and anger burned through my veins at the thought, and I was glad for my helmet hiding my reaction. "Go away, Eris."

"You're always saying that to me," she pouted. "Baby brother, at some point that girl is going to find out just what a monster you really are. May as well get it out in the open now." She gave me a small, knowing smile, and strode off toward the crowd.

I leaned hard against the column beside me, grinding my teeth. What a gods-awful mess.

For centuries I had shared the bed of the most beautiful being in existence. So why, why, why I had I never felt anything like what I had when Bella kissed me? Why had I never seen fire burn in Aphrodite's eyes? Why had the drums of war never beat to the rhythm of my racing pulse when Aphrodite kissed me? *Because whenever I was with Aphrodite, I was only aware of her.* I was never aware of my own feelings or body. I always wanted more of her delight, her pleasure, her satisfaction, only considering my own release later. But with Bella... I'd desired her for my own pleasure, unable to stop myself imagining what it would feel like to be inside her, what her own pleasure would have felt like *for me.*

I let out an angry hiss. This was untenable. Bella could not be more off limits. The memory of the hurt on her face earlier, her anger with me, made that unfamiliar feeling grip my chest again. The one I believed to be guilt.

I couldn't tell her why kissing her was such a bad idea. I couldn't tell her anything, and for the first damned time in my life, I felt guilty.

I tried to rationalize my confused emotions as I watched the party, unwilling to believe they couldn't be explained. I was the God of War, and as such had an innate appreciation for valor and fighting skill. Bella's courage and her fire compelled me to respect her. The thrill of adrenaline I had experienced after fighting the Hydra must have combined with that, resulting in my desire for her. The fact that I could taste my own power within her now just made her feel more connected to me than she actually was.

Yes. That was surely all there was to it.

But she felt it too.

Maybe Eris was right. Maybe the best way to end anything we might accidentally have triggered was for me to do the one thing I knew would make her despise me. Show her what a monster I was. Maybe I should use up all of her power again, in the next fight. It would prove to

Aphrodite that I didn't have any allegiance to Bella, and it would ensure Bella would never kiss me again.

The jolt of loss I felt at just thinking about never having my lips so close to hers again only served to strengthen my resolve.

Whatever it was that was causing these feelings had to be stopped.

29

BELLA

I t was easy to spot the Olympian gods amongst the guests. If they didn't stand out so much for their sheer aura of power, the many other guests fawning over them would have identified them as special. Once again, I was disappointed not to see Hera. I was desperate to ask about Zeeva, and her interest in me.

Hermes and Dionysus both came to speak to me though. I liked Hermes instantly, his cheerful red beard and hair brightening my mood as soon as he began to speak. He asked me about being human, and where my power came from. When I told him I didn't know, he shrugged and told me that he couldn't keep track of his offspring either, and that was one of the many troubles of being immortal. He didn't look troubled though, and was soon waving cheerfully at me as he left to talk to a woman who was over ten feet tall.

Dionysus, on the other hand, I struggled to talk to at all because his words were so slurred and his accent so odd so that I couldn't really understand him. In the end a small troupe of silent women with tree-bark skin - just like the girl at the caravanserai - gave me apologetic grins and carried him off.

"Well fought today," said a male voice as I watched Dionysus disappear with mild amusement. I turned to see Pain, smiling at me. He looked positively regal, in a white robe adorned with gold embroidery, and even more bling than before dripping from his neck and fingers. "I look forward to seeing more of the two of you tomorrow."

"Don't suppose you want to give me a heads up? Tell me what to expect?"

He chuckled. "Absolutely not. You look ravishing tonight." His eyes turned darker, and that uneasy feeling I got whenever he was around shuddered across my skin.

"Thanks. I'm going to find Eris," I said, starting to turn around.

"You're not just any demigod," he said quietly. I stopped, and turned back to him slowly.

"I'm mostly human," I said flatly. "You got a problem with my magic, take it up with Ares." At some point I was going to have to talk to the jackass God of War, just to establish what I was and wasn't supposed to tell people. Since Eris had reacted with so much interest when I told her that Ares had called me the Goddess of War, I now felt reluctant to share the information.

To be honest, I felt reluctant to share any information at all with Pain. He freaked me out, and that wasn't that easy to do.

"You're made of the same power we are," he said, his voice low. More discomfort coiled in my belly. He was right. I shared Ares' power, and Ares said he had created the Lords of War. We did share something.

"If that's true, then I'm glad you got the kinky pain

fetish, and I just got quick feet and a solid punch," I said. His smile widened.

"We are very, very interested in you, Bella."

"Look buddy, I've had plenty enough interest from crazy deities for one evening. I'm going home, I've got a fight to prepare for." I said the words with over-bluffed confidence. The truth was, I had no freaking idea at all how to get back to the caravanserai. I'd only ever been flashed to the fighting pit, and I couldn't even see the city over the top of the high seats ringing us.

But I did want to leave. My simmering temper had reached its limit of dealing with self-important pricks, and the tension in avoiding Ares was beginning to feel suffocating.

If I had to find my own way back, I would.

"I need to rest also. We will leave now." Ares' deep voice made my stomach lurch, and I didn't know if that was because he'd startled me or for a different reason entirely.

"You know that only myself or one of the twelve Olympians can flash a being into my city," Pain said with a smile. He gestured at Ares. "Please, go ahead." Ares didn't move, and it was too dark for me to see his eyes clearly behind his helmet, but I was willing to bet they were furious. Pain knew he wasn't strong enough to do it. *I* wasn't strong enough for him to use my power to do something only an Olympian could do.

"Flash us back to the caravanserai," Ares ground out.

"As you wish, mighty one," said Pain, his voice sly and cold. "I look forward to tomorrow." He gave me one last lingering look, then with a flash we were outside the grand little tower in the center of Erimos.

"Why didn't you go and ask one of the other gods to

flash us back?" I asked immediately. "Why give Pain the satisfaction?"

"Because the more black marks he adds to his list, the more I can punish him when I am divine again," Ares hissed. I raised my eyebrows, but said nothing. "Did you eat?" he asked me abruptly. His question surprised me enough into answering.

"Yeah, that barbecue stuff they were passing around."

"Good. Then I shall retire."

"Right. Good," I said. Why did he care if I'd eaten? He started to walk up the steps to the tower, and I followed after him. "Look, Pain knows I share your power. I don't know what I'm supposed to tell people."

Ares' steps seemed to slow a second, then resumed faster.

"Tell them what you wish."

"What I wish? I don't know anything about my power, you won't tell me!"

"I told you that you are the Goddess of War. That is all you need to know." He started up the stairs, and I hurried after him.

"But Eris and Persephone both said there is no Goddess of War."

"Your existence says otherwise."

"Will you stop stamping off and look at me! This is important!"

He did stop, glaring at me through the eye slits in his helmet. "It is not remotely important. Until I regain my own power, I can access a shadow of it via you. That is all that is important."

"Did you make me, like the Lords?" I demanded, ignoring the twisting feeling in my gut that his dismissal was causing.

"No," he snapped, then flinched, as though he hadn't meant to answer. "Enough." He turned, resuming his stomp up the stairs even faster.

"You're an asshole," I said, but he didn't stop. "You bring me here, turn my life upside down, use me for my power, and are selfish and callous enough to tell me my own history is unimportant."

He said nothing, just marched on until he was out of my vision. A moment later I heard a door slam. Cold fury trickled down my spine and it wasn't all for him. I was angry with myself. I was a fool to think he cared about me. I was a fool to have kissed him. Worse, I was a fool to want to do it again.

I slammed my own door hard when I was inside my room, just to prove that two could play at the stamping and sulking game. I was so caught up in seething with him that the sight of Zeeva on my bed surprised me enough to elicit a small yelp.

"Calm down," she said inside my head. I glared at her.

"Where the fuck have you been?"

"Meeting with my mistress," the cat answered, blinking slowly. The sight of her did something to my slightly fried brain. Other than my little knife and my Guns N' Roses t-shirt, she was the only truly familiar thing I had in Olympus. I had been pouring my issues into the uninterested ears of my cat for the last eight years, and seeing her there, when my brain was so full of conflicting emotions and useless information, made my mouth move before I could stop it.

"Yeah? Well since I last saw you, I defeated a Hydra,

nearly burned my damned arm off, kissed the fucking God of War, got threatened by the Goddess of Love, and attracted the interest of a creepy-as-fuck deity who embodies pain. I could have done with some freaking assistance before now."

Zeeva's tail flicked as I took a deep breath, still glaring. *"You kissed him?"*

I closed my eyes. "Yes. And Aphrodite's crazy, and he's an ass and I just shouldn't have done it," I groaned.

"No. You probably shouldn't have," she said. I opened my eyes and looked at her.

"Zeeva, please. I need more than anyone is giving me. I need to know where I came from, I need to know how to use my power, I need to know if I can trust Ares. Why am I connected to him?" I stopped myself adding, *why can't I stop thinking about him?*

"That is precisely why I have been with Queen Hera," she said. *"I needed her permission to help you. When I saw what Ares did to you in your first fight, I went to her at once."*

My mouth fell open. "I thought you said you didn't care about me?"

"What I care about is you surviving these absurd Trials and catching that demon."

"Why?"

"Because that is what my mistress wishes. Now, I can't tell you where you came from. Before you protest, that is because I do not know. I have my suspicions, but they will not help you until I can confirm them." I clamped my mouth shut, stopping the protestation she had correctly guessed was coming from escaping. *"I can, however, help you access your power."*

Excitement exploded inside me. "Seriously?"

"Yes. Hera and I believe it is important that Ares can't take

it all again. If he went too far, he could kill you. And the easiest way to stop that from happening is to teach you to control it yourself. But Bella, you must use it with wisdom and restraint, or you will drain yourself."

"Drain myself?"

"Yes. Lots of demigods who come into their power late get overwhelmed by it. If you were to do that in Pain's test tomorrow, against a foe, draining yourself could be fatal. It would leave you unconscious and Ares powerless. Do you understand me?"

"Yes. I'm not as impulsive as I seem, I swear." That wasn't entirely true, but her words were hitting home. I had no intention of dying in Pain's fighting pit, power or none. Excited energy was making my palms sweat, and I was rocking back and forth on my slippered heels. "How do I use my magic?"

"Motivation is at the heart of it. Once you know where inside you the well of power is, then needing or wanting something badly enough will activate it."

"How do I find this 'well' of power?"

"Where is your weapon?"

I blinked at her. "You mean my flick-knife?"

"Yes."

I reached into one of the deep pockets in my billowing skirt and pulled out my little knife. "What's this got to do with my power?"

"You are bonded with that weapon. It is small and unassuming, but fast and lethal. It represents you." I looked down at the knife in my palm. I'd never really thought about it like that, but it made sense. *"You have been inadvertently channeling your power into that blade for a long time. It is time to take it back."*

I stared at Zeeva in astonishment. "But the power can't

be in my knife. When Ares uses it I can feel it in my stomach. When I'm fighting I feel it in my vision and my hearing and my muscles. It's not in the knife."

"It is true that a certain amount resides within you. But the real power? The divine power? The more human you became, the more had to pass to the blade. Every time you or Ares has accessed your power since you came here, your blade has been with you. You are the conduit. Now you need to become the source."

I let out a long breath, the hairs on my skin standing on end with excitement as I clutched the blade in my damp hands. Every other crazy thing I'd experienced since leaving that shitty concrete box in London paled to nothing as the knife began to heat in my hands.

"Zeeva, it's doing something," I whispered.

"Yes. Name the blade. Accept it as a part of your soul."

"Ischyros," I breathed, then looked up at Zeeva, alarmed. "What is that word? How do I know it?"

I could hear the smile in the cat's voice as she answered me. *"It is the name of your weapon. It means mighty."*

Heat exploded from the flick-knife, but unlike the searing pain from the inside of the Hydra, this heat was blissful. It spread through my body like an unstoppable force, alighting every nerve ending I had. The knife began to vibrate in my hand, and as the heat moved through my chest and seemed to gather under my ribs, the knife began to shine a bright red. It was growing.

I gaped as my faithful little knife morphed in front of my eyes, transforming into a full-sized sword. I brought my other hand to the hilt, marveling at its weight, and when I drew the blade closer to look at it, the heat inside me suddenly stopped rushing around, as though it had found the place it needed to be.

I knew this sword. I knew the intricate swirling pattern etched up the center of the steel. I knew the two deep dark rubies set into each side of the gold hilt. I knew its weight in my hands as I moved it from palm to palm. I knew it and I loved it. "*Ischyros,*" I murmured, and strength flared in my chest.

I looked up at Zeeva. "This is fucking awesome."

30

BELLA

"**O**h no," said Ares as soon as I opened my door to him the next day. He was wearing his armor but holding his helmet under his arm, so I got the pleasure of seeing his beautiful face fall. I beamed at him, holding my sword up between us.

"Oh yes, armor-boy. I've got a fucking sword."

"How did you-" he began, but I cut him off.

"Let's just get something straight right now. I have no problem with you using my power. But we share."

He glared at me. "I don't even know if that is possible," he said slowly. "And besides, just because you have a sword, doesn't mean you can actually use your power."

"Oh, you mean like this?" I asked cheerily, and pulled on the well of heat now burning steadily under my ribs.

Ischyros grew a foot longer, glowing red.

I wasn't going to admit to him that Zeeva had only taught me how to do that, heal small wounds, and guard my mind against other gods' influence. The last one was the one she said was the most important, and had made me practice the longest before I finally fell asleep.

But glowing swords were way more fun if you asked me.

Ares narrowed his eyes, and I felt a tug in my tummy. He grew a foot taller.

I scowled. I didn't know how to add a foot to my height. In fact, I'd probably have to add four to be taller than him. But Zeeva's warning about using magic wisely rang in my mind. I had a long time to learn more tricks. Right now, I needed to be ready to fight alongside this jackass, not against him.

"See. Easy. I use a bit, you use a bit," I said, schooling my expression into nonchalance.

Ares shrank back down.

"You look different," he said, then instantly looked like he regretted saying it.

"Erm, my hair is still long," I said awkwardly. Plus I was still wearing the jeweled blue headband to keep it back from my face. I really quite liked it. I had also found some proper leather fighting trousers in the closet, along with boots that were nowhere near as comfortable as my own acid-destroyed steel toecaps.

"We should go," Ares said. Our eyes met, and the distant, faded sound of a drum banged somewhere far away.

In a rush, the memory of that kiss filled every crevice of my mind, and I felt heat leap to my cheeks. He looked down quickly at his helmet, then lifted it clumsily to his head.

"Yes," I said hurriedly. "Let's go."

～

If it were possible, the crowd lining the bleachers in the fighting pit was even larger and louder than the day before. Ares had flashed us to the middle of the sandy stage, rather than the plush box we had arrived in yesterday, and as I turned in a slow circle, waving at the spectators, there was a flash of red and the three Lords appeared before us.

"You left the party too early last night, mighty one," said Pain ingratiatingly, bowing his head.

"Indeed. Aphrodite put on quite a show once you had gone. It was a shame you had to miss it. She's quite a goddess." Panic's words caused Ares to stiffen, and irrational anger to roil inside me.

"You know, if we get nothing else out of these Trials, Aphrodite's attentions will have made the whole thing worthwhile," said Terror. His voice was hissing and calm and so much more cruel than the other two.

"Start the last fight," barked Ares, and all three Lords inclined their heads with smirks, before they vanished with another red flash.

Pain's voice boomed out over the pit. "Good day, Olympus! Thank you for gathering to watch the mighty Ares, God of War, take on my Trial of pain!"

There was something about the way he said pain that suggested we really wouldn't enjoy what was coming. I shifted my weight restlessly. Whatever it was, it couldn't be as painful as searing the skin off my arm. I had magic and pastes to heal wounds afterward, I reassured myself. This was just about proving we could endure his Trial and I knew I could handle anything that creep might throw at us.

"And he is joined in the pit by the delightful Bella, Goddess of War!" I froze, looking up at the crowd as fevered exclamations broke out everywhere. *I guess it was a good job that wasn't supposed to be a secret*, I thought, the attention making me awkward. Persephone or Eris must have told them who I was after we left the party. Did it matter if these people knew I was a goddess? Did they know I only had a little bit of power? They'd already seen me fight, so they couldn't be expecting magical fireworks.

I took a long breath through my nose, moving *Ischyros* from hand to hand as I let it out through my mouth. Why should I give a shit what these people thought? I didn't feel like the damned Goddess of War, I was just Bella, except now I had a magic sword.

"And now, to fight! Disable the hundred-hander to win!"

"Hundred-hander? For the love of sweet fuck, tell me there isn't something that has a hundred hands," I said, looking at Ares.

"Of course they have a hundred hands, why else would they be called that?" he snapped back. "They are ancient Titans, and exceptionally strong."

"Fantastic," I replied through gritted teeth. The sound of rushing water reached my ears, and my eyes darted around as the red mist descended. My sword hummed in my hand and I gripped it tighter. A delicious sense of confidence and strength surged through my body, my focus sharpening and muscles alert and tense.

I was born to do this.

With an unearthly roar, a column of water burst from the center of the pit, shooting fifty feet into the air like a geyser, before vanishing as abruptly as it had appeared. But left in its wake was one of the strangest creatures I had ever seen.

Even larger than the Hydra, the thing must have been

between twenty and thirty feet tall, easily the size of a house. Its skin looked rubbery and scarred, and was a weird mix of deep and pale blues. Its eyes were deep-set and dark, and the overly large mouth under its squashed nose was filled with brown and broken teeth. But those details kind of paled into insignificance as I stared up at its torso.

The thing was *covered* in arms. They were everywhere. They came out of every available bit of skin on the creature's chest, ribs, shoulders, back, all the way down to its hips. I could easily believe that there were a hundred of them, each ending in a gnarled, clawed five-fingered hand.

"Cottus," roared Ares, and I looked at him in alarm.

"Is that its name?" I hissed.

"A pleasure to meet you, young lady," the hundred-hander boomed and I looked back to it in shock. "And I'm a 'he', not an 'it'."

"I, erm, sorry. Hi," I stammered.

"It will be a shame to kill you today. I like your hair. But you, little God..." All of his hands pointed suddenly at Ares. "I will be very pleased indeed to kill you today."

Laughter rippled through the crowd, and I looked between Cottus and Ares. "I'm guessing you two have history?"

"We do," he growled.

There was a little shimmer around the Titan giant, and the next thing I knew, many of his ugly hands were holding bows, and small arrows were clutched in others.

"Your Lord of War has provided me with some most interesting weapons," Cottus grinned, and something slimy dripped from the corner of his mouth. I tried to keep from showing how much he grossed me out, concentrating instead on one of the arrows. I couldn't see them clearly enough to glean anything though.

With a sudden jerk, about twenty of his arms moved, and with lightning speed at least ten bows were drawn, arrows pointing straight at us.

The crowd sucked in a huge collective breath and Cottus spoke again. "Time to die, God of War."

No magic sword was going to stop that many arrows, I realized, my stomach lurching. We were in serious trouble.

The wave of arrows soared toward us, and I felt a sharp pull in my gut and watched in muted amazement as they all burst into flame, falling harmlessly as ash to the ground.

"I can't do that many more times," Ares shouted, urgency in his voice as he began to run toward Cottus. "You're not strong enough."

I couldn't help the indignant flash that came with the words, 'you're not strong enough', but I held my tongue as I raced after him. My legs felt stronger and faster as I moved, *Ischyros* hot in my hands.

I was pretty certain that the hundred-hander's arrows would reach the edges of the fighting ring, and he had damned arms all the way around his body. There was no place that would be out of range of the bows except one.

Directly underneath him.

Ares must have come to the same realization because he was pelting forward, racing to reach the giant's feet, his powerful legs moving him faster than me.

But Cottus had already drawn the bows back again

and shifted his arms, half of them now pointing at me, the others straight down at Ares.

A rain of arrows flew through the air, and my stomach twisted with the inevitable realization that I couldn't stop them.

They must have reached Ares a split-second before me, because his shout of pain preceded the first sharp piercing of my arm. I felt arrows bounce off my leather corset, both on my body and the wide shoulder straps, but at least two met skin.

And thank fuck it was only two. These were not normal arrows. The one that had punctured my left arm felt as though it was made of fire, and it was pouring flames into my body, searing heat flashing under my skin. The one that had hit my thigh had only just got through the leather, but it was enough to feel like my whole freaking leg was freezing solid, the icy pain so intense that I could hardly breathe.

As the pain in my leg and arm began to overwhelm me and my pounding run started to falter, I felt a pull in my stomach. As Ares' shouts fell silent I remembered with a jolt that I could use magic.

I drew on the well of power under my ribs, trying to make it focus on the agony in my body. A soothing heat leaped to life in my center, spreading out fast, and I felt my strength and speed returning as the white-hot pain lessened ever-so slightly.

I nearly collided with Ares as I reached Cottus' feet, and the giant stamped and roared. We had seconds before he moved, and my usually impeccable judgment of my opponent's next move was clouded by the pulsing waves of fire and ice burning through my nerve endings. I reached down to where I knew the arrow had hit my thigh, but there was nothing there.

"The arrows are absorbed into your body," panted Ares, as we both skipped to the side, staying under Cottus as he danced around, trying to expose us.

"You can't defeat me from under there!" the giant laughed.

I got a stark visual of when I'd seen men in the ring go for the one area that was always out of bounds, and raised an eyebrow at Ares.

"Can we get him in the nuts?" I asked. We both looked up at the fabric-clad genitalia of the giant above us, and I swallowed a wave of revulsion and unease. Besides being gross, it wasn't really a sporting thing to do. But he *was* trying to kill us.

Before either of us could say another word, Ares jumped at the tree-trunk-like leg of the giant. It was twice his height, and Cottus lifted his huge limb and shook it as Ares pulled himself up the rubbery flesh, reaching the bottom of Cottus' shorts easily. Another wave of pain moved through my body and spurred me into action. I threw myself at the giant's other leg and started climbing.

"Get off!" the giant bellowed, shaking and stamping both legs in turn. I clung on to anything I could get a grip on, trying to ignore how weird his skin felt. Once I reached his shorts it was easier, the fabric offering more handholds.

A hand swiped at me, and I only just ducked my head out of the way of it in time. I was in reach of his lower arms now. An arrow whizzed past my ear and I scrambled round, trying to get to the inside of his thigh and move lower, back out of reach of his freaky arms.

I felt a tug in my stomach and tipped my head back, trying to see Ares.

I knew at once something was wrong.

He was a few feet higher than me, on the front of Cottus's thigh. Arrows were pinging off his armor, but a few must have been getting through because his body was flinching repeatedly. But I was focused on his eyes through the slits in his helmet. They were fixed on mine, and even from this distance, I could see that there was something wrong.

The pull in my stomach turned into a wrench, and Ares began to glow gold, moving so suddenly and so fast that he became a blur again. My vision wobbled.

The traitorous lying, evil fucking bastard was going to use all my power again.

Fury filled me instantly, hotter and harder than the waves of pain the arrows had left behind. The heat under my ribs exploded in a flash, and I yanked back on the invisible cord in my stomach as hard as I possibly could with a scream.

Ares fell. The gold blur whizzed past me, slamming into the ground with a grunt and a metallic clank. But I barely noticed. Because I was fucking glowing.

I stared at my arms, still clinging to Cottus' shorts. They were glowing gold. Cottus raised his leg again, but it was like we were underwater, and he was moving in slow motion. I saw an arm reach down toward me, ready to take a swipe, but it would take an age to reach me, he was moving so slowly.

Seizing my chance, I launched myself up, the strength in my arms and legs, and the speed with which I found myself pulling my body higher astonishing me. When I reached Cottus' waist I began pulling myself up his arms like I was a monkey climbing a tree, leaping from one slow-moving arm to the other like I'd been doing it my whole life. By the time I reached his neck, I was radiating gold light, and I saw the giant's pupil contract, and his eyes widen in blissfully slow detail.

The Titan giant had underestimated me, and now he was paying the price.

I leaped up onto his enormous shoulders, grabbed hold of an ear the size of my head and yanked *Ischyros* from its loop on my belt. Holding the tip of the blade an inch from Cottus' left eye, I spoke.

"Submit."

The world around me sped up again, and I heard the crowd fall utterly silent as they took in the scene before them. Cottus took a heavy breath, his huge eye trained on me.

"You win this one, little lady," he said, then vanished in a flash of green as a gong sounded.

31

BELLA

I pulled hard on the heat inside me as I fell through the air, willing anything to break my fall. I let out a gasp of relief as I hit a cushion of soft air, and then rolled off it, landing on the sandy ground.

"How did you do that?" growled Ares' voice, but I barely heard him over the roar of the crowd and the blood pounding in my ears. I launched myself to my feet, whirling to face him.

"You asshole!" I screamed at him, rage like I had never experienced filling me. I was glowing again, bright and fierce, and I was holding *Ischyros* at Ares' chest. "I trusted you, and you were going to do it again! You were going to leave me empty and broken!" I was furious. And I knew, deep-down, that the betrayal was worse because of whatever we shared. Telling myself over and over that nothing could happen between us had not changed the longing in my core, the belief that something was meant to exist between us.

But his actions had shattered everything.

"It was the quickest way to win the fight and get it over

with," Ares said, only just loudly enough for me to hear him. "You would have recovered."

"No! I don't give a shit about your excuses, you know how it feels to be stripped of your power! You know!" I could feel hot tears of rage and frustration welling behind my eyes, burning. Please gods, don't let me fucking cry in front of him. I drew harder on the rage, and my skin glowed brighter.

"I didn't know you had the power to defeat him yourself. I didn't know you were this strong. How were you hiding it from me?"

"Hiding it from you? Are you fucking serious? You don't get to accuse me of anything, you lying bastard!"

Fire was dancing in his eyes, but there were no drums. And rather than call to me, I felt nothing but the need to douse the flames.

"I made a strategic decision."

"I fucking hate you." The words were out of my mouth before I could stop them, and I loathed how much they made me sound like a petulant teenager. Or a betrayed lover. "I will never, ever share my magic with you. You don't deserve a fucking drop of power, you selfish, arrogant-" My tirade was cut off as the Lords of War flashed into existence around us, Terror clapping his marble hands together slowly.

Pain's voice boomed through the pit. "Ares and Bella win the first Trial! We'll find out what my esteemed brother, Panic, has in store for them shortly." The crowd continued to roar and cheer, but I couldn't take my eyes off Ares. How could he? After fighting alongside me, nursing me, fucking *kissing* me, I genuinely hadn't believed he would leave me unconscious and drained in the ring a second time.

"Shall we continue this elsewhere?" said Terror silkily. "Much as Olympus loves a bit of drama, we should keep some things to ourselves."

Yet more light flashed around us and we were all in the box at the top of the pit.

"Stop fucking doing that!" I yelled, rounding on Pain. "I'm sick to death of being flashed all over the place without anyone telling me!"

"It looks like you'll be able to do it yourself soon," Pain answered with a smile. "You're a fast learner."

"And you're as much of an asshole as him. Send me back to the caravanserai, now."

I needed to be somewhere I could let off this rage, immediately. My temperature was at fever pitch, my blood feeling like it was actually boiling. One more minute in the company of these dishonest maniacs, and I would lose my shit completely. And now that I was glowing and had a big fucking sword, that seemed like a seriously bad idea.

"Do you not want to see your friend before you go?" asked Terror.

I froze. "What?"

"Well you've done so well already," he said smoothly. "We feel you deserve a reward."

Alarm bells rang in my head as I stared at his stone face, the black swirling across it. There was no way these men wanted to help or reward me.

"We've decided that as you weren't the one challenged to the Trials in the first place, you should be given the chance to catch the demon yourself. You don't need to compete."

They were trying to separate me and Ares. They knew he would lose if he didn't have me.

I looked at the God of War. He stared back at me from

under his helmet, and I couldn't identify the emotion churning in his eyes.

And I didn't care.

"How?" I demanded, turning back to the Lords. Terror waved his hand, and a large circular part of the air between us shimmered and rippled. As I stared, the rippling cleared, and the room full of stone beds came into focus. The beds were all empty, but I was sure it was the same room.

"Just step though. If you catch or kill the demon yourself, I suppose Ares can't complete Oceanus' quest and won't get his power back. But you'll be able to save your friend before something happens to him."

My heart was galloping in my chest, a million emotions crashing into each other in my head. I looked back to Ares. If I stepped through that portal I was basically signing his death warrant.

But hadn't he just been willing to do the same? To leave my life to chance? He might survive the Trials without power. He wasn't exactly weak. I looked through the portal. I could see blood, dried onto the stone beds, and a vision of Joshua with his glassy dead eyes and bleeding chest filled my mind.

If I had the chance to save him now, I had to take it.

I opened my mouth, the impulse to tell Ares I was sorry rising in me fast. But as I looked at him, the rage swelled again. He had tried to drain me. Again. After swearing not to. He cared nothing for me.

And I owed him nothing.

Gripping *Ischyros* tightly in my hand, I stepped through the portal.

THE SAVAGE GOD

1

BELLA

Adrenaline tingled through my body as the portal closed behind me, taking the light of Erimos with it. I blinked into the dimness, my sword raised and every muscle in my body tense and alert.

The stone tables that I had seen Joshua's body on stood foreboding and empty in uniform rows, lit by candles set in iron sconces on the walls. I scanned the cavernous space fast, counting five tables across the width of the room, and too many to keep track of stretching the length. I stood as still as I could, ears straining for the sound of anyone else in the windowless space with me but I was sure the room was as empty as the tables were. Reaching out to the closest tentatively, I touched the dark stain I'd seen from the other side of the portal.

Blood.

More tension gripped me, and I felt *Ischyros* heat in my hand. I clutched the weapon tighter, the sensation lessening how alone I felt.

You had to leave Ares, I told myself. *You owe him nothing.*

The rage he had caused by betraying my trust surged

in me, steeling my determination. I didn't need to feel guilty. The backstabbing god had brought this on himself. I was here to save my friend, and that's what I would do.

But the ache in my chest didn't lessen as I shoved the feeling of loss as deep down as I could.

I moved forward, purposefully. There were no exits where I was standing, so I needed to find one.

Checking everything around me carefully as I walked, I made my way through the tables. Any clue could be useful. I noticed that the walls seemed to be paneled in dark wood, but I saw nothing else but tables and flickering candles.

My mind raced, trying to work out how so many bodies could have been moved from this room, and where they might be now. With magic in the equation, I supposed anything was possible. Why would the Lords send me here if there was nothing to be found?

Part of me knew for certain that they didn't want to help me. This was a trap, for sure. But was their intention to kill me so that I couldn't help Ares? Or was it to give me what I wanted so that I *wouldn't* help Ares?

The former seemed the most likely, I realized, and my steps quickened at the thought. I didn't regret my decision though. If there was a possibility of finding Joshua here, wherever *here* was, then I had no choice but to take it.

Joshua was someone I did owe something to. He may not have been honest with me during the time we'd spent together, but he *had* spent all of it trying to help me. Not just using me like that giant asshole had.

.   .   .

I quickened my pace further. I knew I was taking less care to check my surroundings for anything other than a door or window but I didn't want to be in the grim room anymore. I wanted light, and air. I wanted to know where I was, and why. I wanted to find Joshua.

Relief washed through me when after another few minutes, the end of the room finally appeared in the gloom. I half-jogged to a dark archway set in the middle of the wall. It led to a narrow and equally dim spiral stairway, leading up and I took the stairs two at a time, the faint hope that Joshua might be at the top spurring me on faster.

I was not expecting what I saw when I burst through the wooden door at the top of the stairway.

At all.

I was on a ship. A colossal ship, with shiny wooden planks, masts like giant tree trunks, and sails...

My breath caught as I stared up at the sails that were hanging from three masts. They looked like they were made from liquid gold, sparkling metallic colors shimmering across them as the fabric rippled. As if responding to me noticing them, a huge gust of wind blew across the deck, whipping my hair up and causing them to snap taut. I wasn't sure I'd ever seen anything so beautiful.

Something was wrong though, something fundamental, and it pulled me from my awe. I blinked around myself. There were clouds floating by on either side of the ship. Colored clouds, pastel pinks and purples, with glittering dust corkscrewing through them.

There was a distinct lack of salty ocean scent in the air, and my pulse quickened. I took a slow step out of the doorway, glancing back to see that it was set in the raised back end of the ship, a spoked wheel atop the platform above it. A vague memory of pirate movies told me that was the quarterdeck. I glanced toward the other end of the ship, some distance away but close enough to see that there was an identical quarterdeck at that end too. That was definitely different to the pirate ships from the movies.

I walked carefully, knowing it wasn't normal for a ship this size to be apparently devoid of crew. But I saw nobody as I approached the high railings, and tentatively peered over.

My stomach lurched, my heart starting a small stampede in my chest as I stared down at nothing but clouds. We were flying. The fucking ship was flying. Zeeva's words about flying ships pricked at my memory, and exhilaration filled me.

A flying pirate ship.

"No freaking way," I breathed, my words lost to the clouds whizzing past us.

A cold feeling blew over me, and at first I thought it was the wind generated by the ship soaring through the skies. But as my hair stood on end, and an icy trickle snaked down my spine, I realized it was something else. Something magic. Almost relieved that I wasn't alone on the ship, that there was something there that might help me find Joshua, I raised my weapon and turned around.

Shadows that hadn't been there a moment before were crawling down the central mast, and dark smoke seemed to be seeping up out of the wooden planks of the deck. A tangy smell that made me think instantly of blood rose with the misty smoke.

"Show yourself!" I called out, as red seeped down over my vision. A low, keening wail started up, distant at first, but growing in volume fast. It set my teeth on edge and made me want to cover my ears, but I kept my stance as it was, moving slowly away from the railings. I wasn't stupid enough to keep my back to a fall that high. "You don't scare me! I just want to talk."

"Talk?" A voice replaced the wail, hissing and high-pitched and seriously unpleasant to listen to. "Nobody ever wants to talk to me."

"Well, I do. Show yourself."

"You really do not have any fear of me?"

"I don't know what or who you are. So no." I was lying. I feared the unknown far more than I feared foes I could see. If this smoke creature was the Underworld demon, then I would rather it were standing in front of me, giving me a damn clue as to how I could fight it.

The pulsing smoke and shadows whipped up suddenly, drawing together in front of the mast, twenty feet from me. I tried to keep both the awe and fear I was feeling from showing on my face as the keening started again, pitched higher, almost a shriek. The sound filled my mind with images of grief, loved ones hysterical as they wailed over corpses. A surety that I would soon become one those corpses clawed at me. There would be no one wailing with grief over my body though. I was alone. I was always alone.

A sickening desolation took me, and I almost lowered my sword arm when *Ischyros* fired to life. Warmth pulsed from the hilt of my sword through my whole being, forcing out the darkness bleeding through me. *It was the thing's power causing my fear; I had to be stronger than it was.*

But knowing that what I was feeling was being instilled in me by magic made it no less terrifying.

Wings stretched slowly from the dark mass before me, huge and dark and leathery. I focused on them, seeing that they were torn and jagged, the arches at weird and broken angles. Then the rest of the blackness melted away, leaving me a clear view of what I was facing.

I had been wrong about being less scared of foes I could see than those that were hidden. This thing should have stayed in the shadows and smoke for eternity.

The creature had the body and head of a curvaceous woman, but the damage to its wings were nothing in comparison to the rest of it. Her skin was blackened as though she had been brutally burned, the only color coming from gaping red wounds slashed all over her body, rotten flesh and bone protruding nauseatingly. Her face looked as though it had been melted, her features sagging and her mouth hanging too low, as though her jaw was no longer connected to her skull, and just her charred skin was keeping it there. It made her gaping mouth look as though she were screaming. Her eyes were worse though. They were solid black, and utterly devoid of soul, and I'd never seen anything so jarring or unnerving. Even Terror's blank features were preferable to those pits of nothingness.

"You smell like War," she hissed. Her mouth didn't move as she spoke.

I took a ragged breath. "Who are you?"

"I am not given a name in the Underworld. Who are you?"

"Bella," I said. My palms were slick with sweat, and I

could feel it running down my back, despite the cool wind blowing over the ship. "Where are we? And where are the Guardians?"

"You just missed them, baby goddess." There was a high-pitched cackle, and I shuddered involuntarily. "Zeus needs me to move them often."

"Zeus? What's he got to do with anything?"

"He freed me. I do not ask questions, and he lets me have souls." Smoke billowed up around her as she said the word "souls" with chilling excitement.

"Where are the Guardians?" I asked again. My skin was fizzing with adrenaline, and I was struggling to contain my energy. Every part of me longed to lash out, to prove to this threat that I shouldn't be fucked with. It was my go-to response to fear.

"Why are you here? You smell delicious."

My stomach churned at her words. "The Lords of War sent me here. Do you know them?"

Another cackle emanated from her. "The Lords of War are too kind," she screeched, the sound making me flinch. "But I don't think my master wants me to take your soul. I think he has plans for you and the other one."

"The other one? Ares?"

"But you smell so good... I'm sure he can make a new plan."

"What is he planning?" My muscles tensed as she moved, hovering slightly closer to me. I had no idea how to defend myself against her.

"That's not my business. Why is the other one not with you?"

"I... I came alone." Saying the words felt wrong, and guilt about abandoning Ares welled up inside me. "Tell me where the Guardians are, now!" I projected as much power as I could muster into the words, and saw my skin glow in response. *Thank fuck for that.* I was seriously under-equipped in this face off. I didn't know how to fight a demon, Joshua was nowhere to be seen, and I couldn't flash.

I was stuck on a flying ship with a shit-scary demon that wanted my soul. A bit of glowing was definitely what I needed.

A low growl rumbled across the deck, distant screams sounding on the wind.

"You know, you smell even better when you use your power," she hissed. "Like fire and steel and earth."

That's what Ares smelled like, I realized. A fierce wish for him to be at my side speared through my head, and I bared my teeth, angry with myself for being so needy and weak. But as I tried to convince myself that I didn't need the God of War's help, the more I realized just how out of my depth I was. I felt a surge of strength flow through me as my power turned the fear into anger.

"Stop fucking smelling me and tell me where the Guardians are!"

"No. I'm afraid you are too delectable to give up, baby goddess." With a piercing shriek that made pain lance through my skull and terror coil around my chest simultaneously, she swooped at me.

2

ARES

I heaved in a breath as my chest constricted, as though a vice was gripping it. I knew what was causing this latest alien feeling. It was anxiety.

I actually feared for the girl's safety. To the point that my heart wasn't beating steadily, my pulse was racing and my throat was tight. My body was betraying me, behaving like a besotted child when it should be steady and solid and immovable.

Damn this woman!

As strong as Bella apparently was, she could not face an Underworld demon alone. She had no training, no idea what she was dealing with, and no escape.

"Eris, if you care for me at all, you will do as I ask!" I barked the words as my sister sipped slowly from a metal goblet.

It had taken me nearly twenty minutes to find her after I had sprinted from the fighting pit back to Erimos, and now she knew she had me exactly where she wanted me. Desperate.

"Brother, you know I care for nobody."

"If you take me to her, I will wreak havoc," I tried. Something flashed in Eris' dark eyes.

"Well, I do love a bit of havoc," she murmured, setting her glass down on the wooden table before her. I had finally found her in a brothel, and she had refused to leave. A naked young man appeared out of nowhere and refilled her goblet, glancing nervously at me. I was still in full armor. Eris winked at him.

"Bella hates me right now," I continued. "And she will be sure to be causing trouble wherever she is. It's a win-win for you."

"The thing is, Ares, I know who is behind the Lords' new enthusiasm for taking you down. And it's not someone I want to fuck with."

"Who? Who is doing this?"

"I already told you, I'm giving you nothing for free."

Another bolt of worry clawed at my insides and I snarled before I could stop myself. This invasive, constant, useless emotion did not belong inside me, and I didn't know how to remove it, other than assure it of Bella's safety. And Eris was the only person I would ask for help.

"What do you want?"

"I want to know who she is, Ares."

"No. I can't tell you that."

And I couldn't.

Another infernal new feeling flared to life alongside the anxiety. *Guilt.* This one was becoming familiar to me now. And the two combined... How the hell did mortals get a single thing done with all this debilitating emotion churning around inside them?

"Then I can't do a thing for you, brother. It would not be worth his wrath."

I latched onto her words. *"His* wrath?"

She waggled her eyebrows at me, eyes shining. "Oops. Did I say that out loud?"

"Eris, either tell me what you know, or send me to Bella. I swear the chaos will be worth it for you."

I knew she wanted to help me. I could see the struggle on her face as she stared up at me. "Give me something in return," she said eventually.

"I can't tell you who she is."

"Then admit to me that you like her."

I was thankful that my helmet hid my face. I could feel it heating with unease, embarrassment and... *excitement*? What the hell was this collection of feelings supposed to be? Gods, they were endless! The further from Bella and her power I was, the more they invaded my being. It was untenable.

Eris laughed. "Your eyes have the look of someone who has just been caught doing something they shouldn't have been. A look I know well. That will do for now, brother." She was beaming at me and I shifted angrily.

"I have told you nothing! I tried to drain her, just like you told me to!"

My protests were pointless though. Eris' smile didn't change as she stood up. "That love-witch of yours is going to lose her shit when she finds out. I can't wait! Oh, do me a favor? If anyone asks who helped you, don't tell them it was me. Tell them it was Hermes. That'll confuse the fuck out of them."

With another cackle of laughter, the world flashed white around me.

～

The scene that met my eyes was both breathtaking and terrifying, and I was prepared for neither.

The sight of Bella moving across the deck of a ship faster than I could follow, her glowing sword moving like it was performing a dance just for her, was borderline erotic.

But the hell-demon swooping after her, backing away from the light of her sword, then trying to dart around it, would not tire as fast as Bella. I knew exactly what she was, and what she would do to Bella if she reached her.

"Keres demon!" I bellowed.

The demon screeched as she turned to me. Bella froze, shock on her face as she saw me, and possibly a flash of hope.

"He does not smell as good as you," the creature hissed, turning back to Bella.

"Return to Hades, at once!" I roared.

The demon ignored me completely, snapping her rotten wings out at she threw herself at Bella.

Without a second's hesitation, I drew on the cord that connected us, and flashed us both off the ship.

3

BELLA

"What the fuck was that thing?" I half screamed the question at Ares when the light from his flash faded away. My brain wanted to work out where I was and what the hell was going on.

My body wanted to smash everything.

I'd known that I couldn't beat her. I'd felt my muscles tiring, the burning ball of power inside me ebbing away, the rotten stench of the demon getting stronger every time she got closer to me. I'd known that at some point she would get to me, and I had no escape. A refusal to accept my fate had sent me into a frenzy, and my hands were burning as though they'd been inside the Hydra again, my vision blood-red.

"You fucking betrayed me!" I yelled as Ares' eyes found mine, and I knew they would be wild with rage.

"Hit me," he said.

Like the freaking Incredible Hulk, I swung blindly with my sword, roaring and yelling and swearing as it met armor with a ringing clang over and over. Heat fired through me from where I gripped the sword with both hands, each time it made contact sending shocks pulsing up my arms. And they felt good. Over and over again I landed blows on him, barely aware of my actions. I knew he was drawing my power, I could vaguely feel the cord humming in my gut, but I didn't need it.

I kept hitting him until my arms couldn't lift my blade high enough any more, and my breathing was so labored my head spun.

My chest heaved as I dropped the sword to my side, and Ares locked his eyes on mine.

The red mist ebbed away, and questions crashed through my head so fast and thick that pain throbbed at the base of my skull.

"Give me your hand," said Ares quietly.

"No," I spat automatically. He reached forward and grabbed it anyway, and I yelped in pain and dropped *Ischyros* to the ground. There were blisters on my skin. A slow pleasurable tingling spread across my skin, and it dawned foggily on me that he was healing me.

I snatched my hand back, the pain returning immediately.

"I can do that myself," I hissed.

But when I tried to concentrate on fixing the wounds, I found I couldn't, my head a jumbled mess of frustration and confusion. "I have a lot of fucking questions," I said through gritted teeth, giving up on my burns. "And if you don't answer them, I will not spend a minute more with you."

Ares stared through his helmet at me a long moment, his expression unreadable. Then with a sigh, he turned. "Fine. I'll tell you everything I know. But I'm having a drink. Want one?"

I blinked in shock at his back. I'd expected an argument. Not an offer of a drink.

"Yes. Nectar."

I was exhausted. Physically, and magically. I looked around myself, limbs beginning to shake slightly with the adrenaline still coursing through my body. We were in a room made from wooden logs. Ares made his way to a counter fixed to one wall, next to a large bookcase. The room was big and open, with a bed and closets against another wall and couches in the middle. A small kitchenette with a sink lined the wall to my left.

I moved slowly, sitting down on a pale pink cushioned couch. All the furniture looked like it belonged in a retirement home.

Ares turned back to me, carrying two glasses. He passed me one, then sat down on the other couch, a pretty coral color. If I hadn't been so angry and confused I would have laughed, he was so out of place in a room like this.

I opened my mouth to demand he talk, but he started before I could speak.

"The demon on that ship is a Keres demon. They are the spirits of violent death. They are supposed to take souls from battlefields. I do not know why this one has stolen the Guardians' souls."

"Can the souls be returned?" My throat constricted as I asked the question, Joshua's face filling my mind.

"Yes. The demon will answer to Hades when it is returned to the Underworld. He will ensure the souls are replaced."

Thank fuck for that.

"Keres demons are strongly connected to my... our power, as violent death is connected to war. I had hoped for a moment she would obey me. But she is an exceptionally strong example."

"She said she was working for Zeus," I said. "Why?" Ares froze, then took a very long breath.

"Cronos, most powerful and dangerous Titan in the world, is imprisoned in Tartarus, in the Underworld. Zeus recently sought to free him, to remind the world that Titans are dangerous. He then planned to recapture him, to prove his own dominance."

I stared at Ares. "What a dickhead. I'm assuming this history lesson is going somewhere relevant?" Ares ground his teeth a little, but continued.

"It is the belief of the other gods that Zeus was over-confident in his ability to defeat Cronos if he were freed again. The war in which he was originally captured and imprisoned was great and glorious, but it took the help of many other powerful Titans who betrayed Cronos to win."

"Titans like Oceanus?" I ventured. It had been clear when I first got here that Oceanus was more powerful than the others. He was apparently the only one who could restore Ares' power.

"Yes. And Prometheus, and Atlas. These Titans have since vanished, having been made unwelcome in Olympus by Zeus. Oceanus only returned a few months ago. Hades gifted Oceanus his own realm to rule over."

I took a deep breath. "And that upset your precious father?"

Anger sparked in Ares' eyes. "Understandably! He is the ruler of Olympus, and Hades had no right to break the rules. We are not allowed to create new realms."

"Get to the point," I said, my patience waning. I was

still furious with this asshole, and I needed to know what any of this had to do with Joshua and the demon.

"Yes, it upset Zeus. His plan failed, as Hades and Persephone managed to keep Cronos imprisoned. The rest of us confronted Zeus and... You know what happened after that."

"He took your power and fucked off."

Ares exhaled angrily. "Yes, if you must be so crude about it. I don't know what Zeus would want with Guardian magic." He lapsed into thoughtful silence.

"Why would he need so many of them? There were hundreds of tables in that room." Saying the words brought a painful reminder that I had completely failed to find Joshua. I took a swig of nectar, swallowing down my shame and disappointment.

"Of course!" Ares' exclamation made me jump, and I cursed. "That is why none of the gods can find Zeus. He's using Guardian magic to hide himself!"

"What?"

"Guardians hide magic from mortals. It's what they do, they mask power. I think Zeus is using the demon to steal Guardians' souls, and then he's using their masking magic to keep himself hidden from the other gods." There was admiration in his voice.

"If what you just said is true, Zeus won't want to give up the demon. So why have the Lords of War been offered it as a prize for the Trials?"

"I do not know what connection this has to the Lords. But if Zeus has enough souls, he no longer has any need for the demon."

"Oh." I took another sip of my nectar. Ares had not touched his drink. He couldn't. His helmet was still on. At the thought of the face I knew was under the metal, fresh pain panged through my middle, a pain born entirely of emotion.

"Why did you do that to me? Why did you try to drain my power?" I asked, my voice barely audible. I dropped my eyes to my hands, unable to look at his eyes in case I lost my temper again.

"I told you. I thought it was the fastest way to win."

"You are really so selfish? So cruel?"

There was a long silence, so long that I could not help myself from looking up at him.

His eyes were filled with emotion, brimming with sadness and doubt. But as my eyebrows shot up in surprise, they drained completely, as though cold walls had slammed back down around him, dousing out his burning irises. "Yes."

My own hope was doused out just as fast. "Then I won't help you."

"If you want your friend back, you have no choice."

"I always have a damned choice," I said, my voice rising. "Always!"

But I didn't, and we both knew it. He was right. I couldn't flash, I didn't know how to get back to that ship, and I knew deep down that I couldn't best the demon alone. She was far too powerful.

Ares was right. I had no choice.

4

BELLA

Before the God of War could say another word, and I could lose my shit again, I leaped to my feet.

"Where is the washroom?"

He pointed mutely to one of the two doors in the room and I marched toward it, still clutching my nectar. I slammed the door behind me as soon as I entered the tiny space, and leaned my back against it. Hiding from the God of War in bathrooms was becoming a habit. I groaned.

I couldn't forgive Ares for what he had tried to do in the fighting pit. He had betrayed my trust too brutally. But nor did I have the commitment to hate him any longer. I'd seen his eyes when I asked him why he'd done it, and I was sure that I hadn't imagined what I had seen in them, when he thought I wasn't looking. Just as I hadn't imagined the fire, the drums, or the heat when we had kissed.

I couldn't believe that he had acted purely out of self-ishness or cruelty. If he had, the coldness would have been there from the start when I looked at him, not called upon to hide something deeper when my eyes had met his. There was more to the God of War than he was showing. He *did* care. I was almost positive of it.

Maybe I was putting too much faith in one look. Maybe I just wanted him to be better than he was.

I pushed myself off the wooden door, setting my drink down on the tiny lip around the porcelain sink, and peered into what I assumed was the shower cubicle. As soon as I got close, water began raining down from the dark ceiling. With a sigh, I began stripping out of my leathers. I took a moment to heal the remaining blisters on my hands, my racing thoughts slow enough now to do so. The act calmed my anger, my wonder at being able to do such a thing too awe-inducing to ignore. I didn't even know where the blisters had come from.

As soon as I stepped under the warm water my tense muscles began to relax and my thoughts calmed enough for me to start separating facts from emotion.

By the time I had finished scrubbing myself clean, my list of "shit I know to be true" was depressing in both content and length. I'd failed to rescue Joshua. And worse, the god who had taken him, be it Zeus or the demon, was more powerful than I was. The Lords of War had deliberately sent me to my death, presumably in an effort to kill or dominate Ares.

There seemed to be no escaping the fact that Ares and I would have to work together to beat the Lords. Like it or not, the only way to save my friend was to complete their damned tests.

There were lots of things missing from my list, and now that my rage had subsided, I needed to ask more questions. I needed to find out where the hell we were, for a start, along with where the hell Zeeva was, how Ares had found me, and how I was able to do what I had done back in Pain's fighting pit. The memory of my power kicking in during the last fight had come back full-force and I had to know how to do it again. Zeeva had said I needed magic to stay in Olympus, and now I'd had a taste of how powerful I could be, I definitely wanted more.

So many questions. And I was dreading facing the man who had the answers.

I wrapped my newly long hair in a towel and dressed, downing the rest of my nectar and taking a few long breaths before leaving the bathroom. I had to give Ares the benefit of the doubt. I couldn't trust him, but if I had to work with him, I'd rather do it believing he was worth helping.

"May I have another drink?" I asked, strolling as casually as I could into the room. Ares stood up immediately, and I faltered. His helmet and armor were gone, the gold band across his forehead the only remaining metal on his body. His soft hair was pulled back behind his shoulders, the hard planes of his face only accentuated by the loose strands. His lips parted and a bolt of something totally beyond my control hit me in my core.

Don't blush, don't blush, I told myself fiercely.

Mercifully, he turned away from me, moving to the counter.

"Where are we?"

"Panic's kingdom, Dasos."

"Right. Where is Zeeva?"

"I have no idea."

I slumped down on the pink couch. "How did you flash to the ship?"

"That doesn't matter."

I rolled my eyes. "Well, someone helped you. And given what I know about your willingness to ask for help so far, it has to be Zeeva or your sister. And if you don't know where Zeeva is..."

"Fine. It was Eris." I looked at him reluctantly as he approached me, a fresh glass of deep red wine in his hand. He had a loose linen shirt on with a wide collar, and I realized it was the first time I'd actually seen him in a shirt. He'd been bare-chested or covered in hulking gold armor the whole time we'd been together.

Somehow, not being able to see the smooth skin of his chest, his rock-hard biceps and beautifully defined abdominal muscles, was worse than them being on display. *For the love of sweet fuck, what the hell was wrong with me?*

"I still hate you," I told him, as he passed me the wine.

"I know. That is why I am making you drinks like a common peasant," he scowled back at me. "That is how a person is supposed to rebuild favor, is it not?"

I stared at him. "Well, yeah, but you're supposed to do stuff like that because you want to make up for what you did, or to prove you are actually a decent person. Not tell them that you're doing it because you have to. You have no idea what interacting with normal people is like, do you?" I realized the truth of the words as I said them.

"I interact with many people," he said gruffly, sitting down on the other couch.

"Gods and monarchs," I scoffed. "How about normal people?"

"There is no such thing as normal in Olympus," he said quietly, and drank from his own glass. Ironically, it was the most "normal" thing I'd seen him do.

"You know, I think you are completely deluded," I said, matter-of-factly.

"What?"

"I think you are so out of touch with anything real, so absorbed by your godly power, that you are missing everything good in the world. Especially in a world like this."

He gave me a patronizing look. "You know nothing of this world. I can assure you, you are sorely mistaken."

I shrugged. "I will know about this world, soon. And I bet you anything you like that I'll enjoy the fuck out of it. A hundred times more than you enjoy anything."

He gave a bark of annoyance. "I am perfectly capable of enjoying things. Just not you, or this accursed situation!"

"Charming," I muttered. "So, what do you enjoy?"

He looked away from me, discomfort flickering through his eyes. I knew what he was thinking about. Aphrodite. Unease crawled through me too, and I gulped at my drink.

"The ships," he said suddenly. "I like being up on the deck of a ship."

I grasped his words and clung on, relieved to talk about anything that wasn't the Goddess of Love. "Ships! Yes. They're good. I mean, from what I saw. I was a bit distracted." I knew I was babbling, but carried on regardless. "Do all ships here fly? Why did that one have two wheels?"

"The solar sails soak up power from light, so unless it is dark they all fly. There are different types of ship, and that one was the largest class. It is called a Zephyr. It has two quarterdecks simply because it is so large." Ares seemed just as relieved to be talking about something other than Aphrodite as I did, and I couldn't help the boundless curiosity that welled up inside me.

"What other types of ship are there?"

"Crosswinds, Tornados, Whirlwinds."

"I want to see them all," I breathed. Something twitched at the corner of Ares' mouth.

"They are how people travel between the realms. Athena and Zeus have sky realms so people need to be able to fly to reach them. Most other realms are islands in the ocean. Hephaestus has a realm inside a volcano, and Poseidon's is underwater."

A longing so intense it made my chest ache was building inside me as I tried to picture what he was describing. "Are they all run by Kings and Queens?"

"No. My realm is unique for its varied kingdoms. It is also considered unusual for its varied climate, only Apollo's realm matches it for extreme weather." There was pride in his statement.

"What are the sky realms like?"

"Zeus lives on top of Mount Olympus, and wealthy citizens live in mansions built from glass that are set in a ring of clouds around the peak of the mountain. Athena's realm is industrial. It is made up of hundreds of platforms linked by bridges. She is one of the only gods who provides for every citizen in her realm, so it is overcrowded and has lots of places that provide paid work, manufacturing and such."

He was frowning as he said the words, and a pang of annoyance stabbed at me. "Do you feel no compulsion to provide for the people in your realm?"

He shrugged. "They are not my concern."

I shook my head. "You are not a ruler, Ares. You are just the owner of a very large toy." His face flashed dark, sparks firing in his eyes, but I was frustrated enough with him that thankfully I heard no drum beating in response. "There is a difference between owning land and having subjects. Just handing off the care of the people in your realm to others without giving a shit about the consequences is not ruling."

"I have never claimed to be a ruler. I am a God," he spat. "The God of War. In my realm the strongest rule, and they earn the right to rule as they please. That it is how it is, and how it should be."

"I disagree. I'm not suggesting you make Aries any less dangerous, or you remove the ability for those who are so inclined to kill each other for power, but there are plenty of things you could deal with to make it better for everyone else."

"This is about the slaves again," he said, narrowing his eyes.

"Fighting should be about glory and honor, especially in the realm of the God of War. Not loss of freedom and money."

Ares paused with his glass half-way to his mouth. His eyes focused on me, and they were still sparking, but with something other than anger now. Interest, I thought, with a frisson of hope.

"You are saying that there is no glory in winning a fight that you are forced to participate in," he said slowly.

"Yes. If you want a realm filled with glory, slavery is not the way to do it."

"I have not considered it in that way before. The feeling when I fought as a mortal yesterday..." I blushed immediately, the memory of the kiss that followed that fight impossible to shift. But Ares continued. "People would fight for that feeling alone. It was glorious."

"Exactly," I mumbled, gulping wine. "Glorious. Glory. Addictive. You'd fill the pits without taking away people's freedom."

I looked sideways at him, my cheeks still hot. He sipped slowly from his glass, clearly deep in thought.

Why was I so attracted to a man who had the mental capacity of a teenager? A smoking hot body should not be enough to cause this level of reaction when he was fundamentally a jerk.

Because you know he can change. You know he just needs to understand what he has failed to see.

I almost shook my head at the thought. I knew that people who tried to change others were always disappointed. Not from personal experience, but from the many theater shows I'd seen. People could right wrongs, become better people, sure. That was the message behind countless shows and movies.

But to change who they actually were? That wasn't possible.

I couldn't kill my conviction that there was more to Ares though. I was watching, with a front row seat, as the man considered something he had outright dismissed a few days earlier. But didn't the fact that he had never even thought about the fairness of his realm before now mean he was the worst kind of person imaginable?

My thoughts flashed to the many awful places I'd spent time in, from prison, the underground fighting and gambling rings, to the godforsaken foster homes I'd moved through. If I'd stayed too long in a single one of them, I knew who I would have become. I knew the sense of justice and the empathy instilled in me by plays and music would have been snuffed out eventually. The violence within me, the need for confrontation and victory, would have drowned out everything else if I'd not escaped those people, and those environments.

Could anybody be blamed for becoming a product of their surroundings? My salvation had been to keep moving, to limit the amount of time I spent in the places that brought out the worst in me. But Ares was a freaking God. Where was he supposed to go? How could he choose to keep better company, or none at all?

I thought of his face, alight with the euphoria of the battle with the Hydra. His power had denied him that feeling for centuries. Perhaps his power had denied him other feelings too.

Maybe there really was more to him.

Or maybe I was just clinging to the hope that my physical attraction to him could be mitigated by him not being an asshole.

5

BELLA

We finished our wine in silence. I wanted to ask about my power, and the demon, and what we should expect in the next Trial, but fatigue had washed over me, and Ares looked exhausted too, brooding over his drink. Deciding to wait until I had the energy to annoy him into answering my questions, I stood up and stretched.

"I'm going to bed," I announced.

We both looked at the chintzy bed against the wall.

"You know that thing you mentioned about regaining the favor of someone you've pissed off?" I said.

Ares stared up at me. "Yes."

"Well, one way to make me like you again would be to let me have the bed."

He blinked at me. "But then where would I sleep?"

The man was clearly an idiot.

"I don't know and I don't give a shit."

Ares scowled at me, but didn't argue. "Fine. I shall sleep on the couch."

"Good."

I tampered down the tiny part of me that wanted to offer to share the, actually quite reasonably sized, bed. Even if he accepted such an invitation, which I didn't believe he would, it was the worst idea ever. I just wished my body would agree with my head for once.

I slept badly, dreams of fire and ringing steel rousing me regularly. I looked over to where Ares' huge form lay on the floor each time I awoke, but he never stirred. He hadn't fit on the couch, and accompanied by a lot of grunting and muttered curses had instead opted for the rug. I didn't feel the slightest bit guilty in the comfortable bed. I intended to piss him off just as much as he had upset me.

I knew what was rousing me from sleep. The Keres demon would have beaten me. And then either stolen my soul or killed me. I wasn't sure which was worse. I had come up against few people stronger than me, and none by that margin. The knowledge that she was out there made me restless.

Aphrodite using her power on me had been bad enough, along with the knowledge that she could smite me down with a look. Even Ares, who had hardly any power, had managed to put me on my ass.

I needed to get stronger. I couldn't continue to be the weakest in this fucked up game I'd found myself in, or I wouldn't survive.

～

"Wake up, sleeping beauty." My cat's voice filtered through my head and I sat up with a start.

"Zeeva!" She was sitting at the end of my bed, tail curled neatly around her butt. I flicked my bleary gaze at the rug, but Ares wasn't there.

"He's in the washroom." An image of Ares naked and under running water instantly made my cheeks heat.

"Where the hell have you been?" I snapped at Zeeva, rubbing my eyes.

"You and Ares needed some space to work out your differences," she answered coolly. I raised my eyebrows.

"Bullshit."

In a heartbeat, Zeeva grew, her whole body glowing teal and her eyes a blazing amber. A lion-sized cat towered over me and it was all I could do not to shrink back under the covers.

"Do not swear at me, Enyo." Her voice rang fiercely in my head, just as intimidating as her big-cat form.

"OK, OK, calm down," I said, holding both hands up. "Sorry for swearing at you." Slowly, she shrank back down.

"I did not know where the Lords of War had sent you, but I sensed your magic when you returned and came straight here. I listened to your conversation with Ares about the demon and the ship, and relayed it to Hera. I have been here with you since."

"Oh," I said. "Well, erm, thanks. But if you're hiding from me, you can't really blame me for thinking you've just abandoned me." I couldn't help the whiny note in my voice. It was one thing to suspect that your stuck-up pet didn't like you. It was another to suddenly be able to communicate with them and find out that they actually don't. And that they can kick your ass.

"I did not want to interfere with your reconciliation with Ares."

I snorted. "Reconciliation? Hardly. The man is an-"

She cut me off before I could finish the sentence. *"Bella, you are getting through to him."*

"What?"

"He considered your words last night, instead of dismissing them. I believe his lack of power has awakened something in him, and you can take advantage of that."

I cocked my head at the cat. She was confirming what I had hoped, that he was at least capable of changing. But... "What do you mean by take advantage?"

The cat swished her tail, her eyes boring into mine. *"Tell me exactly what happened on the ship,"* she said eventually.

"Only if you give me coffee."

"Tell me," she repeated, and I rolled my eyes and pushed back the covers. I told her everything that had happened as I dressed, and she pushed me for minute details. By the time I was done reliving the memory of being completely useless, and so close to Joshua but failing him, I was mad again.

"It is as I thought. Ares saved your life."

"What?" I stared at the cat.

"He rescued you from that ship, and must have traded something with Eris for her help. You would probably not be here if it were not for Ares."

Zeeva's words smacked into me like a hammer. How the hell had it not occurred to me already that I owed the brutish God of War my life?

My simmering anger instantly swallowed the budding guilt though. "He saved me because I'm his only source of power, no other reason than that."

"I would not be so sure."

"Do you know something I don't?" I asked her, pulling

my hair into a knot on top of my head and using a band from my backpack to secure it.

"A great many things."

I gave her a sarcastic smile. "No doubt. I was referring specifically to Ares."

"I have suspicions. None I may act on or share."

"As usual, thanks for nothing," I muttered.

"You will thank me eventually," she said.

"Hmmm. I want to learn more magic," I told her, putting my hands on my hips.

"Good. But there is a limit to what I can teach you. I do not wield power like yours."

"War magic?" She nodded her feline head. "Ares isn't going to help me."

"He might."

I pulled a face. "I don't want his help."

"Don't be such a child." I bared my teeth at her before I could stop myself, but the sound of the washroom door opening prevented her from berating me further.

Ares walked into the room, wearing full armor, minus his helmet. He nodded at Zeeva. "I see you are back, now that the action is over," he said. Despite the fact that I had felt exactly the same about the cat's untimely absence, I leaped to her defense.

"What Zeeva does or doesn't do is none of your business," I said haughtily, then marched past him into the washroom.

When I emerged, I was surprised and delighted to be met by the smell of coffee.

"Zeeva said you like this muck," scowled Ares, holding out a large mug. I took it from him, inhaling deeply. I'd felt the tug of him using my power while I had been in the bathroom.

"Did you go and get this just for me?" I asked. Ares nodded. "Thank you. I could get used to these 'regaining my favor' gestures, especially if they all involve wine and coffee."

Ares nose wrinkled, and the expression was distinctly ungodly. I couldn't help a small smile.

"Coffee is rare in Olympus. It is expensive and unpleasant."

I barked a laugh. "Coffee makes the world go round."

"Not Olympus."

"Maybe not, but it's a necessity in my world."

Ares opened his mouth to answer, but I didn't hear the words.

An awful creeping cold moved over the back of my skull, and my vision went pitch black. I cried out, dropping the coffee and fisting my hands instantly.

"Little Bella has lots of lovely war magic," whispered a delighted voice, deep inside my head.

"Who's there?" I yelled the words aloud, alarm gripping my whole body at the invisible threat. How could I fight something in my head? Remembering Zeeva's training, I pulled on my power, trying to build a wall around my mind. Nothing happened.

"Calm down, baby goddess. It's just your friendly Lord of War, Panic."

I took a great gulp of air. The demon had called me baby goddess. Anger seeped through my body. "Get the fuck out of my head." More cold slithered down my neck, a feeling like a large band of ice was being wrapped around my head taking over. My vision was still dark but flames flickered at the edges.

"I'm just dropping in to tell you that the Trial announcement will be in half an hour. Ares knows where you both need to go."

In an instant the tight band of ice was gone, and the room appeared around me again as my vision returned to normal. Ares was staring at me, tight-lipped. I took an unsteady breath.

"That was one of the Lords," he said quietly.

"Yes. Why is it so different to when Zeeva talks to me in my head? Everything went dark and my head went weirdly cold." I put both hands to the side of my head, half expecting my hair to feel icy. It didn't. "Why couldn't I block him out?"

Ares glanced at Zeeva, now sitting on the rug beside him. "You are getting stronger. And you share power with the Lords of War. As long as you are in my realm, anyone who has the power of war will be able to communicate with you. Now that your power is growing, you are becoming visible to them."

"Woah, what? What do you mean, I *share* power with the Lords? You said our power was different to them, that they had specific, shitty powers." I tried to keep the worry from my voice but failed. I did not want to be connected in any way with the fucked up creepiness the three Lords had. "If getting stronger means turning into one of them, I'm out. I don't need that in my life."

"I said their power was created by mine. As with all the demigods and deities of my realm. It is not the same, but it connects us all."

"And I'm becoming visible to all of them?" I blinked, mind racing and anxiety building. I could hear my voice rising.

Ares looked at the floor briefly, before taking up my gaze again. "Yes."

I shook my head slowly. "I'm turning into a fucking beacon for your crazy war offspring, and they can make my head cold and my vision black whenever they like? I didn't sign up for this." I had begun pacing without realizing, shaking my head fervently.

"Calm down, Bella. You can learn to block them out." Zeeva must have projected the words to Ares too, because he looked down at her.

"Yes. The cat is right. You can learn to block it. And they are not my offspring. They are not of my loins."

"Who the fuck says loins?" I knew it wasn't the right question to yell at him, but I was pissed again. I hated the feeling of being one step behind everyone else all the time, too ineffective to make a difference and at the mercy of those stronger than I.

Which was apparently everyone.

"Loins are-" started Ares, but I shoved him hard in the chest. He didn't move, but he closed his mouth.

"I know what loins are, goddammit! I want to know how to stop being so weak!"

"You are not weak." Ares said the words with such simplicity that my juggernaut temper stumbled.

"But everyone has more power than me. They can get into my head, and flash me around, and make me feel stuff, *steal my fucking soul.* Everyone in this whole damn world can do more than I can, there's probably an endless amount of magic shit I don't even know about yet. I can't do any of that."

"Wrong. You can do all of that and more, and you're not even at half-strength. You just don't know how to do any of it yet." Zeeva's voice was level and soothing.

"Teach me." I sent the demand into the room in general, not caring which of them answered. Both knew more than I did. There was a long pause.

"I will teach you to keep your mind secure," said Zeeva eventually. I flicked her a grateful smile, then planted my gaze on Ares.

"And you? Will you teach me to use my war magic?"

His eyes dropped from mine before he answered. "No."

Anger spiked through me, quickening my pulse. "Why not?"

When his eyes met mine again, the fire danced in his irises, his dark pupils endless against the mesmerizing flames. "As long as I am by your side, you do not need to use your power."

"I'm not your damn puppet," I growled. A distant drum beat loudly in my mind.

"And I'm no fool. If you learn to use your power, you will not need to help me."

The drum beat again, and again, and the smell of smoke and grass washed over me. "The best way for me to get Joshua back is by completing these tests. I'm not going anywhere."

"You already left once."

His words ricocheted through my head, and the drums beat louder and faster in my mind. There was emotion in his face that I didn't recognize, I realized as the flames in his eyes leaped higher. Was it betrayal? Was he hurt that I had left him?

The Ares who presented himself as stoic, emotionless, get-the-job-done, could not possibly mention the fact that I had essentially abandoned him to whatever fate the Lords had planned for him. But the Ares before me now had fire sparking in his irises and I knew the flames weren't fueled by anger. I knew his anger now, and this was something else.

Whatever it was, I was now a hundred percent sure that I hadn't imagined the look on his face the night before. There was more to Ares than pride and anger.

My eyes moved to his lips of their own accord, and heat flashed through my whole body, settling below my butterfly-filled stomach.

"I won't leave you again." The words came out almost as a whisper, inaudible to me over the rising drum beat, readying my whole being for action. What kind of action, I didn't know. But I was becoming desperate for anything.

Ares took a step back, and the drums quietened. He took another step, his chest heaving under his gleaming armor. The farther those flaming irises got from me, the more distant the drums sounded. Disappointment rocked through me, dousing out my excitement with an unpleasant dose of reality.

Ares didn't want me. And I had just told him I wouldn't leave him. Embarrassment coiled through my stomach, and my cheeks burned.

"I will teach you to fight with a sword."

His statement cut through the heavy atmosphere and I took a breath, burying my arousal and shame as deep as I possibly could with a fierce determination. I clearly needed another word with myself, but I'd be damned if he saw how much he affected me. I would deal with this stupid crush later, alone.

"A sword? How will that help against the demon or war people fucking with my head?"

"Please, stop swearing." He used the word *please* so softly, it took me by surprise enough to elicit a mildly apologetic eye-roll. "I'm offering you training in sword fighting, or nothing. Take it or leave it."

I gave a growl of frustration, but we both knew what my answer would be. "Fine."

"Which Lord spoke to you?" He abruptly changed the subject.

"Panic. He said that the Trial announcement would be in half an hour and you know where to go. Though I guess that was ten minutes ago now."

Ares sighed. "It will be in his throne room. Zeeva, you have twenty minutes to teach her to block unwanted communication. I am going for a walk."

"A walk?"

"Yes."

"Where?"

He gave me a hard look. "Outside," he snapped, then rammed his helmet onto his head and stamped toward the large cabin door. I got a glimpse of deep green foliage on the other side as he stepped through, before he slammed the door shut again.

"Zeeva, do you hear drums when Ares gets mad?" I asked, turning to the cat.

"No, Bella. No, I do not."

6

BELLA

It turned out that trying to build a wall around my mind as Zeeva had taught me before had actually been the right thing to do. Only, blocking out people connected to my power required a bigger, better wall. I didn't feel at all like I'd had enough time to practice when Ares returned from his walk.

"Tell me about Dasos before we go?" I asked him as he stamped into the cabin. He didn't look at me, but he did answer my question.

"It is a forest realm. Filled with traps and unpleasant creatures. Much of it is derelict, and the citizens live in fortified homes amongst the trees."

"Why do they live here at all? It doesn't sound very friendly."

"Panic pays his citizens a monthly wage."

"Just for living here?"

"Yes. Each year the households that have lasted the longest get to compete for prizes."

"Weird, but fair enough," I said, shrugging. "What's the longest anyone has lived here?"

"Eight months."

I blinked. I'd expected him to answer in years. "Oh. So... It's quite dangerous here then?"

Ares finally looked at me, through his helmet eye-slit. "The feeling of panic is a powerful weapon. It causes people to make very bad decisions. Fatal decisions."

The warning in his words was clear. Trepidation rumbled through my chest. "OK. I got it. Don't panic. Don't make stupid decisions." When it came to Ares I felt like I was the freaking queen of stupid decisions, but I didn't need to share that.

Panic's throne room looked like it had seen better days. Much better days.

I turned in a slow circle, staring at the crumbling stone walls around me. I had visited castle ruins in the north of England very similar to what I was looking at. The circular room was massive and the ceiling so high I couldn't really see it properly. Vines and creepers spread across the pale, broken stone everywhere I looked, and the air smelled damp. A breeze whistled through cracks in the walls and I rubbed my arms as the hairs rose.

"This place is a dump," I muttered, eying the only furniture in the room; a large stone chair and iron dish in front of it.

"Isn't it?" Panic's voice rang through the empty space, and with a flash, the three Lords appeared before us. "I only use it for formal occasions," Panic smiled at me. "My other castle is much nicer. If you ever want to see my private rooms, please do let me know." His eyes darkened as he stared at me and I narrowed mine back at him.

"Hard pass."

"Shame."

Terror stepped forward, his marble feet loud on the old stone floor. "How did you fare with your demon?" he asked me, black patterns swirling across the surface of his featureless face.

"You know damn well how I fared," I spat. "Why are you working with her?"

"She can offer us something our once mighty leader can't," said Terror, with a small shrug.

I felt the pull of Ares anger in my gut.

"And why is she bothering with you?" the God of War asked tightly.

"We have something she wants," Panic sang.

"What?"

"As if we would tell you," smiled Pain.

"Is it us?" I asked.

Terror gave a soft chuckle as the other two snorted. "Baby goddess, we already sent you to her on a platter. If it was you two she wanted, she would already have you."

"You will regret your lack of respect toward me." Ares' voice was low and menacing and when I felt the pull in my stomach, I released my hold on the cord connecting us just a little. My lips parted in reluctant appreciation as his skin flared to life with a gold glow, and power rolled from his gleaming armor.

I dragged my eyes from him in time to see a tiny look of doubt pass between Pain and Panic.

"That's a risk we have opted to take," said Terror smoothly.

"No risk, no reward," added Panic, his trademark smile back on his handsome face.

"You had better pray that your risk pays off. My punishment will far exceed your potential reward."

"One is not living, if one does not fear death," the Lord purred. Ares stiffened.

"Let me assure you, you will welcome death by the time I am finished with you." The warrior god boomed the threat, and everyone in the room except Terror instinctively stepped back. Even me.

"Panic, shall we proceed with the announcement?" Terror changed the subject without hesitation, dismissing Ares completely. A low rumble began, and the pull in my stomach intensified. Making a quick decision, I released my hold on my power, letting Ares take it.

The room filled with the sound of ringing steel and the tangy scent of blood. Ares grew twenty feet tall before I could take in what was happening. Raw, unconfined power emanated from him, dwarfing the creepy vibes that rolled off the Lords of War.

"I partake in these tests of my own volition. You do not control me. You worship me." Ares' voice was magnified and carried images of death so strong I could see nothing else. Battle fields, old and new, coursed through my mind's eye. I saw men in furs with huge broadswords that severed heads from necks with roars. I saw ancient warriors in metal plated armor buried in showers of arrows. I saw green helmeted men in breeches praying as shells dropped from the sky before everything was consumed by fire.

When the visions of war ebbed, I saw that all three lords were on one knee before Ares. A fatigue washed over me, and with the tiniest sideways glance, Ares shrank back down. My vision closed in a little, dizziness threatening to take me, and I heard Zeeva's voice in my head.

"Focus on your well of power. Steady yourself." I felt for the burn of restless energy under my ribs, and found it depleted and tiny. It was still fierce and hot though, and I concentrated on it, a feeling of pride buoying me. Ares had used my power to do that. They had been right, I *was* getting stronger. And if Ares could do that with my power... Could I?

Well done, war magic. You did good, I told the remaining little ball of power. My vision cleared, strength seeping back through me.

"Panic, the announcement, if you will." Terror's voice had lost its silky smoothness, a tight anger in his tone now.

Panic moved to his throne, avoiding looking at Ares, and the iron flame dish sprang to life. White hot flames leaped up, before giving way to a gentle orange flicker. A mirror image of Panic appeared in the flames.

"Good day, Olympus," he beamed, all trace of his run-in with the God of War gone. "I am pleased to host the second test of the Ares Trials. Ares and Bella will be facing a little quest. They must find the fighting pit hidden deep in Skotadi, the most dangerous area of my kingdom. Once there, they must defeat a dragon, by plucking no less than three scales from its body."

A dragon? My jaw hung open.

Nobody had mentioned dragons. Trepidation rolled through me and I tried to dismiss it. Surely a dragon couldn't be much different to an acid breathing Hydra? We'd defeated that and survived. Just.

"We shall send the heroes off in style, with a small ceremony in one hour. Until then, farewell."

The iron dish fell lifeless again as the flames died.

"How do I call Eris?" I said, staring at my Guns N' Roses t-shirt with a frown. "I don't think I'm supposed to go to the ceremony in this." We were back in the tiny cabin, and in an effort to distract myself from thinking about the upcoming Trial, I was trying to get ready for yet another pointless ceremony. But the closet in the cabin was empty, and all I had to wear was what was in my backpack.

"I have not been able to contact my sister since we returned." I looked sharply at Ares, where he was sitting on the peach-colored couch.

"Really? Should we be worried?"

"No. She answers to nobody." I didn't doubt that.

I blew out a sigh. "Any ideas on what I should wear, Zeeva?"

The cat looked up from where she was dozing on the bed, her sleek body curled into a small ball. I resisted the urge to go and pet her, as I had for years before. It was too weird now that I knew what she really was.

"I can probably borrow a headdress from my mistress for you. But as for clothes, I can't help."

"Oh, thank you," I said. I hadn't actually expected her to offer anything. She stretched slowly, then vanished in a puff of teal light.

"I too, would like to offer my thanks." I whipped round to Ares at his words, even more surprising than Zeeva's. His helmet was off, his hair loose around his shoulders. And the way he was looking at me... "You willingly allowed me to use most of your power to intimidate the Lords. That means... a great deal to me."

I shrugged awkwardly. "It means a great deal to me too. They deliberately sent me to a demon-y death, and they're all dickholes. They deserved taking down a peg or two."

"Has your power replenished yet?"

I felt inside myself, already knowing that the burning ball of energy was full and ready to go. "Yes."

"Good. That means we did not reach your limit, and you are indeed growing in strength."

"So that was a successful experiment in sharing power?" I said tentatively.

"Indeed."

"So... Can you teach me to use it better?"

"No."

I threw the t-shirt down in annoyance. "Why not? I'm trying to prove to you that I'm not working against you! Show me how to do something useful! How did you make all that war stuff happen?"

"It's what I do. I invoke the power of war."

"Show me."

"No."

"Then show me how to grow."

"No."

"You're an asshole." Ares got slowly to his feet. The single, booming beat of a drum sounded loudly in my mind, and just that one sound sent tingles through my body in heady anticipation. With some alarm, I realized that I was beginning to crave these moments. The aching that spread through me, settling in a delicious desperation, was far from unpleasant.

There was a small flash of teal and Zeeva appeared, a gleaming gold tiara before her.

Ares sat back down.

"This should be enough to make it look as though you've

made an effort," the cat said dismissively, then curled back up on the bed.

"Thanks," I mumbled, and picked up the tiara. It was beautiful, made from fine gold and set with a wavy row of tiny sparkling rubies. "I hope it goes with black t-shirts and khakis, as that's all I've got."

7

ARES

I could not help but admire Bella's confidence as we arrived in Panic's glade. The mossy ground moved under her heavy boots as she immediately sought out a serving satyr, and I saw the raised eyebrows of the other, immaculately dressed, guests as they took in her casual, very human, attire.

She didn't need a dress to look beautiful though. The gold headband Zeeva had given her glinted over her braided hair as she tipped her head back to take a long sip of her drink, and her t-shirt hugged her chest as she moved. An ache I knew was utterly inappropriate pulled at me.

She had left me. Walked through that portal knowing I couldn't beat the Trials and win the Trident without her. And I had deserved it.

I had deliberately tried to take all her power, knowing how much she would hate me for it. In fact, I'd taken her power exactly *because* she would hate me for it, but instead of severing this all-consuming bond between us, it had only solidified my feelings for her.

Whatever connected us went deeper than my burning physical attraction to her. Her excitement was infectious, and I found myself longing to see her smile. How could one person take so much pleasure from the world around her, when she had been treated so unfairly? More blasted guilt trickled through me.

Even her unending questions were annoying me less, and I was finding myself in possession of a reluctant respect for her tenacity. She was desperate to learn how to get stronger, and that resonated within me. I knew she wouldn't give up, just as I wouldn't in her position.

Sighing, I watched her wave enthusiastically, then make her way over to the white centaur she had become so enamored with. At some point, soon, I would have to teach her more about her power. She was becoming strong, and she was right - she would be a lot more helpful in getting this abomination of a gameshow over and done with if she could use her magic properly.

But what if she decided that she didn't need me anymore? Worse, what if she found out who she really was and what I had done?

The thought of her leaving again caused a lurch in my stomach that brought actual queasiness with it. *You just don't want to lose access to your power again,* I told myself. But I knew it was a lie.

Crushing the knowledge that it wasn't just her power I didn't want to be without, I tried to focus on something else. Something that wasn't her.

With a plan forming in my mind, I strode over to where Hermes and Poseidon were talking in quiet voices. The glade was large and completely covered by thick canopies of foliage. Tiny fairy lights danced amongst the greenery, giving the place a hushed, ethereal feeling. I couldn't see any of the Lords of War.

"Ares," Hermes nodded as I approached. He was in traditional ancient clothing, his plain toga contrasting with his glittering winged sandals.

I nodded back at him. "How goes the search for Zeus?" I directed the question at Poseidon.

"I fear your father is as strong as he ever was. We can not find him."

"Do you have any ideas of his plans?"

"There is unrest in the mortal world, and my concerns for Hera are growing. But the Underworld is secure now, and he has not approached any of the other Olympians."

As if they'd tell you, I thought. Poseidon was not our ruler. But I spoke politely. "Is Hades here? I have new information that will be of interest to you both."

When Hades joined us and Hermes was dismissed, I told the brothers what I had learned of the Keres demon, and my suspicions that Zeus was using Guardian magic to mask himself. When I was finished, cold fury was rolling from Hades in long tendrils of smoke.

"I will create a new level in Tartarus to house that demon when I get hold of her," he hissed. "One she can share with my brother."

Poseidon looked to me. "We appreciate you telling us this."

I bowed my head. "I wish to help."

"And regain your power, no doubt." Poseidon did not trust me, and I did not blame him.

"Indeed. But I shall do that by fulfilling Oceanus' quest. I will leave finding my father to you two."

I walked away before they could ask me anything else. I was uninterested in how they would react to my information. I had meant exactly what I said, that my focus was on these damn Trials. Besides, I did not believe for a moment that they could stop Zeus. There was no more powerful god in the world, and all my focus had to be on regaining my own strength before my father made his move - whatever it would be. I would not, could not, be left unguarded when that happened.

I wandered around the glade talking to whomever I passed, with a forced confidence and pride in my voice. I was not going to let anybody think that the Lords had me under their control. If I behaved as though I had instigated the Trials myself, or at least that I was enjoying them, then the Lords lost the upper-hand.

I pulled very gently at Bella's power, and I felt her respond. A warm river of strength flowed through me, and I took just enough to give myself a sense of divine presence. Enough that the other gods would feel it.

"Well, well. Somebody's cheerful." Aphrodite's sweet-as-honey voice washed over me. I felt my insides melt a little, a desire to make her happy swamping my thoughts. But I drew more power from Bella, and the feeling lessened. Aphrodite raised an eyebrow as I turned to her. "She's getting stronger," Aphrodite said, her smile not reaching her eyes.

Her skin was the color of onyx today, her large eyes jet black too, and her lips were as scarlet red as her floaty, sheer dress. She looked like a painting or a piece of art. Breathtaking. "You look beautiful," I said, overly formally.

"Thank you." She didn't mean the gratitude. I could feel her annoyance. "She made a fool of you in the last fight. I thought I would find you more rage-filled than this." Her perfect eyebrows drew together in a frown. "Are you now a wolf without fangs *or* claws?"

Indignant anger leaped to life at her words, but as I opened my mouth to defend myself, a thought bore into my mind, in a voice that I was sure belonged to me, but had been absent from my brain for a very long time.

She doesn't love you.

It was the part of me that had always known that Aphrodite didn't love me, but that had I refused to believe because when I was under the influence of her power, the screaming insatiable restlessness was quieted, just for a while. It was the voice inside me that centuries of never getting enough, never finding the thrill, never reaching the point I knew I was destined to reach, had silenced. The voice that had been replaced by a louder one that led to an unending cycle of pushing the limits of everything around me, all other things in my life unimportant when compared to trying to reach that climax, that place where the thrill and adrenaline peaked, and bliss took over.

I had convinced myself that Aphrodite was the key to that feeling I craved so hard. But she wasn't. Her love was temporary, and weak and false. Aphrodite didn't want to make me better, or stronger. But Bella...

A realization crashed into me, as clear as crystal.

I would take the thrill of fighting the Hydra with Bella over a night in Aphrodite's bed without hesitation. Bella made me better. She reveled in the moment, thrived on the adrenaline, gloried in victory. When she was strong, I was strong. And she wanted the people around her to have strength; she wasn't cruel or greedy.

Something must have shown in my eyes, because Aphrodite's face began to change in front of me, snapping me from my epiphany.

"Ares, you forget who I am," she hissed, a darkness filling her eyes that had nothing to do with their color. The Goddess of Love had a wrath more vicious than any other Olympian, and uneasiness skittered through me. If Aphrodite got even an inkling of my feelings for Bella, it was not my safety I feared for.

"I don't know what you mean," I said, trying to keep my face clear of any of these new emotions. It was not something I had needed to practice in my life, and I prayed I was successful.

"I have power over love," she whispered. "I know when two people are attracted to one another." Her mouth was a hard line.

My heart stuttered in my chest a little. I drew on my pride, and tried to think of what I would have said before I lost my power, before these infernal emotions had begun to cloud my thoughts. "Bella is young, and mostly mortal. I believe she has a crush on me." I filled my words with prideful arrogance.

"And you, my warrior prince?" Aphrodite's tone changed again. Now it was low and husky, and my vision narrowed to her sensual mouth, my body reacting instinctively. "Who do you have a crush on?"

"I do not suffer from crushes."

"Prove it. Prove your love for me. If you ever want to lay your hands on my body again, do not touch her."

Before I could speak, Bella's voice called across the glade. "Aphrodite? I wanted a quick word, if you have a moment."

Fury flicked through Aphrodite's eyes, but vanished as she turned to Bella.

"That's an unusual choice of outfit. But at least you're not pretending to be something you are not." There was a sneer in Aphrodite's voice, and defensiveness leaped to life inside me. I clamped my mouth shut.

"Yeah, thanks. Look, I wanted to tell you that I have no intention of causing you or your asshole boyfriend any issues. Once I've got through these Trials and saved my friend, you won't see me again."

Bella's eyes flicked to mine. I swallowed the pang in my chest that accompanied the force of her words. She was right, one way or another. Once the Trials were over and her power was fully restored, it was impossible for us to see each other again. But she didn't know that.

She was choosing to tell me that she was leaving after this was over.

"You are not significant enough for me to be concerned about your future plans, little girl. I don't care." Aphrodite purred, then turned her back to Bella, facing me again. I expected anger or arrogance from her, but I was almost sure she looked worried, just for a heartbeat.

But then she turned on her brilliant smile. "Come, mighty one. Let us converse with our own kind." She led me by the elbow toward Dionysus and Apollo, at the far end of the glade.

I let her lead me away, and it took more strength than I knew not to look at Bella as I went.

8

BELLA

I'd been stupid to interrupt their conversation. And my announcement was totally unnecessary. But I hadn't been able to help myself. A totally irrational surge of jealousy had taken me when I saw Ares' eyes darken and his posture relax as that witch purred to him.

I hadn't even known what to say when I marched over there, and all I had achieved was being belittled in front of Ares. And now he had gone with her, like a puppy on a leash.

I ground my teeth. At some point real soon, I was going to have to find a way to stop caring. A way to stop this desire for the warrior god. Because so far, no matter what he did, it was not lessening. I was seeing more and more in him that called to me.

I looked around the glade, trying to find something to distract myself. Nestor, the warrior centaur and by far the coolest creature I'd met in Olympus so far, had been called away. Although she might have made that up to get away from my constant questions about how she fought with her war-hammers.

"You seem bored, sweetie," the goddess of Chaos' voice sounded in my head.

"I'm supposed to be able to block people out now!" I exclaimed aloud.

"Ancient deity, remember? You'd have to be about ten times stronger to block me out."

"Where are you?"

"Around."

"Why aren't you here in person?"

"I may have upset a few too many people."

I snorted. "Why doesn't that surprise me? You know, I could have done with your help in the closet department."

"Not at all. I like this look. Besides, you're about to start your Trial, and that would have been a pain in the ass in a dress."

"What? How do you know?"

"Sweetie, I know a lot of things. I know some things that would interest you a lot more than when the Trials are starting."

My heart skipped a beat. "Things about me?"

"Uhuh. And about my baby brother."

"And what do you want from me in return?"

"When I have a trade in mind, you'll be the first to know. Good luck."

"Wait!" But she had already gone. I stamped my foot, not caring how petulant I may have looked.

Everybody knew more than I did, even about *me*. It was infuriating. I was a pawn in a game a bunch of other people were playing, and I was losing patience with it.

"Good evening!" Panic appeared in the middle of the glade, with an over-the-top flash of red light. A hush fell over the guests as he bowed low to each of the Olympians, then nodded his head at me. "Ares, Bella, please. It is time to start your Trial."

So not everything Eris said was untrue. The Trial really was beginning now. I fingered my flick-blade in my pocket as I stepped forward. Ares moved too, toward the Lord of War.

"Find the fighting pit and the dragon, and get three scales. You may not flash at any point. Enjoy." He winked at us both, then we were flashed out of the glade.

The forest smelled bad. Really bad.

"What the..." I could feel my whole face wrinkle in disgust as I looked around myself. The air was heavy and damp, and there was so much foliage above us that only streaks of misty light illuminated our surroundings.

The trees were huge, as big as redwoods I'd seen in pictures before. But their branches started much lower, just a few feet off the ground, and the mass of leaves growing from them were a weird color, as though someone had sucked most of the vibrancy from them. I turned in a slow circle. A low whooping sounded somewhere in the distance, and there was a constant rustling of creatures in the damp fallen leaves littering the mossy ground.

There was no path, or clearing, or any indication at all what direction we should be going in. I looked at Ares, standing out absurdly in his gold armor.

"The smell is rotten vegetation and dead animals, I believe."

I pulled a face. "Gross."

"Use your healing power. Create a thin veil across your ability to smell."

"Really?"

"Yes."

I tried to do as he described, and to my delight, the stomach-churning smell lessened. "Thanks."

He ignored my thanks, and I felt a tug on my power. "What are you doing?"

"Sensing for a dragon."

"Oh. Good idea."

I pulled my blade from my pocket as he stood unnaturally still. "Time to play, *Ischyros*," I whispered to the sword. With a delicious pulse of heat, the blade morphed in my hand, until I was holding the epic steel sword.

"There are lethal creatures everywhere in this forest. The desire to kill is all around us. I can't tell where the dragon is."

A shiver ran down my spine. "You can sense for stuff that wants to kill us?"

"Yes."

"Show me how?"

"No."

I twirled my blade in my hand, taking a deep breath. "Fine. Then which way do we go? Preferably without running into the things that want to kill us." The truth was though, I was ready for a fight. Aphrodite had gotten me fired up, and nervous energy was racing around my body, making me restless.

"I think that the strongest sense of danger is that way." He pointed to a tree that looked the same as every other tree, then stamped toward it. Drawing his sword, he hacked at the low branches, until he'd made a rough hole large enough for him to push through.

"Toward the danger it is," I muttered, and followed after him.

Hacking away at branches seemed like an abuse of my sword's true potential, but *Ischyros* did as good a job as a machete would have. The stuffy heat of the forest was becoming oppressive, the gloom just as suffocating. Alien noises were our constant companion as we forced our way through the dense undergrowth, sharp thorns and scratchy branches catching on my clothes.

"Panic is an asshole for making us go straight from the ceremony. I don't have my armor, or my backpack. And if I tear this t-shirt, I will make him pay."

"Is there anyone you don't think is an asshole?" Ares muttered ahead of me.

I thought for a moment. "Not many people, no."

Ares was silent for a while, then spoke quietly. "You said you would leave once you have retrieved your friend. What do you plan to do?"

His question surprised me, and also caused me an irrational surge of pleasure. *He cared.* "Erm, I'm not really sure."

"Will you stay with him?" His voice was curt and clipped.

"Joshua?"

"Yes."

"I don't know." And I really didn't. "All I know is that there's no fucking way I'm going back to London. Or the mortal world."

"You wish to stay in Olympus?"

"Of course I do. I've spent my whole life not fitting in and knowing with certainty that I'm not in the right place. Olympus is everything I didn't know I needed and missed from my life. I mean, a world where it must be impossible to get bored... That's a dream come true."

Ares had slowed, and he turned to look at me over his shoulder. He had a strange look in his eyes, and I wished I could see the rest of his face.

"What?" I asked him. He turned away. "Ares, what aren't you saying?" I could feel his discomfort.

"Be quiet. I can hear something."

"Bullshit! You just don't want to-"

"Bella, silence!"

He had tensed, his sword raised and his head tipped back. Adrenaline immediately flooded through my veins as I realized he was serious.

I concentrated, straining to hear something. I felt a little rush of heat fire out from the well of power under my ribs, and it was suddenly as though my senses were amplified by a hundred. Every crack of a twig, Ares' measured breaths, even the barely-there breeze, sounded loud and clear in my ears. The muted color of the forest around me came to life, and I caught the bright colors of tiny bugs and the flash of opalescent feathers in the trees that I'd missed entirely before. Unfortunately the rotten smell hammered harder at my defenses, but it was small price to pay.

Before I could tell Ares how utterly awesome this new experience was, a loud buzzing reached my ears. I turned warily in the direction it was coming from.

"What's that noise?" I whispered. It was getting louder.

"If it is a swarm of oxys then we must defend ourselves, now." There was a note of urgency to his voice that he did not normally have, and I snapped my eyes to his. "Bella, we can't fight these easily. If they sting you, you'll have about three seconds to heal yourself, or it will be too late." He gripped my arm, and sparks of electricity shot across my skin. "I'm going to teach you to create a shield, right now."

"OK," I said, a bit breathlessly.

"Draw on your power and picture a shield. A real shield, that you would be willing to use in battle. If you do not believe that what you have imagined could defend you in a real fight, then it will not work."

"Got it," I said, and tried to picture a shield. With a jolt that felt almost physical, a massive circular metal disk flashed into my head. It was beautifully engraved with an image of two rearing stallions, spears and javelins flying behind the riderless horses. A pattern ringed the shield, and looked Celtic or Viking in style.

There was no way I'd invented this shield. I *knew* it was real.

I didn't have time to ask Ares about it though.

The buzzing suddenly surged in volume and Ares crouched down, the plume on his helmet tipping back as he cast his eyes up. I followed suit, holding the image of the horse shield firm in my mind as red seeped fast across my vision, replacing the vibrancy that had been there moments ago.

The buzzing grew so loud I could hear nothing else over it, even the rushing of blood in my ears. But I couldn't see anything in the trees above or around us.

"Where are they?" I yelled at Ares.

"This is Panic's forest; his creatures will try to incite panic before attacking." I caught enough of his words to work out what he had said, and I took a deep breath. The tactic was working. The longer we waited for the threat to appear, the more my imagination built up the foe.

I wouldn't say I was panicking yet, but I certainly didn't want to wait any longer to see what we were up against.

9

BELLA

Something small, bright and freaking fast darted out of the trees toward me.

I felt a slight resistance as it crashed into an invisible barrier a foot above me, then flew off into the tree again. My pulse quickened, and everything around me began to slow as my war-sight kicked in. I felt Ares pull on my strength, and I let go of a little, allowing him to take it. The next oxys that sped toward us was moving just as quickly as the first, but my power allowed me to focus on it enough to see it properly.

It was like somebody had taken a wasp and put it through a Frankenstein machine. It was as large as Ares' closed fist, and its body looked like it had been stitched together out of lots of bits of bright leather. A glowing purple stinger jutted out of its rear end, and it had hairy black wings that beat hard and fast. I couldn't make out eyes on the thing, but it had multiple furry legs hanging down under its tube-shaped body.

It smashed into an invisible wall around Ares, then flitted off.

The buzzing paused, then roared, and my stomach tightened in apprehension as a swarm erupted from the trees. They weren't just around us, they were above us too, blocking the faint light with their sheer mass. I braced myself, and felt my whole body being pushed into the dirt below me as they crashed into my protective shield. It had formed a dome around me, and a sense of being closed-in swamped me as they beat at it, covering it entirely, leaving me in near darkness. I waved *Ischyros* uselessly at them from where I crouched, taking deep breaths and wishing desperately that I knew how to make light.

A weird sense of urgency took over my mind abruptly, and I felt Ares' presence pressing at my thoughts. The second I pictured him, his voice sounded in my head.

"I'm going to create a fireball. And I need a surge of your power to do it."

He wasn't exactly asking for permission to use my power, but he was telling me beforehand, which was a significant improvement on the last Trial. "OK."

I felt a hard pull in my gut, and I didn't fight it. The buzzing upped in pitch into an awful cacophony, then the darkness was suddenly gone, a roaring inferno of orange and scarlet washing over my dome instead. The oxys scattered, the terrible sound of their buzzing fading fast.

I stood up warily as the flames died down and the sensation of being so close to the heat but not being able to feel it was strange.

"The ground and foliage are too damp to catch," Ares said, standing up beside me. Fire licked up an invisible barrier around him too.

A few lingering oxys zipped toward us, but retreated fast as they neared the flames. "They will keep coming,"

Ares said. "In a few hours, they will forget that we have fire and try again."

"This shield thing is cool," I said, reaching out to touch it. My hand moved straight through the magic boundary.

"It is a useful power to have. The oxys sting is lethal."

"So if they stung me I'd have three seconds before I died?"

"No. Their sting does worse than that. It will send you permanently mad. You will become a rabid shell of a being."

I was instantly much more afraid of the oxys than I had been thirty seconds ago. "Why the hell didn't you tell me that before?"

Ares looked at me and shrugged. "I didn't want you to panic."

"Great."

"Speaking of lethal, your power is strong enough now that I think that it's safe to assume that your immortality will have manifested."

"Wait, what?"

"It's not wise to test it, but I believe it would take something extremely rare or strong to kill you now."

"But I thought demigods weren't immortal?" I could feel how wide my eyes were as my heart galloped in my chest. "Only proper gods were?"

Ares stared at me, the flames around us now dying, and the buzzing all but gone. "You are not a demigod."

"Then what the fuck am I?"

"I told you. You are the Goddess of War. We should drop our shields and save our energy."

I didn't tell him that the second he'd said I was

immortal I had totally forgotten about my shield. "Immortal as in - I can't die?"

"That is the definition of immortal, yes."

"Well, fuck." The sheer implications of living forever were too massive for me to comprehend. A cascade of possibilities and fears rushed through me, and Ares turned back in the direction we'd been traveling, raising his sword to start hacking at branches. "Wait! You can't just drop that bombshell and carry on!"

"I thought you had realized this already."

"Hell, I can't even do a fraction of what you can, of course I hadn't gotten to thinking about being immortal! Who else in Olympus is immortal? Does that mean if I fall in love with someone who isn't immortal I'll have to watch them die, like in the Disney Hercules? What if I get like you and I lose the thrill of fighting?" The concerns and fears tumbled from my lips, and I surprised myself by how much they were dominated by worry.

Surely being immortal was a good thing?

But it didn't sit right with me at all. What was the point of anything if it was infinite? How could you live in the moment, if the moment lasted forever?

I didn't *want* to be immortal.

"We need to find this dragon. Keep moving."

I did as he said, but only because I was too distracted to argue. I stepped in his wake, allowing him to clear the path for us as I tried to get to grips with the idea of not dying.

But I couldn't. It was just too... impossible.

"I don't think I can deal with this," I said to Ares eventually.

"Deal with what?"

"Immortality. It's stupid."

"I told you that you have the power of a goddess and that you were getting stronger. How is it you are only considering this now?"

"In case you hadn't noticed, the last few days have been pretty fucking hectic for me, armor-boy. I was concentrating on my magic; I didn't realize not dying came with the package."

"Immortality is the most coveted thing in all Olympus," he said, whacking at a cluster of huge leaves.

"Well, I don't want it. Knowing that you could lose everything makes you treasure what you have all the more. I know that from my shows. People who take everything for granted lose the ability to experience true happiness, or gratitude."

Ares paused, then resumed his hacking. "I have never met anyone like you," he said, quietly.

"Ditto," I answered. "What about the demon?"

"What about her?"

"Well, if I'm immortal, what's the point in fighting her? Nobody can win."

Ares slashed at the particularly thorny tangle of branches that had been behind the leaves. "She steals souls. That would be much worse than dying. She could keep your soul in perpetual torment."

"Is taking their soul the only way to kill an immortal god?"

"There are many ancient artifacts that can harm an immortal, even if they can't be killed. And some very powerful gods who have been granted the right to rule, like my father, can remove your power."

"And therefore remove your immortality?" I asked. Ares nodded. So, Zeus stealing Ares' power must be worse for him than I thought. His father had made him mortal, and removed the protection on his life. "You dad is a total douche."

"What is a douche?"

Suppressing a snicker at the thought of explaining the answer to that question, I answered him vaguely. "Mortal word for asshole."

"Why not stick with asshole? It appears to be your favorite word."

"I've decided to reserve it just for you," I told him.

He glanced back at me, and though I couldn't see his mouth to confirm that he was smiling, there was definitely a glimmer of amusement in his eyes.

10

BELLA

We slashed our way through the forest for another hour or more, and I filled the time by avoiding thinking about immortality, and practicing turning on the thing with my senses that I'd accidentally discovered I could do. I opted not to mention it to Ares, and instead silently marveled at how I could project my amplified hearing and vision at will toward noises and sights that interested me.

I was listening intently to the thud of the warrior god's heart beating in his chest, when the ground beneath my feet gave way.

A shout of shock left my lips as I plummeted downward, grasping at thin air. Before I could get over my surprise enough to pull at my power or do anything useful at all, my back slammed into something cold and hard with a splash, and then I began to sink. I'd fallen into water, I realized, my vision red in reaction to the pain and shock, but my usual focus not able to compete with my thrashing panic.

"Bella!" I heard Ares roar, and I cried out as I kicked

my legs, trying to right myself, but I could feel something coiling around my thighs and hips. My head cleared the surface and I dragged in a desperate breath of air before I was tugged back down again.

I had *Ischyros* in my hand and I slashed blindly under the water with the blade, but the grip on me didn't lessen, the weapon not connecting with anything. I couldn't see clearly, my thrashing causing the murky water to bubble up, but I thought it looked like a tentacle. I kept kicking as hard as I could, and my head broke the surface for another brief moment. I saw a gleam of gold before I went under again.

Ares was in the water with me.

"Stay calm!" His voice was an urgent command in my head, and I thrashed to get to the surface. *"You can breathe underwater."*

"No," I gasped, before I was yanked back under the surface again.

"Yes. You are immortal."

But panic was winning. I was a fighter, not a contortionist. I was trapped and I couldn't get free, I couldn't breathe. I was getting dizzy, and I could feel my strength lessening as the thought of drowning overwhelmed me.

"Stay calm!"

The water around me was cloudy but I could see Ares' bright red plume through it clearly. A painful burn in my chest screamed for air and I tried to kick up to the surface. But something pulled at my legs, and I was jerked further down.

I was going to drown. I was trapped. My lungs would fill with water and I would die.

Huge black dots drifted across my vision as my legs

stopped kicking, the thing coiled so tight around them now that I couldn't move.

"This will hurt, but you will survive. We need your power, Bella. Stay conscious."

Ares' voice was calm and soothing in my mind, and I clung to it, as the last few bubbles of air escaped from my mouth. My chest burned as I turned my head slowly, trying to find his eyes, to focus on something other than the darkness invading my vision. I felt a pulse of pain through my head, and I felt Ares grip my hand, the one holding *Ischyros*.

"Don't let go of the sword. Whatever happens." I was tugged down again, the light from the surface fading. My body gave in to the pain in my chest.

My mouth opened, and I inhaled, with no control over the action at all.

I don't know if I screamed as the freezing water filled my mouth, burning all the way down my throat. I was vaguely aware of the grip tightening on my hand, my weapon becoming too heavy to hold alone as blinding pain took my chest. I squeezed my eyes shut, aware of how close I was to passing out as the agony tore through me, every instinct in my body begging to shut down, to escape.

But I refused to let go, refused to give in to the temptation. Ares said I had to stay conscious.

Just as I was sure I couldn't bear the agony any longer, a rush of cool air seemed to fill my lungs from nowhere, and I choked, expelling water from my throat that burned like acid. My eyes flew open, and I gasped down more air as I realized that it was now almost too dark to see, we were so deep.

I was breathing under water.

Despite the dark, I knew Ares was still there with me, his hand still clamped around mine. As I spat up more water I tried to orient myself, and realized that the thing coiled around my legs was now up to my waist. I felt for it with my other hand, recoiling when I touched a slimy tentacle. I could feel the power under my ribs burning hot, and I drew on it, trying to send some healing tendrils to my raw throat.

"Ares?" I sent the thought to him, saying it aloud too, my voice instantly lost to the water.

"Cut the tentacles with your sword."

His mental voice was weak and strained, and fear for him rushed through me. Something was definitely wrong. *"Are you OK?"*

"Cut them." I felt his hand loosen from mine, freeing my weapon.

"I can't see where they are." After a second, a faint glow illuminated the cloudy water. It was Ares' armor. I couldn't see his eyes, but the gold gleam was enough that when I looked down I could see the purple tentacles wrapped around both of us.

Without hesitation I brought my weapon down. As soon as my blade met with the limb, the thing began to thrash, Ares and I flying through the murky water in its grip. I responded, the red mist tingeing the gold light as my blade met its mark over and over in a frenzy of movement.

I got Ares free first, only a second before severing the last tentacle with a hold on me. I immediately began kicking for the surface, only pausing to see that Ares was following.

He wasn't. I pulled my legs up and did a one-eighty in the water, heading down instead of up. Energy was racing through me now, all of the panic turned to determination.

Ares' glow was fading, and fear caught in my throat as I realized he was moving deeper into the water. The tentacles were nowhere to be seen, thank god, and I swam down after him faster.

"Ares!"

He didn't answer me, his glow almost vanishing as he sank faster. If he stopped glowing completely, I would lose him down in the darkness. New panic swelled through me, and I propelled myself through the inky water after him.

As I laid my hand on his arm, his light went out.

Power flared in my chest, and I knew instinctively that whatever Ares had been using had just returned to me. I had all of my power now, I was no longer sharing it. Which meant Ares was unconscious.

Swearing in a continuous stream of curses, I kicked upward, pulling the dead-weight that was the God of War with me. But he was heavy, and we were so deep, and I was too slow. I knew I wouldn't get him to the surface in time if he had stopped breathing. How did the immortality work if he had no power or was unconscious? Would he survive? Why was there no fucking manual for this?

Anger and frustration surged through me, and with it a blessed hit of strength. My legs seemed to grow as I swam, and a glimmer of hope pushed me further. I drew on the burning heat inside me, willing myself to get bigger and stronger, to reach the surface faster.

And I did. I felt myself getting larger, each kick of my legs more powerful, Ares getting lighter in my grip.

When I burst through the surface of the water I half threw Ares out of the pool and onto the forest floor, scrambling out onto the mossy undergrowth after him.

Heaving for breath myself, I rolled him over, tipping his head to one side and trying to press on his chest to force the water out. But his armor was solid, and I couldn't get his chest to move. I pulled his helmet from his head, revealing his paper-white skin. Desperately, I pressed my hands to his face and I pulled on my power, trying to force it into him through our contact.

"Take my power," I whispered, my throat raw. "Please. Please open your eyes."

Water spilled suddenly from his mouth and he rolled to his side, nearly causing me to let go. But I kept my grip on his face, pouring my healing power into him as relief swept through me. He coughed and choked up water as I muttered about everything being OK, and after what felt like an eternity, he looked up at me.

His breathing was ragged and there was an intensity in his dull eyes as I pushed his wet hair back.

"Are you alright?"

"I am alive," he croaked. "Thanks to you."

Slowly, I let my hands drop from his face, and he moved to sit up. "What happened?" I asked him.

"I... I couldn't take enough of your power without harming you. You needed it to survive the panic."

I stared at him. "You gave up the power for me?"

He looked down at his hands, then stood up, stumbling a little. "It was the only option for us both to survive." His voice was brusque, and he wouldn't look at me as he began banging his armor, getting the water out of it. "If I lost consciousness I knew you'd have enough power to get us both free. If you lost consciousness then you couldn't have saved me. By the time you came around, I would have been dead."

His words were true. I was the one with the power;

without me he had nothing. I was the logical one to have saved. But his awkwardness said something different.

The man acted on pride and impulse, and had demonstrated barely any self control in a fight. So for him to stop himself from taking my power and allow himself to be rescued by me... This was definitely a side to Ares I hadn't seen.

11

ARES

My throat and lungs burned with a feeling I had not experienced in centuries, aside from briefly during the fight with my father. Pain.

Damn my mortality! When Bella was stronger, I would be able to share her power more effectively. Wouldn't I? What would happen if we couldn't both use it to escape death?

An uneasy feeling crawled down my aching spine as I turned away from her. It was true that it had made no sense to let her lose consciousness. I would surely have perished.

But that wasn't what had driven me to let go of her power. That wasn't what had been going through my mind when, for the first time in my memory, blackness closed in around me and very real death had loomed large.

The only thing that had been in my mind, was to save her. Feeling her terror as she thrashed and fought for her life had caused an instinct I didn't know I possessed to take over. She needed all of her power to breathe underwater, to use her immortality. And I had let her have it without hesitation. Why?

Why had I done that?

The power she held over me was becoming dangerous. That was the closest I had ever come to death, and I had put my life in her hands. She may be my most deadly adversary.

I turned a fraction, trying to get a glimpse of her without her noticing. She was standing with her back to me, her hands on her hips, surveying the forest. Her blonde hair hung wet to the small of her back, and I was beset by an image of her stripping out of her clingy shirt. She was taller, I realized, and the muscles in her calves and biceps were larger than usual. Her power had helped make her strong enough to drag me to the surface, and I wasn't sure she had even noticed.

If she was to be the death of me, I did not think she was aware of it.

"I think I know where the dragon is," she said, and I turned away before she saw me looking.

"Where?" I stooped to pick up my helmet.

"There's a distinct lack of birds in that direction."

I took a long breath, then rammed my helmet on my head and faced her. Her eyes caught mine, and I could see concern flash in them, before she looked to where she was pointing.

"Yes. That is where I sense the most danger," I nodded. "How do you know there are fewer birds?"

"I can hear them. Or rather, not hear them."

She was beginning to learn to use some of her powers on her own, which meant I would not be able to avoid teaching her to control them. "You realize you have grown taller? In order to preserve your power, you should shrink back to normal now."

She looked down at herself in alarm. "Shit. You're right. I'm almost as tall as you." There was a wonder in her voice that I instantly wanted to hear more of. Or be the cause of. "How do I shrink?"

"Just will yourself to be normal."

She snorted, raising one eyebrow. "Normal? Fuck that. I've never been normal in my life. Now is definitely not the time to start."

I couldn't help my small smile, but she couldn't see it behind my helmet. "You know what I mean," I said. "As you were before."

She closed her eyes, and started to return to her previous size with a faint gold glow. When she opened them again, she did a little twirl. "I'm going to be good at this magic shit. I can tell."

"Why do you think I'm refusing to teach you anything?" I answered, and immediately regretted the teasing comment. But instead of launching into a tirade of questions and demands, she just shrugged one shoulder.

"Looks like I don't need you to teach me anything. I just saved both our asses on my own. And I know where the dragon is."

Indignation rolled through me. "I'm an Olympian. I could teach you things you didn't even know were possible."

"Armor-boy, literally everything in this world is impossible to me. That's hardly a bold claim."

I crossed my arms. "Infinity would not be long enough to teach you everything I know."

"Oooo, who's a clever boy?" Her grin was doing something to me. Something unexpected and inconvenient. "Go on then. Teach me something nobody else could."

With a rush of unexpected desire, my head filled with ideas of what I could teach Bella that had nothing to do with war or fighting.

The connection we shared must have translated my thoughts, because the second my eyes met hers, fire leaped to life in her irises. A drum sounded in the distance, slow at first, then louder and faster, as though my own heartbeat was setting the pace. Bella stepped forward, her eyes alive, and her lips parted.

My hands moved to my helmet before I could stop them, and as I pulled it from my head Bella let out a breathy sound. My body came alive at her response to me, desire replacing all other thoughts as I dropped the helmet to the ground.

I took the last step, closing the gap between us, and her hand came up to my face at the same time mine moved to hers.

"You saved me," she whispered, and the flames were filling her eyes, fierce and hot and irresistible, the drums of war beating around us.

"And you me," I breathed, and then her lips crashed into mine, and the godforsaken forest around us vanished.

All I knew was her taste, her heat, her passion. Our tongues moved together in a dance more erotic than I had ever experienced, and my mind filled with a desperation to feel every part of her body against mine.

She moaned softly as I broke the kiss, trailing kisses down her jaw, her slender neck. She pushed her fingers into my hair, her nails leaving trails of tingling pleasure across my skin.

I wanted her. And it was more than just her body I

needed. She was mine. I knew it, with a sudden and almost painful clarity.

She was mine.

"Ares." I froze as I realized the icy voice I had just heard in my head was not Bella's. "It is one thing to ignore my command. It is another to do it in front of the world."

12

BELLA

"W-What's wrong?"

Ares had frozen beneath me, one second his hot, hungry mouth on the sensitive skin on my neck, then the next as still as a statue.

"We are being watched." His voice was strained.

I could hear the blood pounding in my head, and my desire was so intense that my whole body felt like it was on fire. But I crouched and picked up my weapon from where I had dropped it, trying to concentrate on the threat. This was one of the most dangerous places in the world, I reminded myself, trying to block out the bliss Ares' kiss had instilled in me. We'd already been attacked by oxys and a monster octopus or some shit. Kisses could wait.

I didn't want to wait. I wanted everything Ares had, and I wanted it more than I'd ever wanted anything. I hadn't even known desire this intense was possible.

"Where?" I whispered. "I can't see anything."

"The Trial is being watched. By the whole of Olympus. I have just had a message from one of the gods."

I turned back to him slowly. "Aphrodite?" I asked, through gritted teeth. My unspent passion was turning fast to rage.

A female voice hammered into my mind, almost painfully loud. "You seek to mock the Goddess of Love?" Aphrodite's cold voice felt like a whip across my skull, and I felt myself wince. "You will pay for this. You will both pay." A searing pain tore through the base of my head and down my neck, leaving me gasping in agony.

"Bella!" Ares was crouching before me, cupping my face in his hands as black dots drifted across my vision.

"I'm OK," I wheezed. "Fuck, that was painful."

"Use your magic, heal yourself." His voice was almost tender, a tone I didn't even know he was capable of.

"The pain's gone now. What did she mean?" I straightened slowly, blinking around.

"I think Aphrodite just tried to curse you."

My stomach clenched tight, fear and anger coiling through me. "What?"

"We need someone that knows about her magic to confirm it, but I'm quite certain we have made an enemy of her."

I looked up at his beautiful face, pinched and angry. And flushed. He wanted me. I had no doubt at all. You couldn't fake a kiss like that twice.

Tentatively, I sent a thought to him. "As soon as we are alone, we are finishing this."

His eyes locked on mine, and for a second the hunger in them was so predatory heat rushed back to my core. But he didn't answer me.

Instead he ducked down, scooping up his helmet and putting it back on. *Ischyros* heated in my hand. This asshole had rendered me unconscious in front of the world, and now he had turned down my sexual advances in front of them too. Red seeped into the edge of my vision.

I opened my mouth, ready to tell him in no uncertain fucking terms that if he was still into Aphrodite, a woman who treated him like shit, that he had better not lay another fucking finger on me, but he spoke first.

"After you." He gestured into the forest.

"You are a trophy to her. Is that what you want?"

A wave of heat rolled from him as I felt a tug in my gut. "Either I hack this forest apart, or you do," he hissed at me.

I bared my teeth at him, raised *Ischyros*, and brought the sword crashing through the nearest bunch of tangled branches.

Once I started, I couldn't stop. I poured all my pent-up energy, all my desire for Ares, fear from nearly drowning, confusion about fucking everything, into the blade, and slashed and hacked with reckless abandon. I wasn't even sure if I was cleaving a path, or just tearing up a chunk of shitty forest.

"Bella, stop." I was panting as I wheeled to face Ares, god only knows how much later.

"Why?"

"The oxys are coming again."

I sent my senses out and snarled as I heard them. "Good. I'll knock them out of the fucking air." I wielded my sword like a baseball bat, and Ares grabbed my arm.

"Bella, if you are stung there is no recovery. You will live trapped in a world of insanity your whole life."

I lowered my arm. His words were serious enough to

snap me out of my sword-wielding rage. "Fine. What do we do?"

"I can sense something below us. Something dangerous."

"More or less than the oxys?"

"I don't know, but it means there must be a passage or caves or something similar underground. We might be able to keep moving somewhere the oxys can't get to us."

It took us less than a minute to find a cave mouth hidden by the dense foliage, but that was plenty enough time for the buzzing to double in volume.

We barely got inside the cave before it was loud enough that I could barely hear my own thoughts. Together we heaved as many loose boulders and rocks as we could find over to the entrance, praying the oxys didn't work out that we were behind the tangle of undergrowth hiding the cave.

I had the distinct sense that we might be making a massive mistake, trapping ourselves inside a cave we knew contained something dangerous. But the oxys were the immediate threat, and we could only deal with what we could see.

"You're going to have to teach me to glow," I said, blinking in the gloom.

"Think of something that gives off a lot of light."

"Like the sun?"

"Yes. I think of solar sails, on a ship."

I thought about the colossal sails on the mast of the demon's ship, like liquid metal gleaming and shining.

"Good." I looked down at Ares' grunt, and felt a smile stretch across my face. I was glowing gold.

"You glow when you are using a lot of power," I said, looking up at Ares. He was giving off a faint light too. "Do you do that on purpose?"

"No. It is just what gods do."

I remembered my skin glowing after I'd used my power to move so fast up the hundred-hander's body. "What gods do," I repeated. "I'm an actual god. Goddess. Deity."

Ares didn't say anything, but turned away from our makeshift barrier and started to head further into the cave.

"You know, you are the worst person to have an existential crisis, or an epiphany around," I said, following after him. "Being a freaking glowing gold goddess would be a lot more fun if I had someone more impressed to share it with."

"All gods glow. It is not impressive."

"Well, I'm impressed. With myself. Not you. Your glow is shit."

He looked over his shoulder at me and I gave him the finger with a sarcastic grin. He shook his head. "Glowing or being a goddess does not make you any less crude," he said.

"No. Seems not."

The cave was wide and cool, and I sent my new super senses out, straining to hear for anything dangerous or interesting. There was a soft scuttling sound, but it was far away, and I couldn't associate the noise with anything obvious. We walked for what I was sure was a few hours, before Ares slowed. His glow had become very faint, and I felt a little pull in my gut as he turned around to face me.

His voice sounded in my head, instead of out loud. "We must rest."

I frowned, but almost immediately schooled my face into indifference. We were being watched by the whole of Olympus. And the God of War did not want the world to know he was tired. The pain of his betrayal in the pits, and the sting of his rejection both times I'd kissed him, made me seriously consider punishing him, forcing him to continue, or admit out loud that he was weak. But he *had* nearly died. And if he wanted to be a jerk he could take more of my power instead of resting, but he wasn't.

"Mortality is a bitch, huh?" I answered him silently. It was too dark to see his reaction, but I made a point of stretching my arms above my head and yawning.

"Armor-boy, I'm freaking starving," I said loudly. "Can we stop and eat?"

We made a small area against the cave wall as hospitable as we could. We found small boulders to sit on, and Ares scraped some moss off a part of the cave roof that I couldn't reach to pad them. I dug about in dark crevices until I found enough bits of branch and twigs to start a fire.

When we were finally seated around our little camp-fire, I looked at Ares. "How do we get food? We're not allowed to flash."

"We could ask for help."

"Ask who?"

Ares cocked his head, thinking. "One of my loyal subjects." I raised an eyebrow. "My daughter," he said.

"Woah now, armor-boy. I'm not ready to meet the family," I said, only half joking. It made me feel weird to think of Ares having kids. He looked the right age to have two beaming, gorgeous toddlers, and it was freaky that I knew he had fully-grown ancient demigod offspring roaming the realms of Olympus.

"I believe that you will approve of Hippolyta. She is Queen of the Amazons."

"*The* Amazons? Like where Wonder Woman is from?"

"I do not know who Wonder Woman is, but Hippolyta is a woman and sometimes wondrous."

I barked a laugh, half excited and half shitting myself with nerves. "Does she have a daughter named Diana?"

"No."

"Shame."

"In order to do this, I will need to teach you to communicate with others who wield the power of war."

"Glowing and mind magic, all in one evening. You're spoiling me."

"I thought you wanted to learn? Do you take nothing seriously?"

"I am serious. I'm nervous."

"Stop talking."

"Fine."

My palms were actually sweating a bit in the cool rocky tunnel as Ares leaned forwards, resting his forearms on his knees. "Hold your sword."

I picked *Ischyros* up and lay it flat across my own knees, gripping the hilt. "Think about leading an army. It can be any group of people or creatures you like, but know that you are their leader, their commander. Then invent your opposition. You know what they plan to do, how they are going to do it, and most of all, that you can beat them."

Ares' voice was deep and intense and I closed my eyes.

I instantly found myself transported to an expanse of grass and rolling hills as far as the eye could see. And covering every inch of those hills were warriors. Hundreds were on horseback, but more were on foot, and almost all carried crudely fashioned spears, swords, or bows. In the distance was a black line of movement stretching across the horizon. The enemy tribe, marching inexorably toward us. The clothes the soldiers were wearing looked medieval, and I could see no modern technology anywhere in my surroundings. Was I in ancient Britain or Scandinavia?

I looked down at the fictional version of myself. I was wearing a plain purple dress draped with a fur cape, and I had *Ischyros* in one hand, and the shield with the two stallions in the other. And I was mounted on a snow-white horse.

"OK," I breathed aloud to Ares, keeping my eyes closed - reluctant to leave the imaginary scenario that had come so freely to my mind.

"Let the anticipation of the fight build, let your instincts guide your plans. And at the moment the battle begins, hold on to that feeling."

I did as he told me, allowing the rush of the impending battle consume me. I soaked up the adrenaline pouring from those around me, and it was as though their heightened emotions were feeding straight into my veins. The warriors began to sing, low and quiet at first, but my skin tingled as more and more voices joined. Before long the battle chant had become deafening, and the enemy were approaching. They were dressed the same as my own army, but at that moment I didn't care who they were. I was only interested in how to defeat them. I scanned the nearing army, noticing instantly that they had less horses, and more bowmen. My mind worked quickly, calculating how fast my own horsemen could get there, where my soldiers with shields needed to be, and how long it would take to dispatch the archers.

I bellowed commands, and the war song dissipated as the men and women surrounding me obeyed them utterly, my instructions shouted along the rows until everyone knew exactly what they needed to do.

A blissful sense of excitement settled over me, as the sound of the enemy's hooves galloping across the earth increased. It would be only moments until they reached us. Until I could prove the steel of the weapon in my hand, until I could prove myself a true warrior.

"That's it," said Ares, and he sounded like I felt, his tone filled with anticipation. "Now, search for that feeling."

"What?"

"Hold on to that feeling, but come back to the cave. Send out your senses, and search for that feeling around you."

"But I need to be here. I need to fight." *I need to win.*

"It's not real, Bella. It's..." Ares trailed off. "It's your power, manifesting in your imagination. Come back to the cave." Slowly, reluctantly, I opened my eyes. "Good. Don't lose that feeling, search for it. Send your senses out."

Suppressing my disappointment at leaving the vivid imaginary battlefield, I did as he told me, trying to keep the anticipatory elation I was feeling intact. I did what I'd taught myself to do earlier that day, but instead of straining my ears I imagined myself listening for the ringing of steel and the cries of war.

My mouth fell open as white-hot fire leaped up around Ares, the plume on his helmet ablaze. But I knew it wasn't real, it was made of light. My hand reached up automatically, curious.

"You've found me. Look further."

I did as he said, pushing my senses out, and all of a sudden it was like I was on a rollercoaster in the dark. I was zooming through an inky nothingness, and flashing up every now and then around me were similar white flames of light, there and gone before I could slow down to look closer.

"Ares?" I could hear the slight panic in my tone, though I couldn't see anything in the cave any more.

"Slow down. Focus. You want to find Hippolyta."

Lacking any visual to hang on to regarding the Queen of the Amazons, I tried to conjure up a picture of Wonder Woman instead, and almost cried out as my mental rollercoaster jerked back on itself. I whizzed through the darkness, then came crashing to a halt in front of a tower of white fire.

"H-Hippolyta?" I whispered.

A woman stepped from the flames, and my mouth dropped open.

"I permit you entry to my mind only because you are born of my own power. Who are you?"

"Bella. Erm, Enyo. The, erm, Goddess of War," I stammered. God, she was impressive.

She was wearing a brown material tied across her chest and hips with coarse looking rope, with bright red slashes painted across it. Her bare stomach, shoulders and arms were corded with toned muscle, and she twirled a large war-hammer in her left hand. Short blonde hair framed a fierce face, with the brightest blue eyes I'd ever seen.

Her eyebrows lifted, then she gave a small nod. "I had

heard of the Trials my father was undertaking, but here in Themiscyra we spurn all outsiders and their nonsense. Why do you seek me?"

"Ares said you might bring us some food. We are in Panic's kingdom, Dasos, in Skotadi, and we are not allowed to flash."

"Why do you not hunt for food?"

"I, erm, don't know," I said, feeling distinctly lame.

Hippolyta scowled. "I shall fulfill my father's wishes," she said, not sounding at all like she wanted to any such thing.

"Thank you," I said, but she had already stepped back into the inferno behind her.

I felt my head jerk as though something was sucking my whole body backwards, and then the dimly lit cave came back into focus around me, Ares staring at me intently from behind his helmet.

"She's..." I started, but before I could finish there was a small flash of red light between us. Something dead, and covered in both scales and feathers, was laid on the floor beside the fire. I cocked my head at it. "I was hoping for a burger."

"She is not happy that I have asked for her help," Ares said wryly.

"No shit. What is that?"

"A rodent."

"It looks like something we could have caught ourselves in the forest."

"I believe that might be the point she was making."

13

BELLA

I couldn't help wondering if we could, in fact, have caught our own food, and Ares had used the idea of asking Hippolyta for help as an excuse to teach me about my war power.

That was what I wanted to believe, at least. We could have tried to contact Zeeva for food, and there was plenty of stuff scurrying about that must have been edible. Asking the Queen of the Amazons for some dinner seemed excessive. He'd refused to teach me anything so many times that it would be hard for him to suddenly backtrack, and I couldn't shift the feeling that something was different since he had nearly drowned. He wasn't using as much of my power either. He could have taken it and spoken to his daughter himself. So why had he got me to do it?

Ares had prepared the animal, and we sat in silence as it turned on a makeshift spit over the little fire.

"Should we sleep here?" I asked him eventually, the quiet too much for me to bear for long.

"I suppose it is as good a place as any, if we must sleep."

"Would carrying on through the night be better? Are dragons any different in the dark?"

He looked up at me, but I couldn't identify his expression. "Take your helmet off," I said softly. He hesitated. "The world has seen your face already."

Slowly, he pulled his helmet off, standing it on the earth beside him with exaggerated care.

"I've seen you quite literally throw that thing at the floor. Why the tenderness now?"

"It's symbolic," he muttered. Firelight flickered across his beautiful face, reflecting in his eyes and softening the hard line of his jaw. He pushed his hair back from his forehead, and I realized I was biting my bottom lip. "Dragons are the same in the dark," he said, and turned the spit with our dinner on it.

"Oh. Do they look like dragons from my world?"

"I have no idea."

"Big scaly things with wings that breath fire?"

"They are large and have scales. They are like winged snakes, with horns."

"Sounds similar," I said.

"They do not breath fire though."

"Oh, good."

"Some are made of fire."

"What?"

"Others from water, but most from muscle. They are very clever. They will try to trick you into doing their bidding, and play games with your mind."

"Right. I can't wait to see which type we get," I breathed.

. . .

When the meat was cooked, I realized with some distaste that the only way to eat it was by tearing bits off. Fortunately, my survival instincts were stronger than my gag reflex, and I knew I needed food to stay strong.

"That was gross," I said, after forcing down the last mouthful that I could manage.

"You will offend Hippolyta," Ares said. He seemed to be enjoying his.

"Sorry, Hippolyta," I said, to the cave in general. "She said she hasn't been watching, so she probably won't have heard that," I told Ares.

"No, she would not have been watching. Her tribe are very insular."

"Ares, how do you kill a Keres demon?"

He looked up me. "You can't kill them. They are bound to Hades while they are in his realm. She must be returned."

"Then how do we capture her?"

"If we complete these Trials then we do not need to."

"I'm just curious," I said.

Ares let out a long sigh, fixing his gaze on me. "Bella, besting an ancient death demon is not a feat you can manage alone, and although I understand your need to beat her, you should let go of the idea."

I hadn't expected a God of War to sound so defeatist. "I have to beat her, to rescue Joshua," I said. But that wasn't entirely true.

I wanted to beat the demon because nobody had ever made me feel so powerless, not because it was the only way to get Joshua back.

"This Joshua," said Ares, dropping his gaze to his knees. "What is he to you?"

"A friend," I said carefully. "He helped me when I was very frustrated and unhappy."

"Why were you unhappy?"

"I already told you, I knew I didn't belong. I had too much energy for the world I was in. I was drawn to extremes, things that didn't fit with what I actually wanted in my heart."

"I don't understand." He looked up at me again, his expression serious.

I sighed. "In my heart, I want justice, fairness, kindness. Love. But the need to feel alive, to challenge everything, to find and push boundaries, drove me to places that were filled with the opposite of kindness and love. And my confrontational urges meant that I caused chaos in those places. Many times, I was close to destroying things, even people. It made me very unhappy, but I didn't know why or how to fix it. Therapy with Joshua helped me understand that there were two sides to my soul, one constantly angry and one constantly seeking joy. He helped me find ways to expel the anger safely."

"I am sorry."

I blinked in surprise. "That's not a word I've heard you use, even when you should have. Why are you sorry?"

A darkness filled his eyes as he stared at me across the campfire. "I did not realize this man was so important to you."

I frowned. Was he jealous? "He's my only friend." I put weight on the world friend, though I wasn't sure why. Ares and I were not a thing. Did it matter if I had a crush on my shrink?

Ares lifted his hand to his jaw, drawing his fingers across his stubble thoughtfully. An intense longing to replace his fingers with mine rose up in me, and I coughed awkwardly.

"We will win the Trials and return him to you. I do not feel like sleeping. We should continue." He stood up abruptly, picking up his helmet. I shook my head. When Ares decided the conversation was over, it was over.

"What if *I* feel like sleeping?" He narrowed his eyes at me, then pulled his helmet on. "Fine. Whatever." I stood, kicking dust over the fire, annoyed. "Why is everything always your way?"

"Because you know nothing about this world." He began to glow faintly as the fire went out, and I pictured the gleaming sails in my mind, satisfied when my own skin began to glow too.

"Tell me more about it then."

"Later."

"You know, you may have been created just to make me roll my eyes," I told him, as he set off through the cave.

We hadn't been moving long when I became aware of the scuttling sound I'd first heard when we entered the tunnel.

"What's that noise?" I asked in a loud whisper.

"It could be many things."

"Real helpful. Glad I asked."

I gripped my sword tighter, feeling it heat in my palm. It had been too long since something had tried to kill us. As if on cue with my thoughts, a sudden gust of air whooshed down the tunnel over us, bringing with it a rank smell of rotten meat. Ares stopped, then turned to me.

"Do you wish to test your power?"

"Yes," I nodded vigorously.

"The feeling of war that you used earlier to find Hippolyta can be used in battle. It will trigger what you experienced with the hundred-hander. Your movements will speed up, and it will feel as though your opponent will slow down. You will be able to anticipate their reactions and decisions with ease."

"OK." Ares nodded, then turned and resumed his march, his steps more cautious than before. "Why are you telling me things?" I asked, following him equally as warily.

"You will need the knowledge to kill whatever we are about to face."

"I thought you were planning to take care of everything yourself?"

"My plans have changed."

"Why?"

"This is not the place to discuss such things."

I made an exasperated noise, but said nothing else. I had suspected earlier that Ares was finding excuses to teach me how to use my power, and something had definitely changed. If he didn't want to tell me in public what was going on then I'd have to wait until we'd dealt with this dragon and we were alone.

Gods, I wanted to be alone with him.

"Stop," Ares hissed suddenly. I did, pushing out my senses as I halted. The rancid smell strengthened first, then the gold glow coming from the two of us brightened as my eyesight improved, lighting areas of the cave walls previously too dark to see. There was a slight film covering them, I realized. It was pale and fine and reminded me of...

"A spider's web," I whispered, a trickle of dread spreading through my gut. "Ares, please tell me there are no giant spiders in your realm."

"What is a spider?" he murmured, his head tipped back as he scanned the ceiling.

"Round body, too many fucking legs," I hissed, following suit. My blood froze in my veins as something as big as a car scuttled across the rocky ceiling over our heads and into the shadows faster than I could make out, even with my super senses.

"It's an arachnida," Ares said, and for some reason he sounded slightly relieved. "You can beat it."

"*I* can beat it? You mean we? We can beat it?"

"No. This time you fight alone."

"Why?"

"To prove that you can." His voice sounded in my head, not aloud, and I couldn't help looking away from where I was frantically searching the shadows for a car-sized spider, and fixing my eyes on him. *"Show the world what I denied you of in Erimos."*

He wasn't looking at me, and nobody watching would have any idea that he was speaking to me at all. He was giving me this fight to let me show off to Olympus. This was his version of an apology, I realized.

Under any normal circumstance I would have been excited. Touched, even, by his thoughtfulness. But why the fuck did it have to be when we were fighting a fucking giant spider?

I opened my mouth to say as much, but my pride barreled through my fear before I could speak. Was I really about to throw away an opportunity to show the world what I was made of? I never backed down from a challenge. I mean, I'd never been challenged by a giant spider before, but still. This was a chance to show Aphrodite that I wasn't as little as she believed I was. Plus, it was a chance to test my growing power, with Ares to back me up for a change, instead of him trying to take it away.

I couldn't turn this down.

"Come at me, spider-scum," I hissed, raising *Ischyros*.

14

BELLA

Whatever an arachnida was, it wasn't an actual spider, I told myself as we moved further into the darkness, me now leading the way. It was just another Greek monster. We'd got past a load of them already. This would be no different.

"Do they bite?"

"No, they sting."

"Everything here stings," I murmured.

"Now you mention it, yes."

My super-sense hearing had lost the scuttling sound, which made me extremely wary. The thing was staying still. I was raking my honed eyesight over the cave walls and ceiling, and therefore totally missed the creature shooting out of the blackness directly in front of me until it was almost too late.

I slashed *Ischyros* down in front of me in a wide arc just in time, and the huge black thing darted backwards and made an awful screeching sound.

It really was as big as a car, and it really was basically a giant spider. It had plated scales instead of fur, and a massive stinger on its ass, but it was definitely a spider. Eight enormous legs held up its disgusting body, and they clicked as the thing moved backwards and forwards, its network of honeycomb-shaped eyes flashing as they caught the gold of my glowing light.

I took a breath as I dropped into a crouch instinctively. I didn't like spiders. In fact, there weren't many creepy crawlies I liked less.

I needed this thing to not even register as a spider in my mind; it was a monster. Spiders were gross because they crawled all over you, fast and tickly and freaky. This creature was something else entirely, that belonged to Olympus, totally new and different. And it reeked.

Remembering what Ares had told me before, I tried to recall that feeling on the battle field as the arachnida and I circled each other. I could make out Ares' faint glow in my broad peripheral vision, far behind me but moving with us. Without warning, the arachnida's ass swerved under its body and a jet of something shot out of it toward me. I leaped to the side and swiped with my sword, immediately regretting it when whatever it was stuck to the end of my blade. I scowled as I realized what it was. Web. The thing was trying to cover me in sticky ass cobwebs.

The clicking of the spider's legs tripled in speed and then it was coming for me again. Pulling on the hot well of power inside me, I raised my sword and threw myself forward, trying to get underneath its body.

"Use the power of war." Ares' voice sounded in my head and as I slid under the creature I groped for the battlefield feeling again.

Just as I got underneath the spider's big body the stinger moved again, curling underneath itself only feet from me. The version of me in the purple dress, mounted on the white steed and holding that epic shield slammed into my mind, and I was vaguely aware of the glow I was giving off bursting into bright life. The web firing from the stinger bounced harmlessly off my invisible barrier, and with a roar, I willed *Ischyros* to grow.

It did, and fast. As the blade made contact with the monster's underbelly it was already twice the size it had been. I filled the muscles of my arms with power as the blade got heavier, feeling my whole body swell in reaction, then rolled as I pulled the blade through the arachnida's body. Its legs gave out immediately and I jumped to my feet as its body followed, collapsing onto the cave floor.

I'd won.

"Good," said Ares, aloud.

I looked between my blade and him. The sword was massive, almost as tall as me in fact. I concentrated a moment, and couldn't help smiling as *Ischyros* began to shrink down. "This is cool as fuck," I said.

Ares stepped around the dead arachnida and I got a glimpse of his eyes. Fire was dancing in them. Swirling energy from the too-short fight redirected itself instantly to the increasingly desperate area between my thighs.

"Your weapon should be warm, not cool."

I blinked at him, then realized what he meant. "The word cool means good in my world."

"That makes no sense."

"No, probably not." I shrugged. "I want to fight more stuff." *Or fuck you until you make me scream.* The alternative flashed unexpectedly into my head, and I felt my cheeks get hot. Fighting and fucking. I knew lots of fighters from the underground rings who connected the two, but I'd never been one of them. Until now, apparently.

"We should keep moving," Ares said.

We walked through the tunnel for what felt like an age, adrenaline and anticipation keeping my golden glow bright and hot. We passed the bodies of many dead things, presumably killed by the arachnida, but nothing living or dangerous. Eventually the tunnel began to narrow, and with some relief I saw a dim patch of daylight in the distance.

"Use your shield when we exit," grunted Ares.

"Yes, sir," I said, giving his armor-clad back a salute. I saw him shake his head a little.

When we emerged from the stinking cave tunnel it wasn't into forest as I had expected, but into a colossal stone ruin. The dusty expanse of broken rock cracked as our booted feet moved over it, the noise loud in the silence. I slowly stepped in a circle, surveying the wrecked structure.

It had once been a fighting pit, I was sure. But the stepped seats that must have lined one side had crumbled to nothing, revealing the maze of rooms beneath. The benches had remained a little intact on the other side, but I wouldn't have risked testing my weight on them. Opposite the tunnel mouth we'd just come from, the circular walls of the pit had disintegrated completely, and the oppressive forest had started to make progress in swallowing the pit, tree roots spreading across what would have been the pit floor like gnarled fingers reaching for us.

I sent out my senses, wary of the oxys, but I couldn't

hear any buzzing. I did hear something else though. Something that sounded like heavy breathing. The hairs stood up on my skin as a feeling I didn't recognize crawled over my body. It was as though I'd been doused in cold water, whilst an utterly certain knowledge that something awful was about to happen lodged in my mind.

"Ares? You feel that?" I whispered.

"I think we have found our dragon."

15

ARES

My desire for the woman raising her sword beside me was becoming so intense I was no longer sure I could manage it. And now I was certain it wasn't just physical. The thought of her coming to any harm caused a blind rage to stir inside me, and fear to coil through my gut. I was Ares, God of War. I was supposed to fear nothing.

I had to teach her to use her power. I had to make her stronger. Seeing her fight and use the power of war was addictive, her glow like a drug I couldn't get enough of. Her fierce spirit gleamed like no aura I had ever seen in a god before.

I needed more.

The sound of stone cracking and wood creaking snapped my attention to where the lethal forest was spilling into the ruined pit. The wood of the trees was moving, the gnarled roots lifting. With lethal grace, a creature morphed into being before us, from where it had been camouflaged so perfectly.

The dragon was made from wood, its body long and

sinewy like a snake's as it slithered into the space on the floor of the pit. Its reptilian head had a mane of sharp horns, and its enormous jaws were lined with ferocious teeth, bared bright at us. Vividly green eyes gleamed in the sides of its swaying head, and it snapped its wings out taut as it came to a stop. They too were born of the forest, the arch and boning of the wings made from thick branches, the matter filling the gaps like sheer leaves.

It was a magnificent looking beast.

"Oh my god, it's stunning," I heard Bella mutter, her voice awed.

"You're too kind," the dragon said. Bella made a small squeak. "You are here to seek me?"

"May we know your name?" I asked the beast loudly.

"Of course, if you are willing to part with yours."

Fierce intelligence flashed in the dragon's eyes. This would not be easy. All dragons were ancient and wise, and it was clear this one was no exception. "I am Ares, God of War, and this is Enyo, Goddess of War." Nerves skittered through me on saying Bella's real name. Depending on the age of this particular beast, he may know more about Bella than I wanted her to know. But if he was who I suspected he was, then it would do no good to lie to him.

The dragon swayed his head from side to side as he surveyed us. He was massive, his coiled body filling half the ruined pit. His tree-bark like scales made up rings that spiraled around his entire length, each individual scale as large as my chest.

"I am Dentro."

My stomach clenched at his words, my worst suspicions confirmed. "I have heard of you," I said. "You are ancient indeed."

"Far more ancient than you, little Olympian."

Anger surged through me, and I reached automatically for Bella's power. I felt no resistance from her. "The *little Olympians* rule the world, Dentro," I said loudly. The creature's lips curled back in an approximation of a smile, and he chuckled.

"Your father and his two brothers rule the world. You can't even hold onto your own power, it seems, let alone rule."

"At least I'm not hiding in a forest," I snarled. It didn't matter how old he was, I would not allow this animal to mock me.

"You are as bound to your situation as I am, little god."

"I am bound to nothing."

"Oh, but you are, Ares. You are bound by everyone stronger than you. You are bound by your own pride. You are bound by your own fear." He hissed the last word and rage erupted through me.

"I fear nothing!" I roared. Bella's power, my power, called to me as the rage spilled over, and she let me take it. I grew fast, tearing toward Dentro.

I heard a roar behind me, and in a flash Bella was running beside me, her face fierce and her skin glowing as gold as my armor. Her power was blinding, all consuming, and she drowned everything else out completely. This was war, and together we would win.

16

BELLA

The mix of fear and excitement I felt as we charged toward the dragon was intoxicating.

Dentro was the most incredible thing I had ever seen, and no amount of my imagination could have conjured him up. His snake-like body was made up of one long spiral of rich brown tree-bark which moved seamlessly as he reared back. Tufts of deep green moss were lodged between the rows of scales and I didn't know if it was growing from his body or had just been gathered up as he slithered through the forest. His wings spread wide behind him and my heightened senses brought the green substance between the bark-bones to life, veined like leaves and vivid in color. The horns around his head appeared to be growing, and large spikes that looked like murderous blades of grass were spreading between them.

He was nature personified, and at its most lethal.

"What do you seek?" His voice rang through the derelict pit, though his mouth didn't move with the words. Ares and I split, he running to the left and I to the right. I had a plan, and somehow I knew that Ares was thinking the same thing. The invisible cord connecting us was humming with life, power flowing between us.

When we didn't answer him, Dentro spoke again. "You will answer me."

The ground beneath us shook so hard I stumbled. Slamming down onto one knee, I only just managed to hang on to *Ischyros* and as I started to push myself to my feet the huge wooden body of the dragon whipped toward me. I tried to move, the war-sight kicking in instinctively and the world slowing around me. But it wasn't slow enough. Dentro's enormous tail coiled around my middle before I could fully stand, and I beat at it frantically with my sword. I tried to raise my shield to force him off me, but he squeezed tighter, the shield useless. The coarse wood of his scales scratched at my skin painfully, and suddenly I was lifted off my feet. With a lurching sensation I was swung around, coming to a stop directly in front of the dragon's gaping maw.

"Now, tell me, Enyo. What do you seek?"

"Dentro!" I could hear Ares bellowing somewhere below me. The tail that was wrapped around me was too huge to see past, and I only had my sword arm free. I smashed my weapon repeatedly against the wooden scales, but I knew it was doing no harm to the awesome beast.

"As you're new to this world, I'm going to let you in on a little secret." The dragon's voice was deep and seductive as he lifted me to look directly into one of his bright green eyes. "I'm even older than some of the Titans. You can't do any damage with that little blade of yours. Now, tell me what you seek."

"Scales," I barked, refusing to stop trying, pouring my power into the blows.

"*My* scales?" The dragon sounded amused.

"Yes."

"What in Olympus do you want my scales for?"

"We were challenged to get them by the king of this realm, Panic."

Something dark flashed in Dentro's eyes, and I stopped beating him with my sword for long enough to get my breath back. "That swine thinks he can use me as a toy in his games, does he? Hmmmm. Why did you accept his challenge?"

"To capture an escaped hell-demon and rescue my friend."

"Interesting. Is this true?"

He swung me violently to the side and moved his head fast, bringing it almost to the ground in front of Ares. The god looked furious.

"Yes! Release her!" He was easily ten feet tall, and his sword was as big as he was.

"No. But, as you are here on a genuinely noble cause, I will offer you an opportunity. How many scales of mine do you require?"

"Three," I said, biting back a curse as my thrashing scratched up more of the skin on my arms and shoulders.

"I will give you the scales, if you get something for me in return."

"We are not puppets!" roared Ares.

The dragon laughed, and the ground shook again, the ruins around us cracking and crumbling loudly. "Then I shall kill you both."

"You can't kill us, we're immortal," I said, resuming my battering with *Ischyros* with renewed vigor, ignoring the lacerations covering my skin.

"No, you're not. Not as long as you're sharing this strange power of yours."

My heart skipped a beat. "What?"

"I am ancient. I can see the cord between you. And only one of you can be a true god - which will leave the other as good as human. For one to be immortal, the other must die."

A trickle of dread slid down my spine. I *knew* he was speaking the truth. We'd as much as proved his words when we had almost drowned. Ares had to give up the power for me to breathe underwater.

But I had hoped that as I became stronger I would have enough power for both of us to be strong. For both of us to be immortal. I found Ares' eyes, my attacks with *Ischyros* momentarily forgotten.

Ares knew the words were true too. I could see it in his eyes. Perhaps he had already known.

"What do you want us to do?" Ares asked, his voice strong and proud, with no hint of the turmoil my brain was currently going through. We were back to only one of us being able to be strong, just as it had been when he'd first found me and wanted to kill me for my power. But things were different now. He was different now. Wasn't he?

"Is Panic watching us?"

"The world is watching us."

Dentro straightened, lifting me high with him, then bent his serpentine neck in a mock bow. "Hello, Olympus," he said, and bared his terrifying teeth. "I'm afraid this conversation must be private."

The sounds of branches cracking suddenly filled the air, and my mouth fell open as forest flowed into being around us, cocooning us in an enormous leafy bubble.

"What I am about to tell you is forbidden knowledge. But for too long I have spent my life a slave to another. I am willing to break my dragon's oath, in the hope that you are noble enough to honor me." Dentro lowered himself back to the ground, taking me with him, and to my surprise setting me back on the stone. His tail slowly uncoiled, and a wave of relief washed through me. Ares stepped closer and then stopped, almost as if he hadn't meant to.

"Heal your wounds," he snarled. I looked down at the smears of blood trickling from the many shallow cuts from the bark, but focused instead on Dentro.

"Who are you a slave to? Panic?" I asked the dragon.

His huge green eyes filled with anger. "When the Titans created beings as powerful as dragons, they needed to ensure we could be controlled. Panic has something of mine that allows him to keep me here, in his forest, to scare people and make himself look more powerful. His lethal pet. I can't leave here as long as he has it. I am trapped. A prisoner."

"What does he have?"

Dentro swooped his head lower, and I held out my weapon defensively as his massive mouth moved close to us. But as he opened his jaws, he spoke. "He stole my tooth." I realized he was showing us the gap in the row of shiny, razor sharp teeth, and I dropped my sword arm.

"Dragons can be controlled by whomever has their teeth?" For the first time since I'd met him, Ares sounded surprised.

"Yes. Teeth, and somewhat more unpleasantly, eyes. If you steal those from a dragon, you can impose your will on them enough to imprison them."

"Can he force you to do things you don't want to do?"

"Not unless he has all my teeth, no. I am too strong. You must swear never to share this knowledge. My kind's persecution and imprisonment depends on it."

"I swear," I said without hesitation. We both looked at Ares when he said nothing.

"I am bound to share knowledge like this with my father," he said slowly.

Dentro snorted. "Zeus is fully aware of this. How do you think he has kept the most powerful dragon in the world, Ladon, under his control for so long?"

Ares was still a moment, then nodded. "Fine. I swear it."

"Good. Steal my tooth back from Panic and return it to me. Free me from this dead place."

I felt my eyebrows raise. *"Steal* it from him? How?"

"I do not know. But as you two are the most powerful beings I have encountered in centuries, you are my best, and likely only, hope."

I didn't know if it was the deep, earnest tone to the dragon's voice, or if it was the fierce intelligence in his huge eyes, but I trusted him. I wanted to help him. Nobody should be held captive against their will. The dark days I had spent in prison flashed through my mind, and I looked to Ares. The god's voice sounded in my head.

"He could be trying to trick us. Dragons are famous for playing mind games."

"I like him," I answered mentally. *"I think we should do it."*

"Liking him has nothing to do with it."

"Yes it does."

Before Ares could say anything else, I spoke aloud. "We'll do it." Excitement danced in Dentro's eyes and his tail swished against the leaf bubble.

"You will earn my eternal gratitude if you succeed."

Ares growled beside me. I'd definitely pissed him off answering for both of us. But I didn't care. This was the right thing to do, I knew it was.

"How are we supposed to get your tooth back from here?" he ground out. "I assume if it was hidden in the forest you would have found it yourself by now."

"I believe Panic has a trophy room in his castle. It is my guess that my tooth will be there."

"We can't leave this forest without your scales."

Dentro paused, then fixed his eyes on me. "I will allow you to take the scales now. But you must promise to return with my tooth as soon as you can."

"Why would you trust us?" I asked, cocking my head.

Dentro stared at me, and I could feel his magic. Not working against me, messing with my mind or forcing me to feel anything fake, but more like an aura, or a glimpse of his soul. He *was* the personification of nature, wild and free and fierce and bright and strong. And he was trapped in a dark, lifeless forest, his essence fading with his hope. "I have no choice but to trust you," he said quietly.

I felt a kinship with this incredible, beautiful creature; I understood him, I felt his pain. I would help free him, whatever it took. I had to. I reached my hand up instinctively, and his massive tail flicked around, slowing to a stop an inch from my fingers.

"We'll get your tooth," I said.

"Thank you." His rough tail met my hand, and I felt a burst of bright hope spread through me, then a warm tingle in my skin as the cuts covering me instantly healed.

Somehow, I had just befriended an ancient, all-powerful dragon.

I freaking loved Olympus.

BELLA

When Dentro dissolved the leaf bubble hiding us from the rest of Olympus, I was clutching the three scales that the dragon had allowed me to gently prise from his tail. With one last pointed look, the magnificent creature melted back into the forest that was spilling into the derelict fighting pit, and I felt a pang of something as I watched him go. Excitement, or anticipation, or maybe both. I could feel Ares' anger with me rolling off him in waves, and I had absolutely zero idea how we would actually get our hands on Dentro's stolen tooth, but I knew I'd done the right thing. Whatever it was I had felt from the dragon was more than just awe or respect, and he deserved to be free.

It wouldn't be easy though. The whole of Olympus would have seen us disappear into the dragon's magic leaf bubble, and it would be obvious that we had not fought and defeated the creature. I took a deep breath, wishing I could talk to Ares in private, so that we could work out our story before we had to face the Lords.

"What do we tell Panic?" I asked him in my head, trying

to keep my face impassive.

"This is your mess. You work it out," he growled back. I locked eyes with him, and my stomach clenched as I saw how dark his were.

"Fine," I said, tightening my arms around the scales, then lifting them higher. "We have your scales, Panic!" I bellowed, holding up the massive sections of heavy tree bark.

"So I see." The Lord's voice echoed through the crumbling pit. "Congratulations. I'll give you the opportunity to tell us all how you managed to coax them out of the beast at a ball in your honor this evening. Put the scales on the ground."

I bent down, doing as he asked. The second they were out of my grip, everything flashed white and we were no longer in Skotadi.

～

I let out a long breath as I looked around at the tiny wooden cabin with the ugly couches.

"If the ball Panic is throwing is at his castle, then that's the perfect opportunity to find the tooth!" I said excitedly, turning to Ares. I almost took a step back as he pulled his helmet off, his expression was so fierce.

"You are reckless and foolish and selfish!"

"What?"

"We are not here to do favors for dragons stupid enough to get themselves trapped! We are supposed to be getting my power back!"

Indignation rolled through me as I took a step closer to the fuming god. "No, we're supposed to be stopping the Keres demon and saving the Guardians. Your Trident of power was an added bonus, if I remember correctly. And besides, it's the right thing to do."

"Whatever the point of our quest, it has nothing to do with damn dragons."

"How the hell else were we going to win that Trial? Dentro could have killed me with one squeeze! He was too strong for us to defeat, and you know it. So did Panic, that's why he sent us there."

Ares stamped his foot and flames burst to life in his eyes as I felt a pull in my gut. I stepped closer to him, as though the pull was physical. "We could have defeated him! We could defeat any foe!"

"Look, Mr Stampy, he nearly fucking killed me. One squeeze, and I was a goner. Panic set us an impossible task, and we won. Take the damn victory." A solitary drum beat loud in the distance. Ares closed the gap between us.

"He would not have killed you. You are immortal." His voice was just as angry, but no longer loud. Fire leaped in his eyes.

"Then he would have killed you instead. Only one of us can be immortal, remember?" I answered, my voice needlessly breathless. My heart was beginning to pound in my chest. He was beautiful. So damned beautiful.

"We need to finish the next Trial, and get your friend and my power back. We do not have time to help the dragon."

His words were like ice water over the heat in my core. "What? No, we get Dentro's tooth. Now, tonight, at this ball."

"Bella, we are not risking the Lords' wrath before these Trials are over." Fury swept through me like a freight train, and I had taken three steps back from him before I'd even realized I'd moved.

"I gave Dentro my word, dammit, and I am not letting him down. *Not risking the Lords' wrath? Do you fear them?*"

I knew the question would anger him, and I was right. His whole body swelled with rage, but when he tugged on my power, I slammed my shields down. His glow dimmed, and his face darkened further.

"It is not the Lords I fear," he hissed, and even without any power he was menacing as hell.

"Then why aren't you celebrating this victory? We won the damn Trial! Why aren't you reveling in the opportunity to take something from that asshole that he values, to return an almighty creature back to full power, to do some fucking good for once!"

"Because we do not know the cost!" he roared back at me.

"Who cares? You're a fucking god, what can they take from you? You've already lost your power, and the Lords can't kill you - the Olympians wouldn't allow it! What cost could be too high?"

"You!"

I blinked at his shouted word, the fire in his irises burning fierce with emotion. "Me?"

"You." His voice was ragged, like the word had been torn forcibly from his throat. My pulse was racing now, a hope I had never known swamping my chest, making my own throat tighten.

"Ares... What do you want?" I half whispered the question, desperate to hear one word in answer. More than anything in the world, I wanted him to say *you*. I wanted him to say he feared losing me. That whatever it was between us was more than physical, that it wasn't just my imagination running rampant. His lips parted and my breath caught. *Say you want me as much as I want you.*

"Knock knock?" I almost jumped out of my skin as Eris' voice rang loudly through the room, then she appeared with an overly bright flash. Disappointment crashed through me, and I heard Ares let out a hiss of anger as I focused on the Goddess of Chaos. Her eyes went wide and she clasped her hands to her lips in mock embarrassment.

"Oh my, oh my, I've interrupted something! I'm so sorry, sweeties." Her smile reached all the way to her eyes, and I took a heaving breath as my pulse continued its gallop. Eris' curly hair was piled even higher on her head than usual, and she was wearing a long, tight dress that glittered with black sequins and barely contained her huge chest.

"You're dressed nice," I said, scrabbling for something normal and not-awkward to say.

"Thanks, sweetie. I'm here to help you do the same. All the gods are coming to the ball, and whilst I'm a fan of this look, I thought you might do a bit better this time."

"Er, thanks."

"I thought you were in hiding," growled Ares.

"I was. Now I'm not."

Unable to stand still, I walked to the bed, dropping my sword onto the comforter, and starting to absently pull bits of forest out of my hair. Waves of emotion were rolling through me, desire and anger balling up into something difficult to contain. It made me furious that Ares didn't want to help Dentro, but was the reason truly that he feared for me? Nobody had feared for my safety in my whole life. Joshua had cared about me, but actually feared for me? I didn't think so.

Dragging my thoughts into line, I tried to work out what to do and say next.

Whatever Ares' motivations were for not wanting to help the dragon, I was getting that tooth. That much I knew for sure. And so long as Eris was here, I was pretty sure she could help.

"Do you know where this ball is going to be?" I asked her, crossing my fingers she was going to say Panic's castle.

"Here in Dasos I believe; Terror's kingdom is not suited to balls."

I suppressed a desire to ask more about Terror's kingdom, and nodded. "Good. I hope it's not in that drafty, crumbling place we were in before when he announced the Trial."

"I doubt it, Panic will want to show off to the gods."

Excellent.

There was a flash of teal, and Zeeva appeared on the bed before me. My heart did a small flutter at the surprise, and my hands tensed into fists.

"I wish everyone would stop doing that," I snarled. Zeeva flicked her tail when she looked at Eris, then focused her almond eyes on me.

"What deal did you make with the dragon?" she asked bluntly, her voice crystal clear in my head.

"It's nice to see you safe and sound too," I said, rolling my eyes.

"You went into the creature's leaf shield his captive, and came out a victor. You offered it something in return for those scales. What was it?"

"That's what I want to know too," smiled Eris, and sat down gracefully on the peach couch.

"Stop listening in!"

"I can't help it."

"Bella agreed to steal something valuable from Panic's castle for the dragon." I looked at Ares in surprise as he spoke. He didn't sound angry any more. In fact, he sounded proud. "And we're going to do it tonight, at the ball, with help from both of you."

My mouth fell open as I stared at the warrior god. His eyes flicked to mine as Eris spoke.

"I do love a bit of theft," she said.

"I know, sister. Your help will be invaluable to us."

"And what do I get in return, little brother?"

"What do you want?"

"Let me think about it," she purred.

"Fine. Don't take too long." Ares turned to Zeeva. "Cat?"

"Theft is not in my remit," she said haughtily.

"But helping Bella is. And we only won that Trial because she made this deal." His eyes locked on mine as he said the words. Was that another Ares-style apology? He *had* just admitted out loud that we would have lost to Dentro.

"I will do what I can to help, if it does not compromise my morals," sighed Zeeva.

"Thank you," I told her. *"You've changed your tune."* I projected the words to Ares silently.

"My anger was misplaced. I do not like meeting beings stronger than I," he answered in my head.

"Me neither."

"I will endeavor to enjoy upsetting Panic by stealing from him. You were right. This will be a victory, of sorts."

"Say that again."

"Say what?"

"The bit about me being right."

18

BELLA

"OK. This is how it needs to go."

We all sat on the squishy couches, listening to Eris.

"Zeeva. If you don't want to be involved in any actual stealing, then we could use you now. All three of us would be noticed by Panic if we entered his castle, as we share his power. But you should be able to get in undetected. Go now, and find out where he keeps his trophies and valuables."

After a small pause, the cat stood and stretched. *"I suppose that is manageable,"* she said, then vanished in a puff of teal.

"You two," said Eris, a smile pulling at her lips as she looked between Ares and me. "You two will need a credible reason to disappear from the party." Her eyes shone with mischief. "Which means making a show of wanting to be alone together. Based on that kiss the whole of Olympus saw, I'm assuming that won't be too difficult for either of you?"

I felt myself blush, and avoided looking at Ares.

"I'll take that as a no," she laughed. "I'll do my best to distract Panic, and trust me, I can come up with some very distracting scenarios, but then it'll be up to you to steal your prize. Do you care if you are caught?"

Ares' shoulders straightened. "Panic can't do a thing about it, I am his ruler."

"We care about getting the prize safely away from the castle," I interrupted. "The idea is to do that without drawing any attention to what we are doing." I looked pointedly at Ares. We'd sworn to keep what we had learned a secret, and that meant we had to avoid questions being asked publicly.

"OK. It's likely you won't be able to flash if you're in a vault or secure place. So you may have to sneak your way out of there." Eris looked at me.

I nodded. "OK."

"We should start getting you ready." Eris stood abruptly, and swirled her hand around until a ball of fabric appeared in it, growing as she swirled more. It was the same purple as the dress that the version of me in my vision of war had on.

"What do I need to do?" I asked her.

Her lips puckered as she looked me up and down. "Keep getting all that forest-shit out of your hair, then shower."

When I entered the main room of the cabin wrapped only in a towel after showering, I saw Zeeva curled up on the bed. "How did it go?" I asked her, excited to find out what she had learned.

"Panic's trophy room is at the top of the third smallest

tower in the castle, on the north-east side. The staircase is rigged so that one false step will send you into a pit below full of oxys. The door at the top can only be entered by someone who possesses the power of Panic. The trophies within are encased in unbreakable glass."

I could feel my face falling as she spoke, each sentence sounding worse than the last.

"It's nothing we can't handle," said Ares, his voice brimming with confidence. I looked to him in surprise. I had expected him to go all *I-told-you-so* on my ass, not sound excited. He wasn't wearing his armor, and my gaze snagged on the open collar of his shirt. "We do possess the power of Panic, it feeds into the power of war."

"What about the staircase?"

"There will be a way through. We will have to outsmart it." His eyes gleamed with excitement, and as I looked into them I felt my stomach flutter.

"And the unbreakable glass?"

"There is nothing the God of War can't break. Trust me." The look on his face sent thrills running through me. I knew, fundamentally, that a man telling me there was nothing he couldn't break shouldn't turn me on. But hell, the truth was that had I been wearing panties, they might have melted off, such was the heat he fired within me. His eyes raked over my bare shoulders, before coming back to my face, and I felt my tongue dart out to wet my lips. I hadn't seen him like this except after the Hydra fight, and his energy was infectious. A buzz of anticipation rolled off him, and I absorbed it greedily.

.   .   .

"Ares, you need to leave. I need to dress Bella. And the way you two are looking at each other, I do not want to be here when she drops that towel. You're my brother. Gross."

I felt my cheeks flush as Ares moved toward the door. "Fine. I will be no longer than thirty minutes."

I heard the door slam as he left, and I reached for him with my mind, unable to help myself. *"I would have dropped the towel for you. If we had been alone."*

I didn't expect him to reply, and I almost let out a moan when his husky voice filled my head a second later. *"I would have ripped it from you with my teeth."*

The whole time Eris was tightening bits of fabric around my body, fluffing skirts and doing something almost-but-not-quite painful to my hair, all I could think about was Ares. Naked. Desire was spilling over every useful or rational thought I had about the heist we were about to try and pull off, and I was unable to concentrate on anything other than the memory of the two kisses we had shared.

I wanted to keep talking to him in my mind, but his answer had been so hungry, so unexpected and so sexy that instead I just hung on to it, replaying the growl of need I had heard in his tone that mirrored my own intensity.

"I don't know why Ares doesn't just tell Panic to give him whatever it is. He is his ruler, after all." Zeeva sounded bored, but I was sure I could hear an undercurrent to her tone.

"Nobody in this realm is honest, least of all those in charge," said Eris. "He would just lie and say he doesn't have it, and Ares is not currently strong enough to challenge him."

"What if I gave him my strength?" I asked.

"No. You are probably level in power with the Lords right now. At his full power Ares would be many times stronger."

"Oh. Are the Lords immortal?"

"No. Not as such. Their hosts can be killed, but the power they embody returns to Ares, until he bestows it on someone new."

My stomach skittered uneasily. "Is that what would happen to my power if I die?"

"Yes."

Which was why Ares had originally planned to kill me, I thought, with an awkward stomach twist. "Why didn't Ares try to kill them and get their power when his was stolen?"

"You'd have to ask him that. But he was the one who chose to bestow Pain, Panic and Terror on other souls in the first place. They are not powers he is interested in possessing. Besides, until you showed up he was too weak to fight them and win anyway."

I glanced at Eris over my shoulder, where she was tightening a choker necklace around my throat. "Did Ares bestow my power on me, like the Lords?"

"Bella, I honestly have no idea where you have come from. I thought I did for a while, but I was wrong."

Zeeva gave a loud yawn, and we both looked at her. *"My mistress knows."*

Excitement flashed through me, making my skin feel tight all of a sudden. "Tell me!"

"I can't. She says you must find out for yourself."

Frustration made my hands fist, and I ground my teeth. "Why mention it then?" I spat. "Just to piss me off?"

"Oh, there is plenty to be gleaned from what your cat has just said," grinned Eris. "If Hera knows where you came from, then we can safely assume she knows where you'll end up. Or at least who you'll end up with."

"What?"

"Hera is the goddess of marriage. And when gods marry, they are bonded. For life. Physically and mentally."

I felt my chest constricting at Eris' words, suddenly distinctly aware of the cord I could always feel connecting me to Ares. But that was our shared power, nothing more. Wasn't it? "What are you saying?"

"Just that Hera knows when two gods are meant to be together," Eris shrugged. Her eyes were sparkling with amusement.

"Gods can't just go around bonding people without their permission!" I spluttered.

"No, of course they can't," said Zeeva calmly. *"My mistress only ever bonds deities who are deeply in love."*

Relief swept through me. It was one thing to wrangle my head into understanding my desire for the ridiculously gorgeous warrior god. That sort of made sense. He was hot as hell, strong, fierce, proud.

It was quite another thing to contend with the thought of being in love with him. He had the emotional capacity of a teenage boy, and didn't seem to have much interest in basic human rights. Not exactly husband material.

"Will Hera be at the ball tonight?" I asked Zeeva hopefully.

"No."

"What's wrong with her? She's not been seen since Zeus fled," said Eris. Her tone was casual, but I could tell she was burning with curiosity. I had to admit to being pretty curious myself.

"She is unwell."

"Olympians gods do not get unwell," said Eris, her eyebrows raised and her hands on her hips.

Zeeva said nothing, just rested her head on her neat little paws. It was exactly the sort of position I would have cooed over when I thought she was just my grumpy pet cat.

"Erm, Zeeva, when you lived in my apartment, did you like being petted?" I asked hesitantly.

After a long pause, the cat answered. *"It wasn't so bad, I suppose."*

19

ARES

Bella was stunning. So stunning that I almost felt inadequate in my armor beside her. Eris had fashioned her hair with some sort of delicate gold headdress, which caged in her pale curls. Tiny glittering swords hung from the sweeping metal curves, catching the light that came from her glowing skin. Her dress was fit for a goddess too. It was purple, and like the last one it was tight around her curvaceous chest, then cascaded down in streams of gold and purple at the skirt. She wore no sleeves and the top of the dress was cut enticingly low. Around her slender neck she wore a tight gold choker, also hung with small glittering swords. It was all I could do to keep my hands off her, instead clenching them hard at my sides.

I had never wanted anybody so badly in my life. In fact, each time my eyes fell on her impossibly beautiful face, I questioned whether I had wanted anything at all as much as I wanted Bella. The thought of her with someone else made rage flood through my veins. She was mine.

Only, she wasn't. And when she found out what I was

hiding from her, the truth about where she had come from, she never would be mine.

I had to stop her finding out. Eris was close to the truth, I could see it in her eyes, hear it in her teasing voice. Would she tell Bella? Was her fondness for me stronger than her need to create chaos?

I knew the answer to that already. Nothing was greater than Eris' desire to create chaos.

Zeeva would find out from her master, my mother, soon enough. Hera knew exactly where Bella had come from. But for some reason, she had not yet shared what she knew with the cat. Why not? And why had she not spoken to me? A flutter of concern for her shimmied through me.

I had long since learned that my mother loved me no more or less than all the subjects she ruled over, and significantly less than she loved my father, Zeus. My parents were stronger than I, and affection within families did not function in Olympus like it did in Bella's world. They were my superiors, authorities that I bowed down to, and not a lot more. I respected that, and always had. War and Chaos were born of the same power but unlike my sister, I knew the importance of order and respect. It was one of the things that made me so strong.

You are not strong any more. You are weak without your power. The voice inside me clawed at my mind, just as it had since the fight with my father. But something was different now.

It was true that I was powerless. Dependent on a woman who should hate me. Dependent on a woman I was becoming obsessed with.

But a slow rumble rolled through me, starting in my

gut and spreading through my chest, up into my throat. A collection of those invasive new emotions.

Excitement. Anticipation. *Nervousness.*

How had I never known these sensations before? We might fail to steal the tooth. I might fall into a pit of creatures who would send me mad for eternity. I might be forced into a panic so intense that I ended up a trophy in Panic's collection. The Lord we planned to cross was as strong as Bella and I were, though he wasn't sure enough of that to test it yet.

But the thrill of that knowledge was intoxicating. I had spent hundreds of years doling out punishment, instilling the need for confrontation into my citizens, overseeing battles and fights that were sometimes breathtaking in their beauty. But despite the strengthening surge of power those events gave me, I had been endlessly unsatisfied. Nothing had stirred so fiercely inside me, brought the light of every moment to life, or relieved me of my mental inhibitions like mortality had. My mind was racing with thoughts I would never have permitted before, almost all of them ending with Bella wrapped around me, her heart beating in time with mine, lost to the fire and the drums, and the pleasure. I would never have permitted thoughts like these before, dismissing them as useless fantasies that did not further my goals or make me stronger or give me power. But now, I reveled in them. Because for the first time in my long life, there was a chance I would only ever experience them in my imagination. I might die before I got what I wanted.

I was not mistaking the intense feeling of being alive for a desire for death. I would do whatever it took to live, and I knew that it would take something truly mighty to end my life. Power or none, I was still the ancient and immeasurably experienced God of War. But even that confidence was new, since having my power stolen. Aphrodite had said I was a wolf without its fangs or claws and I had believed her. But now, Bella was making me wonder. She had survived and fought her way through so much, more than she even knew, with barely a hint of power. She had become an incredible fighter, with an unbreakable spirit, without being a goddess. Was there a chance I could do the same?

With any luck, I wouldn't have to find out. We would win the Ares Trials, and I would receive the Trident of power. Even better, my father would come to his damn senses and return my own power to me.

Thinking about the future made my eyes flick automatically to Bella. If she found out what I had done, she would not feature in my future. In fact, she could ensure there was no future for me at all.

She realized I was looking at her, and her gaze locked on mine. All sensible thoughts fled, replaced by a single, burning need. She was mine.

I would have to make her understand, have to make her forgive me. She was mine.

"Right, I'm ready now. Let's go." Eris stepped out of the bathroom, and I took a deep breath as subtly as I could manage, setting my churning thoughts aside and focusing on the task at hand.

It was time to put on a show.

20

BELLA

I thought that I knew to what to expect when Eris flashed us to the ball. I'd been to too many of these soirees now. But what I saw when we arrived took my breath away.

The arched ballroom was in a castle that was about as far from crumbling as it could get. It reminded me of a church, with high vaulted ceilings and a mezzanine floor than ran around the perimeter of the room ten feet above the floor. The forest existed within the walls of the castle, every stone surface adorned with creeping vines that flowered with buds and petals the color of blood. The vines wrapped themselves around the balustrades that lined the grand central staircase leading up to the mezzanine, then wound their way across parts of the flagstone covered floor, and up the arched ceilings.

The room was filled with people and creatures, of every color, shape and size I could imagine, and all were dressed magnificently. The serving satyrs and tree dryads I'd seen before were moving between groups, carrying trays covered in drinks and exotic looking snacks.

My brow furrowed as I stared at the ceiling. The vines were moving. Some sort of string instrument sounded as I watched, then many more joined in and I gasped as a woman melted out of the foliage high above us. A smattering of applause sounded, and then the music drowned it out, an operatic voice joining the string instruments as the woman began to lower herself to the ground using a vine that appeared to be doing her bidding. When she was halfway down, she stopped, reached out her other hand, and a vine that had been wrapped around the mezzanine railings uncoiled itself and whipped toward her.

She had dark skin and wore a glittering green sheath dress that showed off insanely lovely legs. Slowly, she began to swing between the two vines. Then, when the music hit a high note, she let go, flipping herself high into the air, then turning mid-flight, her skirt whipping out and sparkling as she spun. I felt my hand go to my mouth as she fell, but before she even got close to the ground, more vines flew toward her, and she caught them, revolving and twirling in the air.

It was like the most magical Cirque du Soleil ever, and I could have watched her acrobatics for hours, but I felt a tug on my elbow.

When I looked down, Poseidon, Hades and Persephone were standing in front of me. A wave of deference washed over me, the need to worship these almighty beings built into their very presence. I bowed.

"You are doing well, both of you," said Poseidon. His white hair was pulled back into a tail, and he had a gleaming trident in his hand. He wore a toga, but I could see leather and metal strapping where the fabric parted over his chest.

"What happened with the dragon?" Hades' voice came from his smoky form.

"That is between the dragon and us," said Ares. Poseidon's expression tightened a moment, but then relaxed.

"As you wish. We have been searching for Zeus' ship. We believe you are right; he's using Guardian magic to mask himself, just as the Guardians mask magic in the mortal world."

"Will that harm the Guardians?" I asked quickly.

Poseidon looked at me. "I don't know."

"I believe not. He needs them alive and healthy to use their magic." Hades' spoke with a softness I didn't expect, and I nodded gratefully at him.

"How come I saw Joshua's body dead in my world, but alive on those stone beds?" I asked. The question had been lurking at the back of my mind for days.

"Guardians, along with a few other beings, can move their soul between multiple bodies. They can't flash, so they keep hosts in Olympus and the mortal world, so that they can move between the two."

"Like clones?" The idea was crazy.

Persephone nodded. "Weird, isn't it?"

Before I could agree, Poseidon spoke. "My general came across the demon once, but there's been no sign of Zeus."

"I assume they didn't capture it, or this would be over." Ares' voice was level.

Poseidon shook his head tersely. "No. She is strong."

Thinking about the demon made my skin feel like it was burning. If Poseidon's general couldn't capture her, what hope did I have?

"Ares, there's something you need to know." Poseidon's

tone was awkward, and I suddenly felt like I shouldn't be present for this conversation.

"What?" he asked, standing taller, his demeanor all arrogance that I wasn't sure I believed.

"We may be wrong but... My general reported that the demon used power she shouldn't have. Power she recognized."

Every muscle in Ares' body stiffened. "That's... That's unlikely."

Poseidon's eyes softened. "Ares, I'm sorry. You taught my general yourself, and have sparred with her many times since. She was certain it was your power signature."

An uneasy, sick feeling gurgled through my center, and I was sure it was coming from Ares somehow, but I didn't fully understand what the gods were talking about. Ares looked at me.

"It sounds like my father may have given my power to the demon."

~

I wished I could see Ares' face behind his helmet. All I had access to was his eyes though, and they were as cold and hard as I'd ever seen them.

"I must speak with Eris. Thank you for telling me this," Ares said stiffly, and the other two gods nodded and turned away. Persephone caught my eyes.

"You're doing great," she said with a small smile.

"Thanks," I said, then turned to follow Ares as he stamped toward where his sister was chatting with a pretty man with white wings.

"Eris, I need a word. Now," Ares snapped, yanking her back by the shoulder. A wave of tingling heat washed over me as she turned, fury in her eyes. It faded though as she saw his expression, a smile pulling at her purple-painted lips instead.

"Oh my, what's got into you?" she asked, as he pulled her away from the man, stopping when we reached a narrow Greek style column with warm orange flames flickering on the top.

"You knew. You knew what Zeus had done with my power." His words dripped with icy fury, but I felt no pull in my gut.

Eris' smile slipped for a microsecond. "Yes. I told you I would trade the information, and you refused me. That's your problem, not mine."

"I thought I could trust you," he snarled.

"Then you're a bigger fool than I thought you were," she answered, her eyes as hard as his.

There was an abrupt yank on my power, and Ares shone bright gold.

"If you still want my help tonight, I'd advise calming down, little brother."

Ares' eyes flicked to mine, and he let go of Eris' shoulder. "I will be back in ten minutes, and then we shall put our plan into action." Without waiting for an answer, he strode away. I moved to go after him, but Eris grabbed my elbow as I turned.

"Let him cool off. You need him at full strength tonight."

"I'm assuming that it's pretty bad to give a god's power to someone else?" I asked her.

Her eyes dipped to the floor before she answered me. "It shouldn't be possible. Only a being as powerful as Zeus could do it and it breaks one of the few rules the gods have." She let out a sigh. "A god's power is part of them.

It's the height of fucked up to steal power and then give it to someone else."

"And it was his own father who did it," I said quietly.

"Yeah."

All the angry pride she'd projected at her brother was gone, and I really wanted to believe that she hadn't told Ares because she knew it would upset him. But then why would she pretend to be such a bitch about it?

"Can we still trust you to help us tonight?" I asked her quietly.

"I said I would, and I will. I'm quite used to my brother's temper tantrums." She rolled her eyes and swigged from her glass, and I buried the desire to defend him.

"Good," I said, and headed into the crowd to find the God of War.

"You know, in London we would call your sister a twat. And your dad a total and utter fuckwit."

Ares turned away from the vine covered wall he was staring at to face me. I had expected to see fiery fury in his eyes but there was a hollowness in them that caused a desperate pang of sadness to lance through my heart.

"My father has no duty to treat me differently than anyone else in Olympus. He has broken too many rules already, what is one more to further his plan? I was once going to let Hippolyta die, because the rules of a game demanded it." I was certain I could hear shame in his voice.

"Do you regret that?"

"I am glad she lived."

"That's not an answer."

"Regret is the wrong word. I wonder though, if there is a better way to live my life."

I may only have been around this guy a short time, but the impact of his words were not lost on me. The ancient, angry, arrogant god I had met in London would never have uttered that sentence.

"We'll get your power back from her. I'll help you get it back. I swear."

The hollow look in his eyes flickered, then in a heartbeat was replaced with an *inferno*. My lips parted in surprise as he pulled off his helmet, before closing the distance between us in one stride.

"You are changing me, Bella," he breathed, his hand moving to the back of my head, and pulling my mouth so close to his that I felt his hot breath mingle with my own. "I need you." His words were the most intense aphrodisiac imaginable. Nobody had ever needed me. And sure as fuck nobody like Ares.

The drums of war leaped to life in my ears, no slow and steady build up this time - they were as fast and hard as my heart felt in my chest. As Ares' lips claimed mine liquid fire rushed through my body, building deliciously in my core. I kissed him back as desperately as he kissed me, reveling in his hunger as his tongue flicked against mine, and he pulled me as close to him as I could get, as though any gap between us was intolerable.

A faint part of my brain became aware that we were very much in public, and I moved back an inch, sliding a sideways glance at the room.

Every guest in the ballroom was staring at us. My gaze found the three Lords of War in the crowd easily, but thankfully Aphrodite was nowhere to be seen. I took a massive breath as Ares stood straight.

"Is this not a celebration? Let us dance!" My mouth fell open as the God of War roared the words, and a vibrant tune started up immediately in response. Mercifully, most of the guests turned away from us, finding partners quickly and spinning around the room in elegant maneuvers.

"Well, that's one way to get rid of them," I muttered.

"The Lords will be over very soon," Ares said, tipping my chin up to look into my eyes.

"Aphrodite isn't here," I said.

"No." His expression changed, a darkness taking his eyes a moment, and words tumbled from my lips.

"Do you love her?" I totally failed to keep my emotion from the words. I was well beyond playing it cool. He knew I wanted him, and it was pointless to try to hide it. But if he still wanted Aphrodite, I needed to know now. How could he not? She was the freaking Goddess of Love, the most beautiful being in the world.

"No."

Blissful relief crashed over me and I realized just how much I had feared how far Aphrodite's hold on him went. I couldn't respect a man who let a woman treat him like she had - and I wanted so, so badly to let myself respect Ares. The glimpses of him under the armor, both physically and mentally, made me desperate for more. Tiny hints of his sense of humor, his tenderness, his intelligence, were starting to take their place beside the awe I had for him as a warrior, and I knew I was at real risk of falling for him if I saw much more.

"Good," I said, and couldn't help the smile spreading across my face.

21

BELLA

"The Lords are coming," he said, then ducked down to pick up his helmet. With a shimmer and a tiny fizz in my gut, he turned it into the headband and fixed it on his forehead, before reaching one arm around my waist and lifting my other hand in his, then twirling me around in something akin to a waltz.

"You dance?" I laughed with astonishment.

"When I need an excuse to be close to you, I dance," he said. His words caused a frisson of pleasure to flutter through my chest.

"And an excuse to avoid the Lords of War," I added, as we spun our way past them. I threw a sarcastic smile at the three of them over Ares' broad shoulder as we merged into the crowd of other dancers. Many of them looked at us, and I supposed that whipping his helmet off and kissing girls wasn't a usual activity for Ares at parties. I moved closer to him, almost possessively at the thought, wishing his armor wasn't blocking my skin from touching his. It was warm though. I drew on my power just enough to add half a foot to my height. Enough that I could press my mouth close to his neck.

"I want you out of this armor," I whispered into his throat, so quietly I wasn't even sure he would hear me.

I felt his arm tense around my waist, pulling me even tighter to him, then he twirled fast, making me giggle as he almost took me off my feet. When his eyes met mine as we slowed, his hunger was evident.

"This armor is the only thing keeping me from taking you right now," he growled. Heat flooded my core, and I felt every muscle in my body clench.

"Not all these lovely people?" I said, trying to keep my voice flirty instead of desperate, and raising it just enough that others could hear. "I'd much rather we were alone." That was the plan, as Eris had instructed us. Make it look like we couldn't keep our hands off each other, make it clear we were going somewhere to be alone together. But at that point, I wasn't speaking scripted lines. I'd have done anything to be alone with him.

He stared into my eyes as we danced to the cheerful song that I could barely hear over the beating drums. When he spoke, his lips didn't move and I realized only I could hear him. *"This dragon better appreciate this damn tooth. Because this is the strongest test of my will power I have ever experienced."*

I bit down on my bottom lip and replied, wanting to push him. *"I don't know what you mean? What's testing your will so bad, armor-boy?"*

Desire flashed hungrily in his eyes. *"You. You are fucking irresistible."*

"You cursed," I whispered aloud, smiling from ear to ear. Ares wanted me just as much as I wanted him, and the knowledge was the most delicious thing in the world.

"It's your bad influence," he said, then his mouth claimed mine again, and just like the very first time we had kissed, that feeling of perfect rightness overwhelmed me. This was where I was meant to be, in Ares' arms.

The kiss was too short, but the raging inferno in Ares' eyes told me why. He hadn't been exaggerating, he really was struggling to contain himself. I moved out of his embrace and tugged him by the hand toward the grand staircase. He followed me, and I felt a glow of satisfaction at the surprised murmurs of the other guests. Ares was mine, and they all knew it. The staircase was lined with a moss green carpet that my gold high heels sank into, but I hardly noticed. All I was aware of was the hulking god's finger entwined with mine as he moved behind me. Yes, this was all part of the plan. But holy hell, it could so easily turn into more.

There were guests all along the long mezzanine floor, some leaning over the railings, some watching the acrobat, entranced. A few turned our way, then snickered behind their hands as we half-raced to the nearest finely-carved wooden doorway. There was another staircase through it, this one narrow and made of paler wood. I had already known that, because Zeeva had told us how to get to the north-east tower before we left. Up two more flights of steps, take a long corridor to the left, go through a door that would lead us to a small outside bridge, which would take us to the tower we needed. Once in, we had to find a tapestry of a kraken, which hid a passageway leading to more stairs. The trick staircase that could kill us.

We half ran up the two longs flights of steps, and I almost gasped with relief to see the corridor was completely empty, both to the left and right. I turned to Ares, and with a pull in my gut his armor vanished, his headband glowing brightly for a moment. Then he closed the gap between us, pressing me hard into the vine-covered wall behind me. He pushed one hand into my hair, the other caressing my cheek.

"You are intoxicating," he breathed, as the drums beat.

"So are you," I replied, and he was. I reached up to touch his hard, stubbled jaw, his beautiful eyes mesmerizing.

"I need you. Now."

Fuck, was I ready. The ache of need in my core was almost painful, my lungs barely working properly as my chest heaved. "I'm yours."

With a noise between a groan and a snarl, Ares dropped his head, and kissed my throat, wrapping one arm around my waist and pulling me tight to him. I let out a moan as I felt his hardness through the thin material of his slacks, then fumbled to get my hands between our bodies, needing to touch him. He pulled back a little and kissed lower, across my collarbone and down towards my tightly encased breasts. My skin was alive with sensation, and every time his lips landed I could feel sparks of plea-sure run straight to my sex, making my legs feel weak.

My hands reached the waist of his pants, and I couldn't resist running them up over his solid abs. He was so hard, so strong, so fierce. So perfect.

"God," I moaned, and he moved again, kissing me on the mouth hard. With an anticipation that blew the excite-ment I usually felt before any fight totally out of the water, I reached my hand into his pants. I don't know what noise I made as his kiss intensified, but I had sure as fuck never made it before.

Perfect was an understatement.

"Please," I gasped, breaking the kiss and tugging his

glorious length free of the fabric of his pants. "I need you." He growled something unintelligible, then lifted me off the ground with the arm he had around my waist. I squeaked as my hand was pulled from him, then wrapped my legs around his solid middle, pulling at my skirts so that there was no fabric between us. I wound my own arms around his neck and tipped my head back against the wall as I felt the tip of him against my aching wetness.

"Ares," I breathed, barely even aware I was speaking. I had never needed anything so badly in my life. I'd have given up anything, anything at all, for this moment.

The ground shook beneath us, the wall I was pressed against rumbling loudly.

"You two need to move, now!" Eris' voice lanced through my passion, and Ares froze.

"Shit! Shit, shit, shit!" I cursed as he looked at me, clearly as unwilling to stop what we were about to do as I was. Then the floor actually lurched, and Ares stumbled to the side. I swung my legs to the ground to try to help steady us, my face and body aflame as I brushed against him, but then we were tipping the other way, and it was all I could do to stay on my feet. With a small shimmer Ares' armor was back in place, and grabbing for each other's hands we began to run down the corridor.

"He knows we're here," said Ares, his voice as strained as my tingling body felt.

"Asshole," I spat.

"I thought that was reserved for me?" Ares called, his pace quickening as the corridor lurched again in the opposite direction, flinging us toward the opposite wall. We were too quick though, both of us keeping our footing as we raced on, our hands still locked together.

"Not anymore."

At the end of the foliage-covered corridor was a steel door, and we hurled ourselves against it as the floor achieved its most violent lurch yet.

"Is the whole castle moving?" I panted, as we both tugged at a massive ornate door handle, my feet scrabbling to keep me upright as the floor moved.

"I don't know. This is locked." Ares let go of my hand, and an instant sense of despair gripped me. His eyes darted to mine, confirming he felt it too, before he pulled his sword from the sheath at his waist that had appeared with his magic armor. I let him draw on my power as he slammed the blade down onto the handle. The metal severed from the door, and I leaned forward to tug out the mechanism inside that was keeping it locked. The second the door swung open freezing air washed over me, and I was looking out at a stone bridge being hammered by relentless rain. A medieval-looking stone tower was attached to the other end of the bridge, which had no sides or railings. I felt my stomach churn as the corridor we were still standing in lurched to the other side, but the bridge stayed still. It wasn't the whole castle moving, just the tower we were in.

Before fear could get the better of me, or I could be thrown on my ass by the lurching corridor, I stepped out onto the bridge.

"Fuck, it's cold!" I yelled, as freezing rain pelted down on me. I took a step forward and my heel instantly slid on the sopping-wet stone. I ducked, pulling off both my shoes, and as I straightened a huge gust of wind hit me. My heart leaped into my throat as I teetered, clutching my shoes in one hand and waving my other arm for balance. I was just about to let go of the shoes and try to fling myself to the stone, when I felt Ares' massive hand close around my elbow, catching me. "Thank you," I gasped, heart hammering against my ribs.

"Move," the god barked in reply, and for once I did as I was told, putting one bare foot in front of the other as fast as I dared, Ares never letting go of me.

Thankfully the door on the other side wasn't locked and I wrenched it open and half threw myself inside, out of the horrendous rain. Ares followed me in fast, slamming the door shut behind me. We were at the bottom of another staircase, this one a wide spiral shape. The vines were less here, only sprawling across the low ceiling, and everything was lit dimly by glowing balls of green light that seemed embedded into the rock itself.

"I'm soaked," I said quietly, leaning against the wall and getting my breath, pushing strands of wet hair back from my face. It felt like the crazy-gorgeous headdress Eris had wrapped around it all had held it pretty well, all things considered.

"You can use your power to dry yourself. It's like using your healing power, but imagine it hotter instead."

I looked at Ares, wanting to ask him to do it for me. Better still, I wanted him to take all my wet clothes off and warm me up in a different way entirely. But there was no question of that now. Panic knew we were somewhere that we weren't supposed to be, so we were already on borrowed time. As soon as I thought of the Lord of War, I felt his presence, an urgent agitation at the back of my mind.

"He's trying to make contact with us," said Ares. "Don't let him."

I nodded, picturing my horse shield automatically. The presence diminished. "We'd better move," I said.

"Zeeva said we need to look for a tapestry with a kraken on it."

"Let's hurry. I want this over with."

I knew exactly what he meant. The thrill of the heist was now nothing compared to the promise our bodies held one another. Although the extra bout of adrenaline our dash through the castle had stirred up wasn't doing me any harm. I knew I was glowing, I could see it on my skin. I was as alive as I'd ever felt, overflowing with energy.

Get the tooth, take it to Dentro, fuck the God of War senseless.

This had the potential to be a freaking excellent night.

22

BELLA

There were lots of tapestries hanging in the wide stairwell, and nearly all of them depicted fearsome looking monsters. It didn't take us long to find an image showing a giant octopus type creature, dragging a ship that was hovering twenty feet above the surface of the ocean down toward a watery end. It was heavy as hell, but we managed to pull it down between us, revealing an unnervingly tiny tunnel.

"Zeeva didn't mention it was this small," I said, eying the dark entrance.

"To her, it probably isn't small."

"I've seen her in big cat mode," I said, pulling a face. "She's not as tiny as you might think."

"Do you want to go first?" Ares asked me.

I nodded, then dropped to my knees. A faint smell was coming from the tunnel, but not an unpleasant one. It was a sort of smoky, tangy scent that I thought I recognized. "If this tower starts lurching around from side to side while I'm in there, I will not be happy," I said, looking up at Ares over my shoulder.

"Hopefully it is a defense unique to the last tower."

"Hopefully." I tried to keep the doubt from my voice, and leaned forward onto my hands.

The tunnel was shorter than I had expected it to be, and only properly dark for a few seconds, until it angled up sharply and light poured in from the other end. It was tiring moving up so steeply, but the stone was rough enough to keep a good grip on, and the pleasant smell made the work easier. When I crawled out of the end I found myself at the bottom of yet another staircase, but I could tell immediately that this one was different. There was no doubt in my mind that it was the trick staircase Zeeva had told us about.

It was huge, each step easily big enough for me to lie down on. And it wasn't tall either, only about twenty steps high, a innocuous looking wooden door at the top. Vines snaked their way across the ceiling here too, and coiled around the frame of the door, but they stayed clear of the stone steps. More green light glowed from the rock, mingling with my own gold glow. Ares emerged from the tunnel behind me as I got cautiously to my feet. As soon as I was at my full height I saw that the wide steps had carvings on them, but they seemed to blur every time I tried to focus.

"This feels wrong," Ares said, and I nodded in agreement. There was a kind of bad-shit vibe coming from the stone, like that feeling when the skies cloud over and it gets cold suddenly and you want to be somewhere else.

"Can you see what's carved onto the steps?" I asked him.

"No. The images keep moving." We both moved warily closer to the bottom step. The more I tried to work out the drawing, the more the lines seemed to leap about, evading me.

"Stay still," I snapped, and miraculously, they did. I looked slowly at Ares, my eyebrows arched. "Did I just do that?" I whispered.

"Maybe the magic here obeys war," he said, then turned to the stairs. I felt a little tug as he spoke, apparently to the stairs. "All false steps should reveal themselves now!" he ordered. Nothing happened, and a tiny snort of laughter escaped me.

"What did you expect, talking to a staircase?"

Ares glared at me. "Do you have any better ideas?" I leaned forward, peering at the now clear image on the lowest step. It showed a helmet similar in style to Ares' with a big plume on it, and a wreath underneath it.

I looked at the carving on the next step. It was a lion's head, its mouth open in a snarl, teeth bared. The step after that had nothing carved on it at all, and the one after that had a silhouette of a woman with a severe haircut, and a snake. I couldn't see higher than that without starting to move up the stairs.

"The pictures must mean something. That one with the lady looks like ancient Egyptian hieroglyphs. And her hair... She could be Cleopatra. She had something to do with a snake, I'm sure."

Ares looked at me as I screwed my face up in thought. "We do not have time for this."

"Well, unless you can fly, we'll have to work it out."

He paused, and I instantly got over-excited. "Can we fly? Please, please tell me we can fly!"

"No. Gods don't need to fly, they can flash."

"Oh." I felt my face fall. "And we can't flash in the

castle," I said, putting my hands on my hips. Ares echoed my position, putting his own fists on his hips.

"No."

"OK then. Cleopatra. Do you have one of them in Olympus? Or is she just a mortal world person?"

"She is a minor deity in my realm."

"Ohh, I want to meet her!"

"Focus, Bella."

"Shit, yeah, sorry." I looked back to the carvings. "Does she have any war power?"

"Yes."

"OK. I don't know about the lion. You got any war lions in Olympus?"

"Yes. The Nemean Lion, though she is dead now. Killed during the Immortality Trials."

"OK, so the lion is Olympus only. What about the first picture? That could be you."

"No. The wreath means nothing to me."

"It could be Julius Caesar? He was a famous war general in my world."

Ares shrugged. "I have never heard of him. Athena manages the war and politics in the mortal world. I find it too... restrictive."

I sighed. "So there's no connection there, they're all different."

"Is your Julius Caesar character dead?"

"Long dead," I nodded.

"Like the Nemean Lion. Perhaps we should not stand on steps of warriors who have died?"

I took a deep breath. "It's worth a shot." Ares took a stride forward and I caught his armored arm. "Wait. Try putting something on the step first, as a test."

"Like what?"

I looked around the small space trying to find something that would weigh enough to trigger the trick step.

There was nothing. "Would any of my jewelry be heavy enough, do you think?" I asked him, touching the complicated headdress.

His eyes darkened, and I saw a flame spike in his irises as his eyes swept over me. "Your dress would be heavy enough."

"I am not taking my dress off," I said, giving him a hard look. "I'm already barefoot; if we get caught I'd rather I wasn't in my underwear."

"Then we test it with my life," he shrugged, and I could hear the teasing lilt in his voice.

"You're seriously saying that your life depends on me getting naked?"

"It would appear that way."

I rolled my eyes, then pulled the headdress from my head. My hair tumbled down my back as I worked it free, relieved to feel that the weight of it in my hands seemed to exceed how light it felt on my head. I laid it carefully on the lion step. Nothing happened.

"Take off your boots." I turned to Ares, holding my hand out.

"What?"

"They're not part of your magic armor are they?"

"No, but-"

"Then take them off," I commanded.

"You wish the God of War to tackle a great challenge with no shoes on?"

I lifted my skirt to my knees and wiggled my own bare toes at him. "Yup. Alongside the shoe-less Goddess of War."

There was a long pause, then Ares bent at the waist. "You have a power over me, woman," he muttered.

"Well, it wasn't working up until today," I said. "You have point-blank refused to do anything I've asked you before." He straightened, having tugged both his massive boots off. I looked down at his simple black stocking socks. When I looked back at his face, his eyes were serious.

"I mean it, Bella. I have given up trying to fight it. You do have a power over me."

My face heated with both pleasure and awkwardness.

"I have all the power," I grinned at him, trying to make light of the tension. "That's why I'm here, remember? War-magic battery?"

He shook his head and held out his boots. As soon as I added them to my headdress, the step made a loud cracking sound, then turned completely transparent. Alarm skittered down my spine as the sound of buzzing welled up loud in the small stone room and the boots and headdress fell clean through the step.

Fuck that. I did not want to be standing on one of those any time soon. But the only way was up. We had promised Dentro, and we were not letting him down. I steeled myself, drawing on the flaming ball of power under my ribs to steady my nerves. My trepidation was instantly replaced with an earnestness to succeed that I knew bordered on dangerous. Every victory comes at a cost, I reminded myself, as I turned to Ares.

"I think your boots were heavy enough on their own," I told him. "That was a waste of a damn fine piece of jewelry."

23

ARES

"Do you think the blank step is safe?" I asked Bella.

"Must be. Nobody could reach the fourth step from here. Unless you were a giant."

"Shame we don't have more boots to test it out." I raised an eyebrow at her and she poked her tongue out at me. My body reacted instantly, my arousal unstoppable.

"Put that away, or Dentro will remain toothless," I growled. Pink flushed her cheeks, and she shifted her weight.

With a wrench, I turned away form her and surveyed the step without a carving. "If I fall, do you think you can catch me before the oxys get me?" I asked her.

"Catch you how?"

"You can make an air cushion to bounce me back out. Or send out whips. We can conjure up most weapons with our power." I was becoming comfortable calling it 'our' power, which was remarkable given how I had felt just a week earlier.

"Seriously, why didn't you teach me this shit before?"

"Just picture using the weapon as you draw on your power and it'll appear. It won't be anything like as strong as *Ischyros*, but it will function. You seem to learn fast. I trust you."

She nodded at me, expression resolute. With a quick breath I took a stride long enough to take me to the third step. My heart thudded in my chest as my weight settled, and Bella whooped. The step was holding. I turned to her, holding out my hand and helping her jump to join me when she took it.

I had expected to feel more confident with every correct guess, but that was not the case. Every time we hovered over a step I couldn't help thinking about what would happen if Bella was stung by the oxys, and my chest clenched with apprehension.

It took us much longer than I'd have liked to work out who all the little carved drawings were, but between us we prevailed.

"You know, I could do with a drink," Bella breathed when we finally reached the un-carved section of stone before the plain door.

"It's not over yet." I eyed the door handle suspiciously. Zeeva had said we needed war power to open it. "You are stronger than me. I think you should try and open it."

"You're just saying that so that if it does something nasty it hits me instead of you," she teased.

"Never," I said, emotion flashing through my veins, and my hand reaching for hers protectively. "I would never risk your life for my own." The words were out before I had even thought them, and her surprise was evident.

"Really?"

I nodded. I didn't know when it had happened, exactly, but I knew that I had spoken the truth. When we had been drowning, and the awful realization that only one of use could use enough power to gain immortality, my instincts had made the decision for me. I wouldn't risk her life for mine.

And that fact directly contradicted everything I thought I had known about the Goddess of War for centuries. It challenged everything that had led me to make the decisions I had made all that time ago.

I needed time and space to work this out, to replay those ancient events and understand how I could have got it so wrong. I needed to talk to my mother.

That time was not now though. All I could do now was give in to the fact that Bella had utterly invaded my heart.

"Why?" she whispered, her eyes burning with emotion.

"I wouldn't be able stop myself if I wanted to. I believe we are bound."

She opened her mouth, then closed it again, multiple times. "So... You don't want to feel like this? You just can't help it?" There was an edge of pain in her voice and it felt like I was being stabbed in the gut. I reached for her, drawing her close, running my hand down her soft cheek.

"I didn't know it was even possible for me to feel like this," I told her. "I would trade it for nothing in the whole of Olympus."

A smile, true and warm, lit her face, and she stood up on her bare tiptoes to kiss me softly. "I'm going to need you to say more things like that to me later. When we've got this damn tooth."

"It would be my pleasure."

Bella grinned, then looked down at the handle. It was made from the same rich-colored wood as the door and looked like it had once been carved into something, but years of wear had rubbed the shape away. That same uneasy feeling that I had experience on entering the room coiled around me, making my skin crawl.

"Wait," I said. "Let's do it together. Combine our strength."

A look of relief flickered across Bella's face. "Sure. Good plan. On the count of three?" I nodded.

Together, we clasped our right hands on the handle.

"Three, two, one."

24

BELLA

All the hairs on my skin stood on end, my scalp prickling. The door was moving, but barely by millimeters. My stomach shimmied and fluttered and my lungs seemed to expand in my chest, despite feeling less full of air. I pushed harder, feeling Ares do the same, but the door continued its minuscule crawl.

"Do we need to do war stuff?" I hissed. "It'll take a fucking week to open the door at this rate."

"I don't know. Draw on your war power and let's try," Ares replied, and his voice had the tiniest hit of unsteadiness in it.

"Are you feeling as weird as I am?" I asked, looking sideways at him, but somehow reluctant to draw my attention from the door handle for more than a second. It was as though my hand was glued to it.

"I feel peculiar, yes."

I dug inside myself, finding the burning well of power hot and ready. I blew out a breath, and pictured the mounted version of me on the battlefield.

The moment I got the image in my head, the door

moved faster under our weight. But the uneasy prickling instantly became a tsunami of panic.

I was drowning. I was in the pool again, the tentacles wrapped around me, but Ares' golden glow wasn't lighting the pitch dark water and I was being dragged down, down, down. I couldn't breathe, my head was filled with pain, my lungs were burning as an invisible band around my middle crushed the breath, the life, the soul out of my body. I was trapped, and I was going to die.

"Bella!" Ares' voice sounded in the distance, and the vision changed. I wasn't drowning anymore. He was. He was drowning and I would have to watch him die because I had the all of the power. I had the immortality. Only one of us could live forever and I would be the reason for the fierce warrior god's death.

I would kill the only man who had a chance of caring about me, understanding me. *Loving me.*

I had to watch him die.

Panic overwhelmed me completely, and I could hear myself screaming and thrashing as my limbs went numb, but I couldn't stop.

"Ares!" I screamed, as his body floated lifelessly in the inky water. My mouth filled with water, my eyes burning along with my chest.

Pain shocked through my whole body as though I'd slammed into something solid, totally at odds with the underwater vision that was dominating my mind.

When I blinked, the pool was gone, replaced by pale stone just inches from my eye. The tangy taste of blood in my mouth dragged me fully from the horrendous vision and I realized I was lying flat on the stone floor.

Pain spiked from where my cheek must have hit the stone, and my ribs and shoulder felt as though they'd been hit by a truck as I tentatively tried to move. Residual images of Ares' dead body kept drifting across my vision, and my pulse was still racing at a hundred miles an hour. My chest hurt every time I took a ragged breath, and I didn't know if it was the panic, or true injury.

"Ares?" I tried to call his name, but the pain of moving my jaw brought tears to my eyes. Something was broken. *"Ares?"* I tried again, in my head this time.

"I'm here. Are you hurt?" His mental voice was tense.

"Yes."

"Heal yourself, quickly."

Shit, of course I could heal myself. The intensity of the vision had left me slow and fuzzy, and I reached inside myself, instructing my power to fix whatever was broken. Warm tingles shot out from my center, and my ribs hurt like hell for a split second, before I felt as though I could breathe properly again. Then my shoulder burned white hot, and I gulped down more air as the feeling of wrongness in my torso lessened. Next my face heated, and when it stopped I lifted my head a fraction. There was no pain.

I pushed myself up onto my hands and knees, testing my body before looking around myself.

"Ares!" He was lying beside me, and his face looked in worse shape than mine had felt.

"This is why I wear a helmet," he croaked inside my head. There was no way he could have moved his mouth. He looked as though he had been flung at the stone with the force of a hurricane, blood pooling under the side of his head that was smashed into the floor. I scrabbled over to him and laid my hands on his armor. I felt him pull on

my power and I let him take it, trying somehow to send more through our connection.

"What happened?" I whispered. I was still reeling from the vision, and now, seeing him like this, bleeding and broken... The thought of something happening to him, of losing him, was unbearable. Somewhere along this crazy fucking journey, I had fallen for him. It wasn't just sex. It wasn't just desire. This was serious.

"I think the door opened, and we fell through."

"Fell? How fucking hard did we fall?" I could feel tears dangerously close to spilling from my eyes. He moved, just a little, but enough that I could see the crushed flesh on his face was glowing. *Healing.*

He was OK. He would be OK.

"We survived," he said, this time moving his lips, saying the words aloud. "So, I think we should take this as a victory."

"I like your thinking," I told him, stroking my hand down the undamaged side of his face, trying to get my shit together and contain my churning emotions. "We fucking showed that door who's boss." He gave a forced chuckle. "I... I had a vision," I said, quietly.

"Me too. One that would induce the power of Panic."

I nodded. "We were back in the pool in the forest."

"It wasn't real, Bella. Put it out of your mind." He rolled slowly onto his back, a shuddering breath making his armor move. There wasn't a dent in it. The force of whatever had caused us to slam into the floor had broken my shoulder and ribs but Ares' armor was solid.

"I'm sorry you didn't have your helmet on," I said.

"I'd happily have my face smashed up if it means I can kiss you at any opportunity," he said, his eyes closed as the skin over his cheek and jaw knitted itself back together as I watched.

"That's actually quite a romantic thing to say," I said. "Under the circumstances." I leaned over, and placed a tiny, gentle kiss on his lips. I felt the draw on my power fade as he glowed briefly, then opened his eyes, reaching a hand up and running it through the loose curls of my hair that were hanging down over him.

"I am healed," he said softly. "Thank you." I moved so that he could sit, and for the first time noticed the rest of the room we were in.

The evil-bastard door appeared to have closed behind us, and we were in the entrance way to a long hall. Two rows of pedestals ran down either side of the hall, lit by bright flickering flames that hung upside down from the low ceiling above them. Vines and branches covered the walls behind the pedestals, and the firelight made them look alive, as though they were crawling across the stone with purpose. From my position on the floor, I couldn't make out anything on top of the closest pedestals, only that whatever was in them was encased inside a glass dome, like the rose in Beauty and the Beast.

"We're in," I said, standing up carefully. "We made it into the trophy room."

"Are you fully healed?" Ares' voice was filled with concern as he stood too.

"Yes, I'm fine. I've spent a lifetime having to move slowly after having the shit kicked out of me. It'll take me a while to get used to being able to just bounce back up."

Rage flashed through Ares' beautiful eyes. "I shall murder all those who ever kicked the shit out of you," he growled.

I laughed. "That's very sweet, armor-boy, but most of

them were paid to do so, in a fighting ring. I signed up for it."

His eyes narrowed. "You fought in pits?"

"Sort of, I guess. But as I said, I was paid. And I liked proving the people who bet against me wrong."

"Is that why you care about the slaves?" he asked quietly.

"No, I care about the slaves because it's fundamentally wrong to take somebody's freedom from them," I said. "Look, we can talk about this later. Let's find this tooth and get the fuck out of here, before the Lords show up." I left off the rest of the sentence that was bouncing around in my head. *Don't remind me of the things I don't like about you.* I knew I would have to deal with the serious differences in opinion and nature Ares and I had. But there had to be a way through it. I knew he was capable of change; he had told me himself that I was affecting how he saw the world.

"My sister must be doing a good job of distracting them. It has been a long time since her warning."

"Yeah. I hope she's OK."

Ares pulled a face. "Eris is always OK. It is her victims who you should worry about."

"Hmmm. You make a good point. Right. Where's this tooth?"

I took a step down the hall, renewed determination to get the job done, pronto, flooding through me. So far, Panic's tower had not delivered the evening I was hoping for, but there was still time to rescue it.

25

BELLA

Some of the items under the glass domes in Panic's trophy room made Belle's rose look positively dull.

"What in the name of sweet fuck is that?" I breathed, staring at something that might have passed for a human hand, were it not for the hundreds of eyes and legs all over it. It was motionless on top of the pedestal, I presumed dead.

Ares stopped beside me, and his nose wrinkled in distaste. "I have no idea."

There were lots of pieces of jewelry, shining gems and pretty tiaras, and also many weapons. Ares was particularly enamored with a battle-axe made from gleaming bronze, but I tugged him further down the hall.

"We're here for the tooth. Don't get greedy. That's how they always get caught."

"Who gets caught?"

"Everyone. You know, in plays and movies."

"I don't know what you're talking about."

I sighed. "Nothing new there then. When this is all over, I'm taking you to the theater," I told him.

"Oh. Well, then I shall take you to a theater too."

"Excellent," I said, throwing him a smile.

Eventually, when we were three pedestals from the end of the hall, we reached a glass dome covering a sharp, yellowing tooth.

"Do you think that's it?" I asked, peering at it intently.

"It is certainly large enough."

"Let's check the last few, before we start smashing up the wrong one." Moving quickly, we scanned the few remaining trophies. When I reached the last two pedestals, something skittered over my skin, warm and electric, and I could smell smoke all of a sudden. The sound of steel clashing rang in my ears, and I frowned.

"Can you feel that?" It wasn't the Lords. In fact, I didn't think it was a bad feeling at all. Battle-cries echoed in the far distance, and the mounted version of me, sword raised high, galloped through my mind.

I looked at Ares, about to repeat my question, when I saw that his gaze was fixed on the pedestal in front of him.

The second my eyes fell on the object inside, I gasped aloud, my body filling with a heady surge of my new power.

It was a helmet. Similar in style to Ares' but the plume was purple, and it was smaller. The eye slits were larger though, and the cut out opened higher, so the wearer's mouth would be seen. I reached out as I stepped toward it, knowing for sure that this was not the first time I'd seen this helmet. Just like the shield with the horses, or *Ischyros* in true form. *I knew this helmet.*

"Ares?" My word came out as a question, and when he looked at me his eyes were full of pain and sorrow.

"We must take it," he said, his voice low and resolute. Despite my previous assertion that we take nothing but the tooth, I had no intention of arguing with him. I was connected to that helmet somehow, and at that moment I wanted little more than to free it from its glass prison.

"Yes, OK. But we get the tooth first."

He nodded, and we jogged back to Dentro's tooth, a sudden urgency to our movements.

Ares recognized the helmet too, I was sure of it.

The God of War drew his sword, and the sound of steel on steel set my heart racing faster. I pulled my flick-blade from where it was concealed between my breasts in the tight dress, sighing with pleasure as the weapon heated in my hand and transformed into the magnificent weapon it really was.

"On three again?" Ares asked me.

"Sure."

"Three, two, one!"

Together we arced our blades through the air, bringing them crashing down onto the glass. I poured my power into the sword, and let Ares draw as much as he wanted from the burning well inside me. As we made contact time slowed to a standstill, and the ringing of the weapons against the dome echoed through the stone room. Then, in a rush, the glass shattered completely, cascading onto the floor below. I reached out, scooping Dentro's massive tooth up, and tucking it under my arm.

A freezing wave of air blew through the room in a gust, carrying with it a distinct sense of despair.

"He knows we're here," Ares said, and I sprinted with him toward the helmet. My skin began to crawl again as the gust of air swirled harder, picking up my hair and skirts. I glanced over my shoulder as I reached the helmet's pedestal, breathing in sharply as I saw that the air was tightening into a tornado, and solidifying. It was Panic.

"He's here," I shouted, and turned, trying to raise my sword with my right arm and keep my hold on the awkward tooth with the other. An awful sense of doom was seeping into me, as though my skin was absorbing the power carried by Panic's presence. The sensation brought the visions of losing Ares in the pool dancing back in front of my eyes.

The crash of metal on glass snapped me back, and I focused as Ares pulled his weapon back from the blow he had just landed on the dome. It hadn't broken the glass, just left a widening crack.

"I need you," he barked, eyes wild. I raised *Ischyros*, and without a countdown this time, we slammed our swords into the dome in unison. My blow was awkward, but I channeled enough fear-fueled power into it that it worked, the glass splintering into a thousand pieces. Ares snatched up the helmet from amongst the shards, then I heard his voice bellow in my head.

"Eris! Help us!"

"Your sister has been detained, oh mighty one."

Panic's voice was like nails down a chalkboard, and all the hairs on my body stood on end as we both turned slowly.

He wasn't alone. Pain and Terror were standing behind him, and another wave of hopelessness crashed over me. Together they were stronger than us. If this came down to a fight, we would lose. And I had vowed to return the tooth to the magnificent enslaved dragon. I had to save him.

"You can't contain the Goddess of Chaos," Ares

snorted, all panic and urgency gone from his voice. He sounded like he had zero fucks to give. I did my best to emulate him.

"Yeah, Eris does what she likes," I said.

A slow, creepy smile spread across Panic's face. He was dressed exactly like he owned a castle filled with plants. His outfit was medieval in style, britches and shirt and big leather boots, but it was all in shades of mossy green. "Not any more. I'm afraid her ongoing spat with Aphrodite seems to have come to a head."

Fuck. We were trapped. My power wasn't strong enough for Ares to flash us out of a no-flash-zone, and there were no windows or doors except the one they were blocking.

Panic's eyes flicked between the tooth under my arm and the helmet Ares was clutching. "I see now why Dentro let you go," he murmured. "Clever dragon. He'll pay for his deviousness." A shudder rippled down my spine as the temperature dropped even further.

"You're an asshole. That dragon deserves to be free," I spat.

"That dragon shouldn't have been careless enough to lose his tooth," Panic hissed back. "Now, give me back my property, and we'll pretend this never happened. We'll return to the ball and announce the last Trial." He held his hand out.

"Fuck off." There was no way I was handing over the tooth. He'd have to fight me for it, whether I could win or not. I felt a surge of hot energy, buffering me against his cold, unsettling presence.

"Then we will take it from you."

I threw up my shield as Ares spoke in my head. *"Do you trust me?"*

"Of course."

He pulled on my power, and I let him take it.

In a rush I felt my strength leaving me, the tooth becoming alarmingly heavy, *Ischyros* even more so. I felt my legs bend under the weight, and Panic's eyes lit up as he realized my shield was gone. A wall of air slammed into me, nearly toppling me, a hideous wailing noise riding with it. I almost dropped the sword and tooth to clap my hands over my ears, the sound was so unpleasant. Panic began to crawl its way up my chest, my throat, taking over, unstoppable.

Then I was jerked backwards as a huge arm wrapped around my waist, spinning me around.

"Run!" Ares yelled, and began to race toward the solid stone wall at the end of the hall.

I did as he said, wanting to scream at how slowly I was moving. All my usual speed and power was gone, and the weight of my sword and the tooth slowed me further. Heat flared from Ares, just ahead of me, then a fireball twice my height erupted from him. My mouth fell open, and I stumbled, then Panic's wailing tornado smashed into my back. I cried out as I tumbled forward, catching myself on my hands and knees as I hit the floor, the tooth and *Ischyros* clattering out of my hands.

I saw the fireball explode as it hit the stone wall, and threw one arm up in front of me, as though that would help shield me. A flaming shower of stone and burning chunks of vines came flying toward me, but hit an invisible wall, sliding harmlessly off. I looked up breathlessly as Ares, glowing the brightest gold, couched beside me, tugging me to my feet. I felt power begin to flow back into me, and I pulled gratefully at it, glorious strength flooding back into my muscles. I reached for *Ischyros* as Ares snatched up the tooth, then ran toward the exploded wall, me right behind him. There was a big, ragged hole blasted in the stone.

"Ready?" he shouted as Panic made a strangled sound behind us.

"Hell yes!" I yelled, and we launched ourselves out of the tower.

26

BELLA

My heart was in my throat as we fell through the cold air, rain hammering down so hard I could barely see.

"Shield!" I heard Ares yell, and I pictured my horse shield and tightened my grip on *Ischyros*. With an almighty crash, we hit something, but before I could work out what, the world flashed white.

I sucked in air, looking around desperately for Ares. We were back in the gloomy forest, even darker than the last time we'd been there, now that it was night.

Ares was standing beside me in the pouring rain, his eyes alive with excitement. I tried to focus on what was behind him, to check our surroundings, but he was glowing so bright, and I couldn't look away from him.

"I had no idea that running away could be so exhilarating," he breathed, before stepping toward me and kissing me briefly but oh so passionately. When he moved back the fire was dancing in his irises, his gaze piercing. "What else can you show me, that I didn't know?" He sounded genuinely amazed, as well as sexy as hell, and I didn't know if he was referring to his lack of immortality, his newfound emotion for me, or just sex. Maybe all three.

"Let's get this tooth to Dentro before Panic catches us up, and then we'll find out," I said, my voice abnormally husky.

"Bella, you've made me question everything," he said. "Everything. Please, tell me you know that I can change." There was a plea in his voice that was so at odds with the prideful god's usual tone, and my heart seemed to swell inside my chest.

"Yes. But you don't need to change, Ares. You just need to review some outdated attitudes."

"So... So you don't hold my bad decisions against me?"

He sounded almost fearful, and I cocked my head at him, the intensity of the emotion on his face surprising me. Was he talking about the way he ruled his realm? Or something else?

"We all make mistakes. And we can all try to fix them."

"Bella." He said my name as though it were an apology, pain filling his eyes, and I couldn't help frowning as the rain beat down on us.

"What? What's wrong?"

"I need you to know this, Bella. I need you to know it now."

"Know what?" My nerves were skittering now, a sick feeling swishing around inside me.

"I think I've fallen in love with you."

My heart skipped a beat as I stared at him. For a truly blissful second a sense of rightness slid over us, the rain and the awful forest and everything else shit in the world, fading to nothing. There was nothing but him, and the undeniable knowledge that we were meant to be together. We were two halves of the same thing.

Then agony seared through my head, and I screamed, dropping what I was holding and falling to my knees. My skull felt like it was being split in two, and I barely heard Ares shout over the pain.

A cackling laugh filled the air around us, then Aphrodite's voice rang between the trees, slicing through everything else. "Love, dear ones, is when my power works. Only when you say the words, can my curse come to life. Do you want to see what you have fallen for, Bella? Do you want to see just how savage your god can be?"

"No!" shouted Ares, and I lifted my head, eyes streaming with the pain, to see Ares begin to grow. The cord in my gut fired to life as he drew my power from me.

"Yes, Ares. If you truly love her, and you want her to love you back, she must see you at your worst."

His face was changing as I watched, the beautiful flames in his eyes gone, cold hard darkness replacing them. The air filled with the stench of blood, tangy and cloying, and the golden glow around him was turning red. He was ten feet tall now at least, and he was taking more of my power by the second. I tried to clamp down on the flow, to stop him, but as soon as I tried, he growled, an inhuman, awful sound. His pull got harder, and I cried out in frustration. Something flickered in his eyes, but then I heard Aphrodite laugh again, and his irises turned completely black.

"He's all yours, Bella."

I pushed myself to my feet, my strength diminishing fast. I pulled *Ischyros* with me, but when I tried to lift the sword I found it too heavy. A bolt of fear shot through me as I looked up at Ares.

He had doubled in size, and his red light cast eerie shadows on the forest around us.

"Ares, please. Stop taking my power." I saw nothing of him that I recognized in his black eyes as he looked down from where he towered above me. He took the gold headband off and it began to grow into his helmet, matching his size. Dizziness washed through me as he pulled it down over his head, and another, bigger, bolt of fear raced through me as I felt for the well of power inside me. It was too small. And getting smaller.

"Ares!" I tried again, louder. "Ares, don't drain my power!"

"Your power?" His voice was huge and booming, and totally alien. He stamped his foot as he looked down at me, his whole body beaming with the color of the plume on his helmet. "The power you wield is mine!" I barely had time to react as he kicked out with his bootless foot, throwing myself to the ground and rolling out of the way just in time.

"Ares, stop! It's me!"

"I am the God of War!" he roared, rain hammering against his armor as he continued to grow, his height almost matching that of the trees around us. "You will bow to me! All will bow to me!" The sound of clashing of steel and galloping hooves rang through the air, then cannon fire and gunshots mingled with the noise. Abruptly the sounds were overcome by the screams of the dying, men and women wailing and crying.

"Stop!" My voice was rasping, and I could hear the tears in them.

This couldn't be happening.

The man who had just told me that he thought he

loved me couldn't be the same man who towered over me now, emanating death. "Ares, please!"

"This is the true power of war," he bellowed. "You are not worthy of it. It must return to me." His voice was a savage growl as his cold, dead eyes locked on me, and I had no doubt what he would do next. Fatigue was dragging at my limbs, dark spots floating across my vision, the red-mist nowhere to be seen. I didn't have enough power left to fight him.

I felt like my chest was being cleaved apart, and it wasn't a physical wound. It was so much worse. The connection with Ares that had burned brighter within me the longer I was with him was gone. All that was left was the sickening feeling of him draining my power. There were two cords, two connections, I realized, eyes burning. One was power, running straight to the burning well of magic. But the other, now lifeless, ran straight to my soul.

A sob fought its way up and out of my throat. I would have to run, before the man I was falling in love with tried to kill me.

Turning almost blindly, I felt the ground shake beneath my bare feet, then heard the sound of wood being wrenched apart.

"Enyo." The voice didn't belong to Ares, and I whirled back in time to see Dentro materialize from the forest around us. His bark-covered body was coiling around Ares, and his head flew low across the ground, stopping when he reached the fallen tooth. "You kept your word," he said, his rich voice soft. Green light flashed brightly at the same time as the twenty-foot tall God of War brought his sword crashing down onto Dentro's body.

The dragon hissed, retracting fast, whipping his serpentine tail through the trees around us, felling them all with an almighty crash. Ares had already lost interest in the dragon though, his awful eyes back on me.

I turned again to run, but stumbled as the pull on my power intensified. I didn't have enough power left. I likely only had minutes before I passed out, and then I would die. At Ares' hands. The thought was unbearable, and it felt as though all the love my heart had swelled with just minutes before was now acid, pouring through my body, toxic and cruel.

I felt something hard against my torso, and my vision blurred as I tried to fight against it.

"It is me, fierce one," Dentro's voice sounded in my head, and I stopped struggling as I was lifted from the ground.

I blinked through the rain, my breath catching and my heart almost stopping as Ares tore through the night, his sword as big as I was, and his face filled with murder. Dentro whipped me around, out of Ares' reach, his tail coiling tighter around me. I saw the dragon's wings snap out, massive and taut, through my hazy vision and with a blast of warm air, the creature leaped off the ground.

Ares let out another cry, this one filled with pure rage, as we moved higher. My head swam, then pain ripped through my gut, the cord connecting my power to Ares suddenly aflame within me. I screamed, unable to think or see, and Ares screamed louder below me. Then all of my power flooded back to me, and I opened my eyes, heaving for breath as everything around me sharpened and strengthened. Red covered my vision as it cleared, and suddenly I could see the forest getting smaller below me as we rose higher, the rain cold and hard.

"Take me back!"

"No. He will kill you."

"I am strong again, take me back!" I cried, struggling against the dragon's tail.

"You are strong again because you are too far away for him to take your power. If you go back, he will drain you, and kill you."

A strangled cry left my throat, and I beat my fist against Dentro's bark body. Desperation coursed through me, the pain inside my chest unbearable.

"I love him," I sobbed. "I can't leave him. I swore I wouldn't leave him again."

"I am sorry, fierce one. I can't take you back." The dragon's voice was filled with sorrow.

"What did she do to him? What did that fucking witch do? That's not him!"

"The Goddess of Love is a terrifying goddess to cross. But if you truly love Ares, I will help you lift the curse."

"I do. I do love him. I'll do anything. Please, we have to save him."

With another wracking sob, I let go of all the doubt, allowing the truth to wash over me completely as the dragon soared through the rain.

I loved Ares. And I would do anything to get him back.

THE GOLDEN GOD

1

BELLA

"Where are we going?"

Freezing air raced over my skin as Dentro soared through the sky, my body still clutched in the grip of his bark-covered tail. I could feel the dragon's pleasure rolling from him, his aura blissful as his huge wings stretched out, slicing through the clouds.

He was free.

I, on the other hand, couldn't have felt less free.

I was broken, trapped in an agony I had never felt the likes of in my pain-filled life.

The tears had stopped, but the rage and sorrow had only grown. My chest physically hurt, as though lumps of my insides had been ripped out, and all that was left was a hollow despair that ached worse than any wound I'd ever experienced.

I'd been so close to a contentment I had never even dared to dream of reaching.

Love.

Ares had said he loved me. Nobody had ever loved me. Hell, *I* hadn't even loved me for most of my life.

But Ares did. And I loved him. We were right, somehow. Not because we were the same, but because we weren't. Our differences were what made us fit together so perfectly.

We shared the same fierce desire for violence, confrontation and victory, but we could teach each other so much about how to handle it.

And gods, we could fight well together. There was no doubt in my mind that we could love each other with the same intensity. The thought of being in Ares' arms, our love for each other in every touch, made the acid feeling in my chest spread painfully.

Aphrodite had ruined everything. The jealous, spiteful, cruel goddess had sent him mad with battle-lust, just so I could see how savage he could be. Did she think that would scare me off?

The woman was a fucking idiot. I shared Ares' power. I *knew* how savage he could be. I had the same damn temper, the same violence within me. She didn't need to show me.

I already knew that Ares could control the beast of War, so what he buried inside himself meant nothing to me. I only cared how he *chose* to live his life. His actions were what mattered, not how destructive he had the potential to become. Hell, if I were to be judged on my own potential savageness, I would fare no better than the God of War.

The memory of him lifting his monstrous foot to slam down on my helpless body speared through me. I didn't hate him for draining my power and trying to kill me. It wasn't really him. But hearing his cold words on repeat in my head was torture. It reminded me constantly of how painful the loss of his love was, and how brutally his passion had been ripped away from me.

The dragon banked, snapping my focus down below us. A sparkling blue ocean glittered around a large island in the distance. I could make out lots of forestland, and towns of gleaming white buildings dotting the cliffs. Piers jutted out over the water in several places, and massive ships were docked at them, their solar sails shining.

"This is Hera's realm." Dentro's voice sounded in my mind.

"Hera?"

"Yes. You, fierce one, have a love curse to break. And the only other goddess who specializes in love is Hera."

"But nobody has seen her since Zeus vanished."

"Ares is her son," Dentro said, his wise voice gentle. *"She will see you."*

Hope mingled with fear. "What if she won't? Ares said parents don't care about their kids in Olympus."

"Hera will see you. A bond such as the one you share with Ares runs deep enough that she will be aware of it."

I remembered what Eris had said about Hera's unbreakable marriage bonds between Gods. Last time, the thought had alarmed me. This time, I clung to the notion that something still connected me to the God of War. "I thought you had to consent to Hera's bonds?"

"You do."

"I've never consented to anything like that."

"Not that you are aware of. I believe that there is much you are not aware of."

A sick feeling made my already roiling stomach

clench. If Hera really was going to see me, then I would refuse to leave until I got some answers. I was done letting others tell me that there was all this damn mystery about my past that they all suspected, and only I didn't seem to know.

The dragon tilted so that we flew faster toward the center of the island, where the forest was at its thickest. *"Call to Hera,"* he instructed.

"How?"

"Picture her in your mind."

"I don't know what she looks like."

Dentro let out a snort, and whether it was from annoyance or surprise, I wasn't sure. He began to vibrate, and I gripped his tail tight. Then, with a flash of teal light, an enormous marble column burst up from the trees below us. It rose higher, the carved swirls decorating its perfectly Greek looking top.

The column slowed to a stop thirty feet above the forest, then the air shimmered as a temple took shape before my eyes, fitting atop the column exactly. It was beautiful, with carved columns holding up a triangular facade at the front, and an impressive number of steps leading to grand wooden doors. Grapes were carved all over the marble, I saw as we got closer, and I could also make out lots of images of crabs and peacocks.

The dragon swooped lower and lower, until we were in front of the steps, facing the imposing doors that led inside the temple. My mind darted immediately back to the last staircase I had ascended - the one that could have killed me and Ares in Panic's tower. The one we had beaten together, our lust for each other burning through our bodies as we conquered our challenge.

Dentro set me down carefully on the marble and my

bare feet throbbed as they met the cold stone, but only for a moment. I was still wearing the gown, though the skirts were torn and muddied. *Ischyros* was pulsing, warm and comforting in my hand. The dragon's head moved low, so that one huge eye was level with my face.

"Good luck. I will be waiting here," he said aloud, his voice musical and rumbling.

"Thank you," I said. "For saving me, I mean. Ares would have killed me."

"I owed you."

"Well, now the debt is clear. I don't want you beholden to me. You're free now."

"I will not be waiting here for you because I am obligated to, fierce one. I will be waiting because I like you." Amusement gleamed in his green eye, and a tiny piece of my shattered chest seemed to heal a little. I had a friend.

"I like you too," I said, not quite able to summon a smile, but projecting my sincerity into the words.

"Good. I have a feeling that you will need this." Dentro's tail snaked round, and he deposited the helmet that we had stolen from Panic's treasure room at my feet.

"You took it?" I stared in surprise.

"I believe it is important."

"Why? Do you know where it came from?"

"No. But it emanates the same power that you do."

"War magic?"

"No. *Bella* magic."

I blinked up at the dragon. "Bella magic," I repeated on a breath. I liked the sound of that. I bent, scooping it up. My heart fluttered as I saw how damaged it was. It must have born the brunt of Ares' stamping feet, because the metal was completely caved in on one side, and it would have been impossible to wear.

"It can't have been that strong if it was crushed so easi-ly," I said, trying to hide my disappointment. Ares' armor was indestructible.

"Keep it with you none-the-less," Dentro said. "Now, go."

I nodded, and squared my shoulders. *Ischyros* hummed again in my hand, pumping confidence through me. It was time to meet the Queen of the Olympians.

2

BELLA

The silence that dominated the temple wasn't oppressive or heavy. It was oddly peaceful, compared to the turmoil churning through me. The huge doors had opened of their own accord as soon as I had approached them and a long pool ran all the way down the middle of the expansive space that was revealed. The water that filled it was a joyful, vibrant turquoise and I wanted to run my fingers through it as I walked alongside it. Peacocks roamed the marble floors, moving between the mammoth columns holding up the roof. My gaze followed the columns up, where long slats had been carved from the stone, allowing in the shafts of bright light that illuminated the temple. At the far end of the space, presiding over the pool, was an enormous gold statue of a handsome woman, a proud set to her unsmiling mouth, and wisdom in her intricately sculpted eyes. She wore a toga and a large crown, with vicious spikes that were interspersed with peacock feathers.

It was Hera. I knew the instant I saw it.

"Bella." A deep female voice rang through the temple, and the statue shimmered with teal light.

I dropped to one knee without thought. "My Queen," I answered, the words springing to my lips, unbidden. But I wasn't being forced to say them. I frowned as I straightened. It was more like muscle-memory, something that I had done for so long that I knew to do it.

"You are remembering."

"Remembering what?"

"You were not born of the mortal world. You know that. You have many long-suppressed memories of Olympus."

"Where are you?" I spun, looking for any sign of movement that wasn't a damn peacock.

"I regret that I cannot be with you. I have a task that is occupying all of my time. And strength." She added the last two words in a rueful tone.

I longed to ask her what she meant, but I had questions that were much more important.

"How do I break Ares' curse?"

"I am pleased you are asking me this." There was a note of approval in her voice. "You must visit with Hephaestus. Aphrodite is his wife, and he knows more about her magic than I, or anyone else, does."

I felt my eyebrows jump up in surprise. "You want me to go see Aphrodite's husband? Surely he would hate Ares? Why would he want to help him?"

"It is not our place to judge the relationships of others. How Aphrodite and Hephaestus conduct their marriage is their business."

I frowned, feeling slightly chastised. "Oh." I swallowed, then asked the question burning on my lips. "Hera, am I bound to Ares?"

There was a long pause before she answered. "You know that you are. You feel it."

"Were we bound by you? Is this one of the memories I have lost?"

"No. You were bound by powers beyond my control. And in more than one way. The connection that allows you to share your power is physical, contained by distance. You can only share your magic when you are in each other's company." I nodded. I knew that was true, and it was how Dentro had saved me from Ares' blood-lust. He'd taken me far enough away that Ares couldn't draw my magic from me. "That connection comes from the War power that you share, and is not unheard of. It is similar to how Ares shares his powers with the Lords. But the bond between your souls is different. It is the same as the connection that I am able to create between lovers. Once brought to life by mutual love, it will allow you to feel each other over any distance, and know if the other is happy, sad, or angry. And you will never, ever be whole again without it. I don't know how you two were fated in such a way, but I have done what I can for my son to find you. To find happiness. He may not know, or believe that, but it is true."

"Tell me who I am, how I ended up in the mortal world?" I couldn't stop the words tumbling from me.

"Just as you are bound to Ares, I am bound to prophecy. You must find your own way to your truth." I bit down on the surge of anger I felt at her answer. She was no more helpful than Zeeva. "Oh Enyo, I am so much more helpful than Zeeva."

I hissed, slamming up a defensive wall around my thoughts. "That's not fair," I said, before I could stop myself.

"You are a visitor here, in my temple. Your thoughts in this place belong to me." Her voice was hard and filled with power. I felt my knees weaken and gripped my sword, pulling on its strength.

"Can you tell me anything else?" I asked, through gritted teeth.

"My absence from Olympus is not for nothing. Contrary to what many believe, my husband is worth saving. And I will stop at nothing to do so."

"I can respect that," I nodded. Even though Zeus sounded like a total fuckwad. I was careful to guard that thought.

A rumbling flickered through the stone, and Hera spoke again. "Visit Hephaestus. Take that helmet with you. And... help my son."

There was another shimmer of light over the statue, and the unearthly presence of the goddess vanished.

"Bella." I looked down, startled at the voice, and a rush of relief powered through my tense body.

"Zeeva."

The cat blinked slowly at me. *"I am glad to see you safe."*

"Really?"

"Why do you sound surprised?"

I cocked my head at her. "Because you're never there when I need you? Because you only show up after all the bad shit has happened?"

Zeeva swished her tail. *"You know I can only help you from a distance. I was in the forest when Ares changed."*

"You were?"

"Yes. And if Dentro had not arrived, I would have helped you. My duties and bonds make it hard for me to involve myself, but I would have sought help before Ares could kill

you." Something warm stirred in my chest at the sincerity I could hear in her normally cool voice.

Maybe I had two friends. They may be a dragon and a sphinx-shifter but I'd take that over two humans any day of the week.

"Do you know how to get to Hephaestus?" I asked her.

"Yes. And so will Dentro."

"Good. The sooner we get back to Ares, the better."

3

BELLA

We flew for a long time, and as we did Zeeva talked me through the basics of flashing. There was no question it was something I needed to learn, and I focused on her words intently, pouring my frazzled energy into the task of learning. Anything to stop the memory of those cold, emotionless eyes in the face of the man I loved.

Flashing was dangerous, Zeeva said. If done incorrectly I could end up separated from my soul. I refrained from telling her that my distance from Ares right now already felt like I had been separated from my soul. I didn't understand the depth of my feelings for the god, or how someone as practical and wary as I usually was could feel so passionately about a man I'd known for such little time. But Hera's words played in my head, warring with Zeeva's for my attention.

"You were bound by powers beyond my control. Just as you are bound to Ares, I am bound to prophecy. You must find your own way to your truth."

What did that even mean? Who the hell got involved

with my life before I could even remember and bound me to Ares? And why? What the fuck did prophecy have to do with it?

Ares would have to tell me. I had no doubt he knew more than he had told me so far, and now that he had professed his love for me...

His giant foot stamping down toward me as his savage bellow echoed through the forest flooded my memory. I squeezed my eyes shut, realizing that Zeeva's voice had fallen quiet.

"Do you fear him?" she asked gently.

My eyes fluttered open as I shook my head hard. I was wrapped in Dentro's tail again, and Zeeva was sat on the bark a foot or so from me, her magically enhanced claws set deep into the wood to keep her balance. Dentro had assured us that his skin was thick enough to take it. Pastel pink and orange clouds whooshed by on either side of us, cool air flowing through my hair.

"I don't fear him. I know he would have killed me, but I'm not scared of what's inside him. He was forced to lose control, by another god. There's nothing wrong with his own control."

Light sparked in Zeeva's amber eyes. *"And control is what is important to you?"*

"Of course it is. We are nothing past the decisions we make. I've spent my life making choices to contain my destruction."

"And you agree with the choices Ares has made?"

"Not all of them. But he is not cruel, or unnecessarily violent, which his power could easily make him. He is arrogant and egotistical, but I think I would be too if I were an Olympian god."

"I hope, very much, that you two can be together." The

cat's voice was gentler than I had ever heard it, and I cocked my head in question at her. *"It is rare to see such understanding of a person's darker traits. Such optimism could transform a life. Many lives."*

"It's not hard to understand him. I share his power. Hera said... She said I was bound to him, but not by her. Do you know what that means?"

"No. I don't. I knew that you were connected, and that Hera has a great deal of interest in you two. But no more."

"Do you know how I can get my memories back?" At the question, Zeeva dropped her gaze.

"I can give some of them to you."

My heart skipped a beat as I stared at Zeeva. "What?"

She looked back at me. *"I have been with you for much longer than you know. And I can return some of your memories to you. But not here and now. You need space, and a clear mind."*

For once, I did not argue with her. Concentrating on getting Ares back was more important. And, if I was being honest, a part of me was a little afraid of my own past. What if I didn't like what I remembered? And I had no doubt that I would end up with a whole new set of questions that I didn't have the answers to. I wasn't quite ready for that.

"Why were my memories taken?"

"We will discuss it later."

"OK. What is taking all of Hera's time and strength?"

"That's my Queen's business," Zeeva said, formal once again.

"Fine." I shifted in Dentro's tail, my magical barrier against his scratchy bark now second-nature to me. I didn't even have to think about it to keep it in place. I reached for the well of power inside me, finding it hotter and larger than it had ever been before. My strength now that I was away from Ares was huge.

"Tell me again about the flashing. I have to picture where I want to go? What if I don't know what it looks like?"

Zeeva seemed relieved to answer my question, and as we settled back into the lesson, I tried my hardest to use my ability for laser-focus to concentrate on her words and ignore my gut-wrenching awareness of Ares' absence.

"Dragon?"

A booming, throaty voice filled the sky around us, and my body fired to life as I jerked awake. "What -" My question was cut off as Dentro answered the voice.

"Mighty Hephaestus. It has been a long time."

I blinked rapidly, trying to expel the sleep from my brain. My neck was sore, and my shoulders ached, but I leaned over the tail wrapped around me to peer down. The peaks of three volcanoes were rising majestically from the ocean, and I could see the bright molten lava in each of them. Excitement fizzed through me. We had arrived in Hephaestus' realm, Scorpio.

"Hera warned me of your arrival." The god's voice was deep and clipped, and not remotely friendly. "Will you wait here, Dentro?"

"If you do not mind. The inside of a volcano is a dangerous place for a being made of wood." There was an amusement to Dentro's voice as he answered, and I felt my eyes widen.

"The inside of a volcano?" I hissed at Zeeva. She just blinked slowly at me.

The very tip of Dentro's tail curled up toward me, and he deposited the crushed helmet in my hands. I had tucked *Ischyros*, back in flick-knife mode, inside my bodice when I had realized sleep was going to take me.

"Good luck, fierce one," the dragon said, and then the world flashed white.

4

BELLA

The first thing I was aware of was heat. Serious heat. I looked around myself, feeling naked without my sword and clutching the helmet tightly instead.

I was, indeed, inside a volcano. And it was even more surreal than the flying ship had been.

The only light was coming from a river of blazing orange that bubbled before me. I was standing on dark rock, almost black in color, and I was definitely at the bottom of the epic structure. My neck strained as I looked up. There were rings of rocky platforms lining the inside, and roughly hewn stairways carved into the body of the volcano to connect them. Bridges jutted out at various points, connecting the platforms where there were no stairs and there were waterfalls of eye-wateringly bright lava flowing from huge pools on each floor all the way down to the river in front of me. The sense of being utterly dwarfed engulfed me.

I could only make out details on the first few floors above me, but I could see enough to work out what was causing the ringing, metallic bangs and thuds that were echoing through the volcano.

Giants. Huge shirtless men stood by the pools of lava, dipping pieces of metal into them, then wielding massive hammers and pokers as they worked at long rocky tables.

Hephaestus was the god of blacksmiths, and this must be his forge. I let out a long, awed breath, aware again of how hot I was as sweat trickled down my neck. The smell of sulfur was strong, and I pulled on my power to lessen it.

"Hello?" I called, hesitantly. The top of the volcano was dark, no light from the sky above shining through. A distinctly claustrophobic feeling edged over me, the desire for fresh air suddenly pervasive.

"Bella," said a voice, then a dark figure appeared at the edge of the platform above me. The figure leaped suddenly, and my mouth fell open as it easily cleared the river of lava, thudding down onto the rock just feet away from me.

I dropped to one knee instinctively, as I took in the features of Hephaestus. His face was hard and cold, his features not quite where they would be on other faces. One of his shoulders was hunched high, making him lopsided, and his black toga was covered by a heavy leather apron. A massive war-hammer swung from his right hand as he considered me.

"Hera said you would be able to help me," I said, as deferentially as I could. I needed this god's help. *Ares* needed this god's help.

"You have upset my wife." I nodded, awkwardly. Hephaestus swung the hammer between his huge hands. "She has been toying with the God of War for too long. Her pride turns her into a fool." His words were rough, as though he needed to clear his throat, and his eyes gave away no emotion.

I swallowed, wishing to hell that there was any kind of breeze in the stifling volcano. "How do I break one of her curses?"

"She is the Goddess of Love. Her curses can only be forged and broken with love."

I blinked. "Loving Ares is what caused the curse," I said. "How can loving him break it?"

Hephaestus narrowed his eyes, then they dropped to the helmet in my hands. Interest flickered in his irises, the light of the lava reflecting in the black orbs. "You understand that my wife loves many men?" he said, after an uncomfortably long pause.

"Erm," I said, not having a freaking clue what to say to that.

"Love is the most powerful thing in the world." The god's voice lowered, and a melancholy crept into his words. "All power has to have balance. No immortal is a force for good, or bad. They must all be both. With the greatest love comes the greatest pain. And with the greatest power comes the greatest wrath. My wife must carry that burden." His eyes locked on mine. "You and I will never know the extent of her hardship."

I bit down on my tongue. I understood his words, and a part of me accepted them. They were not a million miles from what I had said to Zeeva just hours before, about Ares.

But there was another part of me that could never understand or forgive the woman who had attacked the man I loved and stripped him of his self-control due to pure jealousy. Every time I had spoken with her, I had seen the cruelty within her, shining from those beautiful eyes. I knew how she had treated Ares before; like a toy, a pet, a trophy. Perhaps Hephaestus was right and it came as part of the package, being the Goddess of Love. But that didn't mean she had to act on it.

"I do not resent the God of War," Hephaestus said, letting out a sigh and mercifully saving me from saying something I would regret. "But I relish the chance to remove him from my wife's life. What were the words of her curse?"

I wracked my brain, trying to recall Aphrodite's exact words. "She said love made her power work, then she made Ares crazy with blood-lust. He tried to take all of my power by killing me. She told him, *'if you truly love her, and you want her to love you back, she must see you at your worst'.*"

Hephaestus nodded. "You must accept him at his worst. If you still love him, the curse will be broken."

"But I do accept him," I said. "Isn't that enough?" Doubt crept over me. What if I thought I did, but on some subconscious level I didn't?

But... That wasn't possible - I knew how I felt. I loved him.

"Ares needs to know that. It must be mutual. He must see that you accept him at his worst."

"How? If I go near him he'll take my power and kill me."

Hephaestus considered me for a long moment. "Do you still believe that you can prove yourself worthy of Olympus?"

"Still?" I blinked at him, trying to ignore the heat pressing in on me. "I don't know what you mean."

The God of Blacksmiths lifted his hammer. "I will

rephrase the question. Are you worthy of Olympus? Of the love of an Olympian?"

"I don't know," I said, staring at Hephaestus. I had no idea what was necessary to be worthy of Olympus. If it meant acting like Aphrodite, then no - I wasn't. And as for being worthy of Ares... "All I know is that I love him. I'll do whatever it takes to save him. Whatever is needed for him to know how I feel."

"I will help you, but you will have to earn it."

Relief washed through me. "I'll do anything."

Hephaestus held out his hand, dropping his hammer to the rock with a crack. "Give me that," he said, pointing at the crushed helmet in my hands.

I stepped forward, placing it tentatively into his enormous outstretched hand. "I made this for you many years ago," he said quietly. "I didn't know that it was you I was welding it for, at the time."

Excitement flared inside me. "Really?"

"Indeed. I make many things for the Olympians." My skin prickled with goosebumps, despite the suffocating heat.

"I'm no Olympian."

"No. You are not." He looked from the helmet to me. "If you can gather what I need from my realm to repair the helmet, then you will be able to break the curse and save Ares."

"How?"

"When you wear this helmet, no god will be able to penetrate it," he said, and took a lop-sided stride toward me. My breath caught in my pounding chest.

"Impervious armor? Like Ares has?"

He nodded. "Yes. But Ares' armor protects his body. This

helmet is different. It will protect everything internal to you. Your body will be just as susceptible to external influence as it was before, but as long as you are wearing the helmet, your mind, your soul and your power will be guarded."

Understanding smashed into me, the meaning of his words sounding too good to be true. "Ares can't take my power if I'm wearing the helmet?"

"He can not."

"Thank you," I breathed, feeling just a smidgen of the tension wracking my body lessen. "Thank you so much."

"Do not thank me yet. My realm is not an easy place to navigate, and you will need to converse with my general. He is not accustomed to visitors."

"Your general? What do I need to do?"

"You understand that this is a test? Of your worthiness?" I nodded. I had enough brute strength and sheer determination burning through my veins that I was sure I could complete any damn test. "I need a bar of gold and a purple phoenix feather." He held up the helmet, tiny in his palm. "Then I will be able to fix this and you can return to Ares."

"I'm ready. Where do I find them?"

"There are many volcanoes in Scorpio. You will need this to enter one." A black orb shimmered into existence at my feet, the size of a large pebble. I crouched and scooped it up. "If you manage to get both items, you'll be flashed back here."

Before I could answer him, he flashed me out of his volcano without a word of warning.

5

BELLA

"Shit!"

I was falling through the air, the crystal clear ocean fast approaching and the black orb clutched in my hand. I ran through my options lightning fast in my head, and deciding I wasn't confident enough to try and flash myself, braced for impact.

I slammed into the water, feeling as though I'd hit a brick wall before sinking under the surface. I scrambled to kick myself up, refusing to let go of the orb and my skirt tangling around my legs as I tried to swim. A dark shadow moved over me and then I was aware of something dipping into the water next to me. Dentro's tail wrapped around my middle and pulled me from the ocean.

"Bastard, asshole, fuckwit god," I spat, trying to push my wet hair out of my face with one hand, still unwilling to relinquish my grip on the orb.

Dentro chuckled. "He's not known for his hospitality. This realm is forbidden. Most who enter it are killed instantly." The dragon moved me so that I was level with his face, his eyes serious. Zeeva trotted along his snakelike body, stopping and staring at me. Cooling ocean spray combined with the breeze caused by the beating of Dentro's wings, and I took a second to revel in the feeling of cool freedom.

"Where is the helmet?" Zeeva asked. *"And what is that?"* She sniffed at the orb.

"If I can find some gold and some purple phoenix feathers, then he'll fix the helmet," I said, hope and excitement rushing through me. "And then it will protect my power. Nobody can get to me when I'm wearing it."

"Including Ares?"

"Yes. I'll be able to go back to him." A sense of purpose was replacing the crushing sense of loss, and I felt my power focusing, doubt and grief forced into a backseat.

"Good. Where will you find these things you need?" Dentro asked.

"Erm..." I held up the orb. "All I know is that they're in his realm and I need this."

"Hmmm," The dragon mused, beating his wings and rising above the sea. "All of Scorpio is within volcanoes. I suppose the orb shows you which one you need to visit."

"It's a good job you're here, Dentro," I said, peering closely at the orb as we rose higher. "I would've been here a week working that out."

The orb was rough, and I could make out a pattern on the black stone.

"Look down. There is Scorpio. Does that help?"

I did as the dragon said, seeing a spattering of volcano tips rising form the ocean. There were at least twenty. I scowled. How was I supposed to single out two of them?

It took another five minutes of hovering over Scorpio and Zeeva asking repeatedly for the exact words

Hephaestus had said, before I realized what the pattern on the orb was.

"Dentro, move around until that big volcano there is on our right," I said excitedly, holding up the orb. The dragon soared through the sky, moving to where I'd asked him, and I fist pumped the air as the pattern on the orb lined up with the peaks jutting out the ocean below us.

"That's it! The pattern on the rock is a map of the volcanoes! Look!"

Zeeva flicked her tail as she looked at where I was pointing. "Well done."

"Thanks," I said, inspecting the orb. "One of them must be the one we want..." I ran my finger over the little bumps that matched up with the volcanoes. One of them was sharp, where all the others were smooth. "I've found it!" I held the orb up, and counted, working out exactly which peak matched the spiky one on the orb. "It's that one, there. Dentro, can you take me down?"

Identifying the correct volcano was one thing. Getting inside it was quite another.

We were low over the basin of the volcano, the heat from the bubbling lava washing over us. No part of me actually relished the thought of being back in the oppressive heat, but I needed to complete the task and show Hephaestus I was worthy of his help.

"I believe that you should drop the orb in," said Dentro.

"What? But what if I need it?"

"I agree with the dragon," said Zeeva.

I gave her a long look, trying to work out any alternative options. Coming up with none, I swallowed and gripped the rock. "Fine."

I drew back my arm, then launched the orb into molten rock below. It made a small splash as it hit, then sank slowly into the lava.

"It didn't work," I breathed as it disappeared. "What in the name of fuck am I supposed to do now? I threw away the damn orb!"

Heat swelled over me all of a sudden, then the lava began to whirl, almost as though someone had pulled a plug underneath it. In seconds, a dark black hole appeared. "I am not jumping into that," I said, staring.

But a vision of Ares filled my mind, his sensual, powerful gaze boring into mine. For him, I would jump into a volcano. For him, I would do anything.

"Allow me to help you," said Dentro, and gently lowered me toward the hole. When I was ten feet above it, I heard his voice again. "I can get no closer to the heat, fierce one. Good luck." Then his tail uncoiled from around me and I was dropping.

I suppressed a shriek and grasped at the thought of the horse shield, dragging it around myself as I tipped into darkness. But almost immediately I felt my weight taken, and a deep fiery glow bloomed around me.

I was floating gently down through another forge lining the inside of the volcano, just like Hephaestus', with platforms housing vats of lava and creatures working with hammers and tools beside them. Lava flowed from the top of the volcano all the way down, filling the vats then spilling down, until it reached a pool at the bottom.

The smell of sulfur was overwhelming and I used my power to block it as whatever was causing me to float started to pull me toward a wide platform. A huge figure was hunched over a slab, beating something that was glowing white-hot with a flat hammer. He turned as my feet met the platform, and ripples of heat washed over me from the vat. I felt my stomach flutter as I found my footing, whatever it was taking my weight vanishing and the sensation jarring. When I was certain I was steady on my feet I looked up. And up.

The man towering over me was an actual giant. And he only had one eye.

"Hello," I said, feeling *Ischyros* hum against my chest. I longed to pull the weapon from my bodice, but was pretty sure that would send the wrong message.

"My master sent you. You had an orb. Why?"

His voice was raspy and booming. Other than the one eye thing, he just looked like a normal guy, if a normal guy was a twenty foot tall wrestler, wearing only a pair of hessian shorts.

"I, erm, need to collect a couple things for him," I said. "I'm Bella, by the way."

He blinked and bent over to look closer at me. The smell of sulfur battered against my defenses. "I am the famous cyclops, General Brontes. I am sure you have heard of me." He beat a giant fist against his bare chest.

"Of course I have," I said quickly.

"Good. What do you want?"

"Some gold and a purple phoenix feather, please."

His solitary eyebrow lifted. "The gold I can give you, if you are strong enough to carry it."

"I'm strong," I assured him.

"You don't look strong." He screwed his face up and peered even more closely at me.

"Well, I am."

He shrugged. "The feather needs to be fetched from the stores."

"OK. Where are the stores?"

He pointed down. "Under there." I moved and peered over the edge of the platform.

"Under where?"

"The lava."

I blinked at the simmering pool of molten rock. "Oh. How do you get to them?"

"You don't, unless you are a telkhine."

"What's one of those?"

He shook his head, then began to lumber along the platform. "Come," he said. I hurried after him. "There. That is a telkhine." My mouth fell open as I looked where he was pointing. Over at the next vat there was a creature working that looked like nothing my wildest imagination could have invented. It was as though a seal and a dog had been combined, and then the thing had been given webbed fingers. The top half of the body was mostly dog like, but the bottom half consisted of a squat fish tail that it was propped up on. It was working on something that looked like a chainmail net, its hands moving so fast I could barely keep up with them. The sight was kind of mesmerizing. "My master created them to work in his forges. They are master smiths and they can swim in lava." Brontes said.

"Wow. OK. Will he get the feather for me?"

"Absolutely not."

I snapped my eyes to Brontes. "Why not?"

"Telkhines hate everyone."

"Oh. Could you ask him for me?"

"No."

"Please?"

"No. If you want the feather, you must go through the lava to get to the stores yourself."

I opened my mouth to argue, but Hephaestus' words came back to me. This was a test of my worth. Of course it would not be as easy as asking someone else to do it for me. "Fine. I'll go myself. Please can I have the gold first?"

"Yes, but I still do not think you are strong enough to carry it."

"We'll see about that, Mister General," I scowled.

I followed the enormous cyclops back to the slab he had been working at, and he began hunting around for something, moving lumps of metal and tools I didn't recognize around. I shifted uncomfortably in the heat, wishing I wasn't wearing a damn dress. The tight bodice wasn't so bad, and kept my sword safe, but the skirts were sticking to my thighs in the humidity.

"Here," Brontes said, and turned back to me. He was holding a small bar of gold in his hand, not much bigger than a candy bar.

"That's it?"

"Yes. That is all the mighty Hephaestus will need. Gold from his forges is like no other."

"I appreciate your help," I said, reaching out to take it from him. He dropped down into a crouch abruptly, and I almost stumbled back in surprise as a single eye came level with me. He had a mop of dark, scruffy hair, and thick lashes.

"When you die in the lava, I would like the sword you are carrying."

"What? Firstly, no. Secondly, I'm not going to die! How do you know I am carrying a sword anyway?"

"I am the general of smiths. I can feel it. It is a fine thing."

"It is a fine thing," I agreed and reached out again for the gold. "And it belongs to me. Now, please may I have the gold and I'll be on my way."

Brontes cocked his head at me, then handed over the shining metal.

"Fuck me sideways," I gasped as he placed it into my hand. It weighed a freaking ton. I almost dropped it before my power kicked in, amplifying the strength in my arms, making my skin glow in the process.

"Huh. You can carry it," muttered Brontes, then straightened with a nod. "You will probably still die in the lava."

"Well, aren't you a ray of freaking sunshine?" I scowled, trying to get the impossibly heavy little piece of metal safely stowed in my bodice. *Ischyros* was hot against my already-too-hot chest, and seemed to burn even harder as the gold slid in next to it.

Brontes frowned at me. "I hate sunshine."

"Then it's just as well that you live in a volcano. How do I get to the stores once I'm in the lava?"

"Just go straight down."

"OK. Anything else I should know?"

"I will take good care of your sword once you are dead."

"It's my sword! Keep your hands off!" I snapped, then shook my head and stamped toward the steps carved into the interior of the volcano, leading down toward the pool of lava.

~

"Well, shit, that's hot." Fear was making my insides clench as I stood over the pool. It bubbled and oozed, mostly a rich orange but glowing white in places. I didn't actually know if I could survive swimming in lava. I knew I was immortal, as Ares didn't have any of my power. And I knew I could use my shield.

But, as much as I was loathe to admit it, I *was* a baby goddess. I didn't really know how to use my power properly, and I was alone.

Ares filled my mind instantly, as though my head was railing against the word *alone*. I wasn't alone anymore. I had Ares. A man who thought like me, understood me, loved me. Didn't want me to be anyone else.

I took a deep breath, and pulled my shield around myself. This was the only way to save him from the curse. If I had to swim through fucking lava for him, I would.

With a muttered curse, I jumped.

6

BELLA

It's so hot, I'm going to die. I sucked in non-existent air as I began to sink through the heat, the sentence repeating in my mind, no other thought able to get past it. *It's so hot, I'm going to die.*

Nothing could survive this heat. I was suffocating, my eyes were burning, I was sinking. The weight of the gold was dragging me down, and my legs were kicking uselessly.

It's so hot, I'm going to die. There was nothing else but the inferno. My skin was melting off my body, my eyes were streaming so hard I could see nothing.

It's so hot, I want to die. The chant had changed. I couldn't take it. I was done. The heat was unbearable, it had to stop. I couldn't breathe, I couldn't move, I-

My feet hit something solid. The mental chant cut off, and I kicked hard instinctively. I heard a faint sucking sound, and then the ooze around me was lessening, lessening, until I was falling though air. I came to a thumping halt on hard rock, knocking what little air I had left in my lungs out of me. I heaved in breaths as I felt the rock beneath me, trying to orientate myself.

The rock was warm, but it wasn't searing.

"Oh thank fuck." I rolled onto my back, pressing myself against the floor gratefully and trying to steady my breathing. My eyes widened as I took in the view above me. It was as though the ceiling was made of glass, a barrier between the room I was in and the mass of surging lava.

"Can I help you? Are you hurt?"

I started in surprise at the timid voice, and tried to sit up. The gold in my bodice was weighing me down, making it hard to move, and I patted myself down, feeling for burns. To my surprise, I could find none.

"Erm, I'm fine," I said, turning on my ass to look for the owner of the voice.

A telkhine, much smaller than the one I'd seen with Brontes, was standing up on its tail a few feet from me. Huge racks of shelving filled the room behind it, and the light was all coming from the glowing lava above us, making everything look orange.

"We don't get many visitors down here. Who sent you?"

There was no aggression in the creature's voice, just curiosity. But Brontes had said telkhines didn't like people. I decided to err on the edge of caution.

"Hephaestus sent me. I need a purple phoenix feather. Do you know where I can find one?"

The little telkhine nodded enthusiastically, its face lighting up. "I sure do. The feathers are my favorite."

Hope surged through me as I looked at the creature. There was no way this thing wanted to hurt me, I thought, as it's weird webbed hands clapped together.

"What's your name?" I asked, getting to my feet slowly.

"Mikro. Because I am small. I work in the stores, because I'm too small to work in the forge." There was a note of sadness to the slightly female voice.

"Well, let me tell you, I like it better down here than up there," I said with a smile.

"Really?"

"Yeah." It was a lie. It was even more claustrophobic with the lava oozing over our heads than it was before, and just as hot. As if it wasn't bad enough being inside a volcano, I was now under one.

Although even that was better than being in the lava. I shuddered and shook myself, trying to rid my body of the memory of sinking through the liquid inferno.

"You know, you're lucky. It would have taken you ages to get to the bottom if that gold wasn't weighing you down. And it's a good job you had something made by Hephaestus on you, or you'd never had got through the ceiling," Mikro said.

"Really?" I assumed she could sense *Ischyros* and the gold with the same blacksmith magic Brontes had.

"Yes. If you didn't have that sword, you would have just sunk to the bottom and stayed there."

I felt a bit sick at the thought, and patted my chest. "Thanks *Ischyros*. Once again, you've saved my ass," I whispered.

Mikro beamed at me. "You make your sword happy, and that makes smiths happy. Come with me and we will find your feather."

We wound through the shelves, Mikro talking fast about her job in the stores as we went. I was only half listening, my body still humming with adrenaline, and filling with impatient hope. I was vaguely aware of the huge sheets of metal and alien looking tools we were passing, but one thought was dominating my mind. Once I got the feather, I could return to Hephaestus. And then I would be one step closer to Ares.

"Here we are."

Mikro had come to a stop and I looked at the shelves next to us. It was like a freaking magical mardi-gras. Feathers of every type I could possibly conceive, and then some more, were fanned out in a display of dancing light and color.

"I can see why they're your favorite," I breathed in awe.

"I know! They're beautiful."

"They are." My gaze was caught on a giant peacock feather that was rippling with teal light the same color Zeeva always flashed.

"That's for Hera only," Mikro said seriously, and I snapped my eyes away.

"Of course. Which ones are phoenix feathers?"

Mikro pointed to a row of feathers on one of the lower shelves and I ducked into a crouch, scanning them. They were as long as my forearm, with soft fluff at the base, tapering into magnificent smooth curves at the top. I pointed to a purple one, the exact shade of the plume on my crushed helmet. "I think that's the right one," I said.

Mikro nodded, and plucked it from the shelf. "Then here you are. Keep taking care of your weapons, and they will take care of you," she chirruped happily, before handing me the feather.

"I will, and thank you." But my words were lost, because the second my fingers closed around the feather, I was flashed.

． ． ．

The God of Blacksmiths stood before me, exactly as I had last seen him at the edge of the pool of lava. He was holding the crushed helmet and he had the hint of a smile on his misshapen face.

I nodded deferentially, then pulled the heavy gold from my bodice. "I have the feather and the gold."

"Good. Bring them to me." He held out his other hand, and I hurried forward to give them to him. Power rolled from him, a sense of calm stoicism that clashed against my own fierce energy.

The god turned away from me, limping toward the mass of lava, and I inched closer impatiently as he crouched down. He flared with a sudden golden light, and dipped the helmet into the liquid fire, along with the gold and the feather. I drew in a breath, concerned his hands would burn, but he straightened and lifted the helmet high.

It was glowing as golden as he was, and something stirred deep in my chest as the god's hands grew, closing around the metal. Heat, but internal - the kind of heat *Ischyros* gave out - spread through my body as Hephaestus' light got brighter and brighter. Just when I thought my skin may actually catch alight, he opened his giant hands.

They moved fast, and I saw that he was molding the now supple metal, a look of intense concentration on his fascinatingly misshapen face. Within seconds, the helmet was the right shape again, and Hephaestus' hands began to shrink back down. He reached out a long arm, the helmet held carefully in his fingers. I took it, warm tingles of power thrumming through me immediately. It felt exactly like *Ischyros*, which flared with heat against my chest from where it was safely stowed.

"Thank you." My voice sounded almost reverent. "I'll be worthy of it, I swear."

"Good. Now leave."

I didn't need telling twice. I had a beautiful, savage god to save.

7

ARES

"**W**hy are you doing this?"
I knew my roared question would receive no answer. And I knew my pain would only give Aphrodite more pleasure. But I couldn't bear the torment any longer.

When I thought of Aphrodite my head cleared, the anger flooding my veins directed purely at her. I knew what she had done. I knew she had taken something from me. Something I deemed more important than anything else. But the second I focused on what that was, the anger boiled over, no longer directed at the Goddess of Love but at *everything*.

I wanted to kill everything. I wanted to fight, to maim, to prove to the world that the God of War could not be beaten or bested, that I was the strongest being alive. The red-mist would descend and then... Then I would come round, I didn't know how much later, my body broken and bleeding. I could not recall the reason through my fury-fueled haze, but I had no power. No divine strength, just that of a well-muscled human. Which I could see was no match for the forest around me.

After the first black-out I had deduced that I had let my rage loose on a tree, the torn skin and blood all over the bark, and the wounds on my hands and bare feet my evidence.

After the second I found a dead wolf at my feet, its throat torn out. Deep lacerations clearly caused by teeth covered my wrists and hands, where my armor did not reach.

The third time, I knew the bones in my right hand were broken. The pain made my head spin and my stomach churn.

The fourth, my left ankle was snapped, the bone jutting right out of my skin.

Each time the rage got the better of me, more of my body suffered. Soon, I would not be able to stand or use my hands at all. But I knew I would still try, when the blood-lust settled.

I took a rasping breath, trying to hold the image of Aphrodite in my mind, and stop the slip of my thoughts to whatever it was that she had taken from me. Whatever it was that I needed so badly, that made my heart pound and the drums beat. An image of a woman, fierce and proud and shining gold filled my mind suddenly, and I screamed as my broken hand closed into a fist, agony lancing up my arm. I was pushing myself off the forest floor before I could stop myself, red descending over my vision, coloring the bleak forest the hue of blood.

Death. Death to all, and victory to Ares. There was no other way.

"Ares!"

I spun at the voice, ready to kill, ready to win. My pain was gone, and I was ready. *Ready for war.*

"Oh god, Ares." The voice broke, and a figure burst out of the undergrowth. I stumbled, then stopped. For a moment, I thought my heart had stopped too.

Bella.

It was Bella.

She was wearing a golden helmet which meant that I could only see her eyes, but I was sure it was her. Memories of the woman standing before me tumbled through my mind, and for a second of pure bliss, I remembered. I fell in love with her all over again.

But then fire was coursing through me, a darkness filling my veins like acid.

Win! Win! She has your power, take it! Win!

The voice was deafening, and I reached out, the cord connecting us bursting to life. I pulled, hard. This was what I needed. I needed my power. Then I would be whole again. Then I would be strong again. *Zeus would respect me again.*

I needed my power back.

But none came.

"Ares, what have you done to yourself?" The woman's voice was choked, and I could see pain filling her eyes.

"Give me my power!" I bellowed, ignoring the scratching pain in my throat. I took a step toward her but my leg gave out. I was aware of the sensation in my lower half, and of the woman's cry, but it only made me more angry. "This infernal fucking body! Give me my power, now!" Desperation was coursing through me, tipping me dangerously close to fear. *Why couldn't I reach her power?*

"Ares, please. I can't see you like this. Please, let me help you."

"Never! I take help from nobody!"

She moved toward me and I lashed out. I missed. More anger swelled through me, impotent rage making my vision cloud. I was Ares, Olympian God of War. I was afraid of nothing.

"You said we would help each other. You said you loved me." The rage stuttered a second, and I tried to focus on her but my other leg gave out. "Ares, you need to know that I love you too. I feel the same. I love you."

Almost as though I'd taken a blow to the head, I fell backward. My armor hit the moldy earth, my broken body bouncing inside it, but I didn't notice. The woman's words echoed through my head as everything faded around me.

I love you.

Nobody loved me. My subjects revered me, the gods respected me, but nobody loved me.

"Why?" I heard the word leave my own lips as my vision swam in and out, shining gold moving in a blur over the top of my prostrate body.

"Because you are strong and proud and good. You're fierce and magnificent, and you're mine. Mine, Ares. And I am yours." Intense emotion filled her voice, and I knew her words were true. I knew it as surely as I knew that I was dying. "I love you."

The cord that connected us seared white-hot all of a sudden, and I heard her cry out.

"Bella!" Concern for her overpowered everything else. The red mist drained away instantly, the toxic rage filling me receding into nothingness.

"Ares! Ares, I need to heal you." Her voice was both relieved and frantic, and my vision cleared long enough for me to see her lift her helmet away from her beautiful face. Tears streaked her cheeks, and she clasped her cool hands to my burning skin.

Then her face faded into blackness.

8

BELLA

"Please, please, please heal." I felt sick to my soul as I stared down at Ares' scratched, pale face. Any skin that his armor didn't cover was ruined; torn and bloodied. One of his hands was clearly broken, the bones at nauseating angles, and his left ankle was practically split in half, blood pouring from the wound in terrifying quantity.

I knew it was a risk to remove the helmet. If the curse was still in place he could come round and drain my power. But he had already lost so much blood, it was clear that if I waited a moment longer he would die. He had no power, no immortality, and no ability to heal himself while I was wearing the helmet.

He had recognized me, before he had passed out. I had heard it in the way he had shouted my name, seen a flicker of it in his unfocused eyes.

"Please heal," I said again, hot tears tracking down my skin. "And please remember me. Believe me. I love you."

. . .

"Well, aren't you two cute?"

I whipped my head round at the sugar-sweet voice that I knew belonged to Aphrodite. My instinct was to leap up, to draw my sword and take the evil bitch's head from her neck. But I couldn't take my hands from Ares. He needed me. He couldn't draw my power from me; I had to pour it into him.

The Goddess of Love took a step toward us, a beacon of beauty and light in the miserable, faded forest.

"Fuck off, Aphrodite. If he dies, I will find you and I will end you."

She gave me a smug smile. "If the almighty Goddess of Chaos can't best me, I highly doubt a backwater baby deity like you will fare any better." Alarm trickled through me.

"You fought Eris?"

Her smile widened. "I outsmarted Eris," she whispered. Her voice was lyrical, sensual, compelling. I slammed my protective walls around my mind. I couldn't put the helmet back on; Ares needed my power.

"Where is she?"

"As if I would tell you. Let's just say it will be a long, long while before she finds her way back home."

Red tinged the edges of my vision. Eris might have been a colossal pain in the ass, but I had become inexplicably fond of her. She had helped us. And I believed that she cared more for her brother than she admitted. "What happened to you to make you so cruel?"

Aphrodite's eyes darkened.

"There is nothing more cruel than love, Bella. I am responsible for providing the most intense feeling of bliss anyone is capable of feeling. Love. There's nothing like it. But everything exists in balance." A bitter look crossed her ethereal features. "I was born with the ability to cause more pain than any other God alive."

"That doesn't mean you should!"

She straightened abruptly. "My motivations are none of your business, little girl."

"Why are you here?" Tension was making my muscles ache, and fear was building in waves that crashed through me. To fight her, I would have to let go of Ares. And that might kill him. I couldn't let go.

But I sure as fuck would not go down without a fight. Carefully, I pictured the horse shield, willing a protective dome around us that she would hopefully not see.

She chuckled. "Bella, I'm ancient. I can sense your pathetic magic."

I snarled, keeping the shield up. She wouldn't be the first to underestimate me and regret it. "What do you want?"

"To say goodbye." Her voice was quiet, and carried a lethal danger. "To Ares."

Fear tore through me, rage taking over and feeding my power like rocket-fuel. The dome around us burst into flame, and Aphrodite stumbled. "You will not take him!" I screamed.

I could only see her silhouette through the flaming dome around us, but her voice was clear. "I am as bound to my power as every other god. You genuinely love him, and I can't interfere with that. But trust me when I tell you Bella, I will not stop until you are both dead."

The flames leaped and grew, and with a roar I pushed as much power as I could spare from Ares into the dome. The boom was so loud that pain lanced through my skull. Everything around us flashed white as the flames became impossibly hot, bursting out like a nuclear explosion.

"Next time, little girl." Her voice rang in the aftermath of the boom, but before I could answer her, I felt Ares stir beneath me. Heat surged through my palms. I snapped my eyes to him, hope and relief and a million other emotions filling my chest.

"Bella." The cord that connected our power flared to life, and I felt the tug in my gut.

"Ares, take it, take my power. Heal yourself." My voice came out as a sob. He was alive. He had spoken my name.

"Bella," he said again, his eyes still closed. The pull got stronger, and I glanced away from his face to his ankle. The blood had stopped flowing.

Reflections of the inferno all around us danced across his golden armor, and I tipped my head back, trying to stop my tears.

"Aphrodite?" I yelled. But I knew she had gone. Something touched my hand, the one glued to Ares' face, and I gasped, looking back down.

Ares' palm was over my fingers, the bones straight again. His eyes were fixed on my face, and for a heart-stopping second he just stared at me. Fear that the curse had not been broken bubbled up inside me, my breath getting short. But then he spoke.

"Mine."

And I knew he wasn't talking about the magic. Intense, soul-deep adoration took over his face as he stared. He was talking about me.

I was his.

9

BELLA

"I thought I was going to lose you," I breathed, gripping his face harder.

"Never. I will never lose you, and you will never lose me." His voice was getting stronger, and the pull on my power was steady now.

"You were so... broken." A lump the size of a golf ball seemed to have lodged itself in my throat. "I couldn't bear to see you like that."

Shame washed over his features, but his eyes only dipped from mine for a fraction of a second. "I am truly sorry that you saw me like that. I... I know I tried to kill you." He looked sickened.

"No, you misunderstand me," I told him. "I meant seeing your body broken, the life leaving you. I couldn't bear to see you like *that*."

Ares' beautiful face creased up in confusion. "But what about the blood-lust? The wrathful, savage rage?"

I gave him a small smile as I shrugged my shoulders. "I knew that was within you the first day we met. It's your ability to control it that makes me admire you so much."

The confusion leaked from his face, replaced by wonder. "You are like nobody I have ever known," he whispered to me.

"Ditto," I told him.

"All those years..." He trailed off, fear flicking through his eyes.

"What? What do you mean?" It was my turn to frown.

"Just that I wish we had found each other sooner."

My shoulders relaxed. "We have found each other now, and that's what matters."

"Aphrodite will not make our lives easy," he said, trying to sit up. Reluctantly, I released my hold on his face, helping to pull his shoulders up. He was almost a dead-weight, and the color leeched from his face again, but he persisted. His jaw dropped when he looked around himself.

We were sitting in what was essentially a crater, the rest of the forest burning and crackling gently around us.

"What happened?"

"I, erm, caused an explosion. To try to stop Aphrodite from killing you." Ares blinked at me and I shrugged again. "I think it worked." My smile slipped as her words crashed back to me. "She fought with Eris, and she says she won. She said that it will be a long time until Eris finds her way home."

Anger crossed the god's face, but it melted away as he gripped my hand in his.

"Eris is strong. We will help her if we can, but only after we finish what we have started."

"The Ares Trials," I said quietly.

"Once we are free of these abhorrent games, we can..." He didn't finish the sentence, a haunted look crossing his face instead.

"I don't love Joshua," I said in a rush, suddenly scared that he might think I would leave him if we rescued my friend.

"I know. You love me. I can feel it." Warmth filled my whole body as he gazed at me. "But we must finish the Trials."

I nodded. "Yes. I can't leave Joshua a soulless victim of a rogue demon - he's my friend. And we need to get you that Trident."

"Bella, I... I need to tell you many things."

I nodded again. "I know. I saw your mother."

He stiffened. "What? What did she tell you?"

"That we were bound, but not by her. That I have lost memories, and that prophecy won't permit her to tell me more. That she loves you." Ares closed his eyes. A tree cracked nearby as it lost its battle with the flames, causing a loud thud as the wood hit the earth.

"Bella, I need you to trust me. I need you to wait until the Trials are finished before I tell you what you want to know."

"Why?"

He opened his eyes, looking intensely into mine. "Because if we fail the Trials, one of us will surely die. Only one of us can be immortal."

"What has that got to do with you telling me about my past?" Apprehension skittered through me, my stomach knotting.

"Please, Bella. Trust me." It sounded like the words pained him, and I was sure I could see guilt in his tight expression.

But, I *did* trust him. I couldn't help it. "You're making me nervous," I told him. "Is it really bad? Whatever it is that you won't tell me?"

It was definitely guilt on his face. "It is... not good. It will take some time to understand. Time and focus that we can't spare until the Trials are over, and the demon is returned and your friend is safe."

I considered his words. He wasn't lying or sugar-coating anything, which strengthened my trust in him, despite it worsening my feeling of dread. He was being practical, true to his nature.

For the first time since arriving in Olympus, I thought about what it would be like *not* to find out where I came from, or how I'd ended up living so many miserable years away from Ares and Olympus. If it was as bad as it sounded, perhaps I'd rather not know.

Either way, Ares was right about one thing. Making sure Joshua was safe and regaining his power and immortality was more urgent. I knew how important mindset and focus were in a fight. His words rang through my mind. *"If we fail the Trials, one of us will surely die."* I'd survived this long without knowing whatever it was he didn't want to tell me. The knowledge wasn't worth risking our lives, or Joshua's, for now.

"OK. We fuck the Lords over by smashing the shit out of these Trials, and then you tell me everything."

A smile pulled slowly at Ares' lips as he let out a sigh of relief. "You know, you swear too much."

"So I've been told."

A shadow moved behind Ares and I almost jumped to my feet before recognizing Dentro's form.

"I have to be honest, fierce one, I was quite looking forward to destroying this accursed forest myself," the dragon said.

"Sorry, Dentro. It was kind of an accident."

"You have done a thorough job."

I grinned at him. "Thanks."

"I wanted to warn you though, Panic is not pleased. And nor are many of the previous inhabitants of the forest. I would advise leaving Skotadi with some haste."

I looked at Ares. "Are you strong enough to flash us?"

"Yes. I think so."

"Thank you for everything, Dentro," I said, standing up and reaching out my hand. Slowly, the dragon slid across the charred ground, his massive body seeming to repel the burning embers. He stopped when he reached me, lowering his head until it bumped against my palm. A sense of peaceful contentment washed through my whole body.

"It is I who needs to thank you. Call me if you ever need me."

10

BELLA

Flashing us drained the strength from Ares completely, and I was so caught up in breaking his fall as he crashed to his knees that I didn't even register where we were.

"Ares!"

"I'm fine," he slurred, then his eyes rolled, and he fell unconscious again, sliding down my body, his huge weight almost taking me with him.

"Shit," I cursed, trying to lower him to the floor gently. He had color in his cheeks and his wounds were healed, so I knew it was just exhaustion that had taken him this time, but a small flutter of panic rippled through me regardless.

I noticed the floor as I carefully laid his head down; a rich, shining wood. Running in planks... I looked up sharply, examining my surroundings. I was on the deck of a ship, shining solar sails standing out against a soft, cloudy sky. I yanked *Ischyros* from my bodice, the blade shimmering and morphing immediately.

Had something gone wrong with Ares' flashing? Had someone else flashed us back to the demon's ship?

But as I turned warily on the spot, I realized that I was definitely *not* on the demon's ship. This vessel had only one raised quarterdeck, and was much smaller, and the front formed a sharp triangular peak, almost like a Viking ship. The deck was made from a richer, darker wood, and the finishes over the doorway that I could see ten feet away were gleaming gold. As I looked closer, I saw images of weapons carved into one of the two masts. The ship gave off an air of arrogant opulence, somehow.

"So this is the God of War's secret home?"

Zeeva's voice didn't startle me, a sure sign that I was becoming used to her appearing out of nowhere.

"Secret home?"

"All gods have their public palaces, and the places they actually like to spend their time. The latter are generally kept a secret." Movement caught my eye, and I looked over to see her sauntering toward the railings. I walked to her, peering down over the side of the ship.

"That's freaking awesome," I breathed.

Below us, under the clouds, was an island that looked like a patchwork of little worlds. A jungle city spread across the south-east cliffs, and I could see sand-filled deserts nestled between expanses of moorland and snowcapped mountain ranges. A colorless forest with a blackened center caught my eye. "Skotadi," I realized. "This is Ares' realm."

"Yes."

"It's stunning."

"It's lethal," answered the cat, wryly.

I suddenly felt as though I should be sharing this moment with Ares, and turned away, moving back to him.

The world below us wasn't going anywhere, and I wanted to wait for a guided tour from the god himself. "I need to get him comfortable. He needs to rest."

Summoning my magical strength, I managed to get Ares through the door and down a small flight of steps.

"Fuck, your armor is heavy," I told the sleeping god. I stepped into a wood paneled corridor with massive double doors at the very end. They were grand enough that I was sure there would be a nice room behind them, so I headed that way.

I was right. The room was beyond nice. It was freaking epic.

Columns of mahogany shelving lined the walls like ribs, and between each one was glass, from floor to ceiling. Glittering clouds floated by on either side of us. A plush red rug dominated the room, flanked by two huge black leather couches. I carried Ares to one, and set him down carefully, before spinning to look more closely at the room. Another set of massive double doors faced the ones I had come through, and on either side of them were cabinets filled with weapons. A glowing spear, a bow strung with something gleaming gold, a war-hammer with etchings that moved even as I looked.

The shelves intersecting the glass sides of the ship were covered in books, weird little artefacts, and many different bottles.

"Zeeva, which of these is nectar?" I knew how much the stuff had helped me when I had been drained.

"Behind you. Third shelf."

It was Ares' voice that had answered me, and I spun to him, heart leaping. "You're awake!"

"I am."

"Good. Where the fuck are we?"

He was sitting up, looking groggy. "This is where I live."

"You said you liked ships; you didn't say that you lived on one!" I moved to the shelf he had indicated, finding the nectar and an array of glasses on the one below.

"This ship doesn't sail very far. I have the best view in Olympus here."

"I saw. Will you tell me what all the different kingdoms are?" I couldn't keep the excitement from my voice as I turned back to him, two filled glasses in my hands.

"Of course I will." He smiled at me. "Your enthusiasm is alien to me."

I scowled as I sat down beside him, passing him his drink. "Is that good or bad?"

"It is good. So very, very good. I had forgotten what joy and excitement had felt like. Until you."

I felt my cheeks heat, and happiness made my stomach flip. The man had no filter for his thoughts at all, and it appeared that included the gooey ones. "Well, thank god for that, because not everyone appreciates my enthusiasm. I have been called annoyingly hyperactive in the past."

"Anyone who insulted you is an asshole."

I barked a laugh. "Hey! That's my word. You're not allowed to use it."

"I've come to quite like it."

"I've come to quite like you," I said playfully, then instantly felt stupid. Ares was the God of War, a giant of a man, a freaking legend. How did one flirt with a god?

"Just *like*? Maybe there's something I can do to increase my appeal a notch or two." Hunger gleamed in his now clear eyes, and I gulped. It looked like normal flirting worked just fine with this god.

. . .

Ares drained his glass of nectar, the wicked gleam still in his eyes. "Come," he said, and stood up, proffering his hand to me. I took it, expecting him to lead me through the closed double doors, but instead he headed through the doors we had come through. I turned my head, catching Zeeva's eye.

"I'll leave you two alone," she said, a lilt of amusement to her voice.

We emerged on the deck a couple of minutes later, and Ares paused, inhaling deeply. Then he pulled me to the railing, looking between the island below him and me.

"My realm, my woman," he said, his face set and strong. A drum beat in the distance. *My woman.* I was his woman.

"You're feeling better then?" I said, my voice coming out a little breathless. A flame fired to life in his eyes.

"With your power running through my body, I feel invincible. With you, I feel like I can do anything."

More flames danced to life in his eyes, and the drum beat again. He reached to his side, and with a few movements his armor fell with a clatter to the planks. His shirt beneath was torn and bloody, and his pants loose at his waist. I looked back to his tangled hair and fierce eyes. He looked like he had been dragged through hell and back. *And survived.* It was the hottest thing I'd ever seen.

Heat flooded my core, an ache building instantly, all the fire and passion and intensity from the castle rushing back like a tidal wave. He took a step toward me, towering over me.

"You have turned my world upside-down. You have made me question everything I thought I knew. You have made me new enemies. And you have given me a reason to *live*."

The drums beat harder, and louder, my heart hammering in time with them. My pulse raced as I stared up into his flaming eyes; his power, his strength, his sheer presence utterly dominating me. I was his. Completely and eternally. I had never needed anything more than I needed him.

"You are everything," he rasped, voice choked with desire, then he was there, his arms around me and his lips crushed against mine. He kissed me with almost frenzied intensity, and I matched him, my need as strong as his. His hands were in my hair, pulling my face to his, but mine immediately went to his chest, pushing their way between us. I was desperate to feel his hot skin against mine, to believe that this was really happening.

He stepped back, breathless, and pulled his shirt over his head as I raked my nails down his rock-hard abs. I bit down on my lip as he hooked his thumbs into the waist of his pants, and pushed.

"Holy fuck." I actually said the words out loud, though I didn't mean to. The glitter-filled skies of Olympus and the liquid gold solar sails of the ship paled into non-existence in the presence of Ares' nakedness. He was perfect. Thick and long and so, so hard.

He growled deep in his throat, then pulled me to him, his fingers trying to work at the corseted dress. I couldn't stop my own fingers reaching for him and I gasped as he tensed. I couldn't close my hand around him.

"Leave the dress," I panted, letting go and pulling the

skirts up around my waist. I wasn't waiting a freaking moment longer.

Ares grasped me around the waist with his huge arm, then spun me with his other, pressing my front into the railings, and his chest into my back. With his other hand he reached around, grasping my jaw and pulling my head back. For a second I thought my knees would buckle as his hot mouth met my neck, his teeth nipping at my skin as he worked his way down to my shoulder. I pulled at my skirts, wriggling my panties down and moaning as I felt him press against my bare cheeks.

"Bella," he growled, moving himself between my legs and pressing me harder against the railings. His hand pulled my jaw further round so that he could kiss me.

"I need you," I murmured into his lips. He pressed into my wetness, just a little.

"I love you," he breathed back, then his mouth took mine as he pushed hard into me.

Pleasure like none I had felt before rocked through me, and I cried out even as he kissed me. The arm that was wrapped around my waist tightened and lowered, holding me close as he moved, pressing against the rest of my exposed sex. He kissed me everywhere he could reach as I gasped over and over, firing tingles from my neck and shoulders right through my body, as though they were wired to my core. Wave after wave of new sensation and pleasure pulsed through my body, and I gripped the railings so tight my knuckles were white, as something incredible built inside me.

He moved harder and faster, keeping time with the drums, and I lost myself utterly to the rhythm. Then he moved his hand over me faster, slowing his pounding thrusts, and suddenly every single inch he moved felt exquisite, and I was exploding around him, a noise I didn't even recognize erupting from my throat. My legs did buckle then, and the railing cracked loudly.

Before my alarm could detract from throbs of intense pleasure running from my head to my toes, Ares scooped me up. I protested at the sudden lack of him inside me, but within seconds he had me pressed against the main mast, guiding his huge self back to where he belonged.

"You're fucking beautiful," he breathed, kissing me, resuming his thrusts with even more power than before. The receding aftershock of my orgasm fired back to life, and I found myself in a state of bliss I couldn't even register properly, somewhere between releases, every stroke of his tongue, his fingers, his cock, divine.

When I felt him stiffen, then let out a roar of pleasure, my second release came instantly, and I wrapped my legs tightly around him, burying my face in his neck. I was exhausted, in the most incredible way. A way that was completely new to me.

"So good," I mumbled into his skin as he pressed me to the mast, our skin slick with sweat.

"So good," he agreed, his voice hoarse.

"You swore," I said, pulling my head up and looking at him. His skin was glowing gold, I realized, and I could see an expression in his eyes that I thought might be contentment.

"It was worth it. You are fucking beautiful."

I kissed him softly, my lips hot and swollen. "I love you," I whispered when we parted. A solitary drum sounded in the distance as Ares looked deep into my eyes.

"I will always love you."

11

BELLA

"So what's that one?" I pointed to a tundra-like wasteland at the north-west point of Aries, far below us as I leaned over the railings.

Ares tightened his grip around my waist before he answered, pulling my back against his bare chest. "That's Pagos. And see that mountain range just a bit further along? That's Terror's kingdom."

Unease tightened my chest, and I pressed myself closer to Ares' warmth as I stared down at the jagged, snow-covered mountains. I had been very deliberately avoiding thinking about the last Trial, not wanting the bubble of bliss I was experiencing on Ares' ship to end.

"I guess it won't be long until they announce it," I mumbled.

"I imagine not, no."

"Terror is the worst of the Lords, isn't he." It wasn't a question.

"He is the strongest, and hardest to control."

"What do you think he'll make us do?"

I felt Ares shrug behind me. "Something terrifying.

But we're stronger than them, Bella. We were strong before, when we were at odds with each other." He gripped my shoulders, gently turning me to face him. "Just think how strong we can be together."

"Like when we fought the Hydra," I whispered.

"Yes."

"Ares, only one of us can be immortal at any point. And... I don't know how you feel but..." I trailed off as I stared into his determined face.

I wasn't sure how to say what I was thinking. Or even if I should say what I was thinking.

All fighters had a weakness or two. It wasn't possible to have none. But the good ones had very few. *Almost* nothing to lose. There had to be something at stake, or nobody would fight at all, but for the winners that would often be pride or ego.

The truth was, I had never fought with so much at stake. With so much to lose.

Ares could die. And deep down, I already knew that I wouldn't let that happen. When pushed to the point of making a decision between losing him, and living my own life, I knew what I would do.

Which was bat-shit fucking crazy. Everybody I knew who had fallen in love in the past had fallen out of it again. I'd barely known the guy a week, and I still had serious reservations about some of his personality traits.

Our relationship could surely not have reached die-for-each-other levels this fast?

I would set the world alight to keep him alive.

The thought speared through the doubt and confusion, hot and permanent. And I was ninety-nine percent certain he would do the same for me. There was zero point in denying it, the knowledge that his life was bound to mine felt like it was branded on my soul.

"I dislike seeing you so serious," Ares whispered, and leaned forward to kiss me. His touch was like a tonic for my spiraling concerns and they scattered back to the shadows of my mind.

One thing at a time, Bella, I told myself as I fell into his embrace.

We got three more hours together to enjoy the ship and each other's company, before the urgent presence of Terror pressed against our minds.

Cold anger wound its way through me at the intrusion. The longer I spent lounging with Ares on his bed or on the couch, talking, laughing and kissing, the more I wanted that life to be normal. I wanted the Trials over, his power back, Joshua safe, and the secrets of my past dealt with. So that we could get on with being together. So that I could show him everything he had been missing in his own world.

"You have not made things easy for yourselves," Terror's voice hissed through my skull as I lay against Ares, dozing in and out of a lazy sleep.

"Where and when is the Trial?" barked Ares, moving to sit up and dislodging my head from where it had been nestled on his chest.

"My mighty Lord, I am pleased to hear you sounding so well." His tone dripped with sarcasm.

"Where and when?" Ares repeated.

"The final ceremony will be in my throne room in two hours."

His presence vanished and I scowled and flopped backward onto the pillows. "Do the gods in Olympus not mind that everything is done with fuck all notice?"

"They have to make an eternal life exciting somehow," he shrugged.

"By having spontaneous parties? I can think of better ideas."

"And I can't wait to hear them."

"Really?" I rolled to my side to look at him. His playful smile dipped.

"Bella, I have thought hard about mortality. And glory. And what our power stands for. I think that we can try some new ideas in Aries."

Hope made my smile widen, and I sat up on one elbow. "I have so many freaking ideas. And I want to see everywhere, and meet everyone."

Ares chuckled, then moved quickly, pushing me onto my back again and covering my body with his. My skin fired with heat, all my muscles clenching. "Just remember, it's my realm. Not yours. Got it?" He dropped his head, nipping at my neck. A small moan escaped me as he pressed his hips against mine and I felt how hard he was.

"I'm sorry, I couldn't hear you," I told him, and he raised his head from where he was planting kisses across my collarbone.

"I said, it's my realm, not yours."

"Nope. All I'm hearing is Bella, do whatever you like in my realm."

Fire flashed in his eyes. "I do believe that you are trying to wind me up." I had time to see the predatory hunger flash in his eyes before his mouth met mine and all other thoughts fled.

~

"Dare I ask why you have women's clothing here?" I heard the dangerous tone in my own voice as I stood in front of the open closet in Ares' bedroom.

"Eris. She hides here sometimes, when she has angered the wrong person." Trepidation rumbled through me at the mention of the Goddess of Chaos.

"Is it our fault that something has happened to her? If she hadn't been helping us then Aphrodite might have left her alone."

Ares stood up, the toga he had donned falling to his knees. His expression was hard. "Bella, let me assure you that the feud between those two runs far deeper than you can imagine. And Eris is one of the strongest beings in Olympus. If Aphrodite bested her, she did it with help. You must not blame yourself."

I let out a sigh. "The first thing we do, after all this is over, is find out what happened."

Nervousness flitted across his face, and I didn't think it was to do with Eris. "The first thing we do is talk. About you. And then we can try to find my sister."

"Right," I nodded. An innate reluctance rose in me. There was no doubt that telling me about my past was a conversation Ares didn't want to have, which meant, by proxy, that I didn't want to have it much either. Anything that threatened the bliss we were creating for ourselves was unwanted.

But it couldn't be avoided. Eventually, I would need to know, and it seemed to be weighing heavily on him. What could be so bad?

What if he's done something you can't forgive?

That was my true fear, I realized as the question

settled. That was the real reason I no longer burned with curiosity about who I was. Because my feelings for Ares now burned hotter.

"Will her clothes fit you? I can show you how to change them with magic if not, but it won't be as good as what Eris can do." I forced my attention back to the closet.

"That's sweet of you, thanks."

Ares screwed his face up. "Sweet? You may be the first woman in the world to describe me as such."

"And I'll be the last. If I hear any other woman call my warrior god sweet, I'll punch them in the nose." I narrowed my eyes at him and he grinned. Seeing a playful smile on his serious face was still new enough to me that it made my heart flutter, and heat swirl through me.

"You know, I might like to see that. Perhaps I will start trying to get girls to call me sweet."

"Don't even think about it, armor-boy."

12

ARES

Having Bella on my arm when we arrived in Terror's throne room felt more right than I could understand. I needed the world to see her with me. I needed everyone to know that she belonged to me.

She had selected one of Eris' more formal dresses, and to my surprise she had chosen to keep it the way it was. I was both pleased that I could see so much heavenly cleavage, and furious that others could too. I had a suspicion that that was exactly why she'd worn it. The corseted top half was a deep grey, like iron, but the color changed slowly in what she had told me with a chuckle was called ombre, into creamy ivory at the bottom. The whole thing was covered in a lace decorated with gold feathers, and together we had used her magic to change them into plumed helmets. "After all, we both have helmets now," she'd grinned at me.

We spelled the helmet itself to transform into a headband, like mine, though hers was more delicate and had a deep purple gemstone in its center. Against her ash blonde hair it looked sensational. *She* looked sensational.

I would kill to see her smile. Hell, I would do any damn thing she told me to, without question. Not that I'd tell her that.

What would she do when I told her the truth about her past? About what I had done?

A part of me that I wasn't even sure had existed until I met her, held some hope that the connection between us would be strong enough for her to forgive me. But the larger part of me feared that I would lose the one thing I had ever cared about.

I thought I'd cared before, about war, glory, honor. Aphrodite. But everything paled next to the fierce Bella, her power and strength and courage burning brighter than anything in Olympus.

She was true love. She was my purpose. She was everything.

"You're sure he's not going to make us go straight to the last Trial from the ball? I am not doing anything in this dress," she hissed next to me. We were waiting in a line of guests to walk through a shimmering portal at the end of a corridor. I knew this was the only way to reach Terror's ballroom, as I had been a guest before, but I didn't want to tell Bella what to expect. I wanted to see the surprise on her face when she saw it. Terror was the most mysterious, dangerous and egotistical of the Lords, and both his kingdom and his palace matched his personality.

"You have your sword and helmet if he does. That is the most important thing."

She nodded. The guests in front of us were turning frequently to look at us, muttering and smiling excitedly. We were the guests of honor.

. . .

Bella was fidgeting by the time we reached the portal, energy thrumming from her.

"Are you ready?" I asked, tightening my arm around her smaller one.

"I've been ready for fucking ages," she answered impatiently, and stepped through the portal, tugging me with her.

Her mouth made an O shape and then she blew out a long breath as she took in our new surroundings. We were standing on a long platform jutting out from the side of a snow-capped mountain. Twinkling blue lights danced overhead, not bright, but strong enough to add to the dusky light coming from the sky above us. Short columns acted as tables and guests gathered around them with their drinks and canapés. A dark archway set in the mountain had a steady stream of servers moving through it with trays. Snow, powder soft, fell but never settled on the floor, and an artificial warmth encompassed the whole platform.

Bella moved toward the edge immediately, staring out at the looming mountains. There were jagged blades of rock jutting from the snowy peaks and spearing the sky, and pitch black crevices everywhere that could be hiding any manner of danger. They almost seemed alive with menacing energy.

"The mountains are impressive," I said.

"Foreboding as fuck," she answered, still staring.

"Do you fear them?"

She glanced at me. "They call to me," she said quietly. "Danger and mystery and the thrill of the unknown."

"I am flattered, but you should be careful what you wish for." Terror's voice was as unpleasant as it always was, and my muscles tightened in reaction. We both turned to him, and I was surprised to see that he was alone. Ink-black shapes crawled unsettlingly across his marble frame. There was no better body for the spirit of Terror and, although I was sure I had chosen well, I took no pleasure in his company.

"Where are the other two?" asked Bella.

"Around," he said dismissively. "Did you wear a dress covered in helmets to anger Panic? I like that." His tone dripped with malice. "You should have added some dragons too. He's most upset about the loss of his pet."

The bond connecting me to Bella was so much stronger now that I felt her surge of anger. "That creature is no pet," she snarled.

"Not any longer, no. Are you ready for my Trial?"

Fear trickled through me and I knew at once that it was his influence. Here, in his palace and without my full power, I could not stop his magic. Bella pulled her arm out of mine and the fear intensified alarmingly before she twined her fingers with my own. Heat rushed me, forcing out the tendrils of building terror. But she was gripping my hand hard enough that I knew it was affecting her too.

"We are ready," I said, glaring at him. "And when we have won, we expect the demon to be handed over without delay."

"You know, we never discussed what would happen if you lost." I opened my mouth to reply, then realized with a sickening jolt that he was right.

"If we lose, we likely die," I ground out.

"An immortal Olympian?" There was a delight in his tone, and it was clear that he knew that I was no longer immortal, unless I took every ounce of Bella's power. "No, no, mighty one. We need a bigger risk than that for you. If you lose, then instead of us giving you the demon, we get you."

~

"No. Absolutely not." Bella's grip turned vice-like and her voice was as sharp as a blade. Her reaction was just what Terror wanted. Fear, anger, challenge. I would make sure that he got nothing he wanted.

Before Bella could say any more, I began to laugh. A small chuckle at first, that turned into a mocking boom. Terror stiffened, his featureless face fixed on mine.

"What do you plan to do with me?" I asked, plastering my best maniacal smile on my face. I drew power slowly from Bella.

"Whatever we wish," hissed Terror, the cockiness gone from his voice. He definitely hadn't got the reaction he had hoped for from me.

"OK, little Lord. If we lose, you get me." I stepped forward, growing a foot suddenly, and dropping my voice menacingly low. "But when we win, I assure you that I will be shattering this pretty body of yours into a million tiny pieces, and finding a new host for Terror."

To the Lord's credit, he didn't step back, though his stone body did twitch. I kept my eyes locked on his featureless face, focusing on the power of War. Screams sounded in the distance, and the cries of battle and the stampede of hooves were joined by the booming of explosions. The smell of fire and blood washed over us, and heat rose around me.

The challenge hung in the air, Terror's black swirls the only thing moving.

"May the best man win," the Lord said eventually.

"We will."

Terror turned, stalking back to the other guests, and no doubt the other two Lords.

"You know, you're sexy as hell when you do that."

I looked at Bella, happy to see a flush to her cheeks that suggested she really did find me attractive. "I'm glad you think so." Power was circulating through my body, the encounter firing me up, leaving me longing for a fight.

"What if we lose?" Bella asked quietly, her flirtatious tone replaced with just a hint of doubt.

"We won't. We can't." There was already enough at stake in these stupid games. I wouldn't accept that there was any chance of us losing, so there was no harm adding one more thing to the list.

"Why do they want you?"

"Dominance. If they rule the God of War, they rule the realm. The desire for power is in their nature. It's what they were created to do."

"But you control your nature, why can't they?"

I took a breath, her words making me uneasy. So fast had we fallen for one another, yet there was still so much she didn't know about me. About my power, and what I was made of. About what I had done to keep my sanity.

"Bella, they are the reason I *am* able to control myself. When Pain, Panic and Terror were a part of me I was... different. Bad. The only way to control them was to split them up and put them into exceptionally strong-willed hosts, with their own kingdoms to keep them occupied. When they are combined in one being they are too strong. They are the very essence of the worst parts of War." I shrugged. "But they are still forces to be reckoned with, and they always work together. This is not the first time they have tried to rise against me and it won't be the last. The difference is that I have never been without my power before."

"Well, you have your power now. You have me."

A blue glow from the fairy-lights danced in her eyes, and after a second's hesitation I pulled the helmet from my head, using her power to turn it into the headband.

"You're stunning," I told her, my chest fluttering as she took in my face.

"A perfect match for you then," she grinned, as I leaned down to kiss her.

We strode around the ball like we owned the place, exuding a confidence I knew would anger the Lords. Whether Bella truly carried that confidence, I wasn't sure, but she seemed happy to act as cocky as I was. Panic gave us a grimace-like smile when we neared him, but did not speak with us. And, as I had expected, Aphrodite was nowhere to be seen.

The mountains really did seem to call to Bella. She seemed to be zoning out of polite conversation with the endless stream of curious guests who wanted to meet the girl who had coaxed the miserable God of War out of his helmet, staring at the looming summits instead.

I felt the same. I could sense the danger within them and it was like a magnet, pulling me to prove myself. I needed to fight, to win, to revel in victory. And I knew with the same certainty Bella seemed to have that the sharp, ragged mountains held a mighty challenge.

By the time Terror drew everyone's attention to him, I actually wanted him to confirm that the last Trial would involve this stark and lethal kingdom.

"Thank you all for joining me," his icy voice rasped. "The last test in the Ares Trials is a simple one. Climb one of my mountains. If you reach the top, you win. If you do not reach the top, you lose."

Excitement surged through my veins. It was exactly as I had hoped. I felt a bolt of energy from Bella, her skin glowing briefly gold.

It was time to show everyone how strong we were together.

13

BELLA

My excitement to tackle the mountain fizzled out slightly when the light from the flash faded and the reality of our task set in.

"Wow. That's quite a long way."

It was freezing cold, and although I was wearing a shirt with sleeves under my leather armor, and my helmet over my head, the cold air still bit at my skin.

We were at the base of a mountain formed from shining black rock, and covered in snow. Everything was jagged, not a smooth line in sight, as though a giant had taken a hammer to the whole surface, leaving jutting angular spikes and deep crevices everywhere. There was the hint of a path before us, twisting up into the mass of rock. And when I tipped my head right back, I could only just see the white peak of the mountain.

"Climbing will be hard, and I expect there will be some added challenges on the way," Ares said, armor-clad and humming with pent-up energy.

"It looks like Terror. All black and white," I mused as Ares started forward toward the path.

"You're right. It does."

"I like hearing that." I followed him, my boots crunching on the snow. *Ischyros* was warm in my right hand. "Feel free to tell me I'm right as much as you like."

Ares threw a glance over his shoulder at me, his eyes sparkling. "You'll have to earn it."

I shrugged. "Not hard. I'm always right."

The God of War snorted. "I highly doubt that."

We bickered playfully for an hour or more, before it began to snow. The path wasn't really a path, just a groove that meandered between the sharp boulders. The incline was steep, and I wasn't sure how well I'd be doing if I didn't have my power. The magic-less version of me was fit for sure, but we weren't climbing an ordinary mountain. There were no trees or scrubby bushes at all, just craggy black cliffs and rivulets of ice. There were no sounds of animals or birds, or anything living, even when I used my new super-senses to hunt for signs of life. All I could get from the mountain was an ominous magnetism. It was creepy and compelling all at once.

My power kept me from getting numb from the cold, but it didn't stop the snow being annoying. The visibility dropped quickly, forcing us to slow our pace a little.

"How long do you think it'll take to get to the top?" I asked.

"Two days. But I believe there will be obstacles to overcome. So perhaps longer."

I nodded, even though he was in front of me and couldn't see me. There was no way Terror's mountain didn't have more in store for us than just snow.

"What was that?" We had been trudging up the ever steeper mountain-side for longer than I cared to know, and I had just seen movement that wasn't snowfall for the very first time.

"Where?" I felt the slight tug of Ares drawing my power and I knew he would be enhancing his senses just as I was. We were entering a reasonably level clearing, surrounded by dark boulders, and I pointed as we slowed.

"By that rock," I whispered. I could just make out the sound of soft footfall, and the slow, steady breathing of something that wasn't Ares. The climb had yet to be steep enough that we had needed two hands, so we had both been walking with our swords drawn. I felt a burst of excitable heat from *Ischyros*, tingling down my arm and causing adrenaline to flood my system.

There was a flash of white, and something green moved again behind the rough boulders.

"Show yourself!" Ares shouted the command, and my heart hammered in my chest as we stood side-by-side.

A rumbling snarl echoed through the clearing, then everything fell silent again.

"What is it?" I hissed.

"I don't know yet," Ares answered, through gritted teeth. We were both beginning to glow.

Out of nowhere, a huge blurred mass of white and brown and green barreled into Ares, knocking him to the ground just a foot from me. I invoked the power of War, snapping the image of myself on the stallion into place instinctively. As everything around me slowed and turned red, Ares leaped back to his feet, sending the creature that had attacked him skidding backward.

It was like nothing I had seen before, even at the ceremonies the Lords had thrown. Most of it looked like a snow leopard, with beautiful spotted markings, huge green eyes and small tucked in ears. But the rest of it...

"It has two fucking heads!" The exclamation was out of my mouth before I could stop it. There was a second neck protruding from the snow leopard's body, and it ended in a vicious-looking mountain goat's head. Coarse black horns curled angrily from its skull and its eyes were beady and red. The leopard head pulled its lips back in a snarl, baring its teeth at the same time that the goat head hissed, clacking its jaws together.

"Three. Check the tail," Ares said. He was right. The end of the snow leopard's fat bushy tail was a freaking snake head, bright green and as dangerous-looking as hell. "It's a chimera."

The creature pawed at the snow-covered ground before us, and I tried to suppress my admiration and astonishment at seeing such a beast.

"How do we stop it?" I didn't want to kill it. "Will fire scare it off, like the oxys?"

"The cold on this mountain will douse magical fire quickly."

The chimera growled, loud and menacing.

Before I could offer another idea it pounced again, this time at me. I was ready though.

I threw myself to the side a second before it hit me, swiping at its legs with my sword as it landed on the ground instead of on me. The snake tail whipped around, forcing me to bring my sword up to defend myself as a forked tongue darted out.

Ares' golden glow appeared behind the chimera, and before it could turn to where I was crouched he brought his sword down. There was a ringing clash as the goat head moved to meet him, its horns blocking his blow.

I rolled, keen to get out of the snake's reach, and as I straightened I found myself face-to-face with the leopard head.

"Fuck, you move fast," I cursed as I jumped backward, only narrowly avoiding the snapping jaws. The goat neck was longer though, and pain slammed through my shoulder as it butted hard into me. I stumbled backwards, then the thing shrieked, an ugly animal noise that made my insides feel weird. Ares had hold of the chimera's tail and was yanking it hard away from me, the snake's head snapping and straining to reach him. The creature turned, its legs moving fast to try to get out of the god's grip, but Ares was too strong. The chimera stilled as Ares brought his blade down, stopping just an inch from the tail he was gripping.

"You can't beat both of us. Come after us, and you will lose one of your heads," Ares said loudly. All three mouths hissed in response.

Ares let go, and I held my breath, sword ready.

The snake head reared back now that it was free, but just as it looked like it was going to launch at Ares, the leopard head made a screeching sound and it froze. With one last hiss, the chimera turned in a slow circle between us, then bounded away, lost in the shadows of the boulders in an instant.

I relaxed my sword arm a fraction, and sent some healing magic to my bruised shoulder. "Is it me, or was that too easy?" I asked slowly.

"Chimeras are usually solitary creatures. But if she returns with a pack, we will be facing a tougher adversary."

I stared after the incredible animal, and hoped like hell that she didn't have any friends on the mountain.

We resumed our trek, and were forced to sheath our swords when the incline steepened and the ground became less stable. Soon we were climbing properly, using both hands to pull ourselves up crumbling slopes, The physical activity would have felt good if the mountain wasn't sending such increasingly bad vibes at us.

"Why didn't you cut off the snake head?" I asked Ares, when we stopped for a short breather.

He looked at me from behind his helmet. "Put it down to my new appreciation of mortality." I raised my eyebrows at him. "And I knew you would rather I didn't. It's the chimera's home we're invading after all."

"If we weren't wearing helmets, I would kiss you," I told him. I knew mercy was a part of war, and I also knew that Ares did not kill indiscriminately. But the red mist was a powerful thing, and instincts often prevailed in a fight for most people, let alone those with divine strength. My admiration for his self-control was only growing.

"If we were wearing nothing, there is no part of you I wouldn't kiss," he said, and heat flared through me, chasing away the cold.

"Let's get this over with, so that you can prove that to me."

14

BELLA

The ground we were covering showed no sign of leveling out, and it wasn't long before we were practically scaling a cliff. The almost vertical slope was icy cold, and if a person didn't have magic to keep their skin from freezing or some seriously epic gloves, they would not have been able to use their hands at all.

I was surprised by how much concentration was required to keep me moving up the rock, and the constant draw on my power to keep myself from freezing to death was starting to worry me too. Only one of us could be immortal, and a fall to the jagged peaks below would surely be fatal. If we both fell...

The thought caused a very unwelcome fear to hover over me, and I began to pray for flatter ground. Or even more chimeras.

Every time the rock crumbled under my grip or my boots slipped on an icy patch my heart lurched and a little more of my composure fled. Not knowing where the top was made it even worse.

"You're doing great." Ares' deep voice filtered through my mind, providing a massive wave of comfort to flood through me. I had paused, clinging to the rock for a moment to gather myself while I had a fairly decent ledge for my feet. He must have noticed. I glanced down, seeing him ten feet or so below me, and tried to ignore the dizziness that accompanied looking in that direction.

"So are you," I told him.

"I am used to climbing; I sense that you are not?"

"It's not something I did back in the mortal world, no," I admitted. *"I'm becoming tired, having to concentrate so hard."* I didn't voice my worry about only one of us being able to survive a fall. And now that I had looked down I was pretty sure that even if I did survive a fall, it would take a colossal effort to try again. That's if I didn't freeze to death whilst healing.

There was no question that this mountain was dangerous for immortals, I realized. That was probably connected to its twisted lure. Danger personified.

"Don't let the fear get to you. Use your confidence. This is Terror's trial, he thrives on fear. So will the mountain."

I tried to wrap Ares' words around me like a blanket, taking comfort from them. *The mountain makes you more scared,* I told myself. *You don't get scared. So climb the damn mountain.*

When the ground finally started to level out, I didn't let myself believe it at first. I had found a rhythm that I didn't dare risk disturbing, one that buried the growing fear of falling under the simple practice of putting one hand and foot in front of the other.

But as the snow fell softly on us, I couldn't ignore the

fact the ground was starting to catch it, and that my body was starting to tip forward more with each step.

When it was flat enough that I could stand upright I turned, waiting for Ares.

"Are you alright?" he asked as he reached me, eyes full of concern.

"Yes. Relieved."

"In that case, something worse is likely coming. We can rest soon, my love."

I nodded, pleasure filling my chest at the endearment. I had never been called "my love" by anyone before. With renewed determination, I hauled my tired ass up the rocky mountain path.

"Trees!" It probably wasn't normal to get so excited about the piss-poor excuses for trees that had somehow managed to grow on the bleak mountainside, but I was sick to death of looking at snow. They were scrubby and spindly and barely had any leaves, but they were definitely trees.

Ares gave a small snort. "Barely," he said.

"Well, they're better than rocks."

"Hmmm."

The ground was a lot less steep now, but the path was twisty and narrow. We were likely wasting time following the path instead of trying to find a more direct way up, but the rocks clawing their way out of the ground on either side were spiky and awkward, and some were three times my height. It would be too hard to try to navigate them. So we continued to stamp along the path, and I continued to admire the crap trees interspersed between the crap rocks.

"I don't like this mountain as much as I thought I would," I said into the silence.

"Stay alert," was Ares' only response.

I blew out a sigh, then frowned as I felt answering warm breath on my shoulder. I turned my head quickly, but there was nothing there. Slowing my pace, I blew out hard again. A warm gust blew over my back and I whirled.

There was nothing.

"What's wrong?"

"I can feel warm air."

I could make out Ares' scowl behind his helmet. "That seems unlikely. I can't sense anything here."

I pushed my own senses out. He was right. No animal sounds or smells nearby. Frowning, I began walking again.

The next time I felt the gust, I could swear it was accompanied by a shove. Not a hard one, but I was sure I felt something make contact with my shoulder. I slashed with *Ischyros* as I spun, but my blade met thin air.

"There's something here, Ares."

As if in response to my words, the snow flurried suddenly, making me unable to see more than about ten feet in any direction. Something shoved into me again, harder this time, and I yelled out. Ares' armor clanged and I looked over in time to see him stumble.

"What the..." Before he could finish the sentence the snow stopped as suddenly as it had started, leaving us both looking stupidly around in circles.

"Do your show yourself thing," I hissed.

Ares cast me a look, then shouted. "Show yourself!"

Nothing.

We waited a moment more, then Ares shrugged. "We're wasting time. Let's keep moving."

I didn't argue, but I kept *Ischyros* clutched in both hands and my body stayed tense as I followed him. I didn't like foes I couldn't see one little bit.

15

Nothing had happened for another hour or so, when my skin began to crawl, unpleasant tingles snaking down my spine. Something was watching us, I was certain. But when I sent my senses out I could find nothing.

The feeling of being watched increased minute by minute. The number of trees was increasing too, and the new ones were actually able to hold some foliage. I scanned the leaves warily, trying to feel for signs of life coming from anything that might be hiding in them. The path had narrowed even further and started to wrap around the body of the mountain. There was now a steep slope to our right heading down, and an even steeper slope on our left, heading up. We had checked to see if we could scale it but it was covered in a sheen of solid smooth ice, impossible to grip.

The wind had picked up, causing the sparse leaves to rustle and cold flurries of snow to gust over us. One such gust whipped across the path, and for a moment I was sure I heard a voice, as though it were carried on the wind. A child's voice.

You're tired, I told myself. *There are no voices on this mountain.*

But another breeze blew over us, and this time the voices were clear. High-pitched childlike voices, repeating the same three words.

Blood. Die. Eat.

Goosebumps rose on my skin and my chest tightened. "Ares? Do you hear that?" I could hear the uneasiness in my own voice.

Ares didn't answer, he just keep walking ahead of me. "Ares?" I called louder. Another gust hit me, harder, and the childish voices were loud whispers, rippling with excitement.

Blood. Die. Eat.

Blood. Die. Eat.

"Ares!" There was fear in my voice this time when I called out, and my legs began to move fast, jogging to catch up with him.

I grabbed at his arm when I reached him and he jerked in surprise. "Bella! Something is here." His eyes were wild and unfocused.

"I'm hearing a bunch of kids who want to eat me on the wind," I said, my voice breathless. "It's creepy as fuck. What are you hearing?"

"The same," he said, and I knew he was lying. But now was not the time to try to find out what exactly creeped out the God of War.

"What is it?"

"I don't know, but there's nothing living here, or we'd feel it."

"So... It's dead?" My voice caught on the word dead.

"I don't know. I suppose it must be. Or something powerful enough to hide its presence."

I hoped fervently for the latter. Somehow, the idea of a powerful magical creature was easier for me to stomach than the idea of ghosts or zombies.

The snow started to flurry again, and a juvenile laugh rippled through the air. There was a screech, an awful sound that made me feel sick, and I felt fear bolt through me. I gripped Ares harder, looking uselessly around myself.

Blood. Die. Eat.

Something shoved my back, and Ares went down with me, both of us landing hard in the snow. More laughter sang around us, and as I scrambled to my feet I realized that the red mist wasn't coming.

"I can't fight what I can't see," I blurted, hating my rising panic.

"Use your shield," Ares said. He moved to me, gripping my waist. "We'll do it together."

"Yes. Shield," I repeated, staring into his eyes and trying to swallow my fear.

The next time we were shoved, it bounced off an invisible dome around us.

Blood-

Before the child's voice could say the next word I poured power into my shield, and the words cut off. Immediately the terror that was building inside me, spreading though my body, lessened.

"Good." Ares still had a slightly unhinged glaze over his eyes.

"Ares, I'm too tired to keep the shield up and walk. But there's no fucking way I'm sleeping here, with whatever's out there. What are we going to do?"

"We have to get rid of it," he said after a moment's thought.

"How? It's freaking invisible."

"We think it's connected to the wind?"

I nodded in agreement, rubbing at my arms. I could feel pressure against the shield, an awful scratching sensation against my power. I hated it. "Yeah."

"Then let's make our own wind. Blow it away."

"Really?"

"I can't think of anything else to try."

Making wind was as simple as making fire, Ares explained to me. I just had to think about it, and throw my power behind it.

"We'll do it together on the count of three. Drop the shield, then blast this whole cursed path with wind."

"What if it blows us off the path?"

"It won't. But get low, in case whatever it is blows back."

I nodded, dropping into a crouch. The ground was cold, the snow piled inches high.

"Three, two, one!"

When the shield dropped the voices were shrill and taunting, a hideous screeching sound whistling through the air.

Blood! Die! Eat!

I poured everything I had left into what I pictured as a tornado, and with a roar the swirling column of wind burst into existence. Red tinged the edges of my vision, and hope lit up inside me, forcing out some of the tension and fear.

"Go," I willed the tornado, and it began to move along

the path. The voices warped, the words no longer clear, and the tornado was louder than the screeching as it roared along the path. I willed it to grow and move, clearing away whatever it was that was trying to haunt us. It pinballed around on the narrow path in a zigzag, whipping up the spindly branches on the trees and causing a torrent of snow to splatter in its wake.

It avoided the place Ares and I were crouched though, and by the time it started to die down my power was completely spent.

"Did it work? Are they gone?"

Ares didn't reply, his face set in concentration. I tried to do the same, but fatigue was setting in. I didn't feel like I was being watched though, and the creepy as hell voices were silent.

"I think so."

"Thank fuck for that. I need to sleep."

We heaved a few boulders together, and pulled a few leafier branches from the trees around us to build a makeshift shelter. I was keen to get as much rest as we could whilst the cannibal kids were gone. They could come back at any time, and the thought frightened me. Invisible scary spirits were seriously not my thing. Ares assured me that my power would keep me warm enough while I was unconscious and, trusting him completely, I was out the second my head hit my trusty backpack.

When I awoke, Ares had one arm wrapped tight around me, pressing me against his golden armor, which even in the mountain weather was always warm. I was alert the second the sleep cleared from my mind, wary of what might have woken me. Sparsely-leaved branches were propped across the top of the two boulders we were between, and I took it as a good sign that they hadn't blown away.

"Ares," I said, lifting his arm and sitting up. I reached instinctively for my helmet, sitting proudly next to his. Energy tingled into my gut from the cord connecting us as he stirred.

"Kiss me," he murmured, and I dropped my head, planting a soft kiss on his mouth.

"We've got to get going," I said, pulling back. His eyes were bright, the sleepiness leaving him fast.

"I am bored of this mountain now," he said as I crawled out of our shelter and pulled my helmet on. It was featherlight once it was on my head, as though it became a part of me. It obscured none of my vision and I never felt it move.

"Me too." I scanned the snowy path. It looked identical to how it had before we slept. I felt inside myself for my power, finding the ball of energy under my ribs full and hot. Ares emerged from between the boulders and yanked on his helmet.

"Let's try to get to the top today," he said.

"Definitely."

16

ARES

"One of the realms must be your favorite," Bella pushed, as we kicked our way through deepening snow. The path was still winding its way up the mountainside, occasionally turning steep and rocky, and sometimes icy and flat.

"Only my own," I answered from behind her.

"You can't choose your own, that's cheating. Pick one." She clambered over a particularly sharp outcrop of rock.

"My father's realm is most spectacular. His citizens live in glass mansions in the electrical clouds surrounding Mount Olympus. His palace is at the top of the mountain."

"Less mountain talk," she grumbled. "And besides, you dad sounds like a prick. Pick another one."

I sighed and she threw me a grin over her shoulder. "Fine. I like Poseidon's underwater realm. It is made up of many golden domes under the surface of the ocean. And he has lots of extremely dangerous water creatures living there." Excitement tinged my words at the thought of Poseidon's ocean monsters.

"What's your least favorite realm?"

"I do not like Taurus. That's Dionysus' realm; he is the god of wine and madness. His citizens live in large tree-houses that are impressive, and there are also many dangerous wild creatures, but you can trust nothing. Whole buildings can turn on their head with no notice, and everything is spiked with hallucinogens. I find it unsettling."

"I want to visit," Bella pronounced immediately.

"Of course you do. Is it me, or is the snow getting thicker?" I was sure that the snow was falling faster, and settling heavier around us.

"Yeah, maybe."

Within another hour the snow was falling hard, and we were having to kick our way through a layer that completely covered our boots. Visibility was poor and our pace was forced to slow considerably.

"When should we start to worry about the snow?" Bella called back to me.

"I don't know." Admitting that I didn't know things was new to me, and I wasn't sure I liked it. If it were anyone other than Bella asking, I would have ignored the question, or made an answer up. But the truth was, this whole mountain was as wild and unpredictable as she was, and I didn't have a clue if the snow was a threat or not.

"As long as those creep-ass cannibal kids don't come back," I heard her say.

Whatever the ghostly voices had been, they had upset her. They hadn't done much for my calm control either.

. . .

A deep, distant rumble caught my ears, and Bella paused in front of me. "You hear that?"

"Yes."

She glowed briefly as she stretched the limit of her senses. "It's coming from deep within the mountain," she said, turning to face me. There was a slight spark of fear in her eyes. "The rock itself. It's not a creature. We can't fight a mountain."

"Stay calm." I caught up to her and reached out, touching her warm skin. The rumble came again, louder, stronger. I felt it through my boots.

"Ares, we are surrounded by tons of rock and snow." Panic edged Bella's voice. "*Tons.*"

"And we have magical shields," I told her, projecting confidence through our connection.

"What if we're separated?" She practically whispered the words, and I realized that was what was causing her fear. Something separating us on the mountain.

"We won't be." I gripped her hand, and the rumble gained more volume. "And even if we are, we are bound. We will find each other." I looked into her eyes, and flames flickered to life as she stared back at me. Flames of will and determination, driven by the strength of her love for me. I knew what she was feeling because I was feeling exactly the same, and our emotions flowed through our bond like a raging river.

She nodded. "OK." The ground lurched under our feet, and we stumbled. "And if we fall down the mountain?"

"Then we start again." *If we fell off the mountain, one of us would die.* I didn't add the statement that ran through my head, though I was sure she knew it as well as I did.

"Fuck starting again," she said, her face fierce as the

rumbling grew and the rock beneath us shook. "We need to get away from the edge."

We moved through the snow as fast as was possible, tucking ourselves close to the mountain as we powered on. The tremors continued, but they weren't strong enough to take us off our feet.

We walked for another hour or more, the terrain becoming invisible through the pelting snow, and we were unable to relax for even a second with the frequent lurches of the ground. Rocks crumbled and rolled past us, and great slabs of snow regularly tumbled from ledges above us, forcing us to throw up our shields.

"Something's here." Bella had to shout the words back to me, the growling of the ground and the cracking and crumbling of rock was so loud. I pushed out my senses, finding a mass of something ahead of us. Something powerful.

Fighting whilst trying to stay steady on this cursed mountainside would not be easy. Excitement and adrenaline fired through me, forcing out the doubt. Bella and I could defeat anything. "Good! I am bored of this trek," I shouted back.

"You know what? Me too." Her words were strained and I knew she was forcing as much confidence into them as possible.

"We will not be separated, my love." I sent the words to her mentally, and a wave of warmth flooded my gut, flowing from our bond.

Before she could reply though, the whole mountain shuddered and a brilliant flash of teal light seemed to erupt through the snow. Freezing powder flew everywhere, sharp lumps of ice accompanying it, and we snapped our shields up. Bella moved, throwing herself as far away from the edge as she could as the ground shook even more violently. There was a slow, echoing crack and I threw myself after her as a tidal wave of snow began to crash toward us.

17

BELLA

"Bella?"

"I'm here. What happened?" I rolled, the surface beneath me feeling like warm glass and everything in complete darkness.

"I got the shield up in time... but we're submerged."

A faint light filled the space as Ares began to glow. I sat up, getting my bearings as I looked around myself.

He was right. We were in a bubble completely surrounded by snow. "Erm, how much air do we have?" I tried to keep the rising fear from my voice and failed.

"Plenty, don't worry."

"How much is plenty?"

"Enough for many hours. And besides, it won't take us long to dig ourselves out." He moved to my side. "Are you hurt?" I shook my head. The ton of snow that had crashed down over us had made me cold, but had not been painful.

"Just a bit cold," I told him.

"We're safe in here, for now. Why don't we rest a moment? Warm up."

I raised my eyebrows at him. "Whilst buried in snow?"

"Why not? No weird voices, no chimera."

"What happens if the shield fails?"

"It will be fine, as long as we don't need to use any other magic."

I cocked my head at him, unsure how comfortable I was with the idea of being buried alive. "How much snow do you think is above us?"

"Not so much that you couldn't fireball your way out of here in a hurry if you needed to." His eyes creased at the corners, and I knew he was smiling behind the helmet. I instantly felt myself relax at the sight. His eyes were so beautiful.

"OK. I guess we could do with a rest."

"It would be good if we could find a way to warm up without using magic," Ares said mildly, pulling off his helmet.

"Huh. Got anything in mind?"

He moved, shifting so that he was sitting with his arms across his knees, facing me. All the serious tension had gone from his face and his eyes had darkened with delicious promise. "Oh yes. I can picture what I'm thinking of very clearly indeed."

I looked at him incredulously. "Are you suggesting what I think you are?"

He shrugged, a wicked smile settling over his beautiful face. "I don't know. What do you think I'm suggesting?"

"Something that we absolutely can not have broadcast to the rest of Olympus," I hissed.

"The shield is keeping them out."

"Really?"

"Yes. Check for yourself."

I sent out my senses, probing. The shield was solid,

that was for sure, but I had no idea what I was looking for. I pulled my own helmet off, and ran my fingers over my hair, pushing back what had come loose from my braid.

The truth was, nothing would make me feel better than to be intimate with him. What better way to force out the fear and trepidation, the anxious energy, than to remind ourselves what we were fighting for? To take strength from one another. There was a tiny voice in the back of my mind that I couldn't quiet, adding its own argument. *This mountain is lethal. There is a very, very real chance we might not survive. This could be your last opportunity.*

"I'll tell you what will warm us up without magic," I said, making my mind up and shrugging out of my backpack.

"Please do."

"This." I yanked the heavy bottle that I had carted all the way from London across most of the most dangerous realm in Olympus, and grinned at him. "Tequila."

It was Ares turn to raise his eyebrows this time. "It warms you? Like nectar?"

"Er, sort of. It's more of a burning than warming, really," I said, unscrewing the top and inhaling the sharp, familiar scent. The amber liquid glowed in the golden light coming from Ares.

"I will drink it with you on one condition."

"Oh yeah?"

"That you are naked."

I stared at him, heat already building inside me with no help needed from the tequila. "I assume you're going to be naked too?"

"Oh yes. Naked and making sure you stay warm."

"Well, I think that sounds fair. You first." I crossed

my legs, wedging the tequila bottle in the crook of my knee, and folded my arms. "Get that armor off, warrior boy."

There wasn't enough room for him to stand up in our snow cocoon, but that didn't stop him. He was down to his shirt and pants in seconds. I watched hungrily as he picked up the bottom hem of his shirt, then pulled.

Holy hell, he had a body to freaking die for. My muscles twitched as I stopped myself reaching for him, and I schooled my face into a mild expression.

"My pants don't come off until yours do," he said.

I narrowed my eyes at him, then picked up the bottle and took a swig, before handing it to him.

The liquid burned its way down my throat, and I was pleased that having godly powers didn't dull the sensation. Tequila was still excellent, even as a goddess. Keeping my eyes fixed on Ares, I began to unlace my leather armor.

"This shield better be keeping out the rest of the world," I said once I removed it.

"It is."

"Good." I pulled my own shirt up and over my head.

Ares' eyes widened, then darkened as they dipped to my chest. Slowly, his gaze came back to mine, and he took a swig from the bottle.

He swallowed, then let out a long breath before smiling. "I like tequila." With a swift movement he leaned forward, pulling me onto his lap. I squealed as he tightened his grip around me, and raised the bottle with his other hand.

"More?" Desire danced in his eyes.

I tried to snatch the tequila from him, and he lifted his arm high so I couldn't reach it. I saw my skin glow as I stretched up for it, and he spoke. "Be careful, Bella. No magic, or the shield might fail."

"I don't need magic," I said, and wriggled out of his grip.

"Oh no?"

"Nope."

I stood up over him, barely an inch between me and the top of the bubble. I had a foot on either side of his knees and he wet his lips as he looked up at me, then moved the bottle low to his side, where I couldn't get it.

"You'll have to come back down here for it now."

"Oh, no I don't. I have a better plan." Slowly, I hooked my thumbs into the waistband of my pants.

Flames burst to life in his eyes, and a drum began to beat in the distance. My heart rate sped up instantly, matching the pace.

I pulled, wriggling my ass deliberately as my panties dropped with my pants. They both snagged on my boots, but I didn't have time to do anything about it. Ares' face was inches from me, and he took a ragged breath as he took in the sight.

"You win. Here's the tequila." He held up the bottle. I took it with a grin, then yelped as his now empty hand grabbed my ass and pulled me forward. His lips pressed against the top of my thigh, and I gasped, clutching the bottle. His mouth moved fast, across the sensitive skin between my legs, then heading lower. I instinctively parted my legs, allowing him in.

His other hand came up, steadying me as he closed his lips around my most sensitive part.

"Oh god." I almost stumbled, bringing my hand down and pushing it into his hair, pulling him harder onto me. His tongue moved expertly, like it had its own kind of magic, and I felt my knees weaken as pleasure rocketed through my whole body. I felt his fingers moving up the inside of my thigh, and then he was stroking and teasing me in time with his tongue, each movement sending aching pulses of need through me. "Oh god," I breathed again as his finger finally dipped into my wetness. "I need you. Ares, I need you."

He pulled back and looked up at me, and my breath caught at the fierce hunger on his face. "You have me," he half-growled. He let go of me and eased out of his pants, revealing himself hard and ready. Desire pounded through me at the sight of him. The drums beat louder.

"Wait," he said, as I started to move. He reached down, and began to untie my left boot. "I need you to be able to move your legs." He looked at me, wicked and beautiful, and torturous longing burned through my blood. I took a deep breath as he lifted my foot from my loosened boot, then moved to the other one. Remembering the bottle in my hand, I took another swig. More fire burned through me, and suddenly, I didn't care about my boot.

Before he could stop me, I sank into his lap, wrapping my left leg around his waist and winding one arm around his neck. "I need you, Ares. Now." I kissed along his jaw as he pulled me to him, his chest heaving. His hard length pressed against me, and I squeezed my leg, lifting myself up.

He let out a long groan that matched mine as I eased myself down. The feeling of him inside me, filling me, was beyond anything I had words for. It was more than a feeling - it was a euphoria. A rightness that took me all the way to my soul. And fuck, it felt good.

I felt myself tighten as I sank fully onto him, and he froze a second. Then his strong arm was lifting me achingly slowly back up his length. Our lips met, and I sank down again, relishing him, losing myself to the waves of pleasure.

We rocked together, and I took every drop of enjoyment from each movement, letting my mind abandon every other thought I had. The small movements; the brush of his fingers across my nipples, the flicking of his tongue over my neck and lips, the soft moans he gave as I moved my fingers over his divine body, combined with the ecstasy of our bodies connecting was causing a pressure to build that I knew I couldn't contain for long. He began to move faster inside me and I ground against him, the feeling of fullness making me gasp for breath.

"Tell me you love me," he growled as he gripped the back of my neck, driving hard into me and pressing his other hand flat to my stomach. "Tell me you're mine."

I arched back as the pressure reached a crescendo, and he growled again as I gasped the words. "I love you."

They were barely audible to me through my orgasm, waves of release smashing through me, making my toes curl and my head spin. But he heard them. The connection between us flared searing hot as he came, pulling me so tight to his body that we could have been one person.

"I'm yours," I said, kissing his face and squeezing my legs around him. "I'm yours. Always."

18

BELLA

The mountain was eerily quiet when we emerged from our snow cocoon. The whole mountain side had turned white, a layer of thick snow obscuring everything. I couldn't even see the edge of the path I knew we were on. The snow was no longer falling, and barely a thing moved.

"We'll have to walk tight to the mountain, to avoid the edge," Ares said. I nodded, and we set off.

As we walked, carefully, I couldn't help the nagging feeling I'd had since the avalanche from growing in my mind. I'd recognized that flash. The color... I was sure it was the exact color Zeeva flashed with. Zeeva was Hera's minion, and Hera had teal everywhere. Was one of Hera's monsters here? Or her magic? But why? She had wanted me to succeed.

Just as I was dismissing the entire train of thought, my cat's presence pushed at my mind, through the helmet. I let her in at once, my surprise evident in my mental voice.

"Zeeva?"

"Bella, I am sorry," was all she said, and then she was

gone. I stopped walking, confusion and apprehension washing through me.

"Ares, something is going on. Zeeva just spoke to me. She said she was sorry." He gave me a grave look. "Do you think something has happened? Off the mountain, I mean?" Fear for Joshua's safety bolted through my chest.

"No." Ares' voice was a rasp.

"What then?"

"I think Terror is a cruel being indeed. I think... I think he is truly going to make us feel fear. I hope I am wrong."

"Wrong about what?" Uneasiness was gathering in the pit of my stomach at his intensity. "Is Zeeva here?"

"I think so, yes. And I think Terror knows that one way to make someone as courageous as you feel true fear is to force you to fight an enemy you do not wish to. One you fear hurting."

I gaped at him. "You think he's going to make me fight Zeeva?"

"Maybe."

"No." I shook my head. "I can't. Terror couldn't force her to do anything she doesn't want to do anyway, she's too powerful."

No sooner had I said the words than there was a bright flash of teal, and a creature appeared on the path ahead of us.

My heart pounded in my chest as I took in the sight. A cat, for sure. But not the one who had lived in my shitty apartment for eight years, nor the large, intimidating cat Zeeva had turned into when I pissed her off.

This was... majestic.

She was fifteen feet tall at least, taking up almost all of the mountain path. Her tail was wrapped around her as she sat, her fur shining with light reflected from the snow.

Lethal claws tipped her front paws, and where her eyes should have been were two gleaming turquoise gems. Power rolled from her, a sleek sense of danger that immediately garnered my respect. I had no doubt at all who I was looking at.

"Zeeva," I whispered, my heart hammering in my chest.

"You may not pass," she said, her voice loud on the silent mountain, but her mouth not moving.

"Zeeva, why are you here?"

"You may not pass."

"How are they making you do this?"

The gemstone eyes flickered with light for the briefest second and her voice sounded in my head. *"For this Trial, Terror is allowed to test your fear, and he is allowed to use whatever would scare you most. I have no choice."*

"You may not pass, without defeating the sphinx," she said aloud.

"I won't fight you!" The red mist was tingeing my vision, but not in readiness to fight. It was in reaction to my fury. Who the hell did Terror think he was, taking the only friend I had and making me face her? That did not instill fear in me, but anger, hot and fierce.

"You may not pass without defeating the sphinx. And the sphinx's strength is deadly."

As if to prove her point she moved fast, her claws swiping out and snagging something from the huge snow-drifts beside her.

Ares and I both had our swords ready, but then I saw what she was holding in her giant paw. It looked a lot like raccoon, but bigger and mostly white. With her gemstone eyes fixed on me, Zeeva tossed the squealing creature in the air and flicked her claw. The thing was disemboweled before it hit the ground, spattering the bright white snow with crimson.

"You may not pass without defeating the sphinx."

"No!" Panic was starting to war with the fury that was boiling through my blood. We had to get past her. We had to finish the Trial. But I couldn't fight something as strong as her and win without hurting her. "Terror, you're a fucking prick!" I bellowed the words, *Ischyros* burning in my hands. "Ares, what do we do?"

"You may not pass without defeating the sphinx," Zeeva said again.

"I know! Stop saying that!" I could feel my temper taking over, my control slipping.

"Bella, I think she's saying it for a reason." Ares' voice was inside my head, and he wasn't looking at me. *"She's emphasizing the word defeat. I think she's trying to tell you something."* I looked between him and my enormous, vicious cat. "You may not pass without defeating the sphinx." I replayed her words. She was saying *defeat*, not *kill*.

"Sphinx," I breathed, the realization hitting me. "She's a sphinx."

"Tell me a riddle," I blurted out. "If we get it right, you must let us pass."

There was a spark in her gemstone eyes before she spoke. "Three riddles, and you may pass. If you get them wrong, you will die."

"Fine." I looked to Ares. "Please tell me you're good at puzzles," I hissed.

"No."

"Shit."

"Are you?"

"Not really."

"Are you ready?" Zeeva's voice cut through my rising

panic. Without waiting for me to answer, she continued. "I am the beginning of everything, the end of everywhere. I'm the beginning of eternity, the end of time and space. What am I?"

Oh god. "We should have fought her," I muttered, fear trickling down my spine. "Maybe we could have disabled her without doing any lasting damage, maybe-"

"Bella, stop talking, please. Concentrate." Ares' voice was hard and authoritative, and I closed my mouth. "Many riddles are word puzzles," he said calmly. "Let's try that first."

I nodded and tried to remember what Zeeva had just said.

"E," said Ares, suddenly.

"Correct," the cat answered.

"Wait, what?" I blinked at Ares.

"The answer is the letter E."

"Oh thank fuck for that," I breathed, letting out a huge breath. "You *are* good at puzzles. It's not like you to be modest."

"Bella, you need to calm down."

He was right. My head was spinning, the red washing in and out of my vision. "She's *my* cat. My only friend here. My only link to my past. I wasn't expecting this."

"I know, that's why Terror sent her. We can do this, OK?"

"OK. OK." I turned to the bungalow-sized sphinx that used to sleep on my damn bed. "What's the next one?"

"The first two letters signify a male. The first three letters signify a female. The first four letters signify a great. What is the word?"

I repeated the riddle in my mind, not allowing my attention to deviate at all.

"It's another word one," Ares said. "What is *a great*?"

The answer came to me in a rush. "A hero! He, her, hero!"

"Correct."

Another hit of relief smacked into me. One more to go.

"What is so fragile that saying its name breaks it?"

"Is this a word one?" I looked at Ares, alarmed to see worry in his eyes.

"It doesn't sound like it."

We both fell silent as we thought about the riddle. I repeated the sentence over and over again in my head, trying to work out what the answer might be but dismissing every suggestion that came to mind.

The silence stretched on, and I could feel the calm I'd briefly managed to get a grip on starting to slip away.

"Any ideas?"

"Shhh. I'm thinking."

I bristled at being shushed, the tension and worry in my body making me twitch. "Well, maybe we should think out loud. Standing here in silence isn't fucking helping so far," I snapped at him. He glared at me and started to speak but I held up my hand to stop him. "Wait. I think I know the answer."

Excitement thrummed though me, but I wasn't sure enough to risk shouting it out and getting it wrong. Ares' gaze intensified. "Really?"

"Silence. I think the answer is silence." He said nothing for a beat, then his eyes lit up as he smiled behind the helmet.

"I think you're right."

"Shall we risk it?"

"Yes."

We both turned to Zeeva. "Silence," I said loudly.

There was a pause that seemed to last a freaking lifetime, before the huge cat answered.

"Correct. You may pass."

Without another word there was a flash of teal, and she was gone.

"Honestly, if you don't smash Terror to bits, I sure as fuck will." I was stamping up the mountain path, anger rolling through me as adrenaline pumped through my veins.

"How about we do it together?"

"Ha. That would be a fucked up activity for a date." I kicked at the foot-deep snow as I powered on, the fatigue from climbing for so many hours gone, replaced with rage-fueled strength.

"It would be satisfying though. And I believe necessary. Terror is in need of a new, perhaps less clever host."

"What else is he going to throw at us on this stupid, cold-ass mountain?" I was in the mood to fight now. Fury at being pitted against my own cat had riled me up, and solving the damn riddles, although I was supremely relieved we had, had done nothing to relieve the violent urges.

A little frisson of unease at the thought of the awful kids' voices on the wind pushed through my anger. I wanted a real fight, not creepy ghost people to fight.

Which likely meant that was exactly what we were going to get next. Terror wasn't going to give us something we could defeat easily. "Where's that snow-leopard chimera with its friends?"

"I thought you didn't want to kill it? You sound ready to kill something." Ares had a mix of amusement and respect in his voice.

"Shit, you're right. I don't really want to kill stuff. Just Terror."

"Bella?"

I whirled at the woman's voice calling my name, my skin turning icy cold, and my heart almost stopping in my chest. "Bella, come here!" My gut twisted, and bile rose in my throat as I spun, looking for the owner of that sickly sweet voice.

"What's wrong?" Ares was at my side in an instant.

"My-my-" I didn't finish the stuttered sentence.

"Bella!" Fear bolted through my whole body, *Ischyros* burning white hot in response. Memories crashed through me. Awful memories. Memories I had spent a long time trying to forget.

"My prison guard," I whispered, clutching my sword with both hands.

"I'm here, Bella," Ares said, gripping my arms. "It's not real. It's just the mountain."

But as I looked into his eyes, drawing his words around me, he jerked backwards, his hands torn from my shoulders. "Ares!" I screamed as he flew backward along the snow. He roared in anger, waving his arms but an invisible force pinned him against the steep mountainside.

"Bella!" he yelled, reaching for me but clearly unable to move. I started toward him at a run but slammed into an invisible barrier. I swung my blade at it, and it went straight through. Terror's voice slithered into existence, almost as though the mountain itself were speaking.

"This test is just for Bella. Ares may not help. You must face your fears alone."

"Oh, Bella," said the female voice behind me. I swallowed, barely able to breathe as I turned.

The prison guard was standing ten feet from me, her unwashed hair piled high in a bun on her head, and a cruel gleam in her eyes. "Bella, such a fucking bad name for you." I looked at the woman as she spoke. "You're uglier than you ever were. Ugly and thick and fucking worthless. Why are you even here, Bella?"

"Leave me alone." The words barely escaped my throat. All of a sudden I was back in my cell, dark walls flying up around me, trapping me. She stepped toward me, a knife in her hand. "He doesn't love you, you broken little tramp. He's using you."

I couldn't defend myself. She'd hit me when I first went into isolation. When there was nobody there to see her do it. When I'd hit her back, she'd reported me and my isolation was extended, along with my sentence.

"Time for another haircut, Bella." She reached for my hair, jerking my head back as she caught a fist full of it. I could smell whiskey on her. "You can hit me back, but then you'll just be in here, alone with me, for even longer." Her voice was a gleeful whisper as she bent close to me.

Heat burned behind my eyes as I willed the red mist to come.

But it never had when she had made my life hell in prison. It had come at all the wrong times. It had come when I was around those who didn't deserve it. When I'd needed it against this monster, it had never come. My fear of her suffocated my strength and courage. She beat it out of me, and I could only vent it when I was out of her power, in all the wrong places.

I thought escaping her cruel tongue and starvation bribes when I got out of isolation and back with the other girls would be the end of my fear. But she still found ways to torment me, knowing I wouldn't risk being alone with her again. When I finished my time and escaped her, I vowed never to let fear win again. I vowed never to vent my violent nature in the wrong place. I vowed never to let myself stay in a place where I could be turned into a monster.

Because I knew that she would push me too far one day. She knew it on some level too, I was sure. Her goading, her abuse, was all to push me to my limit. And then it would be too late. I would have spent the whole of my life in prison for doing something unforgivable, instead of just being caught in the illegal fighting rings. She would have released the monster inside me.

Ares controlled the monster inside him. I'd seen it, in all its savagery, and he could control it. The thought spread through me, slowly at first, but buoying me as it gained momentum, my paralyzing fear and shock giving way to rational thought.

As her hot breath hit my cheek, and I felt the knife slide through my hair, I realized my fear was not of her at all. It was of losing control.

"You're not real." I croaked the words, and she paused. Slowly, she moved her face even closer to mine, and drew the knife to my throat.

"I'll feel real when this knife sinks in," she cackled.

"I beat you. I kept control and I got out. You're not real and I already fucking won." Saying the words was like a light going on somewhere horribly dark and buried inside me.

I had always considered my fear of her as a failure. But all this time, I had been the victor. I had kept control.

I moved my sword without thinking, the fear keeping me frozen in place gone. Ischyros pressed against her gut and her eyes widened as her jaw dropped. The knife fell from her hand.

"You're not real, so I could kill you if I wanted to," I said. She stepped backward, fast.

With an eerie screech, she began to morph in front of me, her sallow skin turning to pale smoke. Within a few seconds, she was gone, blown away with the snow.

"Wait!" After all these years harboring such a deep fear of the woman, I wanted more time to revel in my victory, in the realization that I had moved on and made myself a better person, despite what she had done to me. Plus, I'd kind of liked threatening her. She fucking deserved it, even if she was a creation of Terror's.

But she was gone, and the mountain path was empty, save for the snow. I turned to Ares, and Terror's voice rang out again.

"Time for the mighty God of War to take his turn." Terror's voice held barely contained glee, and it made me shiver. My body began to move of its own accord, sending me skidding hard into the mountainside as Ares went shooting to where I had been standing. His eyes found mine as we passed each other, and the fear in them made my heart stutter in my chest.

He was terrified.

He knew what was coming.

20

BELLA

"I'm sorry." His voice sounded in my head, loaded with pain. Before I could respond, a tiny wizened old lady hobbled into view.

"Why do you seek the oracle?" Her voice was deep and crystal clear, nothing like I had expected her to sound.

"No," croaked Ares. "Please."

"You wish to know if you may rule the world?"

"No! I don't want the world!"

It was as though she was hearing a different answer than he was giving.

"Such a young god, such large aspirations," the oracle mused. "You are barely born and you seek answers to questions I can't give you."

I swallowed hard as I realized what I was seeing. Ares was reliving a memory, just as I had.

"I don't need your help," Ares croaked. The oracle laughed.

"Very well. As you have traveled so far, I shall tell you something. You are strong, but you could be stronger. There is one other who shares your strength."

My breath caught and my stomach lurched. Ares turned away from the oracle, to stare at me.

"I'm sorry," he said, barely audible.

The oracle continued to speak. "As long as she lives, you will never be immortal. A god's strength must be his own, and while it is split between two beings, you will be weaker than your brethren. If she lives, you will be stunted."

The oracle shimmered and disappeared, and a large bed snapped into existence over the snow. A young woman was sleeping in it, short blonde hair fanned out over the pillow.

It was me.

"No!" Ares shouted, as a version of him with no armor and much shorter hair strode through the snow. "Leave her!"

I barely took a breath as I watched younger Ares reach the bed and pull a shining dagger from his belt. He cocked his head as he raised it over me, then paused. Slowly, his eyes widened, softening for a split second before turning steely. He put the dagger back in its sheath, and held both his hands over my sleeping form, closing his eyes in concentration. My form began to glow a gleaming red, then vanished.

"I should have told you. I-I-" Ares cut off as the image before us changed again.

It was me, dressed in peasant clothing, bent over and digging with mud all over my face. A horse galloped around the mountain path, a steel covered rider wielding a sword. My face hardened as I straightened, no fear on my youthful features. But I didn't stand a chance against the mounted rider.

I couldn't help the sharp intake of breath as the rider's

sword separated my head from my shoulders. Ares made a strangled sound, and the image changed again. This time I was dressed as a maid, busy with a duster in my hand. I watched, barely breathing, as flames burst to life on the snow, and painfully slowly consumed the apparition of me.

"No," Ares choked.

The image changed yet again, and like a fucked up time-line of human history I watched myself die over and over, in a different time and place.

My mind couldn't turn the images into sense, couldn't process what it meant.

"What is this?"

"I couldn't kill you. The oracle said I had to kill you to get my true immortality, but something stopped me. So I sent you away from Olympus so I didn't have to share my power. And... And instead of you dying at my hand, you died a thousand times over in the mortal world." His voice cracked on the last word, and intense pain rocked through our connection, causing my own eyes to fill with burning tears.

This was what Ares had done that he couldn't tell me.

And now, on this mountain, he was being forced to live his worst fear. Was it me finding out? Or was it having to see the consequences of his actions?

I stared mutely at the image before us, of me bloodied and wounded, lying on a filthy bed in a torn old-fashioned dress. A small cat with amber eyes was curled up beside me as the life left my eyes.

Zeeva said she'd been with me longer than I knew. This was real. I'd lived a thousand lives I had no recollection of. Ares had banished me from the world I belonged to and I had lived an endless cycle of powerless, violence-filled lives instead.

I'd never fit in. And I never would have.

"You came back to get me when you needed your power. When Zeus took yours, you sought me out after thousands of years."

Ares' look was pure anguish as I spoke.

"But if that hadn't happened, I would still be there. Destined to die unhappy, only to start all over again. In a world I would never belong to, never find contentment or joy in."

A hot tear slid down my cheek. The thought of being trapped for an eternity in endless unhappiness made me feel sick. And the pain rolling from Ares straight into my gut made me unsteady. I couldn't sort through the emotions, couldn't put them in the right order. I couldn't work out what was important and what was beyond fixing or caring about. I watched as an ancient Egyptian man plunged a short knife into my chest behind Ares.

"I'm sorry," he said. Never had two words sounded more sincere, more loaded with truth. But they weren't sinking in, the revelation of the life I had lived taking up too much space in my head.

Neither of us saw the chimera until it pounced.

21

BELLA

Solid weight slammed into me. I registered pain in my thigh and shoulder, and then I was crashing through freezing snow. Red descended over my tumbling vision, and my surroundings slowed as my war-sight kicked in.

The chimera was rolling with me, the snow leopard head rearing back to snap. I jerked my head as our roll through the snow continued in slow motion, leaving me on top of the creature. I jumped, then screamed in pain as the muscle in my thigh felt like it was being torn from my body. I slammed back down onto the chimera, my leap thwarted.

Gasping for breath, I looked down at my leg. The snake's jaws were clamped firmly around it. Searing pain lanced through my other shoulder and I realized my distraction had cost me. The leopard head pulled back, a lump of my flesh hanging from its jaws.

Power surged through my body, pain turning lightning fast into fury. The image of me in the purple dress with an army at my back filled my mind, and I blasted as much of the rage as I could at the chimera, thrusting *Ischyros* toward its heart as we skidded across the mountain path.

It worked.

The chimera was thrown backward with more force than I thought was possible for me to possess, and I screamed again as the snake's jaws were ripped from my leg. I realized within a heartbeat though that I had made a mistake. The momentum created by hurling the thing away from me worked both ways, and I was flying backward at almost the same rate as the chimera.

As my back hit the ground I started to skid. I scrabbled in the snow, desperately trying to find anything to cling on to, vaguely aware of the chimera slamming into the steep mountainside. If the chimera had been thrown toward the mountain, that meant I was moving in the opposite direction. Toward the edge of the mountain path.

"Bella!" Ares' roar was deafening, then I hit something soft but firm, sending me skidding sideways. It was his barrier, I realized, recognizing it at once from when he used it to stop me falling.

Magic, you fucking idiot! You have magic!

Drawing on the well of power burning inside me, I threw up my own walls of air, all around me. With a painful slam, I hit the first one, then the second, before mercifully coming to a stop. I closed my eyes and let my head collapse onto the ground, sending my power immediately to my leg, trying to heal it. I didn't look at it. I knew it would be a mess.

"Bella! Are you alright?"

A snarl caused my eyes to snap open again. How the hell had the chimera survived hitting the mountain that hard?

Sitting up as fast as I could, I scanned the mountain

path but it was hard to see more than a few feet through the blizzard. I could see the golden glow of Ares though.

"Ares?" I yelled, then my heart leaped in my chest as he burst toward me, a chimera swiping at his golden armor. But this chimera had a red snake for a tail. It was a different one.

More snarls sounded, growing louder, and my heart began to thud against my ribcage. Ares swung with his sword, causing the red tailed creature to back off just a fraction, as at least six more prowled into view through the blizzard. They all walked low to the ground, shoulders rocking as they advanced. Ready to pounce.

I glanced at my thigh, already knowing I wouldn't be able to stand. Bile rose in my throat at the sight. I could see bone. My magic was strong enough to block most of the pain, but it couldn't heal my leg in time for me to fight.

Fear crept over me, starting in my chest and working outward, an icy dread tingling through my limbs and taking over my head.

"Ares!"

One of the creatures leaped at him, followed immediately by a second. "Ares!" He had his shield up, and was moving fast, landing blow after blow on the huge creatures, but there were six heads with vicious teeth and horns, and only one of him. A third joined the fight.

"I will not take your power! You need it to heal!" the God of War yelled as he ducked and dodged, keeping himself between me and the pack.

I tried to stand, using my sword to push myself up, but my useless leg gave out before I even got halfway.

Frustration escaped me in a roar.

He couldn't beat them alone. And certainly not if he wouldn't take my power.

"You must! Take it and defend us!"

He didn't answer, couldn't answer, as another chimera joined the fray, snapping at his feet.

Fury at being able to do nothing was gripping me, and I tried once more to stand, without using my damaged leg at all. With the help of my blade I managed to get to one knee, but my elation was short lived.

There were too many for Ares to keep back, and I barely had time to throw up my shield before a chimera leaped for me.

Unlike before, I only skidded for split second, knocked backward by the creature's strength. By the time I realized what had happened, it was too late.

I felt an almost detached numbness as I felt the ground beneath me disappear, and heard an animalistic shriek from the chimera as it too realized what was happening.

I was falling. Falling through empty air, nothing but snow around me. I would survive the fall. But Ares would die at the jaws of the chimera. At the thought of his face I felt a surge of agony through our bond, and fear for his life swamped me.

Instinctively, I began to push my power toward the bond, trying to force it to leave my body, to reach him. Everything I had learned about him, my past, what he had done to me became meaningless at the notion of losing him.

For a heartbeat I thought it was working. I could feel the power leaving my body, the connection flaring.

But then I hit the ground.

22

BELLA

I awoke with a jolt of fear, and flashing stars of light crashed across my vision as I sat up gasping.

"I'm alive." The shocked words came out as a croak, which turned into a wail as the pain hit me.

My leg. I looked down, fighting nausea at the sight of the gaping wound. I shut my eyes and sucked in air, trying to gather my scattered thoughts, trying to focus. Everything was hazy, memories and emotions charging around in my head like unleashed animals, and my body half numb and half ablaze with pain. It was as though my leg was taking up so much of my physical awareness that everything else had lost sensation.

Get it the fuck together, Bella. First things first, where am I? And where is Ares?

I opened my eyes and looked everywhere but my injured leg.

It was dark, but I could see enough to establish that I was in a cell.

Panic coiled tight around my chest as the realization that I was some sort of prisoner settled in. I tried to move, and a rattling sounded. "Oh god." My wrists were manacled. The pain from my leg was so bad it had blocked out the fact that I was fucking chained up. I lifted my manacled hands to my head desperately, the chain pulling.

My helmet was gone. And so was *Ischyros*.

"No, no, no." I could feel the panic spiraling, fear and confusion building. But no power came with it. No red mist, no surging strength. Ares had told me about manacles that stopped magical powers being used. He'd said they could be used on the demon.

But he'd also said only the three brothers, Zeus, Hades and Poseidon could use them. Surely that meant that they couldn't be those ones?

I gasped for breath, fighting to get control of myself. I could feel my burning ball of power, hot and ready under my ribs. It was still there. I tried to send it to my leg, to heal the debilitating pain. But nothing happened.

Find Ares. Memories of the mountainside tumbled through my mind, bitter resentment flashing to life in response to seeing my own death played out over and over again...

"Not now, Bella," I hissed aloud. "More important shit to deal with."

I needed to know where I was, and who had chained me up. That was my most immediate problem. That and the wound on my leg.

Surroundings first, I thought, still resisting seeing how bad the injury was.

I was sitting on a wooden floor, and the walls on three sides of the small room were also paneled in wood. The last wall was a series of tall iron bars. Cell bars.

Slow recognition dawned on me as I stared at the

paneling. I'd seen it before, in the room full of stone tables.

I was on the demon's ship.

How was that possible? I was supposed to be in the Ares Trials! Nobody was supposed to interfere with them!

Fresh fear gripped me, but this time for Ares. It was instinctive, and it drowned out the turmoil of what I had recently learned about him. Whatever the hell had happened in the past, I knew I didn't want him dead. Bile rose in my throat at the thought and I searched inside myself for the connection to him. Hera had confirmed what I already knew, that there were two separate links between us. The one that had been there from the start, the one that I felt tugging when he used my power was lifeless, the distance between us too great for it to work. But the other, the one that had blossomed later and carried his emotions, his presence, his very essence to me was the one I sought.

A weak spark of anguish rolled through me, and I knew it wasn't my own. Ares was alive. But far, far away.

With a surge of relief, I tried again to summon my power, finally forcing myself to look at the bite in my thigh. The blood had congealed, so I was in no immediate danger from blood loss, but it was fiercely hot to touch, and many layers of muscle and flesh were visible above the sliver of pale bone. There was no way I'd avoid an infection. *That's if it's not already poisoned.* I knew from my previous experience with the manticore that creatures in Olympus had many other nasty ways of killing, in addition to all the teeth and claws.

When my healing power didn't respond, I tried to summon a fireball, but nothing happened. Impotent rage was building inside me the longer I attempted, and failed, to use the burning energy trapped in my body. It was all I could do not to start screaming in frustration.

I'd spent my entire life feeling like I was going to explode from the inside out. Like a person ten times larger than me was trying to bust out of the body it was trapped in.

And I now suspected I had spent many, many lives feeling like that. With nothing but pain to distract me, Ares' revelation wormed its way through my other thoughts, demanding my attention.

How many lives had I lived? It didn't surprise me that so many of them had ended violently. The need for confrontation was part of me. Had I got better at controlling it each time I was born into a new life?

Zeeva had told me that over the years my power had seeped out of me and into my blade. I felt a bone-wrenching pang when I thought about *Ischyros*. But her words made sense now. The power had left me and stored itself in the weapon over thousands of years, not just this short life-span.

Ares did this to me. His pain-filled words on the mountain came back to me. *"Instead of you dying at my hand, you died a thousand times over."*

But I remembered none of those deaths. In fact, dying repeatedly was not what made my heart wrench with betrayal. Instead, it was the knowledge that every time I started again would be just as awful and unfulfilling as the last. It was the thought of living the same miserable fucking life over and over that made hot fury and resentment boil under my skin. He had chosen to trap me in an endless cycle of misery.

Could I forgive him that?

Would I rather he had killed me in the first place?

No. I'm here now. And he loves me.

I knew he loved me. There was no way the Ares who had stood before me on the mountain would make the same decision now. He had planned to tell me the truth. After the Trials. He had planned to face his fear of me finding out, and the consequences that had carried.

But he had taken from me my life in Olympus, my power, and whatever family I might have had. He must have known I would never belong in the mortal world. Did he know how truly trapped and unhappy I would be, forever? Worse, his motivation had been greed. Desire for strength and power, pure and simple.

I ground my teeth and fell back onto the planks, my shoulder and leg pounding with pain, and frustration and sadness threatening to overwhelm me.

I had never felt anything like what I felt for Ares. I was bound to him, in a way that went beyond anything tangible. My soul, as old and fucked up as it apparently was, was connected to the God of War in a way I knew could never be undone.

I had lived most of this life at least, clinging to the belief that a person could change, could make mistakes and come back from them. If we couldn't be forgiven for our fuck-ups, then I was a lost cause. I needed to believe in forgiveness, for my own sanity.

But could I forgive him?

Ares was not the same man who had sent me to endure that shitty existence any more, was he?

～

The next time I woke, it was to a clear, cheerful male voice.

"Breakfast?"

I sat up quickly, managing to suppress the groan of pain this time.

The raging anger had kept me awake for as long as my body could take it, but the fall from the mountain had won out and eventually I had shut down completely. No dreams had disturbed me, and I had no idea at all how long I had been asleep for. My body ached from being on the wooden planks, though the discomfort was barely noticeable over the throbbing from my leg. I did think it was slightly less than the first time I woke up though.

"Who are you? Why am I here?" I shouted, blinking in the gloom.

Light gently pierced the darkness though the cell bars, making my eyes water.

"I thought you might like something to eat." Pain's handsome face came into focus on the other side of the bars. He was wearing Erimosian style clothes and a massive grin.

"What the fuck is going on? Why am I not in the Trial?"

"You lost, little goddess." Excitement danced through his dark eyes.

"What?"

"You didn't get to the top. You fell off the mountain, and Ares was overtaken by the chimera when he lost access to your power."

"Is he hurt?"

"Yes. He will probably die within the next few hours." Pure delight was written all over his face, and white-hot fury clawed up my chest.

"If he dies I swear to fucking god-"

Pain cut me off. "You can do nothing, little goddess.

When he dies, you will become the new God of War. And Terror made a deal. If Ares lost the Trials, we get the God of War."

"You're- you're taking me in his place?"

"Of course. What would we want with a dead god?"

"The other Olympians won't let him die," I said desperately.

"The other Olympians have no choice. He took part in the Trials willingly and he was fully aware of the risks. And besides, he is useless to them now; he has no power. You have it all."

I felt sick as I stared at the gleeful Lord. My head was swimming, unable to believe his words. "He's a god. He can't die."

"No. You two combined are a god. The power only needs one of you. Now, do you want this food?"

"Go to hell," I spat. "Where is Ares?"

"Far from here, and beyond your help." His eyes flicked to the manacles on my wrists.

"What are these?" I shook them at him. Fear and anger was building in such a crescendo inside me that I was barely aware of my actions.

"They are what will stop you from saving him," he smiled. Bending, he set the tray down on the floor in front of the bars. "Terror will come and get you when Ares has finally given up his fight with death. We are expecting a visitor, and when they arrive you will need to be presented to them."

With a last fucked up grin, he turned and left, taking the light with him.

A desperate noise escaped my throat as I reached inside myself for the connection to Ares. Fear gripped me even tighter as I remembered what Hera had said.

Distance didn't weaken the bond between our souls. The realization made tears fill my burning eyes. The connection was so weak because Ares was weak. In a rush of certainty, I knew Pain was telling the truth.

Ares was dying.

23

BELLA

Any doubt I had that I could forgive Ares was swept away by a tidal wave of emotion so intense I thought it might actually burst from my chest.

He couldn't die. He couldn't.

I loved him, and I couldn't handle the thought of a life without him. He was a part of me, and my life wouldn't be worth living with a hole that size in my heart.

The rational part of me that knew it was fucking absurd to feel so strongly, that I barely knew him, that all my survival instincts were clearly whacked, was silent.

I had to save him.

I shook my wrists as hard as I could, as tears spilled from my eyes. The roiling mass of power was desperate to escape me, but no matter how hard I tried to force it out, it remained trapped inside.

I needed to get to Ares, I needed to give him my immortality.

A sob clawed its way up my throat.

I needed to save his life.

I sought our bond, trying to feel for him. It was even weaker than before, an anguished pain coming from him that caused more tears to burn down my cheeks.

It wasn't physical pain that he was feeling, I realized. It was what he had done to me that was causing him the hurt.

"It's OK," I said aloud, squeezing my eyes closed and clenching my fists in helpless despair. "I forgive you, Ares. You should have taken my power. You should have taken it on the mountain." My voice cracked, more sobs taking over as I tried stupidly to force my power toward him. "You should have taken it," I cried, the heat inside me unbearable, the void I knew I faced without Ares torture to consider.

I felt a pull in my gut, and my sobbing stuttered. "Ares?" The pull got harder, the power connection flaring into life. "Ares!"

I poured power into the bond with everything I had, the burning, boundless ball of energy shrinking fast as I forced every ounce to Ares, to save his life.

It wasn't until there was nothing left burning in my chest at all that I felt the connection cut off abruptly. As though coming out of a trance, I started in surprise. I'd given him everything. He had all of my power. That had to be enough to save him, to make him immortal again. *It had to be.*

Slumping back onto the planks, I let the tears come, this time fueled by relief. He would survive. He had to survive.

I was not a person who ever really allowed myself to cry, but once the tears had started, I couldn't stop them. I realized I was crying for everything I had endured since coming to Olympus. It was as though all the good and all the bad had rolled together and was spilling out of me in a tidal wave of emotion. I cried for the pain and betrayal and frustration I had experienced, but I also cried for the sheer joy of falling in love with Ares. I cried with gratitude because I knew that even if I died now, I had experienced his love. I cried because I missed him already, because I needed him there beside me. And I cried because I couldn't bear the thought of losing him.

After what seemed like an eternity, I mercifully cried myself into a long and dreamless sleep, until a bang resounded through the darkness. I sat up, alert instantly. Just the act of lifting my body was hard. Without the ability to use my power I was weak and tired. But Ares had my power now. He would come, and it would be my turn to be rescued.

"I don't know what you did, but it would appear that I underestimated the strength of both your power and your feelings. And the manacles' effect on internal magical bonds."

Icy tendrils worked their way down my body as I recognized the voice. Light exploded through the cell, making me flinch and causing yet more liquid to leak from my eyes.

I gritted my teeth and spoke as a figure stepped up to the cell bars. "People have a habit of underestimating me, Aphrodite."

24

ARES

"I have to get to her!"

"You will be no use to her in this state. You must rest."

"Mother, let me go!"

Hera glared down at me, her magic pinning me to the lavish bed I'd awoken in. Bella's power poured through my veins, knitting my torn skin back together and filling my body with life-preserving strength and vitality. She was too far away for me to access her power though, and I didn't know how she'd sent me it. At first I'd feared the worst - I knew I'd get her power the moment she died. But I could feel her presence through the bond between our souls. She was angry and frustrated and scared, but she was alive.

"Ares, if you go to her before you are healed, then her sacrifices, and yours, will have all been in vain." Hera, Queen of the Gods and my mother, let out a long sigh before sitting down on the silk sheets beside me. "I am sorry, truly, that this is your burden to bear. But it will be worth it. The moment you are strong enough, I will help you to get to her."

I opened my mouth to shout and argue, but the sorrow in her eyes stalled me. She looked tired, I realized. And gods never looked tired. "Where have you been?"

"You will find out soon enough, I fear."

She was wearing a toga of bright teal, as she often did, but her usual opulent peacock feather headdress was absent, a simple crown in its place.

"The other gods have missed you," I said.

She gave me a wry smile. "I hope, son, that you are trying to tell me that you have missed me."

I glared at her. "Your counsel is honest. The Olympians need it."

The truth was, I did miss her advice. It was never directed explicitly at me - I did not have that kind of relationship with my mother. Heart-to-hearts were not something we had ever indulged in. I didn't think my father would allow it even if she or I had wanted to. But I found her presence a balm at the meetings of the gods. She was even and fair in most things, and fiercely loyal and vengeful in others. Exactly as she should be.

"I have not abandoned you," she said quietly. "I have been required to direct my power elsewhere, but I have done everything I can to ensure your safety."

I couldn't help the indignant snort escaping my mouth. "This is the first time I have seen you since Zeus stole my power! Until I found Bella, I was mortal!"

"And where did you get the idea to find her?"

I paused before answering. "A dream."

Hera nodded, her mouth a thin line. "Sent by me. And Bella's companion?"

"Your spy."

"For a very, very long time. I have been watching over that girl for centuries, once I found where you had sent her."

"Why?"

"Because the two of you are linked. You have been since you were born."

Slowly, Hera reached out, her finger brushing my cheek in the most matronly gesture she had made since I was a child. Flashbacks of her singing to me, smiling, and a feeling of actual love between us rolled through me, making my breath catch. "You know that my power is linked to marriage and true bonds. I am able to bond two people once they have found love with each other, but I am also able to feel the bonds that exist without my input. The ones created by magic or prophecy or true fate. That is what exists between you and Enyo. When the oracle told you that only one of you could be immortal while the other lived, you assumed it made her your enemy. When you went to kill her, you were both too young for the bond to have ignited. But I knew it was there, waiting. I stopped you that day. I sent the doubt that made you pause, that made you remove her from our world instead of killing her. I couldn't let you destroy the one thing in the world that could make you happy, even if it also had the risk of making you mortal."

I stared, wide-eyed. "You have known this my whole life?" Hera nodded, eyes serious. "Why didn't you tell me?"

"You would not have believed me. You are as arrogant and stubborn as your father."

She was right, I realized, thoughts tumbling through my head. I would not have believed her. I had been certain Enyo was the one thing that could cause my death.

I would never have believed that I was destined to love her.

"How were we bound?"

"Powers beyond my control or understanding. We do not know who birthed Enyo, only that it was a Titan. But her power is yours. When you shed Pain, Panic and Terror and removed their power from yours, they were shed from her too. You are a part of one another."

"I know," I breathed. I focused on my mother's face, and her expression softened just a touch. "I love her. And now I know that I have never loved before."

A smile took Hera's mouth, warm and at odds with the pain in her eyes. "A connection to somebody that runs that deep is the most joyous, and the most painful thing a being can experience."

"She knows what I did to her, yet she found a way to send me her power. She saved my life. Again. Even though I stole hers from her."

"Ares, it is only because of the life Enyo has lived in the mortal world that she is able to save you. Prophecy is a strange and often cruel thing. If she had not lived the life she has, she would not have become the Bella you have fallen in love with, the Bella who is morally good and forgiving. The Bella who can save you from the worst parts of yourself. If she had lived in Olympus, able to expend her power in the way you have, she would have ended up just the same as you."

"Then why couldn't I have been the one who had to die a violent death over and over, instead of her? Why couldn't I have been the one who had to become mortal to learn about forgiveness? I got to march around a glorious world, treated as royalty, while she suffered endlessly." My voice cracked, guilt swamping me as the images on the mountainside of Bella dying repeatedly played before me. "I would do anything to swap places with her. Anything."

"Son, she remembers none of those deaths. And Bella needs to be the person she is. It is what makes her strong. It is what brought the bond to life and made you fall in love with one another."

"I can't stand the thought of everything she has had to deal with, just so that she can come and save me from my own monster." The idea was unbearable.

"Ares, do not be so self-absorbed." Hera's voice was sharp, and I snapped my stinging eyes to hers.

"What?"

"Bella did not become who she is to save you; she became who she is to save herself. She is fierce and proud and strong because of it, stronger even than you. You want your chance to make amends? Well, now it is your turn to face adversity. It is your turn to save her."

25

BELLA

"Hera has just announced publicly that her son will survive. You had something to do with this." Aphrodite's eyes were hard as she stared down at me. She was fiercely beautiful, wearing the look of an ice queen. Her hair was as white as her skin, her lips and dress the color of blood.

"Fuck off, Aphrodite." I tried not to let my relief at her words show on my face as I spoke. *Ares was with Hera. He would be OK.*

The woman hissed at me. "You have no respect."

"I have plenty of respect, just not for petty, jealous assholes."

"I would not be so generous with my insults, if I were you. Three of Olympus' most unpleasant deities are willing to do my bidding."

"Ah, so you're going to threaten me with Ares' Lords of War instead of doing your dirty work yourself?" I narrowed my eyes at her. "Why are you here? What have you got to do with any of this? And where is Eris?"

"As if I'm going to tell you anything you want to know.

All that is important is that you lost the Ares Trials. You belong to the Lords of War now. And they work for me." She leaned forward through the bars, a steely smile on her face as she whispered, "which makes you *mine*."

Being leered at through cell bars brought out the worst in me and I acted instinctively. I drew back my head, and spat at her.

The Goddess of Love shrieked as my saliva landed on her porcelain skin, and my lips quirked up into a smile, the dried tears on my cheeks cracking.

Then pain ripped through my wrists as I was lifted off my ass into the air, my body pulled to the extent of the chains attached to the manacles. They bit into my skin, blood welling instantly.

"You are a pathetic little brat," Aphrodite barked, wiping her perfect face. My body moved higher, and the manacles cut deeper. I tried to kick my legs but I was being pinned in the air by an invisible force.

"Why are you here?" I growled, refusing to show how much pain I was in.

"I am here because I am not fucking stupid, unlike that fool you have fallen in love with," she said, venom in her voice.

My mind whirred, trying to connect the dots. "Why would the Lords of War work for you?"

"They may be spirits of War, but they are hosted by men. And all men do exactly what I tell them to do." There was a note of smugness to her icy voice.

I blocked out the pain rolling in waves down my arms and tried to follow my train of thought. The pieces tumbled into place in my mind. "You're working with Zeus."

She cocked her head at me. "Zeus is the most mighty

of us all. Our true leader. Only a moron would fight against him."

"You mean Ares?"

She laughed. "And Hades and that idiotic water god, Poseidon. They're all fools. I found Zeus, despite him using the Guardian's power to mask himself. And I pledged my fealty to him and offered him my help. He is my true king. The Ares Trials were a gift to me to express his thanks. Zeus will not need the demon much longer, as he will have no need to hide from the other gods when his plan is complete. So, when Ares was sent to find the demon, I saw an opportunity to relieve some of my boredom. What could be more entertaining than watching a powerless, overgrown god defeated by his own underlings? I approached the Lords of War and told them to find Ares and offer him the demon if he underwent a series of Trials that would show the world how powerless he was."

"You weren't expecting my power, then," I said, rage lacing my voice. "And when we started winning, you cursed us instead."

Dark shadows swirled through the goddess' eyes. "You made a fool of me, and that can not be tolerated."

"When we broke your curse, you got Terror to up the stakes. Forcing Ares to commit his own being to the outcome." Fury was helping to block the pain, and my disgust for Aphrodite dripped from my words. "You used Ares like a fucking toy for years, then ruined his life when he didn't want you any more. You're worthless scum."

I jerked hard against the manacles as my body was pulled toward the bars, and I couldn't stop the cry of pain as the metal tore further into my skin.

"You have no idea what I am," Aphrodite hissed. "And

you have no idea what Zeus is capable of. I am on the right side of the war that is coming, and I am stronger than them all. How I treat my toys is going to become your whole life, little brat. I own you."

The power holding me up vanished and I crashed to the floor. The pain from my wounded thigh as I hit the planks was blinding, the whole world flashing between black and bright white as my brain seemed to tip upside-down. For a moment I was sure I'd throw up. Dim light crept back into my vision as I gasped for breath and I clutched at the floor, waiting for the dizziness to abate.

When I finally trusted myself to move without puking, Aphrodite was gone.

∼

"Bella?"

The voice dragged me from turbulent dreams filled with death and blood and darkness.

"Bella, wake up."

"Fuck off."

I lifted my manacled arms, trying to wrap them around my pounding head and shut the voice out. To shut everything out. It was all too dark and hazy.

Exhaustion had taken me completely. With no power left burning inside me, and *Ischyros* gone, I felt as weak as a kitten. The wound on my leg was sapping my human strength by the minute and the pain had numbed alarmingly in the last couple of hours. I knew that if I could no longer feel it, I was in trouble.

"Don't speak to me like that." The voice snapped, and I paused, recognizing it through my fog of fatigue.

"Zeeva?"

"Yes." I groaned as I moved my arms. They fell weakly to my sides as I tried to sit up.

Aphrodite's visit had left its mark. The skin on my wrists was shredded and bloody. "Are you here on the ship?" There was a note of hope in my dry, scratchy voice. I was painfully thirsty.

"I'm here." I squinted toward the bars, and saw a lithe little cat squeeze between them in the gloom. She was dragging something in her mouth. "I am sorry. About what happened on the mountain."

"Wasn't your fault," I croaked. Excitement and hope was forcing some energy into my limbs. If Zeeva was here, she could help me. If she had come from Hera, maybe it meant Ares was on his way too.

"Eat this." She rolled the thing she was dragging toward me. It looked a little like an orange, and I winced as the manacles moved against my cuts when I picked it up. "It will help."

I didn't question the cat, and began peeling the skin off what I assumed was a fruit. "Where is Ares?"

"I do not know."

Alarm skittered through me. "I thought he was with your master, Hera?"

"Then you know more than I do. I was under Terror's enforcement longer than I needed to be." Her usually haughty voice was laced with fury.

"He only just let you go?"

"Yes. And he will regret doing so."

"Wait, you just got free and you're here? Instead of with Hera?"

"Before I was freed I heard Pain say that they had you on the ship, and that it was moored off the north coast of Pisces. I should have gone back to my master but... I was worried."

"About me?"

"Yes."

Despite my increasingly shit situation, I beamed. "I knew it! I knew you loved being my cat!"

"I am not your cat. But... I am your friend. Terror was able to take control of me for the purposes of the Trial, but he should never have been able to hang on to my power for as long as he did. The Lords are powerful. Too powerful. Somebody is helping them."

"Aphrodite is working with them and Zeus," I told her, before putting a segment on the orange-thing in my mouth. Delicious tangy liquid instantly coated my tongue, and a out-of-place cheerful feeling spread through me. "What is this?"

"Portokali. It will help with the fatigue. That makes sense about Aphrodite. Hera knew that one of the Olympians was helping Zeus. I do not think she suspected her though."

"She's a coward and an asshole."

"The Goddess of Love is no coward. She is smart and manipulative and ambitious."

"She is a coward," I insisted. "She won't fight me. She keeps storming off."

"Her powers do not tend toward fireballs and super-strength like yours."

"How do I defeat her?"

"You can't. She is one of the strongest gods. There is little more powerful than love. And if she is truly working with Zeus, then your only chance at getting back to Ares is to run."

"Run? I don't walk away from a fight, and that woman needs a fucking beating. And I'm fed up of being told I can't defeat my enemies."

Zeeva sauntered up closer, then bared her needly teeth as she saw the manacles. "I'm pleased to see your fighting spirit is returning. But you will need it to escape, not aggress. Zeus must indeed have been here. Only the three brothers can use these manacles."

"Zeeva, I can't run even if I wanted to. My leg is useless."

"At some point they will have to take the manacles off. Then you flash."

"I have no power. Even without these evil freaking cuffs."

"What?"

"I sent it all to Ares. He needed the immortality."

Zeeva blinked slowly, and I put more portokali in my mouth. "You... you are mortal right now?"

"Yeah. Hundred percent human. And it sucks. Of all the ways to die, a big fucking hole in my leg was not the glorious ending I'd hoped for."

"How did you send Ares your power if he is in Hera's realm?"

"I don't know. I just did. I gave him everything."

"You love him? After what he did to you?"

"Completely."

There was a long silence, only broken by the sound of my chewing on the fruit. I knew, somewhere inside myself, that giving up my only chance of escape from this place to save Ares life was, well, crazy. But it hadn't been a choice. I hadn't weighed up options and reached a balanced, well-informed conclusion.

I had given him everything because that was what I had to do. Picturing his face made my chest ache, and it was nothing to do with my poor state of health. I longed to see him. To touch him, to kiss him.

"He will come for you." Zeeva said the words with certainty, and hope fired through my shattered body.

"I don't know if he will be strong enough. He very nearly died. And this wound is taking more from me every hour."

Zeeva moved cautiously to my leg, and sniffed her little cat nose. When she spoke, her tone was grave. "We must hope he makes a speedy recovery, and knows where to find you."

"Can you go to him? Tell him where I am?"

"I will leave at once."

There was a flash of teal, and when it faded I frowned. Zeeva was still sitting by my numb thigh.

"Err," I said. "I thought you were on your way to my rescuer?"

"The ship will not allow me to flash." The fury was back in her voice, and in the gloom I saw her eyes blaze dangerously.

The glimmer of hope I'd felt oozed out of me. "Shit."

"Indeed."

I blew out a sigh, and ate more portokali. "Zeeva, how did I send my power to Ares with the manacles on?"

"They must only block external magic."

"Oh. Another question, as you're stuck with me. Can you give me back those memories you told me about?"

"You saw how most of them ended already," she said quietly. "But I can tell you some of the happier ones."

"Do you know who I was before I was sent to the mortal world?"

"Many years ago, when the Titans who had helped Zeus become king had all disappeared, Zeus wanted all the Titan descendants rounded up. Hecate, who helps Hades rule the Underworld and is one of the most powerful remaining Titans in existence, tried to get to them first. She found you and a few others who were as powerful as the Olympians, and convinced the gods to let you learn your powers peacefully."

"Do you think she created the bond between me and Ares?"

"No, she's not really... loving or maternal. She is the Goddess of Ghosts."

"Oh."

"Hera championed you as the Goddess of War when it emerged how strong your power was, and how closely linked with Ares' own it appeared to be. When you disappeared, most people believed Zeus had something to do with it, due to his hatred of Titans. When he was accused, he had a fit of rage and removed all memory of a Goddess of War from everybody. Except his wife and Ares."

"Huh. So, I guess I still don't have a family."

"You have Ares. And... I suppose you have me."

26

BELLA

The scant energy I gained from Zeeva's portokali kept me awake for another half hour or so, during which I held the image of Ares, assured and calm, in my mind.

He would come for me. He would heal fast with all the power, and would find me. Somehow.

The strange thing was, I wasn't actually afraid of dying. Now that the flood of tears and overwrought emotion had been allowed the escape my body, I was *angry*.

I had finally discovered the truth about my past, the reason I was such a misfit, such a freak. And even better than that, I'd found somebody that understood me. It would be too damn cruel to find Ares, then lose him like this, so soon. It wasn't fair, and the idea of never seeing his face again filled me with hatred for the people who had done this to us.

Hatred for Aphrodite, mostly.

She had been furious that I'd managed to save his life. She'd wanted him to die. If I succumbed to my wounds in the shitty cell, at least I had saved Ares, I thought, drawing comfort from the knowledge.

I had saved him. Nothing was more important.

"Bella?"

A bubble of air in front of me shimmered and the voice was coming from it. And it was loud. Loud enough that I cried out in surprise. "Eris?"

"Oh thank fuck for that, I thought I was out of power completely. Listen to me, do not interrupt and do not fucking say no."

I opened my mouth to answer her, but she continued speaking before I could.

"That mother-fucking bitch has trapped me in the mortal world, and she's muted my power. I've got fuck all left, and what little I did have, I used saving my brother's sorry ass."

"What?" I couldn't help the interruption. What the hell was she talking about?

"He's my brother, I'm connected to him. I felt his death starting, even from here. I couldn't heal him from so far away, but your bond to him is epic, so I used what power I had left to amplify that instead."

"You're the reason I could give him my power from so far away?"

"Yeah. And I knew it would be difficult but I didn't know it would drain me almost completely. Must be those stupid fucking manacles you have on. I have no way to recharge here. Aphrodite has made sure of that. This is the last time I'll be able to talk to you, and I'm calling in every fucking favor you and Ares owe me. Get me the fuck out of the mortal world."

"We will. I swear, we will. But... I'm not really in a position to help right now," I said, slowing down as I finished the sentence.

"Well, fucking get into a position where you can!"

"Aphrodite has me trapped, I'm mortal, and I've got a fatal wound. Unless Ares gets here soon, I'm dead or spending eternity as her plaything."

"Ares will come for you. He'd better fucking be coming for you."

"He will," I nodded, even though I assumed she couldn't see me. "We'll find you, I promise. Are you in any immediate danger?"

"I'm in immediate danger of having no power and being bored to fucking death. I'm an ancient, all-powerful deity. This is not how I want to live my life."

Relief that she was safe mingled with the suffocating memories of living in a world that was so utterly wrong for you. I knew how shit that was. But, she would be fine for a while at least.

"I'm sure you'll be perfectly good at causing chaos without any power," I told her.

She snorted mentally. *"Come and find me, Bella. Do not leave me here."*

"We will. If we survive this, we will. And, Eris... Thank you. For saving his life."

I slept fitfully for what could have been an hour or five - I had no idea. When I awoke, I could sense a presence around me, but my body was too broken to react. I was sprawled on the planks, and I couldn't feel the wound on my thigh at all anymore. I tried to lift my head to look at it, but it was as though my skull weighed as much as my old punch-bag.

"Aphrodite?" I tried. Somebody was in the cell with me, I was sure.

"You're mortal. You don't need these any more."

The voice was male and unfamiliar, but as I felt the manacles slip from my wrists I realized who must have spoken.

"Zeus?" I moved my hands tentatively. The torn skin hurt as I moved my wrists, but I was grateful that the heavy feeling was gone from my arms. I tried again to lift my head.

If Zeus was really here, I wanted to see him. To speak to him.

"I have never seen my son like this. You have had quite an effect on him." The words were deep and lyrical, and an awestruck feeling threatened to overtake me as I struggled into a sitting position. My head was swimming, my insides unsteady. A well built man was standing over me, with dark hair shot through with gray. When my vision swam into focus for a few brief seconds I could see that his eyes shone purple.

I needed to worship this man. He was the king of the gods, most powerful being in Olympus. He was strong and beautiful and regal.

"My king," I rasped.

"How did you do it? How did you best Aphrodite and save him?"

Zeus' words floated into my addled brain, and I tried to make sense of them. How did I save him? "Save who?"

"My son. Ares. The God of War."

Ares' face filled my mind, blasting out the confusion like dynamite. Anger flooded my system, and I put my hands flat on the planks beneath me to steady myself. "You were going to let him die," I hissed. "You were going to let Aphrodite kill your son."

"Ares is his own man. It is not my responsibility to take

care of him. Particularly when my efforts have been so consumed elsewhere." There was a bitterness to his voice that made me even more angry.

"But he is only vulnerable because of you! You stole his power!"

"He committed treason." The god's seductive tone had hardened, and I heard a rumble of thunder in the distance. "He tried to get in my way, and he paid the price."

"He tried to stop you unleashing a monster into the world."

"He is a fool. He can't see past the tired rhetoric of my narrow-minded brothers," Zeus hissed, and suddenly he was inches from my face. "I don't know how you seduced him away from Aphrodite, and I don't care. But, I am glad that you will die in his place."

Before I could ask the snarling god anything else he was gone. Did that mean he was glad his son survived? Did he feel anything at all for Ares? Or was he just trying to scare me?

"Asshole," I spat.

"It's not advisable to swear at deities like Zeus." Pain stepped out of the shadows, up to my cell bars. I looked around in the gloom for Zeeva, relieved that I couldn't spot her. It was best if nobody else knew she was here. It might give me an advantage.

"So you got him to take off the manacles for a reason, huh?" I tried to sound as casual as I could, even as my heart beat an increasingly irregular rhythm against my ribcage.

"Aphrodite wants to play with her new toy, and she doesn't like it down here. She's asked me to bring you up on deck." An evil glint shone in Pain's dark eyes, and I couldn't help the icy shudder from tracking down my spine.

It seemed that I had run out of time.

27

BELLA

P ain literally had to drag me up the narrow wooden steps that led from deep in the hull of the ship, where I had been imprisoned. My useless leg didn't hurt as it thumped against the steps. There was more light in the stairwells that we were moving through, and I could see now that the wound had gone a gross green color. It made me feel sick whenever I looked at it, so I tried not to. I made myself as heavy and awkward as possible, just to piss Pain off, and eventually he resorted to throwing me over his shoulder and carrying me down corridors and up staircases.

I didn't try to memorize the route we were taking, or work out an escape plan. My brain was too fuzzy, my body too tired. If I hadn't had the fruit Zeeva had given me, I'd probably have died from thirst already.

"How long have I been on the ship?" I asked. My throat hurt when I spoke, but it wasn't in me to keep quiet.

"A few days. Long enough."

Surely that was enough time for Ares to heal? Why hadn't he found me yet?

"If your bitch-mistress wants to keep me alive long enough to play with me, you're going to have to feed and water me. Humans need that sort of shit."

"Aphrodite knows what humans need. Don't you worry about it, ex-baby goddess."

He emphasized the word ex delightedly and I scowled at his back. They knew I was mortal now. He was right. I was an ex-goddess.

The light was so bright when we eventually emerged onto the deck that tears sprang to my eyes immediately. Pain dropped me unceremoniously onto the planks as I squinted around, pain jarring through me as I landed on the wood.

Pastel clouds surrounded us, and the epic solar sails hung from the masts, shining so brilliantly that they hurt to look at.

"That's a nasty looking wound." I peered blearily at Aphrodite. She had dropped the ice-queen look, and now had caramel colored skin and baby pink hair. She wore a black wrap-around dress and had full, sensuous pink lips and onyx eyes.

"Not as nasty looking as your face," I said, and gave her a sarcastic smile.

We both knew she was beautiful. But I doubted many people told her she wasn't, so I got a kick out of the words regardless.

She narrowed her eyes as her smile widened. "Oh yes. Yes, yes, yes. I can see why that oaf fell for you. I imagine that when you are together you are like immature teenagers, fighting and cursing like idiots?"

I shrugged from my half-sitting position on the deck.

"Well, there's one thing we do better than teenagers do, and I can assure you it's not fighting."

Her features darkened momentarily. "You will never live up to me, little girl."

"Aphrodite, I don't need to live up to you. You and I are nothing alike. We are non-comparable."

"So you think Ares doesn't wish that you could make him feel like I can?" Her voice dripped with sex and seduction. And for a moment, I believed her. Doubt filled me. There was no way I could possibly be a lover like her, no way I could possibly make Ares feel as good as she could.

But then I remembered. *Ares loved me.* Ares was a part of me, and I him. We were meant to be together, destined for one another, and nothing in the world could come close to the feel of his skin against mine, his arms around me, his lips on mine.

"I don't need to have this conversation with you, Aphrodite. I'm done. Do whatever the fuck it is that you hauled me up here to do, give me some food and water, and send me back to that shitty cell, where I don't have to look at your ugly-ass face."

The goddess's eyes filled with fury, and she lifted her dainty arm, snapping her fingers. "Pain! She's all yours. Do not kill her though, or it will be the last thing that spirit of yours does in that body."

Pain stepped forward, a smile on his handsome face. "Of course, mighty one." I looked around myself as quickly as I could manage, my head spinning as soon as I moved it too fast.

Panic was leaning against the railings to my left, and Terror was behind me, standing by the main mast. There was no sign of the Underworld demon. Or Zeeva.

Mortal or not, I had enough years of training for my fight-or-flight instincts to kick in. Ninety-nine times in a hundred, they told me to fight. But I had nothing in the tank. I was empty.

I hadn't given up hope that Ares would come, but I wasn't naive enough to think there was a way out of whatever was in store for me right now.

Neither fight, nor flight, was an option. So the next best thing was to give my attackers nothing. No satisfaction, no reason to come after me again. That was how bullies were dealt with, that was how to bore somebody who went after an opponent who couldn't fight back, or win. Give them nothing.

Pain's eyes roared to life with a burning yellow as he thrust his hand out. My body lurched off the planks as though tied to him by a tether, and I flew up into the air just as I had when Aphrodite had visited me in the cell. I closed my eyes, concentrating on slowing my racing heart, but I didn't have time to take the deep breath I wanted to.

White hot fire exploded to life in my thigh, as though all the numbness had been expelled completely. Sheer agony shot in waves up my leg, smashing into the base of my spine and then shooting up into my skull like electric shocks.

Nothing had ever hurt like it, and I couldn't suck in breath, couldn't make a sound, the pain was so consuming. Darkness and stars descended over my vision and before I could work out how to breathe again, I blacked out.

. . .

"She's mortal, you fucking idiot. If you hit her with that much, her body will just shut down."

"I forgot. Do you know how long it's been since I tortured someone completely mortal? They tend to stay out of my way these days."

I could hear Pain and Panic talking as I came round, but I didn't dare open my eyes. Aftershocks of pain were still racing up my back from my leg, but mercifully most of the numbness had returned. I felt sick, but I knew there was nothing in my system to bring up.

My head lolled and my chin hit my chest. I realized foggily that I was still being held up in the air.

"Let me have a go. At least I can't accidentally knock her out." Panic's voice brimmed with excitement and my stomach clenched.

I was trapped. Their plaything to torture as they pleased. And there was no way for me to fight back or escape.

"Fine. But I want another go before she goes back to the cells."

"Deal."

I heaved to the left suddenly, before jerking back to the right. Panic was shaking me.

"Wakey, wakey!"

My eyes fluttered open and as soon as Panic came into focus, I forced a laugh to my lips. They may have had me as helpless as a kitten, but I wasn't going to let them see my fear.

"You think this is funny?" Panic cocked his head at me.

"No, not this," I rasped. "I'm picturing Ares tearing you limb from limb when he gets here, his power fully restored. It's a highly entertaining image."

"You know, you're just like us? Made of the same thing.

You enjoy seeing others in Pain, enjoy seeing their Panic, enjoy instilling Terror in them."

"You misunderstand me," I told him, using most of my energy to hold my head up so that I could look him in the eye. "I find the idea of *you* experiencing those things most enjoyable. But that's because you're a complete fucking asswipe. I'm not a fan of nice, normal folk being terrorized. Just total fucktards like you three."

Panic snarled, and then I was flying through the air, toward the railings of the ship. My body lurched to a stop as I reached them, and my stomach seemed to jump into my throat as I tilted forward, forced to look straight down over the edge of the ship. I could see land, but only just, it was so far below us.

My mind filled abruptly with images, first of me falling from the mountain and the chimera shrieking, then of me hitting water and tentacles wrapping around me, dragging me under. I felt my body begin to tip, the images in my mind mingling with reality.

Then I was falling, the ship shooting past me as I dropped, the wind rushing against me and making my hair whip around my face. My chest was constricting, air was eluding me. No part of me wasn't sweating and fear was crawling its way up my throat, fighting for space with the panic.

There was a flash and then I was above the ship, near the top of the solar sails, still falling. Within seconds I smashed hard into the deck, pain rocking through my ribs as the wood splintered beneath me. I gasped for breath, rolling onto my uninjured side.

Panic's laughter carried across the deck, a feminine chuckle alongside it.

"How many times could you survive that fall, little girl?" Aphrodite asked.

"As many as it takes until Ares gets here," I panted, sucking in air.

"Let's see about that."

28

ARES

A roar of frustration escaped my throat, and I slammed my fist down on the marble table. It cracked, shattering onto the white tiles below.

My strength was back, in full force. All the power that had been stolen from me and I had yearned for so hard was returned.

And I didn't care.

"Ares, if you are going to act like a child then do it elsewhere! I am trying to find Bella and you are not helping."

I bared my teeth at my mother before I could stop myself. She had been standing over the table for what seemed like an eternity, a portal shimmering over it, but it had vanished with my outburst. Hera glared back at me from under her freshly-donned elaborate peacock head-dress, her gaze filled with authority.

Whirling away, I stamped toward the edge of the temple and glared out over the forestland surrounding us, trying to keep my temper from brimming over its too-small container. "I will rip them apart, limb from limb."

"I'm sure you will, if we ever find them." Hera's voice dripped with annoyance.

The only reason I could keep any calm about myself at all was the fact that I knew Bella was still alive. I could just feel her through our connection. It was weak, and growing weaker, but she was a fighter. As my mother had said, she was stronger than I was. She would never give in.

But she was mortal now. I had every ounce of her power, I could feel it. Which meant there was a limit to her ability to fight the Lords of War.

If another Olympian was there, as my mother seemed to think there might be, then Bella did not stand a chance. The thought flashed into my head and rage welled through my center, flooding my muscles and making me swell.

"For the sake of Olympus, Ares, will you go somewhere else so I can work in peace!"

I had finally cracked Hera's patience. I threw her another angry glare as I stamped down the steps of the temple and out into the forest. I let my body grow with power as I went, trying to take some comfort in the return of the ability. But I got none. What was the use in being huge and mighty and powerful, if it was without her?

The sound of wood cracking loudly in the distance made me pause in my furious march. The trees around me began to rustle. I looked over my shoulder at the temple, still only a few feet behind me, before pushing my power-enhanced senses out into the forest.

The second I did, Dentro materialized before me, his body seeming to melt out of the browns and greens until a fully-formed, enormous dragon's body wove its way amongst the dense foliage.

My body started to move automatically into its

reflexive stance, sword drawn and chest squared, but then I slowed to a stop. Bella and this creature had become friends. She cared for it.

"Do you know where she is?"

"I do. It took me some time to find her, and I had some help, but I know where she is."

Hope, relief and pure happiness flushed the rage from my system in a heartbeat.

"Mother!" I yelled for Hera, then turned back to Dentro's massive face. "Let's go."

"Not so fast, Warrior God. Last time I saw you, you were trying to kill Bella. I have become inexplicably fond of that fierce little goddess, and now I sense that you have her power. All of her power."

"I can guarantee you, dragon, you are not as fond of Bella as I am." I snarled the words, feeling the rage returning. I would not be denied her now, not when I was so close.

"I require your assurance that you only have her best interests at heart."

"Her best interests are staying alive, you idiotic beast! She needs me, now!"

I had grown again, and my sword was clutched in both hands. My chest felt tight and the War power wasn't forcing out my emotions like it always used to. My adoration, fear and love for Bella was permanent.

"Would you die for her?"

"Yes." My reply was instant, loud and true.

Dentro nodded his huge wooden head once, then lifted it to look over my shoulder. I turned to see my mother standing at the temple edge, atop the white stone steps. She nodded at the dragon, then vanished in a flash of teal.

"We must go too, now! Where should I flash to?" Urgency made my words tumble together but the dragon understood me.

"Bella is on a ship, and flashing is not possible there. I will take you."

My mouth fell open slightly as the creature lowered its neck to the ground. A dragon allowing a being to ride it was unheard of. In response to my awe, Dentro spoke again. "I do this for her. Not for you. Never will you be offered my neck again." His voice was tight, and I moved quickly, before he could change his mind.

His bark-covered skin was rough, and I was grateful for my armor as I pulled myself into a sitting position at the base of his neck.

"Hold on, Warrior God," he said, and then we were launching into the sky.

29

BELLA

"*I have found your helmet.*" Zeeva's voice cut through the whistling air as I fell.

The spark of hope her words caused was knocked from me completely as I slammed into the deck. Another of my ribs popped, and pain squeezed around my middle, suffocating me. I could hear myself wheezing, but I couldn't lift a limb, raise my head, or even move an inch. I just lay sprawled on the planks, trying to force enough air into my lungs to keep me alive a little longer. Until I could see Ares again. His face filled my mind, forcing out the doubt and fear.

"*Bella, do not give up now. If you can reach your helmet then they can't get into your head anymore.*"

They didn't need to get into my head. They were breaking my body. Even listening to her mentally was a mammoth effort. I had nothing left. My strength was utterly sapped.

"*Roll onto your back.*"

I knew that if I did what Zeeva said, I would be flung up into the air again, then pitched over the edge of the ship, only to be flashed over the deck to land on the solid wooden planks.

"He is here."

This time the spark of hope was so big, nothing could put it out. My body tapped into a reserve of energy I didn't know I had, and I rolled, looking around desperately.

I instinctively felt for our connection and found it immediately, burning bright and hot.

It was true. *Ares was nearby.*

"Look up."

I realized at the same time Zeeva spoke that the Lords had stopped looking at me and were craning their necks to peer up into the clouds. There was a shape in the distance, a dark spot, small but growing. A moment later, I could make out massive wings. Green and brown wings.

And a tiny, brilliant golden light.

"Dentro found him." I breathed the realization a second before Aphrodite's heels clicked loudly on the deck.

"Terror," she barked. The marble man moved forward from the mast in response. "Let's make sure that Ares is given a formal welcome."

With a lurch I was dragged up into the air again. Being slammed repeatedly into the deck hadn't just broken a few of my ribs. My left wrist felt all kinds of wrong and my foot dangled at a weird angle on my numb leg.

I knew that I couldn't take much more. Everything hurt beyond what I thought I was capable of bearing, and I was sure that the only reason I was still conscious was because my mind was so fixated on one thing.

Ares.

I tried to turn my head, to see his golden glow, and

Terror laughed. The sound made the hairs on my skin stand on end.

Slowly, he rotated me to face the dragon, wings beating through the clouds toward us. Ares shone like a gleaming beacon on Dentro's back and love swelled through my body, a brief and blessed relief from the pain.

But as I watched, the dragon pitched hard to the left and the golden light that I knew was Ares slipped from his back.

"No!" My voice was barely audible as Ares began to plummet though the clouds. Fear for his life gripped me, and I had to force myself to stay calm. He was immortal. He had all the power. He couldn't die.

But I could. And if he didn't get here soon, I would.

His glowing body disappeared from view, and Terror chuckled as he turned me back to face him. "Stealth was never really the God of War's style," he said, sauntering closer. It was inexplicable how a featureless face could carry so much menace. The inky swirls crawled across the surface of the stone, dark and foreboding.

"He'll be back," I croaked.

"No doubt. And when he comes back, he'll fall into her arms, not yours." He nodded his head backward, to where Aphrodite stood with her arms folded, her curvaceous body glowing softly.

At first his words glanced straight over me. But then they seemed to permeate through my mind, settling where they shouldn't.

I knew, deep down, that Ares was mine. But... But what if he was right? What if Ares stood before the two of us and chose her?

"And then, when he is at his most vulnerable, she'll strike."

With a rush I saw an image, clear as day, of Aphrodite plunging a knife into Ares' chest. Blood the color of gold spilled from him, his face twisted into agony.

"No! No, stop!" If any part of me knew that what I was seeing was Terror's magical influence, it didn't register. I was too tired, too weak, too broken, to fight it, or even to understand it. The images took over and my brain accepted them.

The pain was worse than the broken bones, than the wound in my thigh. I was being torn open from the inside out.

"Terror!"

That voice...

I forced my streaming eyes open as I dropped once more to the planks. But I didn't feel a thing.

Dentro landed on the ship's deck, shrinking his huge body to fit, and Ares leaped from his neck as the whole ship shuddered. He was twenty feet tall at least, and his armor shone so bright I had to blink.

His fall from the dragon had been one of Terror's visions. My heart began to pound in my chest, I was so desperate to believe that Ares was really there, that he hadn't fallen.

His boots met the planks and then he was moving toward me, lightning fast. "You have taken your last breath, Terror," he roared as he reached my side, dropping to his knees. His armor clanked and I blinked again as he wrapped one arm beneath me, pulling me to him.

"Tell me I'm not dreaming," I whispered. I felt his anger radiating from him, tempered by the intensity of his tenderness.

"I am here, Bella. Take the power. Now." Heat flared to

life in my gut and warmth began to spread through my body. There was a searing flash of pain in my thigh which made me cry out, but then the familiar tingles of the healing magic took over.

With terrifying slowness, Ares rose to his feet.

"You will pay for what you have done to her. With your life."

Bang. A drum beat so loud that the ship vibrated.

Terror hissed as golden light pulsed from Ares, tinged with red. Then the marble man began to rise into the air, just like I had over and over.

"Master, please-" Terror began, his scratchy voice no longer mocking and cool. He was scared. The spirit of Terror was scared.

Shakily, I got to my own feet, unable to put weight on my leg, but gripping Ares' enormous arm to hold myself up.

Bang. A second drum joined the first. They began to beat together, the sound of clashing steel ringing in the air. Heat and the smell of sweat and iron and blood washed over the deck of the ship. My spine straightened, and my body began to swell.

Red descended over my vision as screams filled the air.

"Ready?" Ares said.

"Yes."

Together, we unleashed the power of War.

Terror screamed as a crack appeared in his pristine skull. It spread, slowly at first, then faster, tracing down his whole stone form. His scream cut off abruptly, and I felt the wave of power roll from us as his body froze for a split second. The drums beat faster, the chants of war and sound of explosions surrounding us completely.

"I told you Ares would fuck you up," I said, then he shattered.

A million pieces of marble showered the wooden planks, and I stumbled at the exertion of power. Ares caught me, pulling me close and staring into my eyes. Fire, bright red and orange, and full of the promise of life, flared in his eyes.

"You're really here. On dragon-back, glowing gold. An actual freaking knight in shining armor." I was half-laughing and half-sobbing.

"Did you think I wouldn't come?" Raw emotion flowed from him, straight into my own soul.

"I knew you would. I just... didn't know if you'd get here in time. It was getting hard to hold on."

Before he could answer me, Aphrodite's voice cut through the moment. "I'm so glad you could join us, Ares," she said, her voice venomous.

A gleaming golden shield shimmered into being around us and Aphrodite's tinkling laughter trickled through it. Ares lowered me gently to the planks, then leaped to his feet, putting himself between her and my still healing form. My ribs no longer hurt like hell but my legs weren't functioning properly and I was exhausted. But the healing magic was working, thank fuck.

"I don't know why you're doing this, Aphrodite, but enough is enough."

"She's working with your father," I said, my voice sounding stronger. I didn't want to draw too much power from him but it burned hot, calling to me.

"Why?"

"The same reason you should be working with him too. He is our king," Aphrodite drawled.

"I disagreed with his actions in the Underworld. What he did was reckless and wrong."

"It is not your place to disagree with his actions. It is your place to support and obey him. Pain, come here please."

I pulled harder on the magic connection, allowing the molten pleasure of healing power to flood through my system faster.

The ship lurched and I looked over to see Dentro flying backward as a pink dome of light sprang up around us, encompassing the whole ship. The dragon, now on the outside of the shield, whipped his tail against it and bright fuchsia light sparked from the contact.

"That should keep the meddling beast out," Aphrodite muttered, before turning back to Ares. "You will regret coming here."

"Hand over the demon, and we will leave you and my father to whatever scheme you have concocted."

"No. I have never done as you have bid me, Ares, and I don't intend to start now." She cocked her head, her lips curving into a cruel smile. "I have to admit, I am sorry that I have lost my favorite trophy. The mighty God of War with his claws and fangs and pride was so much fun to play with."

I expected Ares to lose his temper at being mocked, but he was surprisingly calm when he answered her.

"Let it go, Aphrodite. You can't interfere with love like this, and you know it. We broke your curse. You are done. Move on."

Her face twisted, and it was the first time the woman hadn't looked drop-dead gorgeous. "I'm done when I say I am, you fool. You don't know what it is like to bear my burden, to watch as the world around me implodes and explodes on my cue. You don't know how the balance of my power works, what it does to my soul."

I'd never heard anybody speak with such bitterness, and for the first time, I actually considered what it might be like to hold the power of love. Until meeting Ares, I hadn't known its power. I'd seen it, on stage and on screen, I knew the rumors of its intensity. But I had never imagined it could invade every single atom of my being, or that it had the potential to truly change a person.

"I am done with this conversation," she snapped, whirling around. "I have suffered enough. When Zeus' plan comes together, none of this will be relevant. I do not need you, or the little brat, to enjoy his new world."

"New world? What are you talking about?"

"Zeus isn't taking your mutiny lying down. He is going to reward those who have remained loyal."

"What do you mean by new world?" Ares pushed.

"It does not matter what I mean. You will not be here to see it."

Before he could respond, a deafening crack of thunder echoed around us, and purple lightning split the sky as it darkened ominously.

I may not have been a native of Olympus, but even I knew what that meant.

Zeus was coming.

30

ARES

My father materialized on the deck of the ship before me, bolts of hissing lightning scorching the deck in a ring around him. He was trying to be intimidating. And succeeding.

I was partway to my knees before I could help it. The King of the Gods had a presence that went far beyond normal magic. It could not be resisted.

"Son. I see that taking your power from you has not made you any smarter."

"I see that you saw fit to hand it to a rogue demon," I answered, through gritted teeth.

Zeus looked as he often did, ten feet tall and strikingly good-looking, with silver and dark hair, bright purple eyes and a toga that barely hid his sculpted body. He looked as I had wanted to look most of my life.

"You were no longer suitable to hold the role of God of War."

Anger fired through me. "Cronos was imprisoned with the help of allies we no longer have! Letting him go free was an unwise risk, and as the God of War I am well versed in risks."

"You underestimate my might, little boy? You believe I am not strong enough?" Power crackled around the god, pain licking my skin as electricity hummed through the air. His purple eyes darkened as he grew even more in size, looming over everyone on the deck of the ship. I heard movement and glanced over my shoulder to see the remaining two Lords of War moving backward, eyes averted from the mighty king. Aphrodite, however, stayed where she was, a smug smile on her pristine face. "You do not believe that I could overpower that old Titan? Your lack of faith in my ability is treason," Zeus growled.

"Disagreeing with you is not treason. Nor is it a reason to strip me of my power." Bitterness laced my words.

"Treason is what I say it is. I am your king, whether you want me to be or not." Thunder rumbled in the distance with his words and the sky above us darkened. I could not reason with him on this subject, I realized. If a god as mighty as my father wanted to prove himself against the strongest of all the Titans, I could not stop or change that.

I needed to try a different tactic with the King of the Gods.

"Will you not return to us, as our king? Please, father. Lead us as you once did. Why do you wish to release Titans and cause our world such strife?"

Zeus snorted. "This is not a plea that the God of War should be making, Ares. You are supposed to want strife, boy! You should seek chaos and destruction; these powers are all linked to your own." He sneered down at me, his gaze seeming to bore straight through my armor. "You are a shadow of your former self." His eyes flicked to Bella.

My chest constricted, fear bolting through me. Bella was kneeling, frozen in place and her gaze fixed on Zeus. I couldn't tell if it was awe or fear in her eyes.

"She has nothing to do with this."

"Oh, Ares. I rather think that she does," he breathed, stepping toward her. "She is interesting." The gruffness had gone from his tone, replaced with a dangerously low rumble. The fear inside me clawed its way up my chest, into my throat.

The last thing I wanted was for Zeus to take issue with Bella. Even his brothers could not best him, there was no way I could not stop him from hurting her.

I moved between them, fast. "Only one of us could be immortal while the other lives. You need have no interest in her; she is connected only to me."

"There are many prophecies in this world, boy." Zeus' eyes stormed with purple electricity as he looked at me. "I was happy to take your power and let your mother find a way for you to restore it. You were no threat to me, or my plans, and I had hoped it would keep Hera occupied. But now... This woman can make you strong, Ares. She has the potential to change you into something so much greater than you are now. Something... powerful. I can feel it now that you two are together. I can't let that happen."

"You're wrong," I said, even though I knew the truth of his words as he said them. Bella did make me better, stronger, more powerful. But not in a physical way. "Only one of us can be immortal at any one time, and that makes us weak. We are no threat to you." It went against every fibre of my being to deliberately portray myself as weak, and I had to force the words from my lips, but it was the only thing I could think of to keep Bella safe.

"No, Ares. If you learn to share this power properly... Your lack of immortality is exactly what will make you unstoppable."

Lethal sparks danced in his eyes as he looked between me and Bella, and I thought my heart might stop beating altogether as I dropped to my knees. I was out of options.

"I will not oppose you, father. We are no threat, I swear it."

"And you, girl?" Zeus looked at Bella. "Do you swear it too?"

She looked at me, then at the giant god in front of us. "Yes," she said.

There was a long pause before Zeus spoke. "I do not believe you. There is an indomitable spirit inside you, that can not be crushed."

"Father, please. If you ever loved me, leave her alone."

His foot stamped down hard on the planks as he barked a laugh. "Aphrodite, come here."

The goddess sauntered over to him, making sure to throw Bella an evil look as she did. "Yes, my Lord?"

"Am I correct in my understanding that in failing the Trials, you now own the God of War?"

"Technically, the Lords own the God of War," she purred. "But we have an understanding."

"Good." Zeus looked back to me. There was death in his eyes, clear as day.

I felt physically sick as I tried to flash. I had already known it wouldn't work on this ship, but I had to try something. My mind raced, frantic to come up with a way to save her. "You know how I feel about murdering family members myself," said Zeus. "And your mother would never forgive me. So I'm afraid my only option is to kill the girl."

"No!" I leaped to my feet, only to be held in place by his magic.

"My Lord, may I interrupt?" Aphrodite's voice was silky sweet as I struggled against my invisible bonds. "If you kill the girl, Ares will get all of her power."

"You make a good point, Aphrodite. Let me fix that."

A bolt of lightning screeched down into the deck in front of Bella and she scrambled backward. I tried harder to move, barely able to breathe, but the lightning expanded, electricity shocking my skin as the tendril of purple power reached me. I heard the roar of pain ripped from my throat at the same time as I heard Bella's shout.

I tried to speak, to reach her, but I was pinned in place by the lightning, my whole body shaking as electricity tore through it.

"I would say I'm sorry, but it is what you deserve for crossing me, son," I heard Zeus say.

With a surge of power, the electricity reached my gut, and the connection to Bella. There was an agonizing tearing feeling, then the electricity stopped, draining away fast. And with it, my access to Bella's power.

31

BELLA

"**N**o, no, no."

When the pain of the purple electricity ebbed away, I knew instantly that something was wrong. I could still feel Ares in my heart, but the connection we shared my power through... It was gone. An indescribably hollow feeling was left in its place, as though my body knew something was supposed to be there, but didn't know what.

"Don't kill her!" Ares' voice was ragged and I longed to reach for his hand, but I was being held where I was by a magic that I knew I could never best. As I thought about the strength of my power, a rushing feeling started, like when Dentro had flown me away from Ares in the forest, but more.

Healing magic flooded through my body like a raging river, washing away every trace of fatigue and pain from every cell. I felt like my muscles were growing, hardening, filling with strength.

My power was returning to me, no longer able to

reach Ares at all. And... And there was something else. Something new. I probed inside myself, trying to work out what the dark, creeping feeling was.

Terror.

Recognition dawned on me. It was Terror's power. It must have returned to Ares when we shattered his mortal body. And now it was flowing into me.

Zeus stepped forward, and the addition of Terror's power to my own receded abruptly in importance. I summoned a fireball, projecting it directly from my chest as hard as I could, aiming for the giant before me.

It sizzled out before it got a foot away from me. The mass of power pinning me in place thickened, preventing me from moving and squeezing me tight.

Zeus, King of the Gods and all-powerful deity, wanted me dead. And all the spirit and fight in the world couldn't save me from him. Nor could Ares.

"I love you," I said, unable to turn my head, but sure he would know I was talking to him. "Whatever they do to us, I will never regret finding you."

"Bella, don't give up."

"Never," I said. "I just wanted you to know that." I expected my heart to be racing, my stomach to be filled with butterflies, fear to be consuming me. But a weird calm had come over me.

If I was going down, there was one god I was taking down with me.

"I love you too." A spear of emotion accompanied his words, and a sorrow that I would not get to feel his touch, or kiss his lips, or hear his voice for a long and happy life welled up inside me.

It's not over yet.

"Have you finished your goodbyes?" Zeus boomed, and I took a deep breath.

"I've died a hundred times over," I said, as loudly as I could. "What's one more death?"

The massive god cocked his head at me. "I understand your fondness for her," he said to Ares.

"Please, father," he rasped.

It was all the distraction I needed. A fireball three times the size of the first one burst from my chest. But I wasn't aiming for Zeus this time.

It smashed into Aphrodite before she even realized it was coming, such was the speed of my fully returned power. Shrieking filled the air as her dress caught fire. Zeus snapped his fingers, my raging inferno doused instantly.

"You should be paying more attention, Aphrodite," he chided her. I saw that the skin of her beautiful face was charred and blistered, before it began to knit back together. But it didn't disguise the fury.

"It is time for her to die," she growled, a black dress wrapping around her body out of nowhere, to replace the one I'd just burned to ash.

"Indeed." Thunder rolled and lightning flashed.

Teal lightning.

I saw confusion cross Zeus' massive face for a split second, before Hera shimmered into being on the deck of the ship. She was as large as Zeus, and the rage on her face rivaled Aphrodite's.

"You dare to interfere with bonds this ancient? You dare to ruin our son's life?" The goddess advanced on Zeus, growing even larger. My own breath caught. She was magnificent, a powerhouse of dark skin and teal silks and an aura as intense as Zeus'. I wanted to *be* Hera in that moment. "I have been spending every drop of energy I possess keeping you from your own idiocy these last months, but now you have pushed me too far!"

Zeus' eyes darkened as he glared back at his wife. "You do not know what you are preventing me from doing. Release your hold on me and let me get on with rebuilding our world."

Hera gave a humorless laugh. "Zeus, I am the only Olympian who has any control over you. That's what my bonds do. They connect two people. I am as bound to you as you are to me. I will not let you make these mistakes. And I will not let you kill a part of our son's soul."

"That girl could be the downfall of us," Zeus hissed.

"I do not care. You have gone too far."

They were nose-to-nose now, and I was holding my breath watching them. My leg twitched where my knee met the hard planks, and I realized that I could move again. I turned my head, ever so slowly, drinking in the sight of Ares a few feet away.

"Wife, leave me!" Zeus roared.

"Not this time, husband," Hera replied, and fast as lightning she gripped his face in her hands. There was a loud crack, a flash of purple and teal light, and they were gone.

I fell forward onto my hands as the remnants of power holding me in place vanished with them. Strength pulsed through my whole body, and I was on my feet in seconds. Nobody would have known that just hours ago the wound in my thigh had been bordering on killing me. I felt fucking invincible.

Aphrodite was staring at the space Zeus had occupied

a second ago and rage took me in its grip, instinct and power taking over. I still could feel magic filling me, as though my body was its refuge now that it could not reach Ares.

"What are you going to do now that he's gone, Aphrodite?" I hissed, and my voice didn't sound like my own.

"I don't need Zeus to fight my battles," she said, though I could see the uncertainty in her eyes. "Pain! Panic!" she called.

"Ahhh, so you need some folk with the power of War instead," I said, narrowing my eyes. I knew they would be blazing. I could feel the heat rolling from me as my body began to swell, accommodating the massive energy churning through my limbs. "Because you're too pathetic to fight me."

"I am not so crude as to fight with my fists."

"No. You fight with cruel words and unkind manipulations," Ares said before I could answer. He was on his feet, and though he was large and solid in his armor, he had no glow, no aura of power around him. I met his eyes briefly, and projected as much love and confidence as I could into my gaze. I felt the bond between our souls fire, and knew he'd got my message.

We would work out how to get his power back as soon as we could, but right now we had a war to win.

Together, we stepped toward Aphrodite, as the Lords moved to her side.

"I do not need to fight you at all," she spat. "Not when I have a small army to do it for me."

She held her hands out and they glowed brightly. "You have been summoned, ugly one," she called loudly.

Cold descended over the ship as shadows started to crawl over the deck. I recognized the feeling at once. It was the Underworld demon.

32

BELLA

The Lords spread out on either side of Aphrodite, cruel grins distorting their handsome faces.

I scanned the darkening skies quickly for Dentro, but the dragon was nowhere to be seen. The temperature dropped further and the light from the sails dimmed as the shadows stretched.

I knew what was coming.

Lifting my hand at the same time as Aphrodite lowered hers, I threw up a dome around Ares. Physically, he was strong as hell, but he was powerless against the Lords, Aphrodite and the demon. The thought of him losing his soul caused a new wave of roiling anger to wash through me.

Pain advanced suddenly, and I became aware of a sensation sparking up my legs from the planks. It didn't take long for the sensation to worsen, and pain to start causing my still growing muscles to spasm. I used my magic to force the feeling away, and only realized when Ares growled in pain that the shield I had put around him was under attack, Pain's magic able to get to him through it.

I poured more power into the shield, but as soon as I did, the pain in my own body returned, hard enough to make one knee buckle.

I heard Aphrodite laugh as I clenched my jaw against the growing agony.

"Your turn, Panic," she cooed.

Instantly, the shadows lengthened, and the memory of my last encounter with the Keres demon sprang into my mind. *You can't defeat her. Swords don't work, strength doesn't work, fire doesn't work. You can't defeat her, useless little goddess.*

The voice sang in my mind, allowing the panic to siphon my confidence, allowing it to poison my power as it flowed through my veins.

I felt the shield weaken as the waves of agony grew, and my other leg buckled.

"Leave the shield, fight them," choked out Ares.

"I can't! What if the demon comes? I won't risk losing your soul."

"You can't defend me and fight, Bella. And you must fight."

A loud, feline snarl made me turn, and my breath caught as Zeeva leaped out of the door from the closest quarter-deck. She was huge and lethal looking in her sphinx form, moving with an unearthly grace. I had never been happier to see her.

Even better, she was holding my helmet and sword in her massive mouth.

"Zeeva, you're a fucking legend," I breathed as she

tossed her head as she ran, sending them skittering across the planks toward me. I reached out, stopping the helmet with my knee and scooping up *Ischyros*. Heat rushed into my palm as the sword hummed happily.

"I know," the cat answered, then launched herself at Pain.

The Lord shrieked as she made contact with him, and the agony causing my legs to fail me vanished. Aphrodite stumbled backward, out of the way of Zeeva as she hissed and snarled, slashing with her huge paw at Pain.

I jumped back to my feet, then Ares was up too, running toward me.

Our hands caught each others, fingers entwining as he smashed his lips into mine. For the briefest second of bliss, the fight vanished in the joy of a moment I feared I would never experience again. But he pulled away too soon.

"Bella, you must fight, whatever happens to me. You have all the power now, and you are at full strength. You are a true goddess. You can win."

"I won't let them hurt you."

"Let the power take over, Bella. Embrace who you really are. You're the Titan Enyo, Goddess of War."

"I don't know who that is. I don't even know who I am anymore if I don't have you." I could feel my fear of the demon spreading over me, clouding my thoughts. "I can't lose your soul. I don't know how to stop her, she's not made of flesh and bone."

"Then don't become Enyo." Ares cupped my face in his palm and I heard Aphrodite scream for the demon again. "Become *Bella*, Goddess of War. You have all of your power. You have the ability within you to command the Lords of War. You heard what Zeus said. He feared you,

Bella, the King of the Gods himself. You are mighty and powerful. You will win."

Icy cold blew across the deck as his words smashed through the wall of doubt that had been erected between me and the almost overflowing power inside me.

I was powerful. I knew that much was true, the rage inside me was becoming hard to contain, a tornado of brutal energy.

An awful high-pitched wail floated over us, making me want to cover my ears. Instead, I pressed my lips hard to Ares', then stepped back and lifted my helmet. Taking a deep breath, I slid it down over my head.

I raised *Ischyros*.

I will win. Ares believed it. And now I needed to.

I had to embrace who I was. I had to become the Goddess of War. But not Enyo. I had no use for an ancient version of myself I had never known. I needed to be what I had made myself, the same woman who had come back from every shitty existence stronger. The same woman Ares had fallen in love with.

I felt my spine straighten, and my blood run hotter in my veins.

I was Bella, and I was a fucking goddess.

33

BELLA

The Keres demon burst onto the deck in a wave of black smoke so thick I could barely see though it. The Lords and Aphrodite disappeared in the haze, as the smell of blood and rotten flesh overwhelmed my nostrils.

"You came back, sweet-smelling one. And now your scent is even stronger."

The demon's voice made every hair on my body stand on end, like nails over a chalkboard.

"I'm here to send you back to hell," I snarled, raising my sword. "I am fucking sick of batshit-crazy goddesses and soul-sucking demons trying to hurt the people I love. This ends now."

I gripped the hilt of my sword with both hands and held it high, just as I had seen myself do on horseback in the visions of me in the purple dress.

Like the long lost pieces of a puzzle flying back into place, the vision suddenly made sense. I knew exactly what I was seeing as I closed my eyes and let it wash over me completely. The smell of the grassy earth, the roar of my army's battle chant, the beating of the drums, the sound of hooves pounding the ground.

It was one of my previous lives. One where I had won the most glorious honor of them all. One where I was fierce and strong and wise and I led my people to victory.

Ares was right. I could command the power of War. I was *born* to command the power of War.

When I opened my eyes, gold light was pouring from my body in rivers, and a thrill like I had never felt filled me as I watched. The army from my vision, hundreds of well-muscled men and women on horseback barely half-a-foot in height, were galloping along the beams of light, their swords and axes raised aloft like mine. The demon wailed as the light reached her and began to wrap around her grotesque form as though it were a lasso, ridden by an endless wave of warriors. The air was filled with the sound of the army's battle chant and the thudding of hooves.

I gave my own battle cry as power flowed from my center, the light continuing to pour from my chest and the fearless riders tearing their way toward their enemy, growing in size as they reached her. Within moments there was a tornado of golden light whirling around the demon, and I caught flashes of weapons and horse heads and painted faces amongst the gold as they galloped around her, the drum beats echoing loudly.

Something slammed into me and I staggered.

"Zeeva!" It was the sphinx that had hit me, and whilst I had managed to stay on my feet, she had slid across the planks. She had her teeth bared, a terrible hissing sound coming from her as she jumped back up.

"That Lord will die!" she screamed, and before I could say another thing she had pounced back into the billowing smoke that was covering the deck like fog.

"Bella, she has my power!"

Ares' voice rang in my head, and I closed my eyes, focusing.

The demon had Ares power. I had to get it back. "Your power is gone, pathetic little pup." Aphrodite stalked through the smoke, glowing fuchsia. But she was lying. Ares' power was there, I could feel it emanating from the demon. Why wasn't she using it?

Summoning every drop of concentration I could, I launched myself into the dark space Ares had taught me to access when I sought out Hippolyta via her War magic.

Everything stilled as I found myself in the inky nothingness, a blazing column of red and gold light directly before me, ringed by my mounted army. The bright, shimmering forms of Pain and Panic were there too, as well as a number of less bright lights in the distance, but they were all eclipsed by the beacon of Ares' power, contained inside the demon.

"Keres demon! Release the War power, now! Give it back to its rightful owner!" I shouted the words with no real hope that they would have any effect. I didn't have the first clue how to get Ares power back. All I knew was that I needed to do something and I couldn't kill the demon.

Or could I?

The question burst, unbidden, into my head, and it took me a second to realize that it wasn't my own. It was Terror's voice.

You can kill her. Zeus said you were powerful enough to be a threat. Of course you can kill one demon.

"Why would I help you?" The demon's awful voice emanated from the beam of Ares' power. I forced more of my own power into the swirling ring of light.

"It is not your power to bear."

"As well I know." Her voice was bitter, and everything I knew about power in Olympus whizzed through my head. Ares gave power to hosts, like the Lords, to use. But *he* hadn't given the demon this power, someone else had.

"You can't use the War magic, can you?"

"I do not need it. My own is plenty."

"Then you won't mind if I take it back."

I pulled on my bond to Ares, filling my every cell with him, calling his soul to mine. His power was a part of his soul, he had said. And though the connection in my gut was gone, the one in my heart was as strong as ever.

Slowly at first, the beam of light flickered. Then with a sear of heat it began to rush toward me, along my own golden river of light.

I opened my eyes and gripped Ares' hand, at the same time that the demon wailed. He jerked beside me, then his eyes widened as his power began to flow into him through me.

"Stop!" screamed Aphrodite, rushing toward us.

But she was too late. Like a long-lost dog eager to return to its master, Ares' power had rushed to him in a mere heartbeat.

Gold burst from him as he grew, his own river of light pouring from his gleaming armor and smashing into Aphrodite. The army that raced along his light was made up of footmen with helmets like his own, massive Greek shields and lethal spears. The chants of battle and screams of death echoed through the air, and I felt my own army respond, galloping faster on their horses.

"Ares! Ares, release me!" Aphrodite was screaming as the golden warriors surrounded her, whipping into a tornado just like my own and trapping her.

Strength surged inside me as Ares' eyes locked on mine, flaming.

"We can kill her," I said, before I knew I'd even thought the words. "Both of them. We're strong enough together, I can feel it."

"No, Bella. Hades and Poseidon need to deal with this."

But burning fury was rolling through me, needing to be expelled. "She tried to kill you. She tried to keep us apart."

The golden light running from me was tinged red. It looked a little like fire. I cocked my head at it.

"They need to burn," I said. My head was swimming with images of Aphrodite succumbing to flames, her face a mask of fear, her voice a cowering plea.

"Bella, that's Terror's power talking. Not yours."

"Ares, I want her dead."

"I'll leave!" Aphrodite's voice rang out from inside her cage of light. Her face was just visible through the spinning gold. "You'll never see me again, I swear. Just let me go."

"Lies." I stepped toward her, my light turning completely red. The demon let out a choked wail, but I barely heard it. "You lie, little goddess," I spat. "Demon! You can take souls, yes?" I didn't take my eyes off Aphrodite's, now filling with the fear I was so desperate to see. I could feel the power of Terror's thrill at her reaction. And I embraced it. I couldn't help it. This woman had tried to take everything from me. I had done her no wrong.

She had treated Ares like a fucking toy.

"Yes," rasped the demon.

"Can you take the soul of an immortal?"

"No. But... I can take power."

Glee sparked inside me. "Take her power."

"No!" Aphrodite shrieked.

"Bella, this is not you. This is Terror's influence." Ares' voice was calm, his eyes still blazing as he turned me to face him.

"She deserves to suffer as you have."

"I agree, but we should not be the ones to dole out punishment."

"Listen to him! He is wise," Aphrodite choked. Ares' eyes flashed dark as he turned to her.

"You have spent centuries calling me a fool, Aphrodite. I do not plea for mercy on your behalf because you deserve it."

"Then why? Why do you want to show her mercy?" I could hear the jealousy in my voice. I felt my body swell as even more anger poured through me. I had to fight. I had to win. I had to prove what I was capable of.

"Because you have taught me the importance of fairness."

"It is fair that she suffers as you have!"

Ares' jaw twitched. "Perhaps. But you have Terror's cruelty inside you now. Do not act on his will."

"It is my own will that wants to see her pay."

Ares opened his mouth to answer when agony ripped through my spine. I cried out as I dropped to the planks, and Ares rushed to catch me. I felt my river of light cut off, then heard Pain's voice as I doubled over.

"Flash us away, Aphrodite, now!"

"No!" I straightened in Ares' arms, desperate to stop Aphrodite escaping, but froze at what I saw.

The Keres demon had reached Aphrodite before she could flash away. My stomach churned, bile rising in my throat as the rotten corpse-like form towered over the beautiful goddess, pink light pouring from Aphrodite's chest into the gaping mouth of the demon.

Pain made a strangled sound, but I couldn't take my eyes off the horrific scene in front of me. I clung to Ares, and he gripped me hard back. A sense of utter wrongness spread through me, the idea of my own power being leeched from me like that unbearable.

A true understanding of what it must have been like for Ares to have his power stolen settled over me. "You... you were right. This wasn't what I wanted. It feels so wrong."

Ares was silent a moment before answering, his voice grim. "I was going to say the opposite. I think it is exactly what she deserves. I just didn't want you to be forced into doing something by Terror that you would regret."

The demon turned to us suddenly, and Aphrodite slumped to the deck. A sob bubbled out of her.

"I have done as you bid, new mistress. Will you now let me leave?" The demon's voice made me feel even more sick, the headache returning instantly. Dark smoke billowed around us. Aphrodite's sobs got louder.

"Keres demon! You will return with me now!" The voice blasted across the deck, along with a freezing wave of air that made my body want to shrink and hide. With an almost blinding flash of bright blue light, Hades appeared on the deck.

The thick smoke dissipated, but I was too transfixed on Hades to notice anything else. The blue light that had accompanied the God of the Dead was solidifying into people, just like mine and Ares' had. In a rush, they swarmed the demon.

"Mistress! Mistress, help me!" the demon screamed, and I realized with another lurch of my stomach that she meant me.

There was a loud crack, another bright flash of blue, and Hades and the demon vanished.

The sky brightened immediately, the solar sails casting a warm glow over everything as they refilled with light.

"How..." I stared around, my mind thick with oncoming fatigue and confusion.

"I called him and Poseidon," Ares said gently, and I realized with a start that the God of the Sea was standing over Aphrodite's crumpled form.

"You can't beat Zeus, Poseidon. He is stronger than you and Hades combined," she said through tears.

I scanned the deck. Pain was laying down, covered in blood, with Zeeva crouched over him, still in sphinx form. Panic was cowered against the main mast.

"If you are in league with my brother, Aphrodite, then you are at war with us." Poseidon's voice was low and grave.

"I have made my choice, fool. It is the right choice." I had to admit that there was courage to Aphrodite's words. A courage I had previously not credited her with.

"Then you leave me no choice." The manacles appeared in the sea god's hands, and a bolt of satisfaction tore through me as Aphrodite blanched, the manacles magically snapping into place on her delicate wrists.

"Thank you, Enyo," Poseidon said, before they both vanished in his own flash of aqua-blue.

"It's Bella." I whispered.

34

BELLA

"Pain, Panic, recognize me now as your creator and master. Kneel," Ares barked. Panic knelt at once, fear in his face. Pain struggled to a kneeling position, but Zeeva swiped with her paw as soon as he was upright, sending him slumping back to the planks with a grunt.

"Sorry. I couldn't help it," she said.

Ares gave her a look, then spoke again. "Return to your realms and await my judgment. You will suffer for your mutiny. If you even consider defying me, you will die."

"Yes, master." Both men flashed and I didn't blame them. I'd be getting out of there as fast as I could too. Ares cupped my cheek again, and I drank in the emotion on his face.

"You were amazing," he said.

"So were you. I... I'm sorry I went a bit..." I trailed off.

"When I first had to manage Terror's power it was hard. You did better than I did."

"Really?"

"Yes. Bella, I really thought I was going to lose you. More than once." Gently, he lifted the helmet from my head, followed by his own. He lowered his head, his beautiful, serious face inches from mine. "I love you." His lips met mine, and it was the most tender kiss we had ever shared. The fire and drums and heat were simmering under a passion that went a million times further than my physical desire for him.

I pressed myself into him, winding my fingers around his neck and kissing him deeper.

"I love you," I told him mentally. *"I could never lose you."*

He moved back, holding my face in both of his hands, a pained look in his eyes. "I'm sorry. I'm so, so sorry about what I put you through."

"Let's not talk about it. It's done."

"I... I misunderstood the prophecy. I thought that to be immortal, you must not exist. But now, I would take you over immortality in a heartbeat."

"Well, now that you have your power back, you don't need to make that choice."

His expression darkened, and I knew why before he spoke. "I felt alive when I shared my mortality with you."

"I know. I don't really want this either. But it is better than one of us having to live without the other."

"That is true."

I stood on my tiptoes, kissing him again.

"What will happen to them?" I asked, when I pulled away.

"Aphrodite will be a prisoner and the demon will be returned to Hades' care."

"Not going to lie, I quite like the thought of her a prisoner. But what about her power?"

Ares shrugged, the metal of his armor moving against

me. I glanced down, noticing that we were both still glowing. "I'm sure Poseidon will make the right decision."

"And the souls that the Keres demon took?"

"Hades will keep his promise to return them, I am sure."

I nodded, relief taking me under like a wave. It was over. No more Trials, Joshua would be safe, and most important of all, Ares and I were together.

"Ares, can we go home now?"

"Of course. I think I would like some of that silly drink you like so much. What is it called again?"

"Tequila," I beamed at him.

"Yes. Tequila."

"Can we drink it naked?"

"I wouldn't have it any other way."

"I am sorry to interrupt," a deep voice said. The scent of the ocean wafted over me as I turned in unison with Ares.

"Oceanus," he breathed, and we both bowed to the ancient Titan as he appeared to walk straight out of the brilliant solar sails and down to the deck, as though he were on an invisible staircase.

"It appears that you have completed your task," he rumbled. He was wearing a worn looking toga, no shoes, and his grey hair was tied back from his tanned face. Once again, he looked nothing like I expected the most powerful god in Olympus to look. He looked a like a hot older fisherman at a toga party.

"My power is returned, Oceanus. I am no longer in need of your offer of a Trident."

Oceanus' blue eyes sparkled. "I have been impressed

with your commitment to proving yourself a worthy god, Ares."

He stiffened beside me. "Thank you," he muttered.

"Is there something else I can offer you, in place of the Trident?"

Excitement skittered through me, and when Ares looked at me, I knew he was thinking he same thing.

"The connection that Zeus destroyed," I said, my face splitting into a smile.

Oceanus cocked his head. "The one that allowed you to share your power? That made you both mortal?"

"Yes. That one," Ares nodded. "Can you restore it?"

"Yes, but... that would mean removing the power you just won back. Is that really what you're asking me to do?"

Ares gripped my hand, turning me to face him. "Bella, are you sure you want to share power again? We can be immortal for eternity like this, both true gods with the full strength of Olympians."

"I don't want to be immortal for eternity! I want to live my life like it means something, sharing every experience with you." And it was true. The longer we had spent together, the more I had come to love sharing my power with Ares. The tugging feeling in my gut, the way he poured healing power into me when I needed it... It was just so right, somehow.

"So do I. I don't want the life I had before you. I want what you have opened my eyes to. I want to learn what all these ridiculous emotions do, and feel the thrill of taking risks." His eyes danced with excitement as he talked.

"Then the decision is made," I beamed at him.

My stomach was turning somersaults as we turned back to Oceanus.

"We would like to share the power of one god again. It

does not matter whether it is mine or Bella's. As long as it is like it was before."

Oceanus' wise face relaxed into a smile. "Your decision pleases me. I would like to offer you both a gift."

A small bracelet appeared on my wrist, and Ares held his arm out, a matching one on his much larger arm. They were made of twine, and had three tiny sea-pearls threaded onto the band.

"These will not make you immortal but they will stop you aging. Olympus needs a God or Goddess of War; we can't have you going and dying on us in fifty years."

I looked between the bracelet and Oceanus. "So we will live forever as long as we are not killed in battle?"

"Yes. You can still be killed by anything except old age."

"Thank you," Ares said, sincerity bordering on reverence in his voice.

Oceanus chuckled. "Never have I heard such gratitude for the gift of being able to be killed." He shook his head.

With a whip of his hand I felt a warm tingle spread through my stomach, then a laugh escaped my lips as I felt the connection snap back into place. Ares pulled me to him, kissing me happily as the waves of energy rolling through me lessened, the well of heat under my ribs shrinking. Then I felt the familiar tug as what remained of our power moved between us, leveling out.

Our power. Not mine, not Ares'. Ours.

35

BELLA

"I wish you hadn't made me come here," Ares grumbled. I rolled my eyes but didn't turn to look at him.

"You know exactly why you're here. Because I don't trust myself to flash all the way to the mortal world yet."

"Well, hurry up. The announcement about the fighting pits is soon."

Ares was sulking because I had insisted on seeing that Joshua was safe with my own eyes. The truth was, I wanted him here because I knew he harbored some jealousy over my old crush and I thought he'd worry less if he was here too.

I watched Joshua through the window of his office, disguised from view by my shield. He was talking animatedly to a patient, and as far as I was aware, he had no idea I was anywhere near him. Or even that I existed at all, let alone that I had saved his soul.

Hades had kept his word, returning all the souls that

the demon had stolen. Many of the mortal hosts had been killed, but Hades' right-hand woman, Hecate, had worked some sort of magic to help recreate them, and a god called Hypnos, who also worked for Hades, had helped reset their loved ones memories. I was hazy on the details, but Persephone had assured me that my concerns about zombies were unfounded. It was something to do with creating new bodies, and reinserting the souls, with all their own memories. Joshua was still Joshua, just in a brand new body that looked like the old one.

The power the gods had over the world I had called my home was slightly overwhelming, but I had a long time to get used to it. Forever, if I didn't manage to get myself killed.

"I'm done. I just wanted to check I'd achieved what I set out to do," I said, turning to Ares. "Which was save my friend." I emphasized friend but he still scowled at me.

"The way I remember it, you set out to annoy me."

"Then it appears I have achieved twice today."

He gave me a look, then pulled me close to him, brushing my hair out of my face as he stared down at me. "You can annoy me every day for eternity, if it makes you happy," he said softly.

"Then I shall," I grinned back at him. "But right now, we have to go. Your announcement is coming up."

Ares flashed us back of the deck of his ship, and I half-skipped to the railings. We were hovering right over the center of the largest fighting pit in his realm. People were starting to fill the rows of seats, and excitement trickled through me.

Ares had needed to take care of a whole load of issues

after the Trials. First and foremost was finding Eris, but we'd come up blank. While Hades was fixing the damage the demon had done and restoring the Guardians, we had combed every inch of the mortal realm with Persephone's help. But we couldn't find a single trace of the Goddess of Chaos. All we could do was hope Poseidon would be successful at getting Aphrodite to tell us what she had done.

Reluctantly, Ares had moved onto fixing his own realm. And that meant finding a new host for Terror. I'd met all the candidates with him, and Ares made sure I had a say in the final decision. I didn't trust the harpy-hybrid we had chosen one little bit, but I was confident she would be able to keep the spirit of Terror in check for a while at least.

Now, Ares had to prove to his realm that he was still as strong and as mighty as the God who had ruled them for centuries, and that he was still deserving of their respect.

And I had convinced him that the best way to do that was a tour. Right after the announcement that he was due to make, we would be setting sail for a full circuit of his realm, and we would be stopping in every single kingdom, to prove just how strong and worthy of respect we were. I was so excited my head actually hurt when I thought too much about it.

"Good luck today, fierce one. I must return to my brethren now." I heard Dentro's voice in my head and scanned the skies above me. A tiny dot in the distance swooped in response.

"Thank you for everything, Dentro. Drop by any time."

"I am sorry I could not help on the ship."

"You brought Ares to me. That was everything I needed. You could not have done more to help me."

"Goodbye, for now, Bella."

"Bye, Dentro. Have fun."

I heard his chuckle as the dot in the distance disappeared from view.

My sadness that my dragon friend was leaving was tempered significantly by the fact that my cat friend had gone nowhere. Zeeva had been worried that she had broken Hera's strict rules when she shifted and practically saved my life on Aphrodite's ship, but she had gotten a message from her mistress shortly after. Hera had said nothing about where she and Zeus were, only that she had sent a message to Hades, and that Zeeva was released from her duties until Hera could return.

And to my delight, Zeeva had decided to stay with me, on Ares' ship. I knew she loved me really.

∾

"Are you ready?" Ares asked me, as I emerged from the bedroom twenty minutes later.

I was wearing full armor, helmet and all, as was Ares. "Ready as fuck," I answered him. He shook his head, but his eyes were smiling behind the helmet.

"Good. Let's do this."

The ship sank low into the fighting pit as we made our way onto the deck, so that we were level with the now-packed spectator seats ringing the stadium. Together we swelled in size, only stopping when we were both twenty feet tall, and everyone in the pit could see us clearly. Silence met us and my stomach fizzed with anticipation.

"Citizens of my realm," boomed Ares, and the connection in my gut pulled as he drew power to magnify his voice. "From this day on, no man, woman or creature shall fight against their will in Aries."

Instantly, the crowd let out a collective buzz of surprise.

"Prizes for fighting will be large and rewarding, and only those who are willing can compete for them. The penalty for breaking this new law is death. Fight and be victorious!"

A cheer went up, quiet at first, but louder as it gathered momentum. The citizens of the most dangerous realm in Olympus were a special kind of people, brutal and hard and fierce. I couldn't wait to meet them. I beamed behind my helmet.

"Now, we tour Aries. We hope to see many of you on our travels. Good luck to you all."

The ship moved, lifting us fast into the clouds, and I pulled my helmet from my head. Ares did the same. "Where do you want to go first?" he asked, fire dancing in his beautiful eyes, his skin glowing gold.

"Everywhere. But maybe we should start with the bedroom."

"I love you, my golden goddess."

"And I love you, my warrior god."

THE END

FOR NOW...

READ ON FOR THE EPILOGUE AND TO FIND OUT WHICH GOD'S STORY IS COMING NEXT

36

EPILOGUE

"**G**ive me my power back!" Aphrodite screamed from the other side of the grand wooden door.

I closed my eyes and took a deep breath. "No. Not until you tell us what Zeus is planning."

The truth was, I would love nothing more than to hand her cursed love power back to her. I eyed my trident with a scowl. Between us, Hades and I had managed to remove her power from the rogue demon and store it in my weapon. The weapon that was a literal part of my soul.

I was able to keep her power from affecting mine, but its constant tumultuous presence was a distraction I could do without.

"Fine. I'll tell you. Poseidon, open the door."

My brows jumped at her words. She was being held in a nice room in my own palace, but I knew she wouldn't last long without her power. She would relent and tell us what we needed to know.

But I hadn't expected her to cave so soon.

I opened the door to her room slowly.

Her eyes fixed on mine. Even without her power, she was beautiful. Her hair was a rich black, her skin pale as snow. Her eyes were red from crying and I suppressed a pang of guilt. She had put Ares and Bella through hell, all for entertainment. She was not to be trusted.

She lunged for the Trident before I could process what she was doing. Cursing myself for allowing myself to be distracted, I yanked the weapon back, but her small fist had closed around it.

"I curse you, petty god of the sea," she snarled, and fuchsia light exploded from the trident. I drew on my colossal power, wrenching the weapon away from her and slamming the door closed in her face.

"Aphrodite, you can't win this! Just stop fighting me and tell us what we want to know!" I bellowed through the door, unable to contain my temper. Freezing water rushed up from my feet, swirling around my body and slamming into the wood.

"You're too late, Poseidon! Why don't you go and see that pretty wife of yours?"

My heart seemed to thud to a complete halt in my chest. "If you have done anything to harm my wife-" I didn't finish the sentence, whirling and racing down the corridor, Aphrodite's laughs dwindling behind me.

If a single hair on Amphritite's head was out of place, I would murder the Goddess of Love with my bare fucking hands.

READ ON IN THE POSEIDON TRIALS...

Also, if you like your fantasy romance spicy and you're into hot Irish men with big wings, check out my brand new series, Lucifer's Curse.
Read on for a note from the author.

THANKS FOR READING!

Thank you so much for reading The Ares Trials, I hope you enjoyed it! If so I would be eternally grateful for a review! They help so much; just click here and leave a couple words, and you'll make my day :)

Bella and Ares were so, so much fun to write, and they really did run the show with this series. I normally plot my stories quite carefully, but the more I wrote about these two, the more stuff started happening that I simply wasn't expecting. Like Dentro for example - he was never supposed to be in the story! It was a blast to go on this adventure with the sweary, volatile, loveable-at-heart gods of war and I really hope you enjoyed reading it as much as I enjoyed writing it :D

I have to thank my mum, my husband, and my editor - I really couldn't be doing the job I love without you - THANK YOU.

And even more, I want to thank **you** for reading.

I honestly can't believe that I've just typed THE END on my thirteenth book, and that's because you guys are so amazing. Every single page you read allows me to write more and I'm so grateful.

And I promise to keep the stories coming!

xxxxx